HUNTING PIERO

HUNTING PIERO

WENDY MACINTYRE

thistledown press

Thistledown Press Ltd.
410 2nd Avenue North
Saskatoon, Saskatchewan, S7K 2C3
www.thistledownpress.com

Library and Archives Canada Cataloguing in Publication
MacIntyre, Wendy, 1947–, author
Hunting Piero / Wendy MacIntyre.
Issued in print and electronic formats.
ISBN 978-1-77187-147-1 (softcover).–ISBN 978-1-77187-148-8 (HTML).–ISBN 978-1-77187-149-5 (PDF)
I. Title.
PS8575.I68H86 2017   C813'.54   C2017-905318-3
C2017-905319-1

Cover painting: Piero di Cosimo, *Vulcan and Aeolus*, c. 1490
Author photo: Robert Woodbridge
Cover and book design by Jackie Forrie
Printed and bound in Canada

The author would like to thank the Canada Council for the Arts for its financial assistance while writing this novel.

Canada Council   **Conseil des Arts**
for the Arts   **du Canada**

SASKATCHEWAN
ARTS BOARD

Canadä

Thistledown Press gratefully acknowledges the financial assistance of the Canada Council for the Arts, the Saskatchewan Arts Board, and the Government of Canada for its publishing program.

HUNTING PIERO

For Robert Duncan

ONE

A Renaissance Monster

GNES VANE WAS CERTAIN SHE heard the actual thump of a heart coming from the first work of Piero di Cosimo's she ever saw. This was a close-up detail, on the cover of a book in her mother's study, showing the monster from whose clutches Perseus rescued Andromeda. He was magnificently grotesque: part crocodile, part rhinoceros, part duck-billed platypus. She was trying hard not to think about the dreaded consultation later that day, so it was a relief to stare enthralled for some minutes at this fantastic, multihued sea beast with his piebald copper and sea-green flesh, and the great lacy, coral-coloured ruff that was either his ear, or some bizarre fungus he had sprouted from living so long in the ocean. His long curving tusks were beaded with fine bubbles. His eyebrows were erect little thickets. His spiralling, armoured tail culminated in a graceful pennant.

The portrait amazed and confused her. This picture was such a contrast to the flawless angelic faces and bodies her mother usually studied. Was there really a Renaissance artist who specialized in monsters? What on earth was the book doing here?

Agnes's mother was a university lecturer in art history, and her grand passion was for the works of Sandro Botticelli. For as long as Agnes could remember, the fair-haired goddesses and dryads of Botticelli's *Primavera* had stared out smugly from the wall above her mother's desk. Agnes found all these female paragons chilling in their perfection. They had no depth, complexity or surging blood, no quirk of character that made them memorable. They might as well be fashioned of Perspex, or something thoroughly bland, like cream cheese. She did not think she would want to touch them.

On the other hand, were she to reach out, she was convinced the sea monster's flesh would feel warm despite his ocean habitat. His loose upper lip drooped like an old hound's, and his upturned pig-like snout shot a jet of clear water. But more than anything else, it was his visible anguish that made him so terribly real to her. The hurt evident in his eye and in his open, sorrowing mouth, was one she recognized. She had seen this look in her own mirrored pupils so often: the molten core of pain and bewilderment at the countless ways she could still be made to suffer because of her ugliness. As yet, she had failed to grow the "thicker skin" which her parents and the school counsellor were always urging upon her. And here — in the slashes the sea-beast bore on his shoulder and in the blood that streamed down his mottled neck — she saw that not even he had skin coarse enough to deflect the strikes of the little human assailant who stood on his back hewing at his flesh with a curved sword. Agnes now imagined her tormentors straddling her, squashing her lungs, driving their rapiers into the moist, pink chambers of her heart. *Hey Monkey-girl! Freak-face. Do us a favour and put a bag on your head, baboon baby.* In the monster's doom, she saw her worst fears realized: others found him so repulsive, they must kill him.

She knew his pain, and yearned to tell him so. As she bent closer over the image, she saw something else that surprised and thrilled her. Along with the hurt, there was the unmistakable glow of love in the animal's eye. The look he directed at the half-naked woman, bound with scarlet ties to a dead tree on the shore, was unquestionably tender and adoring. The monster had captured and bound this young woman because he was in love. And she understood perfectly, having indulged in such a foolish notion herself. How else would she ever get a good-looking guy into her bedroom, except to kidnap him, or even more degrading perhaps, pay him for sex? "I understand," she whispered, as if the creature in the picture was indeed alive and might take comfort from her words.

She knew it was her own "freakishness" that pulled her to the monster and made her pity his plight. Any normal-looking girl would automatically identify with the captive maiden, and cheer on her handsome rescuer as he slit the sea-beast's vital tendons. The artist showed this smug little hero in his elegant green and gold attire three separate times: first, arriving on the scene, flying through the air with the help of his sleek winged boots; in the centre, slashing away at his prey; and finally, in the lower right corner, being fawned upon by the liberated glowing girl and her friends and family in their elaborate headdresses. How very clever of the artist to depict all these successive incidents, together, inside the one frame: the maiden abducted and bound and her relatives' lamentation, the rescue, the supposed triumph.

[9]

But the painter's master stroke was the way he had set the fantastic monster at the very centre of the canvas, so that all the little human figures seemed to whirl around him, as did the circle of events, and time itself. Agnes was certain the artist loved the sea beast best. That was why he showed the creature clinging so tenaciously and nobly to life. The longer she looked at the picture, the more certain she was of the artist's intentions. This was the portrait of a creature he cherished, who had come to him perhaps in a dream or in a waking vision. All the human figures, despite their pretty profiles, intense emotions, and elegant hats and cloaks, were secondary. They swirled around the monster as planets do around the sun.

"Isn't he hideous?"

Agnes was so wrapped in the picture's spell she had not heard her mother come into the room. An astonishing rage flamed in her head. She had been so happy caught up in the mystery of the painting. Her mother had ruined it.

"The publisher sent me this book to review," her mother sighed. "But there is nothing I can do, I'm afraid. Or not with any degree of objectivity."

"Why?"

"Piero di Cosimo has always made me uneasy; I mean his art illustrating ancient myths, the paintings he is best known for. His religious works don't bother me, or rather, they leave me indifferent. But paintings like this one," her mother gestured to the book's cover, "with Perseus rescuing Andromeda from the repugnant monster, they leave me unsettled. In fact, I find his secular paintings repellent. There are some really nightmarish images that are best avoided altogether."

Agnes felt her mind buzzing, a frenzied bee trapped in a glass jar. "You're wrong," she kept thinking. "You're not looking at this picture properly." She was about to say this aloud when her mother spoke again.

"It's as if Piero di Cosimo was out of step with the humanism of the Renaissance, its very light and hope. Or perhaps he was simply perverse or a misanthrope. Look, I'll show you what I mean . . ."

She flipped through the book until she found the reproduction she wanted. "Steel yourself," she told Agnes, "to look at something brutal and despairing. I saw this canvas when I was about your age, at the Met in New York. It was a school trip and this di Cosimo, God knows why, was part of the set gallery tour.

"When the guide gathered us in front of this painting and started pointing out details, I felt my knees wobble. I came very close to fainting. Our teacher helped me to a bench and told me to put my head between my knees. I was so embarrassed."

Agnes had not been listening for some seconds. She had entered a shrouded wood, where cruel-looking satyrs and men wearing animal skins about their hips were slaughtering forest creatures with pronged wooden clubs and their own naked, murderous hands. A man was strangling a wolf, which he had hoisted up and gripped against his chest. A satyr, his enormous muscular back striped in shadow, swung his cudgel overhead, about to bring it down upon the head of a lion that had torn open the chest of a large grey bear and was chewing on its heart. A smaller bear, perhaps the dead bear's mate, had sunk its claws into the lion's head and back, and at the same time, turned around to snarl at a human figure who gripped the bear from behind. This figure, Agnes registered with some dismay, was a woman. She could make out the shape of her breasts under the tunic of fur.

The entire scene shocked her, and was at the same time deeply familiar. The animals in the painting were so beautiful, even in death. Her heart cheered on all those who were managing to escape, beyond the borders of the painting, toward the west. Among the animals fleeing she recognized an ox, a wild cat, another bear, a stag, a white wolf, and two small monkeys, one dark brown and one slate grey.

Monkeys in fifteenth-century Italy! How astounding. And these two were so lifelike, she knew the artist must have studied the actual animals closely to recreate the steadiness of their bright, round gaze. *Run,* her heart cried out to all the creatures in flight. *Escape the killing ground. Go quickly.*

She scanned the whole grim death-pageant again, forcing herself to look hard at details that had doubtless sickened her mother twenty years ago when she'd stood face-to-face with this canvas in the Metropolitan Museum of Art. She saw a dead dog, on its back, its legs contorted by rigor mortis. She abruptly perceived what was actually happening with the naked man who knelt on the back of a rearing white horse; he was choking the horse to death. She had to look away from the animal's twisted neck and bared teeth. It was then she spied the third monkey, clinging to the top of a tree in the painting's foreground. It had its little face turned around in the direction of the fleeing animals. Was he yearning to clamber down and join them, or was he a symbol of persistent innocence, clinging to his tree-mast high above the slaughter?

"Appalling," she heard her mother say. "How could we bear it, if life were like that?"

The look Agnes turned on her mother was incredulous. Did she really not know? The last desperate kick of the strangled horse, the frantic effort of the little female bear to save her dying mate, the tiny monkeys screeching in terror as they ran — weren't all these things happening now, and forever, and to human animals as well? So stunned was she by her mother's mental and emotional retreat, she felt dizzy. Then it hit her, with a devastating intensity, just how insulated her extremely pretty mother was: adored and protected by her husband, cherished by her two daughters; admired, even adulated, by her students. The sole blot on her mother's existence was the face of her eldest daughter, the "little freak" who spoiled the family's perfection.

When they were children, kindly, sweet-tempered Phoebe had always tried to keep Agnes from eavesdropping on the comments that would inevitably start up among the less sensitive of her parents' party guests.

"What a pity!"

"She will have a hard time of it, poor child."

"Handsome parents, and the other girl such a stunner. Well, one never knows, does one? Is she adopted, by any chance? But surely . . . ?"

"A regular little monster."

This last remark, which admittedly Agnes heard only once inside her parents' home, was the one she could never eradicate. The word lodged with her forever, scored, she was sure, deep into the tissue of her heart and brain.

Was that the reason her parents had offered her the "option" of cosmetic surgery? Because they were ashamed of the way she looked? Or was it because they were sick of being asked if she was adopted, given the fact she looked so utterly unlike them and her blonde, breathtakingly pretty sister, Phoebe?

"Please eat something, Agnes," her mother said, closing the book and pushing it away with a little shudder. "You can't go to your appointment on an empty stomach."

Agnes ignored this stupid remark. "If you don't want it," she said, speaking as calmly as possible to control her quickening breath, "may I have this book?"

The look of doubt that shadowed her mother's face was so fleeting Agnes was not quite certain she had actually seen it. Or perhaps it was a look of foreboding? Whatever, the peculiar expression was gone in a flicker. "Yes, of course. Take it."

Agnes immediately clutched the book to her chest.

"Be careful," her mother called out. "There is a black . . . "

The rest of the sentence was lost to her as she sped along the hall and up the stairs to the sanctuary of her room. He was hers now. She hid the book beneath Granny's quilt in her battered toy chest, as if she were afraid her mother might take it back from her, just as they were threatening to take away her known face.

The day her parents had broached the idea of having her features surgically remade, she'd been utterly unprepared.

"Just for a consultation, honey," her father said.

"We'll be with you, Agnes darling," her mother said.

Agnes had sat still, with the floor lurching up at her. She'd gripped the arms of her chair convulsively and pushed her mother's hand away. She'd flushed hotly; then had felt terribly cold. If her own parents could not accept her face as it was, what hope was there that she might one day find sexual love, freely and willingly given?

She'd begun to sob, soundlessly, but so compulsively her chest grew tight and sore. Her mother and father both had assumed the tears signalled relief. The consultation with the surgeon, they kept reassuring her, would give her all the information she needed to make her decision. They passed her the glossy pamphlets they had collected, with the seductive before-and-after photos of transfigured clients. Her nose could be lengthened and narrowed, her jaw reshaped, and her upper lip shortened. She could not be made into a beauty, but by submitting to scalpel and laser, the chances were very good that she would look "normal". She would know the great joy of passing unnoticed in a crowd.

After the operations, she would undergo a long period of healing. She'd set herself to imagining the pull and throb of new skin knitting together, and the worse agony of waiting for the bandages to be removed and a startling truth revealed. And here her thoughts would stick badly. Would her new "created" face really be true?

As she had expected, Agnes could eat nothing for breakfast. Even sipping milky coffee was an effort because her throat felt so constricted. Every muscle in her body shrank from the looming interview. The word "sacrifice" kept coming to her, its harsh sounds so uncomfortably like the sharpness and hardness of the cutting implements the surgeon would wield. She saw herself, only half-anaes-thetized, splayed on a stone slab. Her body was wrapped in a white cloth, but her face was quite naked. Her face was to be the sacrifice. She would offer up her "ugliness" to the chill purity of the knife.

At the consultation, she was relieved that the surgeon's hands were cool, rather than cold. His name was Dr. Carruthers. He touched her face softly, with immaculate fingertips, here on the brow, there on the nose, then on the upper lip, indicating where the incisions would be made. Once he had finished speaking, she felt tears flowing. She had the small consolation that she was managing to cry quietly. The surgeon passed her a box of facial tissue. He smiled as he did so, a smile she understood he intended to be compassionate. But she perceived no warmth whatsoever in his eyes.

"Take your time," were his parting words to her.

She was grateful that he did not push her to accept this offer of another face. Nor did her parents. "Let us know when you have made your decision," they told her. And then they let her be.

Over the weeks that followed, Agnes had a recurring dream that left her restless and questing after its meaning. She was striding through a landscape she did not recognize. This place had the atmosphere of a desert, yet on either side there were great-shouldered mountains. They looked like sleeping beasts who might suddenly wake and walk with her, keeping her company. Some of the mountains sprouted crags in grotesque shapes like hunched and grimacing gargoyles, yet these ones too seemed companionable rather than frightening. Despite the fact she walked alone in this craggy world, she had the distinct feeling she had been preceded; that thousands upon thousands had travelled this way before her. Ahead, where the mountains parted, she glimpsed a blue so clear she thought it must be the gathering place of kindly spirits.

At this point in the dream, an invisible assailant struck her between the shoulder blades with a weapon like a stout stick or a truncheon. The blow was so vicious she fell to her knees gasping. In that first rush of expelled breath, she felt something else leave her, something warm and fluttering and precious. The pain in her back was nothing to the sick sensation that now overwhelmed her. She felt as if she had swallowed an abyss. She knew that if she was to save herself she must recover the precious thing that had flown out of her mouth when she had been struck.

She got to her feet and looked about. Then she saw a tiny creature writhing in the dust. She immediately recognized this was her own soul squirming there, close to expiring. It was alternately an ugly and an exquisite thing, switching back and forth, now black, now luminously white; now a loathsome grub, now a delicate winged being that might be a glittering moth or even a fairy. It was in its grub shape when Agnes picked it up with shaking hands and popped it into her mouth. She was careful not to swallow. On her tongue, she felt the thing grow moist and begin to flutter. Then she felt it no more and she understood it was home now. She had restored her soul to herself.

Whenever Agnes woke from this dream, she would go over its various parts. Someone had struck her sharply from behind and made her spit out her soul. But she had found it again. She was more and more convinced that the assailant in the dream was the surgeon and the stout stick his scalpel and laser. She began to fear that the psychic costs of a new face might be terribly severe. Still she wavered in her decision, particularly when a very handsome boy at school cursed her without provocation in the hallway. "Fuck-face! How can you stand yourself?" He looked her in the eye and his expression was deadly serious, tinged with disgust. Her stomach lurched and her flesh burned in humiliation. Yet she strove, and succeeded, in keeping her own face impassive. What hurt most was that she had sometimes thought this boy smiled at her in a special way. She had imagined him to be sensitive and discerning, and entertained fantasies in which he stroked her face, breasts and thighs and told her she was beautiful.

One evening Agnes unfolded all the cosmetic surgeon's pamphlets and spread them fanlike on her desk. She stood a very long time staring down at the photographs of joyful transformed faces. Or was it relief she saw in every "after" portrait? She began to cry silently, as she had done in the surgeon's office. But these were her old scalding tears. As they fell upon the open pamphlets, she half expected the pages to smoulder and char about the edges.

She woke early the next day, hours before her parents and sister. She was agitated and restless, as if her body had some urgent message to impart. The difficulty was she could not hear it properly because there was simply too much interference: a buzzing in her ears, and a prickling along the nerves of her arms and fingers. She managed to make herself a cup of tea, struggling to control her trembling hands. Suddenly her fear became a live visible thing, swooping out of the corner of the kitchen like a huge bat with exposed fangs. She held, with all her might, to a single thought. She must not let this bat-thing suck her sanity out of her. She felt she was being smothered and fought for breath under the wings' tight fretwork of small bones and stifling fur.

If she could only distract herself, she might neutralize the panic. It unnerved her that her legs were so unsteady and that she felt as weak as she had the previous winter during a severe bout of the flu. But with consciously slow steps, and deliberately deep breaths, she succeeded in getting herself from the kitchen into the living-room. There she drew back the curtains to reveal a jewel-like dawn. She made herself speak aloud the names of precious stones whose colours she recognized in the sky: beryl, amethyst, aquamarine, sapphire. She was amazed how this simple recitation helped calm her. She sat on the sofa facing the window so that she could focus on the various hues as they shifted one into another. When the sun rose, she had to look away because it struck her as brash and swollen and bloody. This was how her poor face would look after the surgeon's operation, it occurred to her: a bleeding mash of flesh and bone against a white sheet.

"I am sore afraid." Once again, she spoke aloud the words that came to mind. She put her forefinger to her cheek and lip and nose. Immediately she regretted this, for the gesture, added to her spoken confession of fear, triggered the panic again. She grasped the first thing that came to hand in an effort to divert herself. It was a British Sunday newspaper which her mother sometimes bought because the art critic was an old university friend. Agnes shook the paper so that the magazine insert slid out. It would be far easier, she thought, to look at pictures than to try to read.

The image on the magazine's cover grabbed all her attention. Instead of the usual striking human face or figure, dramatically posed, she was looking at the life-sized portrait of a female chimpanzee. The white-type

[19]

caption, set against the animal's wiry, dark hair, told her that this was Noona, aged three, a resident of an animal sanctuary in north Congo. Noona had been rescued from hunters who had slaughtered her parents for bush meat. For her portrait, the chimpanzee had compressed her lips in an apparent smile. Agnes was struck by how human Noona's mouth looked, as did her brown eyes. They had the depth and gleam of warm topaz. She perceived no wariness in the animal's eyes: only an unsullied trust and innocence and a tragic gentleness that made her want to wring her hands in anguish.

She imagined the frantic squeals of Noona's parents as the poachers hacked at their flesh. She felt nauseous, and then overcome by useless fury. Inside the magazine, she found twenty more portraits of bonobos, orangutans and chimpanzees, all of whom had found refuge in sanctuaries. The text under each portrait gave the animal's name and a brief history of the ordeals it had undergone at the hands of hunters or unscrupulous owners or exotic pet traders. Many of these rescued animals were suffering from mental disorders — like Ruella, an orangutan who had been found in a poacher's hut, curled up beside her mother's decapitated head.

A cataclysmic jolt went through her spine. Agnes sat erect under the force of an emotion she could not at first define. The longer she looked at the individual portraits, the more she perceived not just a vague resemblance to her own mirror-face, but an actual bond of blood and being. "Flesh of my flesh," she said aloud. Never before had she understood anything with such clarity. She was connected to these animals through time past by way of an ancient ancestral lineage. But she was bound, as well, through all her personal future time. These bonobos and orangutans and chimpanzees were the beings who had preceded her on the road where she had been forced to spit out her soul. That they were ahead of her meant she could learn from them. She saw how she might strive to emulate their dignity, and cultivate the watchful awareness that made their eyes glow so finely.

Was she romanticizing? Of course she had read about human beings' sacred relation with animals, and this had always struck her as a pleasing idea. But never before had she properly grasped what it meant. Now that she had actually experienced the irrepressible and electrifying nature of this bond, she saw that it must, and would, revolutionize her life. Nothing in her world would be the same again. The very sunlight she walked in and the air she breathed would look and feel different to her. Two other new certainties came to her: that she would never again eat meat of any kind, or allow the cosmetic surgeon anywhere near her face.

Half an hour later, when she heard her parents come into the kitchen, she was able to tell them with absolute confidence: "I have decided. I don't want the operation. I don't want my face to be cut."

"Honey, you're sure?"

It disturbed Agnes to see how deeply furrowed was her father's brow. She saw the same perplexed concern on her mother's face.

"I am sure. I want to keep this face. My face."

It was not her parents, but Noona's trusting topaz eyes she saw as she spoke these words.

She had made her decision with all the clarity and courage she could muster, and was sure it was the right one. Nevertheless, she kept seeing the concern that had clouded her parents' eyes. Could she really bear all her life to come with this face? She began then to think about her mother's reaction to Piero di Cosimo's *Hunt*; her refusal to recognize the suffering that was the lot of living creatures everywhere. With that inane perspective, how on earth could she understand her own daughter's daily fare of pain? Agnes tasted something vile in her mouth and wondered if it was the bitterness of lost illusions. She had always believed her mother felt the pain along with her; that she ached, as much as she did, at the indignities she had to undergo every day, the humiliations that sometimes made her want to claw her own flesh from her face.

My mother has never really understood what I endure. In the cold light of this bleak revelation, Agnes saw herself condemned to a future where she was utterly isolated, subjected to unending sadistic treatment and shame. And there *was* increasing shame these days, as the nasty remarks hurled at her had more and more a prurient cast (*"I guess you like it from behind, eh monkey-girl?"*) What gave them the right, she raged within herself, the greasy-haired men who yelled at her out of the windows of their rusting cars; the twelve-year-old boys in the private school blazers who sniggered at her on the bus? She tried so hard to pity them for their self-damning shallowness and their sad, sick obsessions. In fact, she hated them because they made her feel so dirty. What have I done, she thought. Have I thrown away my only chance to look and feel normal?

She felt more and more sick and overwhelmed by dread. How could she possibly bear her life to come if she was never to feel a genuine empathy from another living human creature? To steady herself, she retreated to her room and took out the precious art book. Turning several of its heavy glossy pages at once, a scene opened before her that seemed uncannily to respond to her need. A lovely young woman lay in a flowering meadow flanked by two mourners: a gentle-faced satyr kneeling at her head on his strong goat legs and a sorrowful brown hound keeping vigil at her feet. So palpable was the grief of these two compassionate attendants that she felt they reached out to embrace her as well, with all the stirring warmth of their creature-life.

She sensed, in her very blood, that this painting conveyed a poignant mystery, a holy secret that the painter had won through the agonized labour of his craft and a belief in something fine and transcendent that lifted all life high above the abyss of bloody deeds and coiling tragic circumstance. Every detail intensified her conviction: the care he lavished on the tiny wildflowers of the meadow; the reappearance of the loyal brown dog on the sandy strand in the distance where he appeared to be stopping a fight between a black dog and a white one; a great heron silhouetted against the misty water, its supple gaunt frame looking so like a keyhole; the way the young woman's rare luminosity, even in death, was mirrored in the sheen upon the blue-white river. If she meditated on this painting, as religious people did on icons, she sensed she might enter the hushed mystery of its world. The more she looked, the more she wanted to look. And the more she wanted to know.

She was certain that the painting contained a life-giving truth, despite the fact it was a death scene. Discovering that truth, and how it connected to the painter's obvious care and attention to the lives of animals, was a task she knew she had to take on.

She lay on the bed with the heavy art book propped on her knees, and turned the pages with a slow and tender care. Many of the book's colour plates drew from her gasps of astonished joy. In the animals she saw there, some with their own and some with human faces, she encountered, again and again, eyes that knew the bloodied, troubled road she travelled. These eyes were benign, wise and sorrowful. They seemed to look out at her directly and to welcome her. So too, she believed, did the artist who painted them.

TWO

The Painter (1492)

PIERO WAS GRIEVING FOR THE Medici's giraffe. The marvellous creature, a gift to Lorenzo from the Sultan of Egypt, had broken its neck when some fool in the family's household led it beneath too low an archway. The animal's needless death sickened and enraged Piero, for the giraffe was a veritable miracle and he had loved it dearly.

The first time he saw the giraffe, its head like an antlered flower atop the astonishing neck, he had wanted to fall on his knees and weep for joy. Had he painted himself at that moment, he would have shown his face shining, his eyes and mouth as round as apples. He was elated, and thanked God for the existence of such an incomparably graceful being. And what a gentle regard the animal turned on all those who looked at him in wonder. Children ran to peer out upper windows to see him as he cantered by, then clapped their hands in delight. The giraffe had seemed to smile upon them. His eyes were mild.

Piero had been privileged to sketch the giraffe on several visits to the Medici menagerie at Poggio a Caino. He had recast his sketches as pen-and-ink drawings for inclusion in his book of portraits of animals, rare and exotic. In these drawings, he had portrayed the giraffe with his head uplifted so that he seemed to yearn toward the stars, where he might meet his mate again and graze upon sidereal delicacies. How nobly the animal bore his loneliness and years of exile. How he must have missed his African homeland. Perhaps it was a comfort to him to be so much admired, Piero thought, and to draw forth so many smiles and cries of joy whenever he went about the city as the brightest feature in the Medici's many pageants and parades. Such was the gift all animals gave to humankind, if men had but the eyes to see and understand this rightly.

Piero began to shape in his mind how he might give the giraffe a memorial more lasting than his pen-and-ink drawings. In oils on canvas, he could render the creature's subtle colouring of ripe apricots and weathered ivory. Against an unmarked sky of palest blue, he could show to advantage the long, pure curve of his neck, and the fine modelling of his face, antlers and ears. And, to offset perfectly the taut strength of the animal's tawny back and shoulders, he would set behind him a mountain of turquoise. He would depict the giraffe in that stance he had so often assumed in life, his pale right foreleg bent slightly at the knee, and his hoof lifted from the ground.

The portrait must catch that exact moment when the giraffe turned his head and his features took on the expression that Piero most loved to see. This was a look of benign curiosity with which the giraffe regarded men and women at their work or daily chores. Piero saw suddenly, on the shining tableau of his mind's eye, the diverse elements of the scene on which the giraffe would gaze. Two gods sit upon the ground, their flesh sagging about their jaws and naked chests, aging as real men age.

The grey-haired Aeolus, god of the winds, pumps bellows to keep alive the fire of the forge at which Vulcan works, shaping molten iron with instruments utterly new to mankind. This was the Golden Age, the painter realized, a time of men and women's innocence — an unreal time perhaps, but one in which he wanted ardently to believe. No blood lust. No scheming cruelty. No slaughter of animals and no eating of their flesh. A time of veneration for every living thing in the natural world.

For Piero, these things included mountains, the craggy outcroppings of cliffs and simple stones. They too lived and had their own individual character. In the foreground of the scene, he saw a cricket sunning itself, content upon the flat, warm stone that was its dear companion. In this scene, he envisioned, fire would also be mankind's loving consort. The sparks Aeolus tended with his bellows glinted, as rubies did, inside a white hearth shaped like a scallop shell. Fire's potential uncontrollable frenzy was here contained and nurtured in its correct proportions by pagan gods who grasped its most capricious nature.

Piero stared into the flames of his own hearth. Their leaping and mercurial shapes seemed a mirror of his mind. The flames' very dance gave birth to faces, forms and figures so distinctive and so numerous he feared he might not live long enough to set them upon paper, wood or canvas. So teeming they were, and so quick and restless in their movement, most especially the marvellous hybrid creatures: trees with human faces, mermen with fishes' tails, satyrs and centaurs. He delighted to see them, each and every one. The satyrs now vaulted from flame tip to flame tip, their hooves gleaming like hazelnuts.

All these creatures' most natural wildness, their shining purity, counteracted the heaviness of spirit that sometimes affected him so sorely he could not abide the company of men. There were days indeed when he could not bring himself to pass through his front door out into the Via della Scalla. In these tormenting hours, he was so conscious of human sinfulness, it seemed to stain his very skin. He would study the backs of his hands, his palms and his naked forearms and see where the shadows had seeped into his flesh. He saw in himself that sombre hue, of mud rather than clay, that the great Masaccio had given the faces of Adam and Eve when they are expelled from the Garden of Eden. What inarticulate cry, what howl, issues from Eve's open mouth? Piero was sure he knew. Whenever he visited the Brancacci Chapel to stare awe-struck at Masaccio's fresco, he felt the need to stop up his own mouth with his hand, lest he sob aloud in sympathy with Eve and Adam's misery and most grievous shame.

Of course, his own ingrained melancholy was in part responsible for the loathsome burden that so often encumbered his spirit. Melancholia seemed to warp both his mind and his eye so that he saw nothing but human-kind's vicious destructiveness and blind arrogance. How could men think themselves superior to the creatures of the forests and seas and skies? What right had they to murder these beings to satisfy their despicable gluttony, vanity and blood lust? In his worst states of despair, his habitually vigorous body would fail him. He slumped upon his chair in a dim corner. When he did manage to stir himself and rise, he shuffled like a man of fourscore years, palsied and drained of strength.

There was an antidote for this poisonous melancholia, one he had first learned as a young apprentice from his master Cosimo Rosselli. His master was always much fascinated with the hermetic process of making gold from base matter. Indeed, it sometimes seemed to Piero that hunting out obscure secrets of alchemy meant more to Cosimo Rosselli than did the art of his fescoes, even those on which they had laboured for Pope Sixtus IV in the Sistine Chapel in Rome. His master early instructed him in the most essential paradox of the arcane science. The *nigredo*, the spirit's most pitch-black state, Rosselli told him, was necessary precondition for the lustrous gold. So Piero struggled to remind himself each time he felt the smothering coils of melancholia grip his soul, and its deadly torpor numb his limbs. He had learned he must suffer these states, groping through blackness like a blind man confined in a room not his own, until at last he perceived a sliver of light.

This light came sometimes in the form of a fleeting mental visitation, a face or figure or scene that by its particular refinement, purity and calm, restored him to himself. Once, it was a vision of the young Saint John the Baptist. The saint he saw was barely more than a boy, with rounded cheeks and lips and a tousled mass of curls covering all but the very tip of his ear. Later that day, Piero took up his brush and strove to replicate the profile of this boy he had seen. He wanted most especially to capture his mild and steadfast gaze that radiated outward, Piero was sure, to embrace the Lamb of God. In the finished painting, he had shown the whiteness of the lamb reflected in a crescent gleam upon the boy's throat.

Sometimes the light that penetrated and roused him from his melancholy was as close as his own window shutter where the sun gilded a slat. This lustre called to him and stirred his blood. He would fling open the shutters and stare amazed at the tumultuous greenery of his garden: the leaves of the grape vines and of the fig trees profuse and shining and wild. Here, at his very doorstep, nature followed her own course freely, for he refused to let anyone prune his fruit trees or cut back the vines. What right had he to make sap bleed or blight the forms that nature made? He would settle himself outside upon a three-legged stool and take up again the study that was the root of his being and his art, breathing in the emerald air and the pungent mint that grew thick at his feet. Within the compass of the following hour, he would be attentive to every species of vegetable or creature life he saw inside the boundary of his garden, no matter how minute. And thus he would find himself healed, the murk of his despondency shed like a filthy garment, his mind lifted up by the sight of an ant's forefoot or the filigreed fretwork of a cricket's wing.

Yes, he thought, it was always in the secular kingdom of animals, birds and insects that he found his sure salvation. No human touch or voice could cure him as these creatures did, or cause him such unselfish joy. This was why he would continue to lament sorely the senseless death of the Medici giraffe. A glimpse of that dear creature's rare form would be more welcome to him than a vision of God's angels. Piero did not consider this a sacrilege. Nor did he think it wrong that, in the portrait he imagined, the giraffe would cast his glow of goodness upon every other creature and, by his gentle nature, bind element to element. His unspotted soul would generate a light to pour forth and bless every object in the world of the canvas: the tiny horse that accompanies him and mimics his gait; the birds of the air; and the turbaned man and his wife in a red cloak, who sit together on the ground adoring their new baby. The light from the giraffe's eye will also touch a gracious youth upon a white horse who watches bemusedly as the two full-fleshed, aged gods demonstrate how metal is made.

The cricket on its hearth-stone watches in his turn a young man who sleeps in the foreground of the painting. This youth is utterly naked, and he sleeps the untroubled sleep of a child, his arms folded easily about his midriff, and his knees drawn up so that he presents himself in all modesty, but also in utter trust. Piero sees that it is this naked, sleeping youth, his face and body turned toward the viewer, who most eloquently declares the innocence of this time and place, this world that flows out of the pure gaze of the Medici giraffe.

It is a world where fire, the terrible transforming element whose extremes Piero dreads above all else, is mastered and confined in the shell-shaped hearth of the gods to warm and hearten humankind. That confinement of the yearning flames is a sign to him that this place will keep its holiness.

As a boy, Piero had been fated to witness the worst that fire can do. Out of a leaden sky the bolt struck, so fast and furious he felt its heat upon his lips and the fine hair stand up on his wrists. He was walking in the woods outside the city, hoping he might spy a boar or a bear. What he saw instead was the death throes of a great ox, felled where it stood by a second bolt of lightning. He would never forget the sound of the animal's piteous bellowing as it sank to its knees. There was a moment when he saw what no human being should see: the organs and the bones of the beast lit up as if for some ghastly spectacle designed by devils who delight in pain. The animal's skin began to burn and to peel away from its frame in long bubbling strips. Yet still it bellowed and still the boy Piero cursed himself that he could do nothing to abate its agony.

That was why, even as a grown man, he shuddered violently and shrank into himself whenever he heard the doleful rumble of thunder. He knew there were those in the city who mocked and reviled him for this fear and for other of his habits they considered strange. The truth was he did not care what they thought of him. They did not see the things he saw: whether of the dark or the light. They did not wake in the night, with the sweat pooling on their chests and in the palms of their hands, because they have had a vision of all the forests of the world burning. They did not see men and women and animals fleeing a world on fire, all of them labouring to speak aloud the heavy grief upon their hearts. Or was it something else they tried to tell him? His own tongue was swollen in his mouth when he woke from these dreams of The Great Burning. He too laboured to speak, and could not. And so he would take up his red chalk and paper from beside the bed and begin to sketch shapes fantastic and majestic: forms that had beguiled him on days previous in the massed and drifting clouds of dawn — persons and creatures and creature-persons that other men might think monstrous, but that he found glorious. As he saw the images in his mind take shape upon the paper, he knew himself, despite his fits of despondency and his solitary nature, to be greatly blessed.

Through work and an abiding humility, he might yet help to prevent the mighty conflagration he witnessed in the thick forests of his dreams.

THREE

Out with the Toads

A T FIRST LIGHT, THE CROWS swooped over the gabled roofs of the town. Sometimes, as she stood watching from the tall window of her college dorm, Agnes would imagine that the birds had just been shaken loose from the cradling hand of God. That was why they looked joyous as they poured out of the east and over the houses.

She recognized the shape and surge of her own happiness when she looked at the birds. She still could not quite believe she was here; that she had won a scholarship for a full four years at one of the finest liberal arts colleges in North America. Everything was new. It was as if she had stepped through one of the magical doors in the children's stories her mother used to read to her and Phoebe. She had always assumed, even then, that it was only lovely, golden Phoebe who would be able to pass through the doors into the dewy lands of fairies and talking animals.

Yet she had found the latch. She had passed through into this dear place where the trees were burnished and every book she touched brought the thrill of imminent discovery. Burckhardt. Ovid. Pico della Mirandola.

Panofsky. And, of course, every scholarly article she could find on Piero di Cosimo. It was to him she owed her scholarship and her new life. She had written a paper on the painter that her art teacher had passed on to an academic board she hadn't known existed. Then, with her teacher's help, she had reworked the paper into a full-blown thesis, most of which she could still recite by heart:

"The Piero di Cosimo known to most Renaissance art scholars is an eccentric misanthrope who cannot stand the sound of church bells or of crying babies, and who eats nothing but hard-boiled eggs, which he cooks fifty at a time. He deliberately leaves the vines and fruit trees of his garden straggling and unkempt. He is best known for his fantasia, an imagination that spawned the monsters, satyrs, centaurs and other unreal creatures that sport, love, laugh and fight inside the confines of his canvases and decorative panels. Had Piero striven to keep the wilder excesses of his imagination in check, had he been less 'brutish' (bestiale) in his personal conduct and domestic arrangements, he would have been a far greater painter, a master who could have rivalled the stature of Leonardo da Vinci himself."

This is the judgement on Piero di Cosimo's work and character that has been passed down through the centuries by Giorgio Vasari in his influential Lives of the Artists. *But Vasari, a highly mannered and largely passionless painter of the Late Renaissance, had a particular agenda to promote in his essays on the Italian masters of the generation prior to his own. What Vasari desired above all else was the "professionalization" of the artist in his society. He wanted his noble and wealthy patrons to relate to him as a social equal, and he sought to be as courtly, well-mannered, well-spoken and well-dressed as they were.*

On all these scores, Piero di Cosimo fell vastly short according to Vasari, and he therefore makes Piero his scapegoat. By emphasizing di Cosimo's alleged eccentricity and brutish behaviour, and his flaunting of patrons' specifications, Vasari conjures up an image of all that an artist ought not to be. It is this propagandistic word portrait of an unkempt and ill-mannered eccentric with a penchant for bizarre grotesquerie that has infected perceptions of this remarkable artist up to the present.

In her historical novel Romola, *for example, George Eliot introduces Piero di Cosimo as a minor character, drawing heavily on Vasari's characterization. Eliot's Piero is curmudgeonly. He lives in squalor, and co-habits not just with rabbits and doves, but also with a trio of corpulent toads. In the twentieth century, W. H. Auden likewise seizes on Vasari's notion of di Cosimo as bestial, and implies that the painter was also sadistic and blood-thirsty. His poem* "Woods" *opens with a description of* "those primal woods that Piero di Cosimo loved to draw, where nudes, bears, lions, sows with women's heads / Mounted and murdered and ate each other raw . . . :"

My thesis is that Auden, Eliot, and most certainly Vasari, all misconstrue and misrepresent an artist who believed in, and delighted in depicting, the power, beauty and moral superiority of the animal kingdom. In the painting to which Auden refers (The Hunt, Metropolitan Museum of Art, New York), *it is in fact men who are the murderers. As if in response to their brutality, the forest setting of* The Hunt *has begun to blaze. Masses of yellow-black smoke blight the far horizon. There is an ominous red glow between the trees just behind the male hunters, who carry on their grim business, oblivious to the threat of conflagration.*

Piero di Cosimo pursues this trope in The Forest Fire *(Ashmolean Museum, Oxford), which some astute scholars now recognize as one of the great masterpieces of the Florentine Renaissance for its drama, sfumato, vivid coloration and disturbingly memorable images of the threatened wildlife. Of the scores of animals and birds who flee the flames, or who stand rooted in the foreground uncertain where to run, two have human faces. One of these is a roe deer, whose profile is that of a bearded Florentine youth. The other is a wild boar, whose grey shoulders and flanks glimmer as if lit from within. The human face the wild boar shows us, framed by luxuriantly flowing hair, could be either male or female. The gentle eyes look out at us from a countenance that is consummately serene and philosophical in the midst of duress and danger.*

Is this the face of Piero di Cosimo himself? If so, what truths does he have to impart about the mystery of fire, and the conjoining of human and animal forms and souls? These questions remain, for now, tantalizing ambiguities at the heart of this extraordinary painter's finest work."

Agnes would never forget how all three of her examiners nodded as she came to this conclusion.

"Indeed," said the slim, elegant man who sat in the middle of the three renowned scholars who had listened to her so attentively. "Tantalizing ambiguity. Quite so. You obviously have your subject, Ms. Vane, and your work ahead cut out for you."

All three had smiled at her graciously when Agnes left the room. At that moment, she'd been happier than ever before in her life, even more so perhaps than when the letter arrived three weeks later informing her she had won the scholarship.

"You obviously have your subject, Ms. Vane, and your work ahead cut out for you."

She recited these words to herself often, and each time she would see the wild boar with the gentle human face she believed to be Piero di Cosimo's. He looked out at her with benevolence and a sorrowful wisdom, while behind him the fleet deer ran to the east and to the west, and the trees put forth their long ruby tongues of flame.

FOUR

Pinto

FOR MANY YEARS, PINTO HAD been at war with his own rage. He had come to think of it as a firestorm he must always be damping down as fast as he could. If ever he were to let his fury escape and flare outside the confines of his body, he knew he could do great harm. He was a large man, and strong. He was terrified of the damage he might do. Sometimes, when he was walking, he would picture his interior glowing like the dull black-red of a coiled stove burner turned on high. This thought made him wince, and unconsciously all his muscles contracted, right down to his sphincter.

Yet no one seeing this ambling big-bodied young man would have guessed at the battle he waged within himself for hours every day. In fact, it was words like "pacific", "benign", and "beatific" that came to his professors and fellow students when they wanted to describe Peter (Pinto) Dervaig. This was because his broad face with its heavy-lidded eyes and sweet mouth seemed always to be smiling. Some people thought he resembled storybook drawings of the Man in the Moon. Others looked at him and saw a huge stone Buddha come to life. Wasn't it wonderful, many people at the college remarked, that such a big man emanated such gentleness, and despite his affliction? Pinto suffered from abnormal skin pigmentation. Large patches of his flesh, particularly on his face, were markedly different colours: pale rose, mocha, and a light green shade almost identical to pistachio. He looked piebald, and that meant it was impossible for any sighted person not to stare on first encountering him.

These days, Pinto often comforted himself that the worst years of his affliction were behind him. Not that his condition had improved, or any of his various patches of colour faded. The pink, the mocha and the green were, if anything, more vivid and clearly demarked than ever. When he was younger, and of course much smaller, people had scrutinized his face long, hard and unfeelingly, as if he were a bizarre object on display in a museum, but now, at the age of twenty, he had the protective advantages of his great height and obvious strength. And he had discovered, too, a wondrous fact, that in the academic setting of a small liberal arts college of sterling reputation, even strangers were inclined to give him the respectful treatment he had yearned for as a small boy when he used to pray ardently each night that the following day would be overcast because on dull days, and most especially on rainy ones, passersby were far less likely to notice his strange complexion.

At school, he had learned to endure. "Yuck!" "Ugh!" "Are you for real?" were the least offensive of the comments he heard each day. The most barbaric remarks he had trained himself to block out altogether. Because his peers feared his condition might be contagious, they would not touch him. Indeed, he was always surrounded by his own ring of space. He taught himself to go deep within, to retreat to an inner world of dream and reflective thought. He became a voracious reader. Among the books inherited from his grandfather were ancient paperback Westerns by a man with the wonderful name of Zane Grey. It was in these books that Peter came across the pinto horse, recognized his own image and renamed himself.

Because what he most yearned for was simple kindness and the respect one creature willingly gives another, he also read all he could about the world's religions. He took on the perplexing study of ethics when he was just eleven. He decided he wanted to be a "good man," by which he meant never deliberately to make another living being suffer, and to help others where he could and they were open to his doing so. He believed he could be content if he could just learn to be as decent and guileless as his beloved dog, Yangtze. She was a red chow crossed with a Labrador so that instead of having a squashed pug face, her nose was long. Yangtze had the indigo tongue of the chow and exotic, black-rimmed eyes. She never learned to bark. Instead, she howled, often at things invisible and at inconvenient hours. She also had a low and thrilling growl that she turned on nearly all other dogs, and most people. She was not at all vicious, only superbly defensive — of herself and of Pinto. She liked to show off for him, becoming a red blur as she ran around the outside of the house. Then she would stop abruptly and dance toward him, her curved fan-like tail and thick skirts of fur swaying. He would bury his face in her thick, dry, briny fur. He felt safe there. He loved her unstintingly and in the depths of her lovely eyes he saw his affection returned. He believed no other creature would ever love him with such intensity and loyalty.

He sometimes wondered if his mother loved him at all, or if she saw him largely as a burden with which she had been unfairly inflicted, but that she shouldered out of an ingrained duty. When he was very young, and his mother brought friends home, she would ask him to stay in his room and not show himself at all. She would even provide him with a plastic bucket so that he did not have to come out to use the toilet. She had tried hard to make these occasions pleasurable, getting him little treats, like big bars of chocolate and rented movies. He must watch these very quietly, she told him. He was an obedient child and eager to please her. Yet he sensed the truth of the matter: that she was ashamed of his appearance and did not want to have to explain his disfigurement to her friends.

"Disfigurement" was the word their family doctor had used. He referred Pinto to a dermatologist who was reputedly a wizard with laser surgery. Foolishly, Pinto had allowed himself to hope. The meeting with the derma-tologist was heartbreakingly brief. In such cases, she told Pinto and his mother, the chances of success were very slim. Moreover, the surgery, which would involve a long and painful healing process, could cost upward of a quarter of a million dollars. Pinto heard his mother groan. Finding this amount of money was, he knew, like asking them to make a soup out of moonbeams. His mother worked in a casino, and they lived in a tiny rented house. There was no other family member who could help them raise such an enormous sum. Pinto's father, whom he could not remember at all was, according to his mother, "a deadbeat who had never contributed even a penny of support."

[41]

The dermatologist proffered crumbs of comfort. "There are new technologies being developed all the time," she said. "In another decade, there may well be something we can do for you with more assured results and far less pain. By then, you'll be — what? — just twenty-one or twenty-two. And your whole life still before you."

Pinto responded with the beatific smile he had already begun practising. He had scotch-taped a picture of Mahatma Gandhi to the mirror in his bedroom because the Mahatma's was the smile he wanted to emulate. Gandhi, the "great-souled," was one of his heroes, the embodiment of a moral daring, courage and selflessness that filled him with awe. He often thought about the ratcheting pain to which this gaunt and often ill elderly man had subjected himself: the hunger strikes and the long, punishing protest marches on naked, bleeding feet. A civil disobedience founded on non-violence. That was Satyagraha. Pinto liked to say this word aloud. It sounded to him holy, and yet solid, like the kind of sturdy, deep-rooted tree that held the cosmos together. Satyagraha meant you turned the other cheek. You did not strike back when your opponent dealt you a heavy blow.

Pinto often had reason to turn his other mottled cheek when he found poisonous words, and sometimes dog turds, flung his way. At fourteen he towered over every boy and most of the teachers in his school. Because of his size, and his schoolmates' persistent fear his skin condition was infectious, they kept their distance. They treated him as if he were a pariah dog and felt free to curse him. He heard himself called "devil's arse-face" and "disgusting dog vomit." He heard many ugly things and tried ardently to rise above it and smile bravely. What hurt most was when the foul words came from girls and young women. Once he got home, he would stare at himself in the bathroom mirror and touch, in turn, each of the diverse blotches of colour upon his face. "You are unique, Pinto," he told his mirror reflection. "You are kind-hearted and you will be loved."

"You will be loved," he repeated because repetition exerted its own magic, like mantras or the choruses of old English and Scots ballads. He found the plots of these ancient songs consoling because they showed him there were many fates far worse than his own.

He took great solace, too, in singing to himself the song Gandhi had sung as he walked all day barefoot on stony ground with only the spotless loincloth covering his rickets-thin frame:

Walk alone
If they answer not thy call, walk alone;
If they are afraid and cower mutely facing the wall,
O thou of evil luck
Open thy mind and speak out alone

"O thou of evil luck." That was him: Peter (Pinto) Dervaig who had the bad, bad luck to be born with such a face. Yet he would persist. He swore to himself he would. He would go on striving to emulate, to some small degree, the illustrious life examples of people like Mahatma Gandhi who defined their own "good" and then lived it.

Above all else, Pinto strove to be kind. In his own neighbourhood, he made a practice of befriending several old ladies who lived nearby and needed help with cutting their lawns or carrying heavy garbage cans and recycling boxes to the curbside. None of them ever commented on

[43]

his "affliction" or even so much as looked at him askance. They gave him milk and cookies for his services (he always refused their offers of money) and showed him photographs of their children and grandchildren, whom they seemed sadly never to see.

Often all they wanted was someone to talk to and Pinto, who had no social life of his own, had time for them. He was a good and patient listener, although he did quite often find his mind wandering. He told himself this was forgivable. While his old ladies chatted on, he would indulge in daydreams — of how it would be when he got into a good college and lived in a real intellectual community. No one there would call him a freak. And he would have professors to guide him so that he would finally understand what Kant meant by the Categorical Imperative, or how he might, like Julian of Norwich, "purify" his motives.

He had a certain plan for his future life when he would escape at last from the small-minded cruelties of his peers. He clung to this plan, as to a lifeline. He studied hard. He got excellent grades in all his subjects except trigonometry. He continually deepened and widened his interior world. He chanted Gandhi's walking song to himself and practised his beatific smile. He kept on in good faith, envisioning the fine and noble-hearted man he would become. And how he would look: no longer disfigured, but transfigured. He would be as beautiful as Yangtze. His skin would have a radiance that wrapped him in a glow of warm light. His very physical being would reflect his striving toward the pure shining Forms of Love and Goodness Plato wrote of, and which the deep work of the soul and small acts of kindness might discover.

It will be so, he told himself each morning and evening. I will transform my evil luck.

Then the terrible thing happened.

It began with an old lady's anguish. Just as he was leaving the house on his way to school the morning of May 5 — a date he was never to forget — he saw Mrs. Eatrides limping along the street half-dressed and with her long white hair streaming unbound. She seemed not to realize that her dress was gaping open at the front. Then he saw to his horror that she was actually clawing at the exposed flesh of her chest. He feared, although he could not quite believe, that she had gone mad.

Mrs. Eatrides had always struck him as one of the most vigorous and self-reliant of the elderly ladies he helped. She sometimes asked him to cut her lawn at the height of the summer when the grass grew too rapidly and thickly for her to keep up. Or to help her get Mikos, her much-cherished ten-year-old male cat, into his carrier for visits to the veterinarian. Mikos was a long-bodied cat with topaz eyes and thick fur the colour of dark honey. He was also spoiled, stubborn and haughty.

"Mikos. Mikos." When Pinto ran out to the distraught Mrs. Eatrides, she could only repeat the cat's name over and over, in a voice made hoarse by calling. He saw that the old lady's bottom lip was bleeding and guessed she had bitten it unthinkingly in her distress. He managed to calm her a little and persuaded her to come inside his house, where he made her a mug of tea, heavily sugared.

Pinto's mother was asleep after her night shift at the casino, and he did not like to wake her. Yet he was reluctant to help Mrs. Eatrides button up the front of her dress or tidy her hair. To try to do so struck him as disrespectful. He was apprehensive as well, that she might at any moment become hysterical again and start plucking at the loose flesh of her neck and chest. He put the mug of tea in her hands. She inhaled the warmth and the scent, took a sip, and then set the mug down, precisely centred on a cardboard coaster imprinted with words "Bonanza Casino." This simple domestic gesture was enough to restore her to herself.

"Such a state," she whispered as she buttoned up her dress with trembling hands. That finished, she began to smooth her hair, gathering the straying lengths into the rucked elastic from which they had escaped, winding and patting until the sliver strands assumed the familiar shape that satisfied her.

"Sorry, so sorry," she gestured vaguely to the front of her dress and to her hair. "Such a kind young man. So rare. Very rare." She nodded to herself.

Then her body sagged. She began to shake and to sob. "Mikos. Mikos."

"Is he sick, Mr. Eatrides?" Surely not dead?

"Gone. Gone. Missing. Two days. Three nights." She held up three fingers and looked at them dolefully.

Pinto escorted Mrs. Eatrides home, and saw her safely inside. He promised her he would go immediately to look for Mikos. He could easily afford to take the day off school. Besides, he was full of foreboding. There was in the neighbourhood a tribe of young boys, all between eight and eleven, who delighted in the torture of small creatures. Pinto had twice come upon them stoning wrens and chickadees, and had chastized them as calmly as his burgeoning rage allowed.

"Fuck off, yuck-face!" the bravest of them had retorted. But he was three times the height of the tallest of the boys and more than twice their breadth and he had seen the fear in their eyes and had managed to save a bird or two from a torturous death. He was under no illusion that his reprimand and warning had curbed the young band's sadistic practices, so when he set off in search of Mikos, he prepared himself for the worst. There was, to the west of the neighbourhood, a railway track long defunct, bordered by three storage sheds that had somehow survived decades of neglect and torrential rain. Ever since he could remember, these sheds had been colonized by successive gangs of young boys indulging in pursuits grubby and bloody. Or so he surmised from the reek in the vicinity of the sheds and the crude drawings of sexual organs and dismembered body parts daubed on the outer walls.

Because he was a loner, Pinto regarded the things bands of boys did together from an almost anthropological perspective. He observed and sniffed the air, and was unsettled by their penchant for cruelty. He was at an utter loss to understand the satisfaction they apparently took from inflicting pain on small animals, themselves and each other. Once, he had sat on the bus beside one of the tribe and been appalled at the suppurating mess on the boy's forearm.

"You ought to have the school nurse look at that," he'd said, striving for a non-patronizing tone.

"It's a tattoo, yuck-face. They always look like this to start with."

The boy stared fixedly ahead, while Pinto tried not to think about dirty needles and pins, and poisonous home-made inks. He went inward, to that place he worked at so hard to cultivate: the cool crystalline corridors where he focused solely on things holy, like Plato's Eternal Forms and Gandhi's selflessness.

All that changed when he opened the door of the second shed and found what was left of Mikos nailed to the wall. The boys had plucked out one of the cat's eyes and torn off his left back leg. They had ripped open his soft topaz belly and pulled out his lungs, and guts and small heart.

Pinto's stomach lurched. His eyes streamed. His fists twitched. He began to pray — he was no longer sure to what — that Mikos had expired long before the boys began to blind and maim him. Then he saw, through his tears and unholy rage, a deathly human face superimposed on the wall beside the crucified cat. He knew two things for certain: that the face was not really there; and that what he saw was the demise of his own imagined soul and the man he had wanted to be. At that moment, the very idea he was a man disgusted him. He turned his back on Mikos because he could not bear to look at the mangled remains any longer. Nor did he have it in him to take the cat down and bury its body deep in the earth. He could not stand the idea of touching the corpse, and becoming any more contaminated than he already was, contaminated by reason of being human. For one of the most terrifying things he'd felt within himself was a desire for vengeance, bloody and exact. He wanted, and loathed himself for the urge, to hurt the little tribe of torturers as they had hurt Mikos.

"I am this," he thought, as the tears streamed down his face and his fists tightened into balls; he imagined pummelling the boys' faces, mashing their flesh together with their bones. Again and again, he saw in his mind's eye, re-enacted for him in heartless detail, the death of the luminous soul he had cherished and laboured at so hard. Its death's-head grinned at him as if at some merciless cosmic joke. His whole life plan had been pure sham and delusion. He did not have the makings of a saint or a mystic. He was too corrupt, too full of self-disgust at his own humanity ever to become a truly "good man." Yet some residue of his old self still yearned to do the decent thing. He must beat back the desire for vengeance, he told himself, even if this meant a physical scourging of his own flesh.

And he must keep Mrs. Eatrides from ever finding out what the boys had done to Mikos. He was certain she would torment herself by dwelling on the cat's agony and ultimately go mad. He could think of only one way to destroy the evidence and that was to burn the building down. There was no shortage of matches in the shed, nor of flammable materials, including greasy pizza boxes, chip bags, pornographic magazines and discarded ragged clothing. Pinto set fires in all four corners and stayed long enough to see the flames leap up the wall where Mikos hung.

Then he went out the door and squatted at some distance to watch the vile place consumed by a conflagration he believed wholly justified. It did occur to him that if he were spotted, he might be charged with arson or mischief-making of some sort. He told himself it was well worth the risk to stay and see the shed burn. He ardently hoped that Mikos's bones would burn as well. *Mrs. Eatrides must never know what I know,* he kept telling himself. *It would destroy her.*

He was surprised what pleasure he took from the spectacle of the fire: its glow and wild mercurial aspect struck him as consummately beautiful. He shifted from his squatting position to his knees and put his hands together in a gesture of prayer. He had not at first understood that by starting the fire, he was initiating a ritual. He was purifying the ground that had been polluted by evil and enabling Mikos's spirit to go free. He concentrated, as fervently as he could, on the image of Mikos, made whole and healthy again, floating high above the flames. What magnificent angels cats would make, he thought, far nobler, gentler and clean-souled than the chubby-faced boys with wings who cluttered the sky in old paintings of the Virgin Mary. Cherubim, he realized, looked far too much like the boys in the gang who had done this unspeakable thing.

The smoke made his eyes smart and he began to cry freely. If Mikos were an angel, why couldn't God be an antelope or a bear or a lion? Weren't animals wholly superior to humans, in any case? Didn't they once rule the world, from horizon to horizon? And deep in the secret caves of the earth, weren't the first paintings humans ever made portraits of animals that throbbed with sacred power? Pinto's eyes watered as he pictured first Mikos, the cat-angel, and then a hand that trembles in awe as it applies lines of red oxide and black charcoal to a cave wall. Revealed in the imagined torch light were shapes of auroch, horse and antelope, swift and eternal.

Ink-black clouds were gathering to the east as the remnants of the last two standing boards collapsed into the pyre. There was an unmistakable buzz in the air that presaged rain. Soon the skies would open, the fire would go out and this foul place would be doubly cleansed. He kept going back to the idea of animals' cleaner souls. No animal would have done to another creature the horrific thing the loathsome boys had done to Mikos, certainly not willfully, gleefully, urging one another on in their perversity.

No animal would have done this. A revolutionary thought seized and shook him. What he saw, with such an astounding clarity it made him almost afraid, was that human beings had taken a wrong turn that corrupted evolution. It had all gone terribly awry after men made those holy paintings of animals deep in the caverns of the earth. What should have come next, he saw, was a natural shift into mutual respect and fraternity; and yes, even conversations between animals and humans. He recalled in excitement pictures he had seen of St. Francis of Assisi shaking hands with a wolf, and talking with birds.

This was no fairy tale, he realized. Once upon a time, animals spoke. And if human beings had only listened properly, men and women and animals might have lived as equals, guiding each other and fructifying one another's thought. He wondered if "fructify" was quite the right word. But he liked the abundant possibility it suggested and the idea of a natural flowering of the spirit. If we had only opened our ears, we might not now be so foul a species, base of heart and drawn to do evil far more often than good. Or was it really that simple? Was he deluding himself?

Did he hallucinate what happened next? For the rest of his life he would swear to himself that he had not. There was perhaps no one he could ever tell what he had seen who would not think him mad. Yet it had happened. Mikos the cat-angel appeared in the sky and tried to speak to him. But to his immense sadness and frustration, Pinto could neither hear nor understand.

You have a holiness we have not. These were his last words to Mikos before the vision faded, and there was only the rain falling and the sizzling sound of the fire dying away under the downpour. When he stood up, he was at first unsteady on his feet. It was as if some essential interior balance had been forever undone. "I am no longer what I was," he chanted to himself as he ran. The repetition of this simple sentence helped repel the image of the crucified Mikos which threatened to invade his brain. He ran on with the heavy rain drenching his hair and pouring over his face and down his neck. His jeans and his shirt clung to his skin. Like seaweed to the corpse of a drowned man, he thought.

I am no longer what I was.

But what, then, was he? "I am a believer in the holiness of animals," he told himself. "I will, wherever possible, strive to be their defender and to keep them from harm." He recognized the overwhelming magnitude of this promise and his own limited resources for carrying it out. He was frail and he was fallible. He knew himself to be every bit as corrupt as the wicked boys. He saw that he had been up to now solipsistic and self-obsessed. He had wanted to be a "good man" so that he might narcissistically admire himself and luxuriate in the glow of his own virtue. Most despicable of all, he had wanted to be "good" so that he could feel superior to everyone who reviled him for his deformity. And his skin condition *was* a deformity. Why did he persist in kidding himself? He was an aberration. And then it hit him, as forcibly as a fist in the gut, why he had been born as he was. His freakish appearance made him alien enough to see the human species objectively. And his consequent role was to bear witness. He must spread the word; become a walking, breathing testament that nothing mattered more than this foundational ethical precept: that as a species, humans had to transform their attitude to animals.

How could he begin to build up the learning and the wisdom to make himself a fit proselytizer? What happens when your whole idea of mortality is upturned and no longer has just a human face? All these things Pinto ruminated on in the shower as the extremely hot water beat down on him, washing away the stink of the fire and of the boys' evil.

It was an irony that nearly choked him. His very first deed in his new identity was to tell a lie. This was something he had seldom done in his life, except to spare someone else's feelings. Which was undoubtedly the case with the untruth he told Mrs. Eatrides: "I am sorry, Mrs. Eatrides. I looked everywhere I could think of. We can try putting up notices around the neighbourhood with his picture. I can . . . "

She silenced him without a word, thrusting her right hand, palm outward, at the air. If he had been standing any closer to her, this hand would have struck him. She did not look like herself, with her right eyebrow raised appraisingly and her whole demeanour stern and judge-mental. She was an ancient seer casting a cold eye on his frailty. He was certain she could see through his duplicity. He had gone on babbling for a moment, about putting up posters and searching further,

Mrs. Eatrides nodded sharply. "Done," she said. "It is done." And she showed him the door.

Mrs. Eatrides never spoke to him again. Although he went several times to her door, and knocked loudly and patiently, she did not answer. A month passed. When he next walked down her street, he saw a real estate agent's bold red sign fixed to the white picket fence. A quick glance told him the house was already empty, even the blue-and-white ceramic pot, with its frilly geraniums, gone from the front step.

As he stood staring at the empty house, where once he had been made so welcome, he realized he was looking at the end of an entire passage of his life: a boyhood that had gone on far too long, where he had swaddled himself in delusions, most particularly about his own potential saintliness.

In the weeks that followed, he sought and found new heroes: like the British scientist J. B. S. Haldane who had experimented on himself rather than use animals, and Barry Horne, the animal rights activist who had died on a hunger strike in prison to publicize the crimes of the people who operated animal laboratories. Pinto regarded Horne's as a supreme death, invested with the deepest possible meaning. More and more, he haunted the websites of groups like the Animal Liberation Front that took the protection of animals as gravely as a religious vow. He read stories and saw images of animals' suffering that made the tears stream down his face and onto his keyboard. Some of the things he saw made him physically ill. But his indignation and rage were stronger than any nausea. He seemed always now to see, at the back of his mind, the iconic image of the rights warrior, his face obscured by a black wool balaclava, and a rescued dog or cat cradled in his arms.

By the agonizingly clear light of all that he learned, Pinto re-plotted his future. He would still study ethics, but he would focus as well on mass psychology. He wanted to know why it was that entire groups of people, and even entire nations, could become infected by, and then act upon, some absolutely vile idea. Salo. Babi Yar. Dachau. Abu Ghraib. If he thought about these things too long and too hard, he found himself wanting to divest himself of his human-ness, strip it off like a foul and maggot-ridden skin. He knew he had to be careful for his sanity's sake. Above all, he determined never to be part of an unthinking cult where his own moral sense got utterly subsumed by the group.

It did occur to him to confront the boys who had tortured Mikos, to see if he could at least stir their remorse. But he desisted simply because he feared he would not be able to control himself. He had burned their playhouse down, and perhaps that was vengeance enough, although vengeance was not what he had intended.

He had thought that fatal month of May could hold nothing worse for him than the crucifixion of Mikos. But then the second terrible thing happened. What he noticed first was Yangtze's limp and the way she held her head oddly to one side. Then he saw how glazed her eyes were. And yet how brave she was, trying to bound toward him and dance in her usual way, but stumbling and falling. He put his arms around her neck and tried not to sob too much into her fur, lest he upset her.

The veterinarian prescribed an antibiotic and a steroid to reduce the swelling in Yangtze's brain. Other than that, there was nothing to be done, except wait and watch and hope. Pinto tried, and failed, to be as brave as his dog. She was so uncomplaining, never whimpering or moping as most humans would have done. He thought he would never see anything as noble as her forbearance. His heart ached when she tried to rally for his sake. She would assume her old dancing pose and then collapse. Toward the end, he had to hold her up while she peed, because her legs simply gave way beneath her. He looked into her eyes and saw she knew it was time. He believed, and time proved him right, that he would never look into eyes more beautiful than Yangtze's.

For weeks after he had her put to sleep, he felt numb. He walked into doors and three times let the bathroom sink overflow. Sometimes it felt like someone was scraping a roll of barbed wire repeatedly across the inside of his chest.

At college, he kept on his bedside table a photograph of Yangtze so that the first thing he saw on waking was his beloved friend's image. But in the first semester of his second year, something odd happened. Now, when he woke, it was another face that entirely dominated his thoughts: that of a young woman in his "Animals and Ethics" course. She was the most exquisite-looking person he had ever seen. He yearned to sleep with her, and to cradle her small body in his arms and feel her wonderful breasts pressed against his chest. He had asked his friend Campbell Korsakov to find out her name. He experienced an exultant joy simply when he repeated its syllables to himself. Agnes. Agnes Vane.

FIVE

The Punjabi Pyjamas

ONE OF THE GREAT SENSUOUS pleasures in Agnes's new life was dressing up. Her scholarship left her enough spare cash to indulge in occasional trips to charity shops where she hunted happily for choice vintage clothing. She seldom spent more than ten dollars on a single item and delighted in the sheer luck by which she stumbled on some of her very best finds. Who would have thought you could buy a dramatic thirties felt cloche for just four dollars, or a gauzy silk bed jacket with cape sleeves embroidered all over with flowers of pale lilac and silver for seven?

She liked to imagine intimate histories for each of her purchases, seeing the little stains and mended tears as evidence of the original owner's passions and thrift. From the dime-sized patch of ochre near the edge of the bed jacket's left sleeve, she conjured up a spill of night-time brandy topped with cream. It even crossed her mind that this silken confection might have belonged to Oscar Wilde and that he had forgotten it one morning, amidst the tumbled sheets in a hotel bedroom while on his reading tour of America. When she held the bed jacket up to her nose, she wondered if it was the scent of lovemaking she inhaled. Whoever the jacket had belonged to, Agnes was convinced it had played its part in some splendidly erotic moments, the embroidered silk draped beguilingly from smooth shoulders, then slipping away, to reveal breasts as round and firm as her own.

The bed jacket inspired fantasies Agnes judged to be elegant and even decorous. At nineteen, she was still a virgin. This fact did not greatly dismay her. Although she was extremely curious about sex, she had decided to wait until she fell in love; and, above all, until she knew with full certainty this feeling was reciprocated. When she had lived with her mother and father and the flawless Phoebe, she was constantly beset by doubts that anyone would ever find her appealing enough to love and desire. Now, far removed from them, she saw her own reflected image in an utterly different light.

She had a small face, full of character. She thought it likely that in the entire history of humankind, no other person had ever looked exactly like Agnes Vane. Recently, she had come upon the French phrase *belle laide* and immediately appropriated it as exactly right for her. To be simultaneously ugly and attractive was surely far more interesting than to be simply, and boringly, beautiful. How extraordinary it was to feel at last comfortable in her own skin. It was this new ease with her physical self, something she had not experienced since she was a very young child, that prompted her to pack away all the clothes she had brought with her to college, the baggy, serviceable shirts and slacks in olive and brown she had worn for many years in the hope she might go unnoticed.

In this small, benignly tolerant liberal arts community where she now lived, she felt buoyantly free to wear outfits she would never have considered in her previous existence. Like her latest six-dollar acquisition, which she had christened her Punjabi pyjamas, a long tapering cotton tunic in a feathery black and white Paisley pattern with matching slim-leg pants. The tunic was bordered with a wide rosy braid embossed with zigzags of amethyst and pale gold. Decorating the widest band of braid, stitched down the tunic's central closing, were thirty-two appliquéd diamonds. She had counted them. Inside each diamond was a flower with a violet centre. Most striking of all was the sunburst of embroidered orange and gold marigolds above the tunic's hem. This vibrant cluster was set just slightly off centre, an asymmetry that appealed to her artistic eye.

She was amazed how light-footed and exotic she felt when she put on her Punjabi pyjamas, particularly with red velvet slipper shoes and a simple black scarf tied around her brow. This was the outfit she was wearing the day she fell in love.

It happened in the third lecture of her "Animals and Ethics" course. This course was very popular principally because the young and charismatic professor, Fergus Jonquil, was so passionate about his subject. He was also an intensely attractive person, lithe and quick-moving. With his trim beard and flashing eyes, he reminded Agnes of portrait photographs she had seen of D. H. Lawrence. The professor's moral authority electrified the hall, his sentences assembling in her head like radiant lines of force, all building toward a great edifice of enlightened thought. By this light, she saw her own ignorance and complacency starkly revealed.

She had not believed she was in any way arrogant in her attitude to animals. His lectures showed her that she was.

"I want you all to consider carefully over the coming week the questions I am about to pose." As he spoke, Professor Jonquil strode briskly back and forth across the stage. Agnes accepted this show of restlessness as a natural overflow of his charisma. It had yet to occur to her that his physical agitation and the wild, swooping gestures were all quite deliberate; that he used his wiry frame and crackling energy to compel their attention, and bind them to his belief.

"First, what would it feel like to be the mouse abruptly upturned by the plough in Robert Burns's poem? Cowering, Burns says. Timorous. Seized by panic. Its heart pounding so hard, its ears are probably ringing. Read the poem. It's on today's handout. You're all smart enough to figure out the dialect. Put yourself inside that little creature's terror. Thought by thought. Perception by perception. Live it out.

"Second, and here comes the plough again, but this time you're an earthworm. And you've been cut, sliced in half by the blade. If you honestly think the worm feels no pain, you probably don't belong in this class.

"Inhabit that worm. Be it.

"Next, I want you to consider what sentience really means. It means that everything that lives — and I mean *everything* — can feel and can suffer. Not just furry creatures. But also toads and salamanders. Bats and rats. Ants and gnats.

"All living things feel and perceive and have experiences that are unique to their particular lifetimes. And the totality of every living creature's experience, the multiplicity of every consciousness, are all connected and interwoven." He flung his arms wide.

"'Each outcry from the hunted hare / A fibre from the brain does tear.' That's William Blake writing in about 1800. Whose brain does he mean? Certainly not just the hare's. But our brains as well. Every individual who hears and reflects on the hare's pain. And something far greater. I think Blake's talking here about the very soul of the world, the Anima Mundi. The soul of the world suffers and is diminished at the cries of every hunted, suffering creature."

His right arm swung up abruptly. He pointed at random at faces among the hundred and more students in the amphitheatre. "I know some of you are sitting there thinking this is all mystical claptrap. Or maybe you see me as some kind of holy fool, standing here bleating on about the sensibility of a creature you would just as soon ignore because it's negligible. It's only an animal.

"For you in particular, but this applies to everyone in my classes, I urge you to examine your assumptions mercilessly. Be rigorous. Remember we spent the first two lectures trying to expose how deeply we in the Western world are conditioned to think of animals as the lower orders of creation. They are mere things that exist to labour for us, or amuse us. Or they are commodities to be eaten and stripped of their skins to make us boots and shoes and belts and ridiculously expensive accessories.

"Plastic," he said, pointing to his narrow tomato-red belt. "Rope and rubber." Holding aloft one rather ungainly looking sandal.

"And according to Descartes, who puts thinking man at the pinnacle of creation, animals are beast-machines. He honestly believed they are incapable of feeling. Which is why, as I told you in our last class, the Cartesian philosopher Malebranche had no problem whatsoever in kicking a pregnant dog who happened to get in his way when he was out walking.

"So the essence of your assignment for next week is to remove yourselves, imaginatively and empathetically, as far from that kind of heinous conditioned response as you can. Write me an essay from the point of view of Burns's mouse or the worm dissected by the plough, or Blake's hunted hare. Enter their experience and ask yourself, is there really any difference between sentience and consciousness?

"And please do all the readings listed on your handout. And please reflect hard on that fibre of your brain tearing each time a hunted hare cries out. So shirk off the arrogance, ladies and gentlemen, and concentrate on cultivating respect, empathy and compassion for every living creature, whose experience — just like ours — is part of a single consciousness. Every one, all connected and interwoven."

This idea resonated strongly with Agnes. It seemed so perfectly to describe the fluent, radiant world of di Cosimo's paintings with their wondrous human/animal hybrids. The week previous she had got on a Greyhound bus and made the journey to the Art Museum in Worcester,

Massachusetts. There she had gazed a full two hours at *The Discovery of Honey*. This painting, much loved by the Surrealists, showed a boisterous procession of satyrs, attendant on a boyish, red-nosed Bacchus. As they danced along, they were apparently making a great clamour as they banged on pots and pans, a fire shovel, and a waffle iron so as to drive away the bees hived in a massive tree.

She focused on the seductive colour and varied furs on the satyrs' graceful goat legs, the smooth musculature of their naked human chests; and their pointed ears, bristling with hair, that looked so astonishing appended to their very human faces. What struck her most was their evident joy, and their courteous and highly civilized interaction. These were not at all the devilish-looking satyrs bent on rape and destruction that showed up in the works of other Renaissance artists, like Botticelli. Agnes was drawn in particular to a contemplative male satyr, who wore a huge scallop shell as his codpiece. He held a chubby baby satyr carefully on his shoulder so that the child could see everything going on.

In the background, a stately lion descended a winding path originating in one of di Cosimo's mysterious cloud-like mountains. The lion, who was in no hurry, was obviously one of the company of beings who inhabited the world of the painting. He intended no harm. Agnes loved the fact that the animals were always there in di Cosimo's work. Even in his religious paintings, which were by no means her favourites, he would include at least one animal with a markedly individual character. In a nativity scene, where the Virgin Mary cradled the Christ child, he even had a black rat walking along an ancient beam of the stable wall.

Even the loathsome, putrid rat. Agnes realized di Cosimo would not have known rats were plague carriers. But surely he could not have loved rats in the way he apparently loved horses, dogs, leopards, boars, or the Medici giraffe? Or was she just projecting her own ingrained prejudice? Whenever she caught sight of a rat, as she sometimes did in her walks by the river, she felt physically ill.

Rats, according to Professor Jonquil, were one of the most abused creatures on the planet. "Every day in every supposedly civilized country of the world, laboratory rats are subjected to tortures of the flesh and mind that can only be described as fiendish." When she first registered for his course, Agnes had not expected to be brought to account for her instinctual aversion to rats and sorry indifference to their fate. But under the influence of the professor's densely persuasive powers, she often felt ashamed of all the ways she fell short. She was a vegetarian, working at becoming a vegan. She had never worn fur. She sent money every year to several animal rights charities, including — in tribute to Noona — an African refuge for orphaned and abused bonobos and chimpanzees. Despite all this, she would leave Professor Jonquil's lectures in the grip of a fierce, almost painful self-questioning. Was she complicit in an evil so pervasive she was blind to it?

The odd thing was that over the course of the week following the "single consciousness" lecture, she started to have niggling doubts. Wasn't it possible that the professor's views were just too extreme? If humans followed his precepts to the letter, wouldn't the world be overrun by rats? Was sentience really equivalent to consciousness? Or was this claim he made purely specious and manipulative?

Yet once she was seated again in the lecture hall, it was as if a beam of Absolute Truth emanated from the mesmeric figure on the stage. This beam enveloped her completely, and she felt grateful to be so indelibly enlightened. His voice itself had a peculiar power, she realized. His pronunciation was crisp, almost barbed. She thought he might be British or Australian. When he appeared most impassioned, he spoke very rapidly, as if he could not contain himself. His words seemed more than ever to be actual living entities that ran on before her, beckoning her, all aglitter with a holy fire. Or was it sometimes an unholy fire? For in each lecture, he described recent examples of animal abuse that left her burdened with grief and a self-disgust she could not properly disown on the grounds of ignorance. He was in the habit of closing the class with an anecdote so graphically horrific, she would find her body tensing in anticipation. She did not really want to hear. Yet not to listen was moral cowardice, was it not?

"Rabbits," he said. "Six baby rabbits. I want to tell you a story about how they went blind. It wasn't an accident or genetic bad luck. These rabbits were bred in captivity in a laboratory where scientists are studying the physiology of the eye. In effect, these baby rabbits were doomed from the instant they issued from their mother's womb because shortly after their birth, laboratory technicians sewed the babies' top and bottom eyelids together. And why did they perform this barbaric operation? It was because they wanted to find out what effect exposure to light has on the development of the optic nerve.

"Ladies and gentlemen, I ask you. Wouldn't the least grain of common sense tell any decent human being what the inevitable result of such an experiment would be: that by depriving a newborn of light we condemn it to a life of sightlessness? How would you characterize this experiment, ladies and gentlemen? Careless? Stupid? Vile? Heinous? Soulless? Contemptible? Despicable? Bestial?

"Personally, I am reminded of the abominations of Dr. Mengele. But here's the rub, as Hamlet would say. Because these rabbits are *only* animals, no one is held accountable for the fact they were quite deliberately blinded.

"And that, ladies and gentlemen, is my parting shot for today's lecture. Try to keep this reprehensible experiment in mind, and the invidious speciesism behind it, in all the readings you do over the coming week."

Agnes sat, feeling as she always did in the aftermath of the professor's "parting shot", numbed and enraged, torn between tears and the urge to stand up and scream. So trapped was she in the idea of the rabbits' snowy white innocence and their utter powerlessness in the hands of their torturers she barely realized she had moaned aloud. Loud enough in any case to make a young man sitting in the row in front of her turn around and stare.

She was shocked. The face of the person who regarded her so intently was one she never expected to see in the flesh. In her dreams, certainly, and countless times in Colour Plate 6 of the cherished book on Piero di Cosimo her mother had given her years ago. She could barely take it in, so uncanny was this young man's resemblance to Piero's curly-haired satyr who mourned the slain nymph. But it was true. She was looking at the same deep-fringed, slightly elongated eyes under straight, dark, silky brows; the same delicately moulded nose and lips. He even had the same downy goatee and soft moustache with its upturned ends which made his face look vulnerable and endearing, as if he were a child who had put on a disguise. Regular rounded human ears, of course, rather than the pointed goatish ones of Piero's satyr. Most astonishing was the profound depth and colour of his eyes. Because Piero's satyr was gazing down at the slain nymph, Agnes had never known their exact shade.

Why had it never occurred to her that his eyes would be the most intense blue imaginable: the pigment made from lapis lazuli, a colour the Renaissance painters called ultramarine because this semi-precious stone came from far beyond the sea in the Hindu Kush? Recently she had learned it was the transparent splinters of calcite crystals embedded in the stone that made lapis lazuli's dark blue look starry. And so it was. Starry. For although she looked down into this young man's eyes, she had the illusion she was looking up, into the vastness of the night skies so thick with stars that she lost all sense of her earth-bound self. She was falling upward into the heavens. Was that possible? *No*, she thought. And then again: *My God! I am falling in love.*

She was reluctant to pull back from this otherworldly state: its blue-black, rushing, velvety radiance, and the undercurrent of enticing fear. *If I touch him, what will happen? If he touches me, what will I become?* Was this how it was to fall in love? To feel you were in the presence of someone with god-like powers who could whirl you through the heavens at will, or shrink you to a mote, to the barest sliver of light reflected in his eye? Get a grip, Agnes! She knew (surely she knew?) that she was indulging herself foolishly here.

"Yokay?"

At first she did not understand him at all. It might as well have been satyr-speech.

"Yokay? Are you okay?"

She had it now. "Yes." But the word got lost in her constricted throat. She nodded.

"It stinks, right? I mean, about the rabbits."

"Yes." She managed this time to say the word. She wondered if he had any idea how extraordinarily beautiful he was. She wanted to tell him she had seen his face before; that one of the most sensitive and inventive artists of the Italian Renaissance had painted him over four hundred years ago; that thousands of people every year gazed at his features in the National Gallery in London.

"Maybe you'd like to come to one of our meetings," he said. "The Ethical Ark, we're called. Next one is this Friday. Our house, mine and Pinto's." He gestured to the large, moon-faced man beside him, who, Agnes realized, must have been watching her all this time. She had seen him from time to time around the campus where he stood out, not just for his size, but also his peculiar complexion. He always looked very kind, she thought.

"Here's the address. We usually start at eight. And bring whatever you like to drink. Oh, and I'm Campbell. Campbell Korsakov. Some friends call me Camel. I don't mind which."

"Thanks." She took the scrap of paper on which he had scribbled their address and smiled as calmly as her state of agitation allowed. Campbell Korsakov. What an astonishing name.

"Cute outfit," he said, as he stood up to leave, nodding at her Punjabi pyjamas.

She sat a while, a bit benumbed, pretending to pack away her lecture notes with painstaking care. In fact, she was watching Campbell Korsakov run lightly down the aisle between the rows of raked seats. He stopped to grasp around the waist, and kiss upon the lips, a tall, slender woman with waist-length red hair. She felt the first of many quick, sharp stabs at the heart she was to experience on Campbell Korsakov's account. She kept watching as he and the woman with the magnificent hair left the hall together. The red-head wore a scoop-neck leotard top of dove grey and a long circular skirt in the same colour that swirled gracefully as she moved. All very spare, simple and elegant.

For a perilous moment, Agnes felt herself to be ludicrously, even clownishly, dressed. Then she felt a trembling balance swing within her ever so slightly, and she knew it was all right. "Cute outfit," he had said. She decided to sleep that night in her Punjabi pyjamas.

Six

The Painter (1495)

H E SAW THE YOUNG MAN outside Santa Maria Novella in the company of an elderly woman, perhaps his grandmother, who had grown faint in the close noon heat. She sat, heavily bowed, on the cathedral steps. The young man fetched water from the fountain in his cupped hand and urged her to drink. When she had wet her lips, he let the water spill from his fingers and then laid his hand gently on her forehead. Piero watched as the youth next deftly removed his tunic and fashioned it into a light head-covering to help shield her from the sun.

He feared for the young man then and cast his eye quickly about the piazza lest any of the Piagnoni be on the prowl. Piero did not doubt that Savonarola's "weeping ones" would judge the youth's naked chest to be a most immodest display; they might well find him guilty on the spot of attempting to inflame lustful thoughts in women going in and out of the cathedral. It was the children who were most to be feared among Savonarola's followers. These youngest members of the Piagnoni melded into ferocious little bands, strutting puff-chested and proud of purpose. They were proud most particularly of their legitimized right to inflict punishment and let rain down blow after blow upon the flesh of the guilty. Their cudgels were cruelly fashioned, with prongs sharpened to draw blood.

A leaden shadow would cloak his soul at the sight of these ardent boys, ten or twelve abreast, moving as one body through the streets. How high their colour was, as if already they scented their victims' fear and blood. How wild the look in their eyes — a look he believed he saw in the face of the Prior himself, the one time he had gone to hear Savonarola preach in the Duomo. This little hunched priest had to stand upon a box in order to look out over the pulpit at the people who crammed into the cathedral to come under the spell of his voice.

Piero was shocked to hear such dense power emanate from a form so bent and shrunken. He could shut his eyes and readily imagine it was an Archangel who spoke, or God Himself, as Savonarola claimed. There was thunder in this voice, and the crack of a horsewhip on frigid air. There was also the harsh music of crows, and it was from this note that Piero flinched in particular for he knew it was the element that would seduce him ultimately, if he listened too long. So complex and variegated an instrument he had never heard. It appeared the Dominican's voice had some unearthly power to pour like liquid night into the ear and flood the mind, so that all ideas except his, the great Savonarola's, were swept away.

Many of these ideas were dangerous, which was why he had gone to listen to the Prior only once. He could not afford, for the sake of his sanity and of his art, to hear all the beauty of the world denigrated as illusory and corrupt, including the shape and substance of living creatures of all sorts. What a grim and terror-filled place Florence had already become after barely a year under Savonarola's tutelage. The Prior preached penitence and made people tremble with his descriptions of how God's sword would smite the city; how He would send unending pestilence and famine if they did not forsake their vanity and self-love, their greed and lust and fornication. Savonarola held his crucifix aloft as his doom-filled voice reverberated throughout the cathedral, reviling those who read Plato, Aristotle, Cicero and the miraculous tales of Ovid. To save themselves, the people of Florence must hold fast to holy scripture, the Prior declared. Piero's flesh tightened as Savonarola recited from the Book of Ezekiel on the filthiness of whores and sodomites: "They shall deal furiously with thee. They shall take away thy nose and thine ears; and thy remnant shall fall by the sword . . . "

To Piero's horror, the militant youth among the Piagnoni had begun to take these proscriptions literally. He heard, far too often, of vulnerable men and women maimed in the street by boys primed by their own righteousness and hot quest for blood. They were too young to share in the Prior's self-disgust, or to embrace, as he did, the imminent destruction of the world when he would at last shed his foul carcass and join the heavenly host. The self-disgust Savonarola preached these youth went outward to become a hatred so exact, Piero heard it in the very tramp of their feet upon the stone streets. How relentless they were, how strong their hands, how sharp and white their teeth.

It was his own secret, saving irony that he had used the repellent single-mindedness of the young Piagnoni as the model for hard-bodied killers in the two panel paintings he had done for Francesco del Pugliese. This Francesco was a devoted follower of Savonarola. He wanted, for purposes of deep reflection, two spalliere that set out in grisly detail an uncivilized man grappling to the death with his animal prey. "Show me mankind in his barbarous, unredeemed state, little better than the beasts he seeks to kill and eat. Let me see the very thick of the hunt: men's thirst for blood and their craving for raw meat torn from the bone. Paint me a panel where I may look upon the corrupt and bestial state into which we sink without the benefit of God's law and the scourge of discipline."

Piero had thrown himself into the commission with a fervour that soon enough became a fever. There were days he felt his own flesh befouled by this scene he painted. He would falter and step back to look aghast at the nightmare his hand was shaping upon the wooden panel. Who would not recoil from the naked, green-hued cadaver he had painted, foreshortened and inverted in a way that compelled the eye to travel its length, from around bare skull to splayed toes? It was an illusion that even he, its creator, found unsettling: to stare down at the dead man's face, the skin stretched so tight against the bones that the lips pulled back from the teeth in a macabre grimace. Yet most horrible of all was the fact the stiffening corpse lay neglected and forgotten by his fellow hunters. Death had rendered the man useless. He was a defunct machine.

These brutish men he painted were dedicated engines of destruction. Across their broad backs, along their muscular arms and legs, he set the shadow of the doom they carried. For he saw they had no souls. To kill was their greatest pleasure, and they did this as one unthinking creature. He gave them faces weathered and puckered and sour. But the hunters' bodies he imagined to belong to the youthful Piagnoni, who had so vilely changed the character of his city and in whose eyes he seemed to see these things he painted now almost against his will. This was a world where one murderous act spawned another.

His brush shaped a magnificent lion that one hunter had caught fast by the tail while another made ready to smash its skull with a club. A naked man knelt upon the back of a rearing horse, strangling it to death with iron-hard hands. Should he weep or groan aloud to paint such things? He gave the ancient trees of the forest his voice. They stood like blasted mourners, stolid and sombre. He could hear them moaning. Their very roots sent up a piteous lamentation.

He knew he had satisfied the requirements of Francesco de Pugliese's commission to the letter. Was there ever before such a scene of brutish early man drenching the world with blood? Yet he could not leave the painting as it was, without a note of either hope or redemption. He must insert some sweet and sustaining ambiguities, some swirl of cleansing spirit upon the painted air to catch the attentive, seeking eye.

Let them loose, his hand and spirit commanded. *Let them loose*! And so at the extreme left of the work, at the very perimeter of this soiled and accursed world, he set down lovingly and with infinite care, a menagerie in flight. Ox and capuchin monkey, deer and bear, wolf and sow and female lion, all ran for their lives. He would have them escape, for their limbs in motion and their very shapes were as dear to him as were the Eternal Forms to Plato.

Then he set yet another secret within the painting's frame to counteract the burden of horror. Clinging to the top of a blasted tree, a tiny monkey with a white-tipped muzzle watched the animals flee westward. His expression was a mix of fear and of care for his fellows. Who would even notice the little monkey, he wondered. Who would look up from the hunters' frenetic mangling of flesh to see him, holding fast to his tree, taut, alert and his round fine eyes alive with looking?

This young man who stripped off his tunic to shade his grandmother's head from the sun — he was one who would soon spy the little monkey. The youth bent over the elderly woman protectively and lay his hand upon her shoulder. Piero stood a moment, captivated by the concern in the young man's face. The youth was of that age where beauty can manifest a singular androgynous aspect. Such faces always stirred in him thoughts of human tenderness and hope. The slight upturn of the nose, the soft, full lips, the long dark eyes, the tumble of black curls falling over his forehead and cheekbones, all these features made the youth a perfect model for the faun who was to be a primary figure in his next commission: a painting for a marriage chest where this young satyr mourns the death of a nymph. The subject was inspired by a tale of Ovid's, where the nymph was mistakenly killed by her lover when she hid amongst the reeds. He was much taken by the name of the dog in this tale, which was Laelaps.

He looked closely at the boy once more, to set his features and his posture in memory, and then set off briskly to his house in the Via della Scala to fetch a head-covering for the old woman so that the boy might clothe himself again. By the time he returned, they had gone. Yet he comforted himself he had seen no sign of the Piagnoni, either going on his way or returning.

After his sighting of the youth, he worked on the marriage chest painting in a state of rare serenity, as if a gentle guiding spirit watched over his shoulder. It was through this spirit's prompting that Laelaps the faithful brown hound appeared, mourning at the nymph's feet. He had seen this very dog just weeks ago when he was walking in the countryside. Noble of head and demeanour, stern and silent, the mastiff sat in the courtyard of a farmhouse guarding a child who dug in the earth with a spoon.

It was the spirit presiding over the work who also showed him how fine and fair was the tufted down on the satyr's long pointed ears, how strong his forearms and how graceful the hand that cupped the nymph's naked shoulder. The long-necked herons upon the pale sands in the distance, the dawn light whitening the river, and the pure deep blue of the hills — all these things flowed from his brain as if planted there by a power that had known the story of this painting long before he did himself. He filled the green meadow in which the dead nymph lay with wildflowers whose petals seemed to tremble in a quiet lamentation: violets, daisies, marigolds, narcissi. He stands back with tears in his eyes, such an ache rises in him for the loss of this lovely girl, perhaps barely fifteen, her innocent life drained away through the wound he has just set, a scarlet gash, in the hollow of her neck.

With that fatal stroke of his brush, he saw revealed the story's full and astonishing truth: that the slain nymph was the human soul, and that the javelin which struck her has pierced that organ in her throat which enables speech. He understood well that this was the story of his own time. It was the doctrines of Savonarola that had killed and silenced her, cutting her off from the joy in the meadow, the river's tremulous light and the graceful birds that walked upon the strand. Piero knew they all awaited her rebirth. And that when this wondrous event transpired, it would be the soul's faithful companions of the animal kingdom, the young faun and the dog, who would greet her first and help her learn again to be who she was.

By way of covenant with this sacred truth, he swirled the wet paint of the pale blue sky with his naked fingertips. Then he began to heat walnut oil for the glaze so that the colours of this world might shine through vivid and clear, for a century at least.

How long, he wondered, before she woke and sang and danced again upon the strand in their dear company?

SEVEN

An Incident in the Ark

AGNES HAD NO TROUBLE FINDING the house, despite the fact most of the street numbers on the weathered clapboard houses were obscured by hanging baskets of bedraggled plants or six-foot-high towers of beer cartons. She spotted "The Ethical Ark" sign almost immediately after turning on to the short street. Nailed to the front porch (she marvelled at the landlord's tolerance), the sign was both large and garish. Yet charming too, because whoever had painted it had an arresting faux-naif style. On a sea of aquamarine, a nut-brown boat floated, its bright cargo of animals and birds jostling each other happily. Orange giraffe, silver bear, rosy flamingo, emerald tortoise, red chow and other vividly painted creatures all looked out at her with the same oddly familiar gentle smile. By the time she knocked on the outer screen door, she'd realized their sweet-tempered expression was uncannily like that of the huge man called Pinto.

It was with this smile Pinto greeted her at the door, and a little of her nervousness fell away. College life had made her newly aware of just how limited her social skills were. She had never been to a dance or even joined a club.

Apart from her sister Phoebe, with whom she had to be always tempering an eruptive envy, she had no real friend. Agnes was impatient, and consequently inept, with small talk. She hoped at this gathering simply to be able to listen, because animal rights was certainly something she cared about passionately, and also to stare, as much as she dared, at Campbell Korsakov. The prospect of seeing him again had her extremely agitated, so much so she had considered not coming at all. She had changed her outfit three times, settling at last on a dark brown, ankle-length Indian rayon skirt and a scoop-neck, long-sleeved leotard top in terracotta that she thought flattered her chestnut hair. She was letting her hair grow out after years of having it cut severely short, scorning anything that might soften her features. As her hair grew, she was surprised at how glossy and thick it was, as though all the years of harsh cropping had stimulated its sheen and luxuriance.

If only the same principle applied to her social self: that from her years of seclusion with only books and laptop for company, she would emerge gregarious, witty, sensitive and "interested in others." It perturbed her that, despite her new ease with her physical self, she was still at some deep level on guard. When would it come: the next unthinking or deliberately hateful remark ("Freak. Monkey-girl. Are you for real?") that would make her flinch, and retreat?

As she presented her bottle of Chianti to Pinto, she found herself wondering if he had also suffered acutely on account of his unusual appearance. She hoped not.

"Wine," he said. "Wonderful." She had not been at all sure about the wine. But he looked at her so benignly, she felt reassured.

"Come into the living room and say hello to Camel and meet the others."

He led her down a dim hallway lined with miscellaneous footwear: running shoes, sandals, hiking boots, a pair of fuchsia crocs, Tai Chi slippers, high green rubber boots.

"Should I take off my shoes?" she asked, pointing.

Pinto laughed. "No need in this house. Most of this collection was already here when I moved in a year ago. We've just got used to the look of them."

He turned abruptly left and ushered her ahead of him into a room filled with many more people than she had anticipated. She froze. For an excruciatingly long moment, she was confronted by floating blotches of pink, beige, ivory and tan. Faces, she told herself. How she detested these ghastly tricks her nervousness played. Then she felt the light touch of hands upon her shoulders, and everyone and everything took on their proper shapes. Campbell Korsakov was standing before her, crystalline and perfect. To her surprise, he kissed her European fashion. She felt the brush of a butterfly's wing, on one cheek and then the other. He stepped back, and said: "Agnes, so glad you could come."

Hearing him speak her name, she felt she was stepping into it fully for the first time. On his lips, "Agnes" no longer sounded quaint, plain and tediously forbearing, but electric and absolutely consonant with her boundless imaginative world. She was Piero's nymph, and Campbell the young satyr gazing down at her. But she was not at all dead. Pinto showed her where she could sit: a bunchy lime green beanbag pillow on the floor. As she nestled into it, tucking her long skirt under her legs, Campbell began rapidly introducing the others. He sat with his knees drawn up on an old armchair, once covered in a proud maroon velvet, its gentility now as distressed yet comfortable as the rest of the furniture in the room. "Kit McCready," he announced, as the striking redhead from Fergus Jonquil's class entered the room with a glass of wine in her hand. She wore an open-necked shirt of watered silk: an iridescent peacock blue that made her magnificent hair look even more glorious. This was the first time Agnes had been able to study Kit's features closely. She saw, with some rankling discomfort, that Kit's angular beauty was remarkably like that of Botticelli's Venus floating on her gigantic scallop shell. So perfect I could spit, she thought childishly; then she upbraided herself. In her fixation on Kit, who had positioned herself gracefully on the wide arm of Campbell's chair and begun ruffling his hair, Agnes missed the names of at least two of the others.

She vowed to pay closer attention. She hoped she did not look ridiculously squat or pugnacious, ensconced in her lowly beanbag. It was a relief when Pinto brought her a glass of wine because it gave her something to do with her hands. He then somehow folded his great height into the space on the floor beside her, and sat with his back against the wall and his massive trunk-like legs stretched out in front of him. She did not feel at all crowded, but rather shielded and comforted by his proximity. Perhaps he sensed this because he bestowed on her one of his gentle smiles, and then shut his eyes as if sinking into a meditative trance.

Pinto's return had interrupted the introductions, which now resumed. Next was Minnie, a woman with very short white-blonde hair. The name must be ironic because Minnie was not at all small. She was obviously dedicated to working out, and the skimpy sleeveless T-shirt and spandex leggings seemed deliberately chosen to show off her formidable musculature. Then there was Zeke Jones, whom everyone called Zebra. "I've loved them since I was a kid," he told Agnes. Zebra was wiry and had a narrow, chiselled face with fine brown eyes. He projected a highly charged, restless energy, and kept crossing and uncrossing his legs, and tapping one foot and then the other on the floor. "And yes," he responded to her unspoken question. "I always wear something with black and white stripes; at least . . . whenever I can. At my grandmother's funeral, for example, it was a bit difficult . . . "

"Okay, Zebra. We get the point." This from a very small man in a brown velour jacket with a hood. Although the house still held the heat of the late autumn day, he had his hood pulled up and the jacket tightly zipped to the neck. He was sitting on the edge of the couch to Agnes's right. Looking up at his pale, pinched face and his mouth with its small, badly spaced teeth, she was put in mind of a bad-tempered elf. Horace's brow had a permanent vertical crease, which gave his features a gloomy, censorious cast as he stared out from under his dark hood.

"Horace," he informed her. "Horace Fairhaven. I'm the voice of reason in this bunch."

Someone (was it Campbell?) made a sound like a seal's bark. Pinto sighed deeply.

"Did you say something, mine ever-elegant host?" Horace fixed his malign frown on Campbell.

"Bugger off, Horace." Campbell put his knees down and sat very erect in his chair. It pained Agnes to see him looking so upset. Kit, she observed with envy, was stroking Campbell's forearm just as one would soothe an agitated child.

Pinto said to Agnes: "Some of the other members couldn't make it this evening. There's Harriet and Lupo . . . "

"Those dithering old farts!" exclaimed Horace.

"Horace, that's enough!" Kit said sharply.

"No it's not, Kit, darling. It's not nearly enough. Because tonight we're going to roll in the same warm cuddly crap you so-called activists always cart out. You'll raise a glass to that sucky framed portrait of Fred the Bear and say how wonderful it is that he was liberated from the dreadful circus in England where they fed him stale cake and made him ride a little unicycle around the ring, and then chained him up the rest of the time. You'll say: 'He looks so happy now in the animal sanctuary in Northern Ontario, ambling about freely with snow on his nose.'

"You'll talk about how saintly Jane Goodall is and what a selfless, inspiring example Barry Horne set for animal rightists everywhere. Not that any of you would have the guts to do what he did.

"Then you'll yammer on about whatever guilt trip that pretentious idiot Fergus Jonquil has inflicted on you this week. And finally, when you've all had enough to drink and smoked a few joints, you'll start to wallow in sentimentality. We'll hear what your dear old dog or cat or tortoise meant to you, or how excited you were when you first saw real live giraffe running in the wild when Mummy and Daddy took you on a South African safari.

"But you never *do* anything. You never even talk about any of the real nasty stuff. Like . . . "

Zebra groaned and put his head in his hands.

[83]

"Like the sheer sadism that drives vivisectionists to clamp animals down and cut them open without any anesthetics. Over 100 million animals all around the world, splayed on operating tables, having their eyes and guts ripped out."

"Shut up, Horace!" Zebra's face was as white as the stripes of his shirt.

"No, I won't, fetish boy. You know what you need — what you all need? You need to wake up and face the ugly facts. Take one of those tours of the Cambodian killing fields and watch the North American college kids fork out $500 for the pleasure of firing a rocket launcher at a real live cow. Talk about participatory history! All those piles of human skulls really get these kids going. Disgusting little sadists, every one of them!"

"That's sick, Horace," Minnie said.

"Of course it's sick. To be human is to be sick. Sickos. That's us. Isn't that correct, jolly green Buddha?"

Pinto shifted his weight ever so slightly on the floor beside her. How keenly she empathized with him as he strove to ignore the little man's mockery. She felt her own muscles tighten in the old conditioned response. Would it be her turn next?

What did happen next took Agnes utterly aback. Kit stood up, and in one fluid movement was kneeling on the floor in front of the cross-legged, frowning Horace. She put her hands on his shoulders and spoke to him so softly Agnes did not catch it. Then Kit began stroking the back of Horace's hand.

Everyone in the room watched this odd, tender scene in silence.

When Kit stood up, she was holding Horace's hand. They made a discordant picture, given that Kit was a good foot taller than the little man in his hood. Was she the only one thinking how like a classic fairy tale princess Kit looked — one who had found herself fatally stuck to a malign little creature under whose spell she had unwittingly come?

Yet Kit sounded completely self-possessed and in control as she announced: "I'm going to give Horace a drive home. Unfortunately, I won't have time to get back for the meeting. Regrets." She included them all with a graceful sweep of her hand; then kissed Campbell on the brow and left quickly with Horace still grasping her tightly by the hand.

Agnes sat rigidly, feeling uncomfortable and confused. What on earth could the relationship be between queenly Kit and spiteful Horace who had succeeded so well at poisoning the atmosphere?

Pinto started to say something to her, then apparently changed his mind.

"Horace is Kit's uncle," Zebra told her. His voice had a new tinny quaver.

"Half-uncle," Campbell corrected him. Campbell had his head down, intent on manufacturing what Agnes assumed was a joint. He had a book on his knee on which he had laid out three rolling papers glued together accordion style, and a little pile of leafy herb. Agnes's only knowledge of recreational drugs came from television, films and novels. She had never even taken a puff of a regular cigarette. Would it be impolite or impolitic to refuse if she was offered marijuana?

"Horace has had a difficult life," Campbell said as he sprinkled the herb liberally along the seam of the central rolling paper.

"What crap!" Zebra exploded.

Minnie laughed ruefully. The others either frowned or shook their heads.

"Horace," Zebra addressed Agnes, "is our group's burden. He shores up our moral development by testing our forbearance. Isn't that right, Pinto?"

"He doesn't always come to the meetings," added a rosy-cheeked, fair-haired young woman whose name Agnes later learned was Perdita.

"And we thank heaven for that," Zebra sighed, rolling his eyes.

"Agnes should be told his story," Pinto said.

Campbell, who was now applying the tip of his tongue to the glue edge of a very tightly packed slim joint, nodded.

"Yeah. Sure." He lit the joint and took two deep draws, then passed it to Perdita, who inhaled once daintily and handed it to her partner. "Pablo?"

Pablo did not look at all Spanish or South American, but was as fair and rosy as Perdita. They might be twins, Agnes thought.

"Can you explain, please, Pinto? Sometimes I just can't bring myself to talk about Horace calmly."

Campbell then abruptly left the room.

Pinto angled his shoulders so that he could speak more easily to Agnes face-to-face.

"Kit's grandfather suffered from Alzheimer's disease," Pinto began.

"Completely gaga," Zebra chimed in. "Loco."

Pinto sighed before continuing. "Yes, okay, Zebra . . . Kit's family is very wealthy and for some reason — maybe duty or shame? — they decided to care for the old man in their own home . . . well, it's a mansion really. So he was on an upper floor."

"Madman in the attic," Zebra put in.

"I doubt it, Zebra. Probably an upper floor, as I said. But her grandfather was very well cared for, Kit says . . . "

"How would she know, Pinto? She wasn't even born then."

"Well, Zebra. That's what her family told her. That's the official story."

"Story. Exactly." Zebra rolled his eyes.

It dawned on Agnes that this explanation amounted to a privilege. She was being taken into a confidence that was initially Kit's but now belonged to the group as whole. She experienced a distinct buzz of pleasure, wholly inappropriate to the tale's dark substance. Yet the frisson persisted at the simple delight she was accepted.

"Kit's grandfather had round-the-clock nursing, of course," Pinto continued. "There was a whole roster of private nurses and care providers. One of them was a very small woman. She was Irish, and she was wonderfully good with the old man because her accent made him happy.

"Kit is of Irish heritage," he added.

"Anyway, one day the unthinkable happened and he overpowered this Irish nurse and raped her."

"Oh," exclaimed Agnes, gritting her teeth in reaction to this act of raw violence and its consequences. In her mind's eye she saw the tiny figure of Europa overcome and mounted by a huge shaggy bull.

"Thus occurred the gestation of the horrible Horace," Zebra said.

"Don't fuck around, Zeke. It isn't amusing — for anyone!" Campbell glared at his friend, who squirmed in his chair.

"Sorry, Camel."

"Yeah, well . . . " Campbell shrugged.

Agnes thought how much she would hate to incur his anger.

"The family felt responsible, of course," Pinto continued. "They offered to make provision for the child and ensure the Irish nurse was financially comfortable for the rest of her life. Legally, it was all pretty murky because Kit's grandfather wasn't in his right mind and couldn't be held criminally accountable for the crime."

"It must have been dreadful for the nurse," Agnes said.

"Yes," Campbell said. "But it was one of those really strange things where a disaster turns out to be a gift-in-disguise. The nurse — her name was Kelly Fairhaven — was a young widow. She was lonely. She thought about it carefully and decided she wanted to keep the baby. She was one tough lady, I guess . . . resilient, I mean. And she and Horace never wanted for a thing . . . materially anyway."

"Yeah, because he certainly . . . " Zebra broke off abruptly and looked at Campbell with apprehension.

"It's okay, Zebra. You're absolutely right. Horace lacks sensibility and sensitivity. He's nasty and he exploits his victim-hood shamefully, particularly as far as Kit is concerned. He's made her feel implicated in her family's guilt even though she wasn't even born when her grand-father did what he did. She feels at least partly responsible for the fact Horace is a vicious mess. Which is ridiculous, but that's the way it is," Campbell concluded.

He comes and goes," Pinto added. "I mean, Kit doesn't have to put up with him hanging around all the time. But a little of Horace goes a long way."

"He's a kind of a curse," Minnie said. No one contradicted her.

"And the disease seems to be a family curse as well," Campbell added. "Because now Kit's mother is in the first stages, even though she's still pretty young. She can't remember sometimes who Kit is when she goes to visit. Her brain just kind of whites out."

"Plaque and tangles," Pinto said.

"What?" asked Zebra.

"It's what kills off the nerve cells in the brain of people with Alzheimer's," Pinto explained. "Plaque is a sort of protein and tangles . . . "

"Plaque! Ugh! Like filthy teeth. Could we change the subject please?" urged Minnie.

And so they did, with Campbell asking Agnes how she had first got interested in animals' rights. Caught off guard, she began telling them about the fateful morning she had seen Noona looking out at her, with all her vulnerable dignity, from the cover of the British Sunday magazine. She did not of course speak about the context; grappling with the decision her parents had pushed at her to get rid of her own "monkey face." That was long behind her. What she must convey, as frankly as she could, was the force of the connective bond she had experienced, looking into the liquid eyes of a being who had suffered so much and endured.

"It came," she told the group, without fear she would be mocked, "the way I imagined mystics might have a vision. I mean, up to that point, I suppose I had always thought of my own being as distinct and single, like a stem or branch. But afterwards, I seemed to be looking up into a great canopy of leaves and I understood I was part of a mighty, many-branched tree. And that really, it mattered intensely *how* you related to all the creatures in the entire company of beings; that you be empathetic and respectful and protective, where need be."

She stopped talking, worried she had gone on too long; that they would think her foolish, or jejeune, or even worse, insincere. In fact, she found when she glanced about her that they were all regarding her intently, and that some were smiling at her warmly. One of these, she was delighted to see, was Campbell.

"Yes," he said. "A mighty, many-branched tree. What a neat image."

She felt elated at his enthusiasm. She had never spoken of these things to anyone before. Was this what acceptance was like — this heady warmth? As to the other part of her story, would any of them have guessed? Were they focusing on her features now, thinking that of course anyone who looked like her would be bound to empathize with a chimpanzee? She was very glad the bitter-tongued Horace had left.

These solipsistic thoughts deflated her. She renewed her vow to focus outward on these people who had listened to her so attentively.

"But don't you think," Minnie was saying, "that Fergus takes it just too far? I mean rats and worms! Ugh!"

"Fergus is a crusader and an idealist," Campbell said. "He's challenging us to examine preconceptions and undo learned aversions."

"I can't love or respect a worm," barked Minnie. "And do you really believe Fergus would smile sweetly if he woke up and saw a rat at the bottom of his bed? He'd go out and buy a box of Warfarin like everybody else."

"Does Fergus ever come to your meetings?" Agnes asked.

A heavy silence followed on her question.

Pinto finally broke it: "Fergus has to be very careful. He's under a caution. He got in a bit of trouble at the college where he taught previously. Some parents complained about his conduct to the university board of governors. They said he was propagandizing and inciting his students to commit acts of violence. There was a girl who apparently got hurt in a demonstration outside an abattoir."

"Fergus was there," Campbell interjected. "But it wasn't his fault. The meat plant brought in some very heavy security guards who were into excessive force.

"Essentially, he'd be risking his job if he was seen with any of us outside the university — even in a pub, which is just so stupid. But that's the way it is. He's in a delicate situation, a kind of everlasting probation, and it's going to be very hard for him to ever get tenure anywhere.

"Of course, he's still absolutely vigilant and committed to the cause. His probity . . . "

"His *what*?" asked Minnie.

"Probity. It means honesty, being morally upright."

Agnes noted with delight that Campbell's explanation to Minnie was free of condescension.

"In fact," Campbell continued, "I want us to talk tonight about some information Fergus passed on to me. And we must all swear never to reveal he was the source. I'm deadly serious here. Are we agreed? Whatever happens, we didn't find out what I'm about to tell you from Fergus Jonquil."

Everyone including Agnes nodded their assent. She felt flushed and jubilant because she had just taken an oath as part of a group and was about to be privileged with secret information.

"You know that chocolate factory at Bridgewater?" Campbell asked.

Zebra, Minnie and Pinto all said yes. Agnes had never heard of Bridgewater.

"Well, apparently one of the Big Pharma companies has bought the plant and it's going to be turned into an animal testing laboratory. It's top secret."

"Christ!" said Minnie.

Pinto moaned.

Agnes, meanwhile, did battle with the nauseating images that bombarded her: cramped cages, metal restraints, muzzled jaws, spilled blood and viscera, deliberately exposed organs, broken bones, inexpressibly sad eyes.

"We have to stop it," Campbell was saying.

She clung to his words and to the pure glistening idea behind them. Stop it, yes. At last, she could do something more than sending her few paltry dollars every month to help support animal sanctuaries around the world.

"Dogs, cats. Rabbits. We know when the first animals are due to be delivered. After 1:00 AM on the morning of October 27. So I suggest we be there to meet them. We'll do a peaceful sit-in demonstration in front of the main doors. I went up there on my bike last week to check the place out. There's a wooded area behind the plant where we can hide and keep a lookout for their headlights; then take up our position in front of the doors. And we'll bring along some sympathetic people from the media."

"You don't mean that crazy Trot from the student union paper, do you?"

"Minnie, do you know how much you sound like Horace right now?" Campbell asked.

"God!" Minnie grimaced.

"Anyway, Tom's all right. He'll come, even if no one from the city paper does, or *The Chronicle* or CNN."

"CNN!" exclaimed Perdita.

"Well, we can try," said Campbell, with such brisk certainty they all seemed to take heart.

Agnes felt a surge of energy from crown to toes; something speedy and bright was rushing through her cells, making her skin buzz all over. She saw their little group shot into the future by a bolt of pure will, its source an unquestionable moral rightness. She had never experienced an emotion quite like this before, even at her most rapturous moments of insight. When she'd first turned the corner and seen the Ark sign, she'd had no inkling she was embarking on so vast and noble an undertaking. If she was ruthlessly frank with herself, she had come mainly to gaze at Campbell Korsakov. Now she found herself looking, with an admiration akin to affection, at every single person in the room. She belonged here. It was an astonishing feeling. So astounding, and so heady, that she did something she would never have done otherwise and accepted the joint Perdita held out to her.

"It's quite strong," Pinto murmured to her.

Agnes inhaled and shuddered at the sulphurous rasp in her mouth and throat, and the very unpleasant skunky odour in her nostrils. It did not take long for an insidious cookery to begin in her blood and brain. The effects were at first pleasing enough. A soft glow surrounded, or perhaps emanated from, all the objects in the room. Everyone — not just Campbell — looked exceptionally beautiful, benevolent and sensitive. She wondered if this was the way mystics saw the world, with the natural goodness of the human soul so readily apparent in the flesh. The light seemed to spill outward, from every individual countenance, so that they were all floating in the same lucent sea, a holy company.

Abruptly, it all changed: their faces turned shadowy and angular, the glow disappeared. A worm of panic began wriggling in her belly. She saw Perdita lean over and whisper something in Pablo's ear. They smiled at one another cruelly, and sent a furtive glance her way. Agnes understood, with a dreadful unassailable clarity, that they were laughing at her. She began to grasp, under the sure prompting of the wriggling worm, that she had been invited to this gathering specifically as an object of mockery. Her panic fed on every simple gesture: the way Campbell rubbed at his left eyebrow, and then stared stonily into space, as if he had had enough of the game and simply wished her gone; Minnie's deliberate flexing of her fingers, one by one, which she then regarded studiously; Zebra's attempt to keep a silver-coloured CD spinning upright on the palm of his right hand. All these gestures, she recognized, were coded and pregnant with meaning.

How terribly cold and abandoned she felt. Then the fear came rushing in: first that she would disgrace herself by losing control of her bladder or bowels or temper; then, that she could actually feel the others' harrowing, hate-filled thoughts penetrating her brain. She began to dwell obsessively on the brain's awful physical vulnerability. She pictured the plaque and long tentacles that might even now be choking and consuming the moist pink tissue inside her skull.

She stood up in great fright, only just managing to find the words she hoped would allow her to escape with some modicum of dignity — before she fouled herself, or declared aloud how wretchedly paranoid she felt. She kept telling herself she was in this very uncomfortable state of mind because of the drug. It would pass. She would shortly feel normal and perceive rightly again. But each time she tried to grasp this fact tightly as her salvation, it eluded her. She was engulfed again by a sickening wave that made her dizzy and nauseous.

Out on the front porch, beneath the gaudy Ark sign, she inhaled and exhaled as deeply as she could, while holding fast to the wooden railing. Then she launched herself deliberately out to the sidewalk and began to walk with all the determination she could muster. She would not fall down. She would not get lost. She would not, above all, become hysterical or blubber or babble. She looked at her feet, willing them to perform the forced march that would ultimately bring her to the safety of her room in the dorm. She wanted, above all, to feel safe, and secluded. Had there been one of those massive anthropomorphic trees Piero di Cosimo loved to paint, with a gaping hollow in its trunk, she would gladly have crawled inside, and curled up to sleep until it was all over. Why, oh why, had she been so foolish as to try the stupid drug?

Pinto's multi-coloured moon face swam suddenly into view. "Agnes? Are you all right? It's very pokey weed, according to Camel. That's why they're all navel-gazing back there, or just staring into space."

How huge he was, like a kindly giant come to rescue her. She found the sound of his voice steadying. Surely she could trust him?

"Paranoid," she said.

"I get like that," he told her. "That's why I don't toke anymore. I just say no and then sit and watch them all go zombie-like for half an hour.

"It would be good," he confided, "if there was somebody else in the group who didn't indulge. Then I'd have someone to talk to when they all fly off to their zone."

He looked at her with such hope, it made her smile. Was she starting to feel normal again? But the instant she posed herself the question, the fear struck again. Plaques and tangles will eat my brain up. There will be nothing left of me.

"Would you like to walk by the river?" he asked. "The rippling . . . the sound of water . . . it might help."

She nodded. She realized she had put herself in his care, but was uncertain when exactly this had happened. There was a great comfort, she discovered, in walking beside so large a man with so gentle a disposition. The thought crossed her mind that this was the way she had imagined God when she was a child. She had a sudden urge to tell Pinto this, but then thought better of it.

He found them a bench beside a particularly fine willow. "It might help," he counseled her gently, "to keep your breathing in rhythm with the flow of the water."

She tried and then sat, quietly, as Pinto began to tell her stories. Because of the potency of the pot, she found she was picturing very vividly what he described, as if it was indeed happening in front of her: the red dog dancing, then making a bright ring about the house; the boy burying his face in her soft fur.

At one point she looked up and saw how full the moon was. She had not realized it was so late. As she turned around to ask Pinto the time, she caught sight of a man sitting very high in the branches of a tree farther along the bank. He was a small person, delicately made, and Agnes could see, even at that distance, that he was wearing a kind of cream-coloured smock or tunic, and that his dangling legs were bare. He was staring out at the river and the floating moon. Perhaps he felt her eyes on him, because he turned his head and looked at her and nodded. She did not point him out to Pinto. She knew that he was there for her alone, just as she knew that if she looked away for even a second, he would be gone.

Of course, she thought, he would have sat that high in the ancient trees in the *contado* outside Florence, with a drawing pad on his knee and a pocketful of brown and red chalk. Where better to observe the forest animals, and catch their lineaments and very character upon the paper, without disturbing them?

She felt quite peaceful and filled with wonder at his appearance. "I should get back to the dorm," she told Pinto. "I am fine now. Thank you. You've been so kind."

Pinto uttered a gruff sound, shifted his bulk upon the bench, and stared stolidly out at the river. "It's very late," he said. "The main doors to your building will be locked. Do you have the code to get in?"

How could she have been so stupid? Because she had never before been out past eleven, it had never occurred to her to bring the code for the electronic lock.

"You can sleep in our spare room," he told her.

She was immediately excited by the idea of sleeping under the same roof as Campbell. Just thinking of him lying naked, or half-naked, in the room next to hers or just down the hallway, sent ripples of heat through her belly and thighs. She could feel her clitoris getting erect, her labia swelling. She had already had several orgasms brought on by intensely vivid fantasies starring Campbell Korsakov and half-feared she might come spontaneously right there on the bench, beside this finely moral and upstanding man. She had never before met anyone to whom the word "upstanding" applied. These thoughts touching on Pinto's exemplary character helped temper her ardour, and she knew this to be a happy result.

They walked back to the Ethical Ark in an easeful silence that seemed to be one with the thickly clustered stars and the creamy-white moon. Whenever she glanced at Pinto she thought how noble he looked in that light, which softened his cruelly variegated complexion. She chose a bright star at random and made the child-like wish that Peter Pinto Dervaig would some day meet a woman who gave him the love he so much deserved. As they made the final turn into Pinto's street, she stumbled on the curb, perhaps because of her mounting excitment about staying the night under the same roof as Campbell. Pinto gave her his hand to steady her. She had a fleeting sensation, before he let it go, that he had caressed her palm with his thumb. She must, she thought, have been mistaken.

She was delighted to find that Campbell was still up, talking with Zebra. The others had gone. He bestowed on her a smile that made her catch her breath, so swiftly did the tide of desire rise in her again.

"Hi guys. Have a nice walk?"

"Yes," Pinto replied. "Agnes is going to sleep in the spare room since it's so late."

"Sure. Great. Glad to have you."

Have me. Have me. Have me, Agnes chanted to herself as Pinto led her up the stairs and showed her the bedroom and where the bathroom was. He took a towel and clean sheets from a jumbled linen cupboard.

"Do you want help making up the bed?" he asked.

"I'll be fine, thank you. I really appreciate all your kindness to me tonight."

He took a small step toward her, hesitated, then let his large hand rest a moment on her shoulder. "Goodnight, Agnes. Sleep well."

Closing the door of the bedroom, she had a quick look about. It was a narrow space, sparsely furnished: just a futon on a single-bed frame and a chest of drawers with an old oval mirror hanging above it. There was a pull-down blind rather than curtains at the window and this she chose to leave open so that she could lie in bed and gaze at the moon. After she had made up the bed and plumped the pillow, she took off everything but her vintage slip, with its openwork cream lace at the bust. That she might at any moment hear Campbell coming up the stairs made her skin prickle. Of course, he had no reason whatever for coming to her room, but the meagre possibility he might tantalized her and kept her restless. After fifteen minutes of lying rigid, trying to quell the riotous jumble of erotic images in her head, she got up to use the toilet. She was as quiet as she could be, and saw and heard no one in the hallway on the way back to her room. She did not think she had drifted off, and was therefore surprised when she heard her door creak open and someone whisper her name.

"Just checking to make sure you're all right."

It was Campbell. She could see him quite clearly as he approached the bed. He looked even more exquisite and fine-boned in the moonlight. He was wearing only cotton pyjama pants and his naked chest was as tawny, smooth and gleaming as the young satyr's in di Cosimo's painting. She felt her nipples harden and she involuntarily shuddered.

"Are you cold?" he asked. "You're not still upset, are you? I'm sorry if the dope was a bit strong for you. Is that why you left?"

She nodded. As if her gesture implied a far more general consent, he came closer still, and sat on the edge of the futon and cupped her bare shoulder with his hand.

"Pretty lace," he said and his hand moved to the creamy froth that covered her breasts. So quickly and deftly did he insert his hand inside her slip, she was utterly surprised and somewhat shocked. She took a deep, sharp, very audible breath.

"I can stop if you like," he said calmly. "Just tell me." As he spoke, he was already caressing her nipple in a circular motion with his palm. She had not thought it possible, but her nipples got even harder. Like two proud little towers, she thought. Just before he put his lips to her bared breast and began to nibble and gently suck, she had one last purely rational thought — that she was swollen with pride that this exceptionally handsome, graceful, intelligent and cultured young man had come to her bedside, willingly, to seek her out.

None of the erotic literature she had read prepared her for the intensity of the sensation she now experienced as he pulled the slip over her head and began to run his hands over her body, here, there, everywhere, even into hidden places she had imagined no man would want to touch. She was certain that if he stopped doing what he was doing to her, she would die. Then he did stop, but only long enough to stand up and drop his pyjamas.

Agnes was astonished, and a little frightened by the transformation, as he stood briefly in profile beside the bed. It was like looking at a mythical being, born with a magical thrusting horn. She wondered if it would hurt her; if indeed she wanted this to happen at all.

He got on the bed and knelt over her; and began stroking and nuzzling her body in a way that made her utter sharp little ecstatic cries. She tried very hard to keep quiet, thinking of the others in the house, and of the good-hearted Pinto above all, not wanting to disturb him. She was very close to climax when Campbell slid down the bed and pushed his hot tongue between her labia; then he licked her clitoris so cunningly she could no longer hold off the excruciating mounting wave of pleasure. She began contracting wildly on his finger which he had thrust deep inside her. Where did she go then? Out of her body certainly. Out and far above the naked form of Agnes Vane, who was quaking under a surfeit of incomparable sensations.

Was it Campbell's lovemaking that triggered the vision? Or would she have seen what she did regardless of who brought her to her first engulfing climax? She felt the mist above the lake touch her lips and eyes, and the pale blue dawn light swathed her around. She was a creature compounded of clear light and air. She was close enough to the grey heron to make out the luxurious plumage on his neck. Then the miracle happened and she witnessed the impossible moment when the slain nymph revived and put out her arms to the young satyr who cried out in joy. As the great heron soared aloft, Agnes looked out of its eyes and felt her soul shake.

A kiss in the hollow of her neck brought her back to the Ark, with Campbell Korsakov kneeling over her, grinning.

"That was fun," he said. "Now grab hold." And he guided her hand, and showed her how, with a rapid firm pumping motion, she could make him orgasm. His exultant cry when he came sounded uncannily like the satyr's in her vision when he saw the dead nymph revived. His semen, spurted across her belly and hips, felt warm and silky on her skin. It dried quickly to a crystalline sheen, which in the moonlight resembled a multitude of tiny stars.

"You have a beautiful body. Do you know that, Agnes? Beautiful." He ran his fingertips lightly over her collarbone. "And you've got this kind of powerful quietness about you." He kissed her lightly on the forehead; then he pulled her against him so that she lay with her head nestled on his shoulder, and her body pressed against his side. She told herself she would never be happier than at this moment. But already, the melancholy was seeping in. She was agonizingly aware that people called this wonderful thing that had just happened to her a "one-off." It would never happen again because Campbell loved Kit. It had only happened at all because Kit had had to leave to look after the dreadful Horace.

She strove hard to banish these shadowy thoughts. If ever there was a time in her life for drawing all the savour from a moment, it was now. She moved her head a little so that she could drink in the astonishing beauty of his face. She concentrated on the warmth and strength of his body beside her, and let her mind touch in turn each of her new incomparable experiences: all the places he had touched her with his deft fingers; the next-to-unbearable arousal he'd brought her to with his lips and tongue. This flutter of thought raised various shapes in her mind. Now she could remember only a lofty window of ruby and ultramarine stained glass and a vast nest, made of woven rushes and bright fragments of silk, set extremely high in the same tree where earlier that evening she had glimpsed the figure of Piero di Cosimo. When the tree's branches swayed in the wind, so too did the nest. Yet she knew it was solid and secure, its structure sustained by Campbell's unconscious breath mingled with hers.

When she woke several hours later, he had gone. The sheet on his side of the bed was pulled taut. It looked as if he had even smoothed out the hollow in his pillow. She stretched out all ten fingers to feel on her belly the fine spangled remnants of his climax. Yes, it had really happened.

The chorus of early morning songbirds had already begun. She decided to leave once the light was fully up. An hour later, she let herself quietly out of the Ark's front door, relieved that everyone else in the house was still asleep. She walked down the street with a brisk, light step, but carefully, as if she carried some fragile treasure.

From his upper window Pinto watched her go, the tears streaming down his face. He had often had cause to wrestle with, and neutralize, extremely acrimonious feelings toward the blithely oblivious Campbell. Camel had some wonderful qualities: he was a loyal friend and utterly committed to the movement. But he was still a spoiled rich kid, overindulged by his doting mother. He took his abundant good looks and charm for granted, and he was an inveterate womanizer. Pinto knew that Camel did not really care about Agnes. All he had wanted was to get laid.

Shortly Pinto would have to begin a gruelling process of mental purification. He could not afford to let this animosity toward Camel fester within him. He recognized this moral undertaking was going to be more difficult than any he had attempted before; even when he'd had to transcend his sick vengeful desire to beat to a pulp the boys who had murdered Mikos.

But now, for the briefest interlude possible, he would allow his feelings free range. He confronted his hatred for Campbell and saw how hard and sharp it was, like a pit inside a luscious fruit. He looked then at his love for Agnes and saw it was a wild bird, trembling inside his chest. He plucked it out of himself, painfully, and sent it flying away after her. Its cry was so plaintive it set his teeth on edge, and he struck at his heart, again and again, with his closed fist.

EIGHT

The Vulcan

"ONE-OFF" WAS A CRUDE PHRASE but it caught her situation with a mocking precision. As Agnes kept reminding herself, what had happened with Campbell was down to pure chance. If Horace hadn't behaved so badly, Kit would have stayed. Then it would have been Kit in bed with Campbell. Extravagantly beautiful, long-limbed, peerless Kit.

They belonged together. Anyone could see that. Physically at least, Campbell and Kit inhabited another realm of being, and all Agnes could do was gaze at them in covert envy, or better yet, an ever-yielding acceptance. Although she was now more reconciled to the face she saw in the mirror, she knew no one would ever think her truly pretty. Despite this, she replayed obsessively the extraordinary moment when Campbell said: "You have a beautiful body." She got hot every time and the ensuing sexual fantasies sent her reeling off into a humid, voluptuous picture-world dominated by his face and hands and by her body, in that edge-of-madness arousal on tangled sheets beneath the moon.

She would come back to herself with a little groan; look at the page in front of her and realize fifteen and more minutes had passed without her absorbing a word. This faltering attention had fateful implications. Poor grades on essays and exams would lose her her scholarship; and then, quite conceivably, she would lose her reason for living.

She summoned up the vision of the bare-legged figure sitting high in the tree, watching, like a tutelary spirit, over her and Pinto. It did not matter if her glimpse of Piero di Cosimo was a hallucination generated by strong pot. Her recollection of the figure's calm presence and fluid, all-embracing attentiveness fed her in a way she could not doubt was truth.

It was to Piero she turned for an image to fasten her resolve to keep at a studious discipline. The painting was by no means his best, but its subject was most certainly to the point: a bug-eyed, buck-toothed, cartoon-like horse grinned foolishly and kicked up his legs in a rambunctious pose that showed off his tumescent genitalia. This was Lust, or how Piero chose to depict Lust, in all its willful, wasteful, shameless folly.

He was a purely allegorical horse, just as the figure of Chastity, with her erect bronze wings, small marmoreal breasts, smooth braided hair and cool regard, was a wonderfully imagined symbol of consummate restraint. Chastity's hips were decently covered by a triangular swathe of crimson drapery. She held the horse by the merest gossamer thread of a rein, looped around his thick, muscular neck. Agnes thought the gossamer was most percipient. Her resolution to keep her thoughts chaste was just that evanescent and easily torn.

She next saw Campbell, accompanied by Kit, at the Wednesday Animal Ethics lecture. She took notes in a desultory fashion, but could not focus properly on what Professor Jonquil was saying. The topic was the altruistic behaviour of the great primates and other mammals, and she ought to have been noting his every word. But her eye kept returning to the backs of the two gleaming heads three rows in front of her: Campbell's glossy raven hue and Kit's breathtaking burnished red. That superb colour was just the last straw; as if the gods themselves were so besotted with Kit's lovely features they could not stop giving and giving.

Agnes's envy coiled as she saw Campbell's fingers twine through the rippling red-glow mane. Those fingers had stroked her everywhere, even deep inside. Why did she so stupidly want it to happen again, so badly that even her teeth ached with desire? Why was she deluding herself? She knew the possibility of any repeat performance was ludicrous. Why would he choose her with her odd little face?

She was being ridiculous. Like Piero's buck-toothed, grinning horse, his head empty of everything but carnal craving. What she was feeling was primitive and raw, and she must at all costs get it under control. She was beginning to understand the extreme iconography of eremites flagellating themselves in their desert hovels; even if the rein to subdue the lust was gossamer-thin, it was nevertheless a rein. She would hold firm. She would not be a naked body on a bed, legs splayed, tongue lolling from her mouth, as she begged for pleasure. This scenario was degrading and would be the ruin of her intellect, one of the few real assets she had.

She uncrossed her legs, sat erect, imagining the towering wings of Chastity at her back. She then refocused on Fergus Jonquil who was enthusiastically miming the death throes of an elephant matriarch who has sacrificed herself to roving hunters for the sake of the herd. He moved speedily to her burial, waving an invisible trunk, lifting one foot and then the other heavily as he mimicked her inconsolable relations in their ritual of grief. How would his performance strike a new student coming into the hall? Possibly as more than a little mad, or flagrantly uninhibited. There was definitely an unsavoury aspect to the professor's histrionic demonstrations. Was it because he appeared to be enjoying himself a little too much, thus cheapening the very point he was trying to make? Or was that unfair? Perhaps Fergus Jonquil genuinely believed he took on the characters of the animals he imitated. She wondered briefly about the contents of his dreams and had an unwanted vision of him swaying in his lugubrious dance, dressed in the animal's flayed skin.

This horrific picture jolted her. Where had it come from? Could she be projecting her own prickly angst about Campbell on to the innocent Fergus? The gruesome image of the weaving figure in his bloody elephant's robe would not let her go and it spawned its own steely thought: that Fergus Jonquil's claim to understand what animals felt and thought was vain and foolish, and perhaps dangerous, for himself and those he taught. This led her to the young woman who had been injured in the demonstration that ended in Fergus's dismissal from his previous teaching position. No one at the Ark had said exactly how she was hurt. Had she recovered? Was she sitting somewhere now in a wheelchair, unable to walk or talk? Did Fergus ever think of her? Did he feel in any way responsible? Judging by his antics on the lecture stage, Agnes guessed not.

The air in the hall now seemed tainted. Her head ached. She felt dizzy. She wanted to leave but shrank from the idea of everyone's eyes fixed on her as she made her awkward way past the students sitting to her right, and then down the stairs and out the heavy door of the lecture hall, with its disruptive clunk and swoosh.

How tense she felt. She clenched and unclenched her fists at her sides. She could not rid herself of the stupid idea some kind of miasma was polluting the room. At last, the lecture was over and she wrote down, with a disproportionate relief, the details of the readings required for the next class. She left quickly so that she would be spared any further witness of Campbell-doting-on-Kit and Kit-doting-on-Campbell. It was only when she was outside, taking in long draughts of tart autumn air, that she realized Pinto had not been at the lecture. She hoped he was not ill. As her mind touched on the idea of him — the gigantic man with the gentle face — she felt a great swell of gratitude. How would she have fared if he had not come after her when she'd left the Ark, distraught and buzzing with paranoia? She might have got horribly lost and ended up in a dangerous part of town, or begun raving in the street.

She recalled how sensitively he had calmed her needling anxiety; how, in his company, the bench facing the river had become a secure anchorage. She had an urge to go there now and see if she could find the tree where she'd had the vision of Piero di Cosimo perching. She was not so foolish as to think she might be granted such an apparition again. What she really wanted was to revisit that state of still clarity Pinto had helped her find. She needed to sort through and settle her thoughts — most particularly, how might she throw off the pathetic craving to be with Campbell again? She must try to exhume, as well, whatever nasty element in her own psyche had cast up the gruesome image of the well-meaning professor cavorting in an elephant's newly flayed hide.

When she got to the little park that bordered the river, nothing was as she remembered. Night and the moon had made it seem larger, almost vast, and denser somehow. In that recollected scene, the crowns of the trees had looked round and full, although naturally she had not been able to see their burnished colours in the dark. In the last few days, strong winds had stripped the trees almost bare. The leaves, many already crisp and sere, lay heaped about her feet and in crested mounds against the iron legs of the bench. The overwhelming odour of decay stirred in her the old remembered dread of all the autumns of her high-school years. Those first few months back were always the worst. After the blessed respite of the summer, she'd had to relearn how to bear the sadistic onslaught: the crude, thrusting gestures; the wicked caricatures passed furtively beneath desks that showed her naked, with pendulous breasts and coarse hairs sprouting from her chin and buttocks. Freak. Monkey-Girl. She'd had to master again how not to flinch, how to keep her face impassive and her posture dignified, no matter how unexpected or vicious the strike.

She shut her eyes against these lacerating memories. She began to wonder if what drew her to Campbell was not so much physical and emotional desire as a childish need for acceptance. Through his touch, she had proof she was not utterly repulsive.

She shook herself; stamped both feet angrily. How she hated her tendency to run to self-pity, and even worse, self-loathing. She was *not* a freak. She most absolutely was not. But how complex it all was: this turbulent business of desire and love. For, yes, she was sure she did love him, and not just because he was so damned beautiful and looked so like Piero's grieving satyr. She loved him because he was sensitive and intelligent and because he cared so passionately about the welfare of animals. She loved him because he was organizing the protest at the animal lab and that took courage. She loved him because he had come to her bedside and willingly and generously "made love to her." She did not know how else to describe what he had done, so lavish and delicate and fluid were his attentions. Like an erotic choreography.

Choreography! This was the first time it had occurred to her that those clever caresses Campbell used were the result of long practice. How naïve she was. All along she has been hugging the delusion that what took place in the tiny moonlit bedroom in the Ark was as brilliantly spontaneous and unrepeatable as a work of art. Deflating as the cold truth was, it had the advantage of clarifying her position and wrenching her focus back to her work. To be a scholar delving into wonders must remain her prime passion.

It was Saturday morning. Agnes sat at her desk, head lowered over the same page of Burckhardt on which she had been focused for the past hour. Her essay on the character of the Renaissance ruler, what Burckhardt termed "a strange mixture of good and evil," was due Tuesday. As yet, she had achieved nothing but the sketchiest of outlines. She had decided to tackle Sigismundo Malatesta, Lord of Rimini, rather than the more obvious choice of Lorenzo de Medici. According to Burckhardt, Malatesta combined "unscrupulousness, impiety, military skill and high culture." She could have written pages on Malatesta's "high culture" as easily as pouring water from a jug. She had seen photographs of the gracefully proportioned temple he had commissioned for his dead lover Ixotta, with its carvings of elegant goddesses, dolphins and elephants on its pediments and columns. It was an exquisite construction verging on the ethereal.

It was the other strands of Malatesta's character, especially the unscrupulousness, which stayed her hand when she tried to write anything. Of course she recognized that many patrons of the arts, and artists themselves, were not necessarily *good* people. The men in particular seemed often to be egocentric, condescending and vindictive. They were in the habit of treating their models, lovers and wives abominably. But, for the most part, they weren't rapists or murderers, as reputedly was Malatesta. She pressed her knuckles into her temples, an old childhood habit she believed renewed her powers of concentration.

At that moment, someone rapped on her door. She sat bolt-upright. She never had any visitors. Her first thought was that something had happened to her parents, or to Phoebe. When had she last spoken to them?

"Agnes? Hi! Are you in there?"

She opened the door to see Irma, a round-faced woman with an infectious laugh, who had a room two doors down the hall.

"You've got a visitor waiting outside," Irma told her. "I just bumped into him on my way back from getting coffee." She held up the giant banded paper cup, as if compelled to show the evidence.

"He's hot. Very hot," Irma confided. She rolled her eyes, and blew on the coffee's rising steam. "Well, have a nice day!" She smiled, and hurried away.

"Thank you," Agnes called after her, doubtless a little late for anyone more practised in common courtesy.

She was perplexed. *Hot.* She knew only one person who fit Irma's description. But it couldn't be. Campbell hadn't even spoken to her since their "encounter" in the Ark, other than "hello" with a smile he could have easily bestowed on a sparrow.

Nevertheless, she glanced quickly in the mirror, fluffed her hair with her fingers, and patted on some lip gloss. Then she ran downstairs to the lobby where her heart leapt so high in her chest, she pictured it as a salmon, pink and sleek, cresting sea spume. Flying. She was. Through the glass doors, she could see him sitting outside on the stone steps, with what looked like (but surely it couldn't be?) a black leather jacket slung over his shoulder.

"Hi," she said, as she pushed through the doors, armed with her best guise of cool dignity. "Did you want to see me?"

Her heart was no salmon now, but a creature whose wild battering might at any moment break through the confines of her ribs. And she shivered because she was cold, dressed in only a thin T-shirt, leggings and her little red velvet slippers with their flimsy soles.

He swung around and stood up to face her. The sensuous smile and his unreal beauty, more breathtaking even than she remembered, completely undid her. "Dissolved in a dew." That was what was happening to her fatuous resolve to maintain a self-protective distance from him.

"Beautiful day," he said, his right hand sweeping to take in the crystalline air and the pure light that seemed to bound from point to point.

"Yes, it is." She smiled, but with her lips compressed. It was true. How sharp and clear everything looked.

"I wondered if you'd like to go for a ride. It's not too cold, and there's no wind. We could spend a few hours touring along the coast. Interested? Or are you too busy?"

Already, he was pulling on his jacket, making it evident there was no time to waste if he was to make the best of the day.

"Ride?" she asked. Did he mean bicycles?

"The bike," he said. "The Vulcan. There." He pointed to a gleaming machine parked across the road. What most surprised Agnes was how much it looked like an art object: the bike declared its own power through its bold marriage of crimson and black, and the immaculate curvature of the casing over what she assumed must be the engine.

"I've never been on a motorcycle," she said. She felt she had to be honest in case her inexperience posed some risk.

"Great! All the better! You'll love it. But if you're coming, we have to start soon. You'll need a warm, windproof jacket and shoes with good thick soles." He looked down at her slippers. "I'll be waiting over there." He pointed to the Vulcan. She saw how powerfully the bike magnetized him, his whole body inclining a little toward it.

Like a boy with his horse eager to surge into the world, she thought fondly, as she ran upstairs. The salmon back again. Flying. She told herself she would not think. She cast a baleful glance at the abandoned Burckhardt, and immediately looked away again. She hurriedly pulled on jeans, put on socks and running shoes; then rummaged in her closet for the periwinkle blue windbreaker, with hood, that she had found a couple of weeks ago at a garage sale. She remembered to pick up her wrap-around sunglasses, but forgot about gloves, an omission she would later regret when she had to chafe at her chilled, benumbed fingers every time they stopped. Much later, she wondered whether her cold hands on that ride were a premonition, of which she ought to have taken note. But even if she had registered such prescience, how could she have stopped the calamitous train of events that followed?

As she listened carefully, Campbell rapidly went through the essentials. Sit up straight and keep her feet on the foot rests. Put her arms around his waist. Trust him; he knew what he was doing. Do not move abruptly or do anything to startle him.

He handed her a helmet which she tried to put on over her sunglasses. But the glasses were too wide and she found herself stuck, the helmet wedged halfway on, halfway off. She winced. How damned ungainly she was. He was probably thinking she looked like a huge insect; doubtless he was wishing he had never asked her to accompany him at all.

"Here." She could hear him, but not — at least for the moment — see him. She was relieved he did not sound either irritated or impatient. She felt his breath on her face and then a little tug at her temples, as he extricated her sunglasses. Then he took off her helmet.

She blinked in the sunlight. He kissed her lightly on the nose. Yes, he did. Her lips parted in a tiny "o" of astonishment she hoped he did not notice.

"Try these," he said, handing her a pair of sleek, light-weight goggles. Only after she put them on did she wonder if these were the goggles Kit usually wore. I must not think about that now, she admonished herself, as she slid the helmet on and pulled the strap taut under the chin. Then she mounted the bike, settled in behind him, and put her arms about his waist as instructed, trying to keep her hands steady so as not to betray her nervous anticipation. Of the ride, or what might follow the ride?

An inarticulate cry escaped her as the bike lurched forward with a roar. Her whole body reverberated to its headlong, inexorable demand. She had never before felt so physically fragile: she was a creature made of eggshell riding the back of a dragon. This bizarre picture actually made her giggle and for a moment she shed some of her constricting fear. She became wholly alert then to the startling new way of being in the world that Campbell and the bike offered her. It was as if they were flowing unimpeded into the very heart of things: the rusty gold of shorn corn fields on either side; the invigorating air spangled with speedwell blue; and the pearly shimmer on the horizon she supposed must be the sea. She had not expected this extraordinary transformation of self and perception. She and Campbell and the Vulcan were particles in the flow of the world.

She was wrenched from these fanciful thoughts by Campbell's sudden swerve around the sad remains of a blown truck tire. She only just managed to rein in her panic, certain his abrupt manoeuvre would tip the bike. But, as he straightened out and they roared forward again, she felt the fear return in earnest, creeping up her spinal column and the back of her neck. She told herself this rising anxiety was just the flip-side of the exhilaration she had felt only a few moments before; that if she just turned the terror inside-out, like a glove, and wore it well, she could recover the cleanly alert attention that gave her such a fluid stronghold in this precipitate, speeding world.

They accelerated to pass two cars driving slowly in tandem. Perhaps the drivers were lost, she thought, or searching for some elusive crossroads. Very soon, Campbell turned right and she saw ahead a brilliant sheen from which rose an evanescent fan of rainbow light. The sea, she thought. In fact, it was a small bay and as they drove past she caught sight of a rocky outcrop whose deeply incised crevices suggested one of those hidden faces she often glimpsed in Piero di Cosimo's mountain crags. She was never sure whether these secret faces were glowering or benign.

As they rushed on through the bright clear morning, she thought that of course the animistic features she had seen in the rock must be kindly. How could they be anything else on such a day? She had been so certain she would never touch him again; yet here she was, on the back of his bike, her arms circling his waist. Tendrils of his hair, which was rather long at the back, escaped his helmet and blew across her lips. Although she still rode inside her fear, the marriage of dread and bliss gave everything about the ride a scintillating sharpness. When he pulled into a travellers' stop, he kissed her lightly on the mouth as he helped her off the bike.

"Hungry?" he asked.

She was not — at least in the sense he meant. She was feeding greedily on the vast resource love was. Like an infinite honeycomb, a sweet, sticky substance you lapped up, and then shivered in delight. She saw herself reflected in the plate-glass window of the restaurant as they walked forward together. How mysterious and powerful she looked in the helmet and goggles. "I am perfectly happy," she told herself. "Nothing will ever surpass this."

But something did. An hour later, after guiding the bike down a hard-beaten path between swathes of dried rushes and salt-hay, he took her inside a half-moon shelter the sea had carved in the rock. She barely had time to stare up at their craggy roof before he pulled her close and thrust his tongue deep in her mouth. She was overcome. He had not kissed her on the mouth at all in the Ark. She read this new intimacy as symbolizing a great advance in their relationship. Joined to him in this way, she felt she was disappearing into a vast red cavern where desire kept overleaping itself. She became aware he had taken off her jacket. His left hand slipped under her T-shirt, his right under the waistband of her jeans in a quick-silk movement that partook of magic. His fingers were both inside and outside her, taking her deep down again into that undertow of saturating pleasure where she would willingly drown.

She was embarrassed at how wet she was, but he did not seem to mind. "You are very, very sexy," he whispered in her ear. "Did you know that, Agnes?" She came then, and swayed against him, almost sobbing because everything was so intense. Not just erotic and emotional, but something else, she was certain. Some fragment of soul they had exchanged in this place.

"I really want to have you completely this time." He spoke in quiet earnest, enunciating each word carefully, like a prayer. He extracted a wrapped condom from his pocket. "Is this all right with you?"

"Yes." What other answer could there possibly be?

It hurt at first much more than she'd anticipated; like the rasping burn on her palms when she'd had to shimmy up a rope in gym class. He strove, in his practised and considerate way, to bring her along with him, but she was too conscious of the residual discomfort, and above all of the way he filled her, to achieve another orgasm. When he came, she was for some seconds inside a dark red rippling tunnel, where she ceased to know her own bounds and his shudders and moans were hers. But her chief sensation was an unqualified wonder that he was inside her. She was no longer virgin, but for this instant queen, because he was unspeakably beautiful and had taken her fully out of desire.

He did not stay beside her as long as she would have wished. He pulled on his clothes and sat, face turned away from her, looking out at the water. He lit a cigarette.

She was pulling her T-shirt over her head as he spoke. "You okay?"

When she could see again, it was still his back he presented to her, and she felt an irrational hatred for the cigarette on which he seemed so intent.

"I want to ask you something," he said.

She felt her stomach lurch. What was he going to say? Why was she always expecting to be hurt? She made herself ready.

"You wouldn't tell Kit, would you?" He looked so worried, she almost cried out in alarm.

"It's only," he went on urgently before she could respond, "that she's going through a tough time right now. Her aunt in Ireland died suddenly last week. Kit's there now with her mother, for the funeral. But with her mother the way she is, on track one minute and totally off the rails the next, the whole thing is going to be a real strain for her. So . . ."

Did his request make her angry or just sad? She was uncertain. "No," she said. "I would never tell her."

"Or anyone?" he asked, concern still a visible cloud in is eyes.

"Or anyone," she repeated.

In some curious way, this concession struck her as a sacrifice. She was taking a symbolic bullet in the breast for his sake. Yet she was jubilant as well that he had not said: "Well, it's been a blast, but you understand why it can never happen again."

Or the unthinkable: "I've never made love to a girl as ugly as you before."

There was still a chance, in other words, that this might happen again and again. And because he had said nothing to wound her irrevocably, she could still keep the memory of being with him sacrosanct.

He came and put his arms around her. "You're sweet and understanding, as well as really sexy," he said — words she was sure she would repeat to herself every day, without irony or rue, until she was a very old woman.

As they rode back, she was amused to see that the shadow-shape he and she and the Vulcan made on the tarmac resembled a single hybrid, its elements as strongly forged as a satyr's with his human torso and goat-legs. She felt exhilarated; the bike's vital, primitive energy was speeding them to a future so potently charged, her body buzzed with awe, wrapped around the core of abiding fear.

When they neared town, she spotted the church spire not far from her dorm and behind it a dense dark-grey cloud whose bulging scallops suggested a doleful face in profile. This shape was disturbingly familiar, yet she could not place where she had seen it before.

"Thanks," he said, as he dropped her off. Then: "Would you like to do it again some time?" His smouldering look told her he did not mean just the bike ride.

"Yes." Dazedly, she watched him ride away, then ran up to her room, wanting to trill madly like a lark.

She did not shower or even wash her hands because she wanted to keep his scent on her as long as possible. Almost immediately, she sat at the computer and began to write her essay. Something about the bike ride, the machine's sculptural perfection and the dangerous lure of its air-cleaving speed, allowed her to slip inside the contradictory character of Sigismundo Malatesta. When at last she finished, at two in the morning, she went wearily to bed, her head filled again purely with thoughts of Campbell and everything he had said and done to her.

At six, she woke from a dream that had her clutching at her throat in panic. She had dreamt she was the elegant, bare-breasted young woman in Piero's portrait of the great Florentine Renaissance beauty, Simonetta Vespucci.

Behind her, setting in relief her delicate chin, fine nose and smooth high forehead, was the ominous scallop-edged cloud like the one Agnes had seen above the spire.

The portrait had another unsettling torque, an attribute the eye fastened on with fascination and loathing in equal measure. This was the slender, green, live snake twined around the base of Simonetta's white throat like a necklace. And if the lovely woman were to move just a millimetre, Agnes always worried, or even took just a slightly deeper breath, might that not cause the living necklace to inject its venom into the white neck or the high little breasts with their proud nipples? And what then would become of the lady's calm, pure regard?

Why had he created such a cruelly mesmerizing image, a picture that made one catch one's breath in apprehension? The snake must be a viper, nurtured and warmed by the Tuscan sun. Agnes could not begin to imagine baring her breast and then slipping such a creature about her neck, regardless of its exquisite emerald scales. In bed, she shuddered, put her head down again and tried to sleep; but she could not. The dream image was still too strong and far too close for comfort. She could not begin to fathom its significance.

The lethal snake-necklace continued to haunt her over the following days, even sometimes blighting the recollected bliss of all that had happened in the cave by the sea.

NINE

Piero and the Snake Necklace

P IERO HAD CAUGHT SIGHT OF Simonetta Vespucci once, when he was a boy. She rode a white horse and was flanked by her mounted attendants, forming a majestic train en route to an entertainment hosted by one of Florence's great families. What had struck him most about the noble lady was the overwrought artifice of her coiffure. Pulled tightly back from her brow, her thickly braided golden hair was looped into fantastic shapes, like the twining tentacles of the squid he sometimes saw for sale in the market. The plaited coils were encrusted with jewels that winked in the light of the torches her attendants carried. He thought they might be rubies and pearls. But he had then seen few real jewels and could not be certain.

Of one thing he was sure. The ornate sculpture of her hair arrangement was sorely burdensome to the lady. He noticed how her head drooped slightly under its weight, how she must make a constant effort to keep her delicate chin tilted upward.

When, many years later, he received a commission to paint a memorial portrait of the lady, he understood she had borne a far heavier burden: that of her fabled beauty and her fame. During her brief lifetime, many Florentines saw in Simonetta, who was as good and pious as she was beautiful, the embodiment of Plato's most sublime Form, the Love that surpasses perfection. She was resplendent and peerless; most could adore her only at a distance.

The most passionate of her admirers was Giuliano de' Medici, younger brother of Lorenzo. On his twenty-second birthday, in 1475, at a magnificent pageant and joust Lorenzo staged in his honour, Giuliano entered the Piazza Santa Croce bearing a banner with Simonetta depicted as Pallas Athena. The message was clear. Simonetta was not only lovely as a goddess, but consummately wise as well. *Sans pareil*, the French inscription on the banner read. The unparalleled one. At the joust, she was crowned "The Queen of Beauty."

Within a year this paragon of womankind lay on her deathbed, felled by a disease of the lungs. Lorenzo de' Medici sent the finest physicians to attend her. But no earthly skill could save her. She was barely twenty-four and at the height of her fame and beauty when death seized her.

All of Florence mourned her passing and Marco Vespucci graciously acceded to the public's request that his wife's coffin be open for her final journey through the city's streets to the family's crypt in the church of Ognissanti. Thus all who loved and admired her might have a last glimpse of that exquisite countenance. Thousands followed her coffin, among them Sandro Botticelli, who pressed in close for a last look at the lady, whose image he could fold away inside his heart. For he too was besotted, and in the years to follow he would paint her features again and again — for the Venus on the half-shell who was to make his name immortal, and Flora of his *Primavera*, for whom he fashioned one of the most extraordinary confections in the history of dressmaking. The flowers woven into Flora's gauzy skirt, bodice and sleeves gave the illusion they had wafted there on a wind out of the south. The gown evoked the very essence of spring: evanescent yet perpetually renewing.

In those memorial portraits Botticelli painted of Simonetta, her serene gaze was directly on the viewer. Her lips, compressed in a gentle half-smile, promised a rarefied bliss, far removed from illness and toil and the base urges of humankind. By contemplating her image, a man who sought the highest spiritual truth might find his longing realized and behold a divine radiance.

When, many years after the lady's death, a scion of the Medici family commissioned Piero to create a posthumous portrait of Simonetta, it was the coiled arabesques of her extravagant hairstyle that came first to the painter's mind. He remembered well the deliberate grace she had summoned in order to bear the heavy burden of her beauty. He had by then come to understand that physical perfection such as Simonetta's was as much curse as blessing.

His Medici patron wanted an image of Simonetta that would show above all the luminous raiment of her soul, which he could contemplate at leisure in the privacy of his study. The portrait need not be an exact resemblance of the exalted lady as she had been in life, he instructed Piero, but rather an eidolon that caught the essence of her unmatched purity. By gazing at her portrait, the young man hoped to leave behind the shadowy cave of mundane matter and achieve a place at the Platonic Academy the Great Lorenzo had established at his court. As a guide for Simonetta's expression, he gave Piero a quotation from the poet Poliziano's paean to the lady: "She is regally mild; her gaze could quiet a tempest."

As always, Piero began the work by first conceiving the subject fully in his imagination. He saw the lady in profile, just as he had seen her many years before when she rode by him on her white horse. He let his inner eye follow the cunning coils of her hair, the thick loops entwined with their milky ropes of pearls, the elegant scattering of larger milky stones. At the nape of her neck, below the thick outermost loop of her bright hair, a single ruby dangled, like a solidified drop of blood.

He saw then in quick succession three things that gave even him a jolt; yet immediately the vision appeared he knew it could not be otherwise. First, as proof of her unspotted soul, she would show the world her naked breasts, as small and innocent as a nubile girl's. Second, she would display her marmoreal stillness in a setting where no semi-nude Florentine noblewoman would ever show herself — out in the countryside, with umber and dark sage hills defining the horizon. Just behind her head, in counterpoint to her porcelain quietude, an inky storm cloud glowered, swollen with the seeds of a tempest. Simonetta's reflective purity, so evident in the unsullied profile, kept the tempest at bay, just as Poliziano's memorial poem described.

The third element of Piero di Cosimo's vision for the portrait was the one that most perturbed him. He found it very strange indeed, even given his predilection for the fantastical. Through the necklace of tiny linked chains hanging above the lady's naked breasts, a live snake wound in sinuous twists of green and gold. Just above her collarbone and mere inches from the puckered flesh of her small nipples, the reptile's sinister thread-like tongue and tail tip almost touched.

Piero saw immediately that the slender green-gold viper was as mesmerizing as the woman herself. It was only when the work was finished, and he had painted the last tiny scale on the live peril which rode upon her breast, that he recognized the snake's true significance. Its serpentine twists symbolized the very vagaries of Fortune. This was the same Fortune that endowed Simonetta with a beauty that could inspire rapture, and had then just as capriciously struck her down.

Who knew, he reflected, where it would strike next – for good or for ill — the shadowy serpent that all mortal beings wore in blind ignorance about their necks?

When he saw the finished work, Piero's young patron at first appeared displeased. He frowned at the boldness of Simonetta's nakedness and shuddered at the sight of the viper's flickering tongue so near her tender breast. Then, even sooner than the painter had hoped, the young man began to praise the enigmatic balance of these disparate elements. The snake necklace, he told Piero, paid a most fitting homage to Simonetta's eternality.

Piero wisely said nothing. He had worked, in tempera on wood, a composition in exact keeping with his vision. He smiled at his creation for the last time, and pocketed his payment.

TEN

Pinto Reflects on a Soldier

PINTO HAD TRIED EVERYTHING TO shut out the sounds that now tormented him at night. Little balls of absorbent cotton stuffed in his ears had only a muffling effect. What he heard might be coming from deep beneath the sea. Perversely, he would then strain to catch any single whole words that emerged from the undertow — "No." "Yes." "Please." This last was always the worst. It pierced him to the core.

He had bought earplugs designed for air travel which promised to insulate the wearer from the ambient roar of engines and the wails of distressed babies. The plugs came with a dull black eye-shade. This conjunction of sensory deprivation devices made him smile grimly in the dark. He felt ready for his own execution. With ears stopped up and eyes covered, he lay as still as he could, intent on the oblivion of sleep. Was it his nerves or his skin that continued to register the cacophony through the walls, the little sharp cries: "Oh, oh, oh"? Like machinegun fire, he thought. He lay on his long bed, clutching his midriff, digging his nails in where the pain concentrated its assault.

He had also tried humming quietly, with his pillow bunched up around his ears. When that did not work, he put on his clock radio with the volume turned low. He had the radio set permanently on the public broadcast station that played classical music non-stop. When he yearned for a musical cocoon, it was the melodic, melancholic Brahms he most wanted to hear. He thought of Brahms as a kindred spirit because of his unrequited love for Clara Schumann and wondered if the composer had ever struggled to subdue a corrupting rage against all the expert lovers in the world. Pinto tried very hard, as he lay in bed listening to Agnes's protracted cries of delight, not to hate Campbell.

He had so far endured a full week of this torture. In part, he was disappointed in Agnes for succumbing to Campbell's heartless ploys in the first place. He experienced, as well, a palpable disgust at the idea of what the two of them were actually doing just down the hall. He refused to let his imaginings go too far: of hands and tongues and . . . If he thought too much about it, he would surely go mad. What he did glean from the wild cries he tried to obliterate was that this sexual activity had an exceedingly vulgar aspect. Sometimes it sounded as if they were spanking each other. "Go. Go. Faster, baby, faster!" This was Campbell's urgent voice, and it was horrible.

He was appalled to think of Agnes being so devalued by Campbell's lust. Lewdness. Pinto pondered the word, which conjured up a sickly stew of hormonal urges and secretions. He wanted Agnes liberated from all this cheap nastiness. If she willingly came to him, how high a place he would prepare for her, nurturing her true self in his mind and heart. Soul enfolded in soul. And a love-making consonant with this: a gentle rocking rather than the rambunctious, crude copulation that was Campbell's apparent preference.

If Agnes were only willing, he would worship her with his body. He would share with her the quiet yet intense Tantric techniques he had studied; the matchless joining of blood, breath and life-force that would bring them both to true ecstasy. *True.* Not tawdry and brutish.

"Fuck, baby," he hears Campbell yell. "Fuck. Fuck."

Pinto thrust his index fingers so far into his eardrums that it hurt. Well, since he already hurt all over, what was the difference? He wondered if this ache was even worse than his mordant grief when his dear dog Yangtze died. He had never wanted anything so badly as for Kit to come home. Surely it would be soon?

"Arghhh . . . "

He gritted his teeth. Had Campbell achieved his greedy climax at last? But if the past few nights were anything to go by, they would soon be at it again. It was already 2:00 AM and Pinto had an early class at eight. Two nights ago he had tried going out for a walk to escape the disturbance. But he had deeply resented having to do so and as he walked that resentment fuelled his old mindless, destructive urge to a degree that shocked him and made him question whether he had progressed at all in mastering his core rage.

He'd gone to the river to the same bench he'd taken Agnes when Campbell's strong pot upset her. He sat, staring into the dark water, wondering if the huge snapping turtle were down there somewhere, its claws stirring the muddy bed as it dreamed of fresh and yielding prey. He had seen the turtle in the spring when the new ducklings were skittering about on the water. They'd looked tiny and vulnerable, more like water-bugs than waterfowl and so his heart had lurched in his chest when the mother duck began sending out anguished warnings to her six babies. She swam up rapidly behind them and then circled the group, quacking her alarm all the while.

The snapping turtle was so monstrous and formidably armoured compared with the minuscule, crushable ducklings. How leathery and grey and ancient the turtle's head looked, and how sharp the claws of the webbed feet that churned the water so steadily and slowly. Yet this steadiness and slowness were all illusion, for the massive turtle kept gaining on the ducklings, who remained apparently oblivious to the danger. It had been the reptile's relentlessness he'd found most chilling, as though it had been swimming toward its prey forever, a slow missile out of a prehistoric time that nothing whatsoever could deter. For an instant he'd stood transfixed by its wrinkled head and lidless eyes. He'd had the hideous notion that what he saw there was the antediluvian shape of Fate itself.

How ridiculous his actions had been, flailing his arms and waving his knapsack back and forth over the water and the reptile's head. "Leave them alone," he'd bellowed. But although his shouts had had no impact on the turtle's resolute trajectory, they had succeeded in frightening the ducklings, who'd paddled toward the safety of the bank in a neat little V-shaped flotilla.

As the noises continued on the other side of the wall, he closed his eyes and again saw the turtle swim on, unblinking and unperturbed, to feast elsewhere. He tried hard not to think of the creature as malevolent. Had he interfered with an elemental process? What would have become of the principle of natural selection if well-intentioned humans had always been intervening in this way? This question perplexed him. Had he been right or wrong to try to save the ducklings?

He was delighted to find that by plunging back into this unsettling scene and its attendant moral dilemma, he had finally managed to blot out the noises coming from Campbell's bedroom. In the hope he could repeat the trick he turned to another ethical conundrum that had recently preoccupied him. The week before, while researching an assignment for Fergus's class, he had come upon an article whose revelations continued to haunt him. Each day since then, he had found himself passionately wishing he could speak with the protagonist in this story.

This was impossible on two counts: first, because the individual in question had died in the fifth century; and second, because he had probably never possessed any form of human speech. How well the author had set him up for the unexpected twist. He began by describing the grave of a Roman soldier archaeologists had unearthed earlier that year in the Pyrenees. Only then did he reveal that the young warrior, buried with honours in his finest uniform and with his gleaming metal belt or *cingulum,* was an adolescent macaque, originally from North Africa.

He kept visualizing the young monkey laid in his grave, while his comrades wept and saluted. He reasoned the macaque must have been much loved to be interred with such care and ceremony. But how had he come to be part of a Roman legion in the days when the Empire was crumbling? And was he really a soldier who took part in battles against the Barbarians or was he a mascot?

Had he been kidnapped, torn from his family? Did he lament his fate? Or had he come to love what he did, marching and fighting with his fellow legionnaires? Did he understand he was not the same as them? Was he willing to do what he did, even if initially he had been coerced?

Yet the macaque *belonged*. They would not have buried him in his best uniform, with his belt shining about his waist, unless they felt he was one of them. Pinto felt a sudden, absurd stab of jealousy towards the long-dead macaque. I will never belong, not really. Not to any one, or any group. This bald self-pity shattered his lovely speculative globe. Now he could hear again, all too clearly, Campbell's crude, greedy cries.

"Harder, baby, harder!"

He will hurt her with his selfish crudity, Pinto thought. Unconsciously, he had tightened his big hands into fists. He struggled hard, as he had so often of late, against the terrible desire to wrap his huge hands around Campbell's elegant neck and choke him until he turned blue. Until Campbell was ugly, and spat out his life's blood.

Pinto pressed his fists into his closed eyes, until they smarted. How he loathed himself for these violent thoughts. Whatever his faults, Campbell was still his friend.

His ceaseless tossing had made a tangle of his sheets. He unwound the top one from his legs and spread it carefully over his thighs. Then he began to breathe as deeply as he could, as necessary preparation for a calm clarity. But a single wish continued to flash neon-like in his brain.

Oh, if only Kit would come home soon. Campbell would drop Agnes then, and he, Pinto Peter Dervaig, would comfort and love her as she deserved.

Please come home, Kit. Please.

ELEVEN

The Demonstration

GRIEF AT HER AUNT'S DEATH and her mother's continued decline had transformed Kit. Her porcelain skin had a bluish cast and there were hollows in her cheeks where none had been before. These were changes that would have made most women look wan, ill and undesirable. But on Kit, they served only to dramatize her fine-featured, fairy-world beauty.

Agnes could not help but gaze awestruck at the picture Kit made on the back of Campbell's bike. She sat like a tall stately elfin queen, with everyone's eyes (or so it seemed) drawn by the magnificent river of red hair that streamed from beneath the motorcycle helmet as Kit strapped it on. Agnes was unsure if it was the same helmet Campbell had given her to wear and told herself it did not matter. The principal fact was obvious and humiliating enough: it was not that she had been supplanted by Kit in pride of place behind Campbell on his bike and in his bed. It was that she had been "whited-out," apparently obliterated from his memory altogether.

She kept watching for a particular smile or covert gesture he might send her way as a token of affection;

some sign of gentle remembrance she could hold to assuage the hurt. She found nothing. Not a scrap.

Yes, she had been a fool. An utter fool to enter into an undertaking whose rules she does not comprehend. She saw the dangers clearly now and just how easily a person can be undone by an addiction to sex, an obsession that could ruin one's life as surely as would drugs or alcohol. If she let herself dwell on the ways he had touched her, and the heavenly sensations he aroused in her . . . But she must not.

Work, she told herself each day. Work would be her salvation. That and a passionate, unflagging commitment to animals' rights and welfare. Wasn't that the reason she'd gone to the Ethical Ark meetings in the first place? She knew this wasn't strictly so, or that it certainly had not been her only reason. But the compulsion to take action was, if anything, surging in her more strongly than ever before. She was obsessed with the pitiable plight of the cats, dogs and rabbits that were even now on their way to the new laboratory where the stark metal operating tables and torturing instruments awaited them. She could smell their terror as they fouled themselves, crammed into wire cages stacked floor-to-ceiling inside the frigid transport trucks.

Here hell began, and therefore anything she and the other Ark members could do to stop this evil business would be worthwhile. Campbell assured them that representatives of the media were on their way. But as yet, at the assembly point outside the Ark, there were only people she knew: Pinto, Zebra, Minnie, Pablo and Perdita. Much to her surprise, Horace had shown up. In his velour jacket with its tight little hood, he looked more wizened and malign than ever. His tongue had lost none of its acidity.

"What!" he exclaimed on arrival. "No Harrier or Lupo? Have our aging Alpinists defected? Don't tell me. They had a prior pressing engagement. They're off stomping the northern tundra, feeding starving caribou by hand. Or down on their dear old arthritic knees praying for the survival of Icelandic whales. My, my. However will we manage without their electrifying presence . . . ?"

"Shut it, Horace," Zebra exclaimed. "They're old, for crying out loud."

"I had noticed that, fetish boy. But doddering might be a more accurate description, don't you think? And have any of you noticed that Harriet is starting to smell just a little bit rank? Incontinence can be such a problem at her age."

"You're disgusting, Horace! You're a sick little . . . " Zebra rounded on him.

Agnes began to fear there would be a fight.

"Guys!" Minnie glared at both men. "Just drop the adolescent crap, okay? This is a mission, right? Remember why we're here and let's behave like adults, for God's sake."

"Mission!" Horace guffawed.

His defining cynicism seemed today more offensive than ever. Agnes felt her skin prickling in revulsion at the back of her neck and down her forearms and shins. Why did he have to demean everything and everyone?

"What's that, Missy Agnes? Lo! She speaks! A rare occurrence indeed. And did you say 'demean', Missy?"

Agnes flushed. Had she really spoken her thought out loud? Was she so keyed up she'd been unaware of doing so?

"Au contraire, Missy Agnes. I am the only one here who grasps the meaning. I am your group's reality check. Face the facts, kids. This isn't a mission. It's an escapade. It's self-regarding, self-indulgent folly. So why don't you all put down the silly crusading guise and toddle back into the Ark before one of you gets hurt?" Horace had raised his voice and was looking pointedly at Kit.

"But it is a crusade, Horace," Agnes piped up. "Why can't you see that? Even one act of defiance . . . "

"Stop right there, Missy, because your thinking is muddled. And haven't you been indulging in extracurricular activities lately that may have gravely undermined your ratiocinative powers? In fact, utterly screwed them up, one might say. That's S-C-R . . . "

"Leave her alone, Horace!" Pinto interposed his great bulk between Agnes and the acerbic little man.

This intercession annoyed her because she felt she was capable of dealing with Horace's rudeness herself; on the other hand, she was glad to have Pinto's massive back obscuring her face, which must be blanched by paranoid worry. *Screwed*. Horace had definitely said *screwed*. But how could he know? Or was he simply cunning or clever enough to have guessed? Horace's unfailing devotion to Kit might well have given him some kind of super-sensory power. There was probably never a moment in his existence when his niece (or was she his half-niece?) was not foremost in his thoughts.

Indeed, as Pinto stepped aside, Agnes saw Horace's eyes fixed on Kit. She had removed the helmet so as to better arrange the mass of her hair under it, and Campbell had got off the bike to help her. He was looking down at Kit so lovingly his expression was besotted, if not worshipful.

He had never looked at her like that. Never. It was the difference between mud and gold. He had just wanted to play. She clenched her teeth on the obdurate truth of the matter. He just wanted to get a little dirty before he went back to his proper god-like realm.

And Kit and Campbell did look like gods, the setting sun gilding them in miraculous lilac and bronze light. Then the delicate shades dissipated. There was only the huge star dying on the horizon, looking hotly crimson and swollen. Like a massive face with the skin peeled away. She was reminded of the rising sun on the fateful morning she'd decided against the cosmetic surgery: its repellent pulsing redness a projected image of the awful mash of exposed tissue, nerves and blood her poor face would present on the operating table.

Now as she watched the sky drain of colour, it was the animals in the cargo trucks she thought of: their skin and fur peeled back; limbs broken or sawed off; eyes plucked out or propped open with mechanical pincers so that they could not sleep.

Her stomach was in knots. How could anyone do these things to living creatures who looked back at you with fine, trusting eyes? Why did billions of people remain oblivious to the sacred functions animals fulfilled, when the consequences of their indifference were sickening and catastrophic? After thinking about it deeply, she could see no ethical difference whatsoever between the torture and deliberate extermination of animals and the torture and deliberate extermination of human beings. She recognized that to voice such an opinion in unsympathetic quarters was to invite a whole host of accusations, from anti-Semitism to insanity.

Her eyes sought automatically the one person present who might subscribe to such a view. She found Horace standing beside Kit, his palms pressed together in an attitude of prayer.

"Please," he was saying. "Please, Kit. Don't go." His tone was so plaintive and heavy with foreboding she felt her own anxiety swell. The little man dropped to his knees and lifted up his face to gaze beseechingly at the lovely woman on the back of Campbell's bike. His hood fell back. Agnes was reminded of the figures of kneeling saints in altarpieces, their eyes brimming with the ineffable light emanating from the Virgin Mary who floated just above them. Horace's expression projected the same nobility and transfigured grace. She was more than a little chagrined to witness this transfiguration because she had come to think of Horace as irredeemably coarse. And not just because of his habitually barbed comments. If she were truthful with herself, she had judged him as polluted by the way he had come into the world. Which was so very wrong of her.

"Leave her alone, Horace." Campbell's voice was abrasive. "She wants to go. It's her decision."

"I can speak for myself, Campbell!"

Everyone looked at Kit.

Agnes had never heard her address Campbell in any other way than caressingly. Did this mean some tiny fracture was opening between them? Might she still have a chance with Campbell? Her blood quickened at the possibility. She felt quite warm, despite the bitter wind that sought out her bare neck and hands now the sun had gone down.

"It's time, people," Campbell announced. He revved the bike and raised his right arm in a gesture that conveyed both command and solidarity. "Let's roll out."

"But, Camel, where's the media guys?" Zebra's question was drowned by the bike's roar. The Vulcan, with its two god-like riders, shot down the street like a well-aimed lance. What could do they but follow?

Minnie had brought a battered emerald-green van into which Agnes climbed to sit in the back with Perdita and Pablo. Pinto got into the front passenger seat, with a quick apology for taking up so much room. Zebra, who had borrowed a friend's Austin mini, was talking to two men Agnes recognized from Professor Jonquil's class. Zebra briefly had introduced them. The slighter of the two was called Ewan, and the taller man had a German name. Klaus or perhaps Gerhardt? She had forgotten.

She was surprised to see Horace slip into the back of a red sports car which had only just pulled into the little street. The driver and the man seated beside him both had the muscular shoulders and arms that can only be obtained through serious training, and square jaws so similar they might have been twins. She wondered if Horace had enlisted their help so that Kit would have a trio of bodyguards if the need arose.

It would take about forty minutes to drive to the "death factory" as Zebra called it. What if Horace was right about the danger? What if they arrived to find several brawny security guards who would not hesitate to use force against any intruders? A buzz of panic ran up and down her arms and legs. She glanced sideways at Perdita and then at Pablo. As usual, the fair-haired pair sat quietly composed, as though contemplating their boundless inner reserves of peace and fortitude. She had recently learned they were Quakers. She envied them their calm confidence and, not for the first time, wondered whether a deep fund of traditional religious faith might make her a stronger moral agent, and a more resilient and unflagging crusader on animals' behalf.

Once they arrived at the turn-off for the laboratory, they continued for some minutes before she could see anything. She had not expected the lab to be located so far from the highway. As their convoy drove up, sensor lights came on to reveal a very long, one-storey building built of dun-coloured blocks that was otherwise featureless. There were not even any windows. It could have been an industrial plant for the making of something as innocent as cardboard boxes or children's cots. Was this what the "banality of evil" looked like? It had never before occurred to her that this description could apply as much to a place where unspeakable things were done, as to the soulless perpetrators themselves.

Minnie parked the van close to the towering pines directly behind the laboratory, the headlights revealing the perimeter of a dense wood. When she got out, on legs shakier than she'd anticipated, she immediately looked about for Campbell. He was fastening his helmet and Kit's to the bike, which he had parked on the road paralleling the laboratory. With the help of the sensor lights, she could make out that this road looped back down to the highway. They had driven up the entrance road. The exit road led off from the far end of the building. That must be for trucks that picked up and took away the animals' remains. She struggled against an upwelling nausea as they approached the massive corrugated metal door, about thirty feet in width, where the animals would be driven in and then unloaded.

"God," Minnie said. "It's ghastly."

For a moment they all stood in silence, as if benumbed by thoughts of the appalling uses for which this chill hell was conceived. The animals would be alive and without any kind of anaesthetic when these things were done to them. How desperately they needed unflinching defenders.

"Let's get in position," Campbell urged them. "As we agreed. We form a human chain in front of the door. When we see their headlights coming, we join hands and stand fast. Right?"

"Camel, when are the media guys going to get here?"

Campbell sighed. "I don't know, Zebra. Maybe nobody's coming. But we've all got cameras, don't we, on our phones?"

Agnes, who still did not own a smart phone, said nothing. She was, in any case, becoming more and more agitated. She kept seeing the round, fear-filled eyes of the animals in their cages; kept thinking of their warm bodies and bright, soft fur; of how they should be stroked and held rather than killed by slow degrees.

Help me! She did seem to hear them crying out to her. And it was only then it dawned on her with a crushing clarity how puny and even potentially counterproductive their little demonstration was. Nine men and women — for Horace and his two companions had chosen to remain off to one side — joined shoulder to shoulder in front of a massive metal door. And no journalists present to film the arrival of the sacrificial animals and the young people trying to save them. Perhaps all they would accomplish would be a reinforcement of security at the lab. An electric fence would go up, or guards with guns would patrol all the time.

Was this whole exercise a folly? Were they doing more harm than good here?

Then Perdita began to sing "We Shall Overcome" in a light, lofty soprano that made Agnes newly aware of the brilliance of the stars clustered in the thick blackness above them. She felt reassured and strong. Yes, of course they will overcome.

Everyone joined in the secular hymn, with the exception of Horace and his two companions.

As if on cue the headlights of the first truck in the convoy bore through the dark. Agnes counted four sets of headlights.

"Stand firm," Campbell said.

They squeezed one another's hands for courage, and pressed their shoulders, spines and buttocks tight against the metal door. Kit, Campbell, Zebra, Pinto, Agnes, Perdita, Pablo, Ewan and Gerhardt/Klaus. Horace and his two friends approached the far left corner of the building, close to Kit, as the four trucks pulled in and lined up facing the metal door with its flesh-and-blood blockade. The drivers kept their high beams on and they were drowning in harsh light. It was disorienting, and to some extent, it hurt. Agnes understood this was the intent.

Then, as if flawlessly synchronized, all the high beams dimmed. Now the light was sinister and glutinous. Into this soupy pall four drivers emerged. They were all burly men, with wide solid chests and arms. Their large faces were grim-lipped. They advanced in tight formation. They wore identical uniforms, like modified soldiers' fatigues, in a drab olive.

One of them said: "This is private property and you are trespassing. We will give you until the count of ten to remove yourselves and get into your vehicles and go. You have been given due warning, and if you do not comply we will have no alternative but to remove you forcibly."

He spoke these words rapidly and without inflection. As if he were an automaton, Agnes thought, a barrel-chested robot built for intimidation and battle. But something even more chilling had occurred to her; and this was that the drivers had showed no surprise whatsoever at finding the Ark members blocking the door. *It was as if they knew we would be here.* This rattling thought came entangled with the notion of betrayal. A cold worm crawled through her spine.

"Stand tall and hold your ground," she heard Campbell say.

She gripped Perdita's and then Pinto's hand tighter.

"Go home, you stupid little shits!" a second driver yelled. "We don't want to hurt you."

Campbell laughed derisively, his seal's bark.

"One-two . . . ," the driver began.

"Be brave," she thought she heard Pinto whisper. But the blood was pounding in her ears so hard, she could not be sure exactly what he'd said.

"Nine, ten." On ten, there was a metallic crash as the back doors of the four trucks banged open. Agnes, who was not thinking at all rationally, had the nonsensical idea the animals were coming to save them. In fact, what the trucks disgorged were several more stolid, uniformed guards. There were four more at least, she observed in her shock. But these new ones wore helmets with protective visors and had heavy batons swinging from their wrists. She held on to one last clear thought — "But this is ridiculous. We are not armed" — before the world disintegrated. It was as if a huge mirror reflecting the Ark members' human chain smashed, and in each jagged piece she saw her friends suffering in a way that only seconds before had been unimaginable.

This cannot be happening, she kept telling herself, even as she saw Pinto doubled over with one of the guards pummelling his back with his baton; Zebra with blood pouring into his eyes; and Perdita and Pablo huddled together on the ground, each trying to protect the other from the darts of the stun-gun that had already blighted Agnes's shoulder. Now it hit her again, this time in the right hip. But it hurt much more this time, as if they had thrust her entire leg into a gigantic electric socket. She was for some seconds immobilized by the needling strikes; then she managed to stagger out to the road paralleling the building. She must go and fetch help, even if she had to crawl down to the highway. She must get help for her friends, and then they could all free the animals. How had everything gone so terribly wrong?

She felt increasingly dizzy as she tried to walk. Her head was swimming, yet at the same time so heavy she could no longer stand erect under the weight of it. She went down suddenly on her knees, and for some time — she was never to know for how long — she blacked out. It was in this state she smelled the fresh blood of the slaughtered grey bear Piero painted, and felt within her chest the explosive panic of the white stallion as the steely hands choked off its breath.

Then she came to. She was still kneeling on the ground. She looked up and saw Campbell astride his bike. He was screaming at Kit to jump on behind him. But one of Horace's friends had grabbed Kit around the waist, holding her back. Horace was jumping up and down in a frenzied fashion, telling Kit again and again to come with them; to get in the car.

Campbell started the bike and put out his arm to Kit in a last imploring attempt. But Horace's friends held her fast, as she called out to him in obvious anguish. Then the bike took off, faster than Agnes had ever seen it go. She remembered Campbell's proud description of the Vulcan's powers of acceleration.

How wonderful, she thought. Campbell was going to get away unhurt. For the moment, this was the most important fact in her world. She saw him glance back at Kit, still caught fast by Horace's two friends. Even at this distance, Agnes saw how his lips twitched and then tightened before he turned away, steering the bike toward the exit road that led back down to the highway. On and on the mighty machine roared, faster and faster. Campbell was their blessed outrider. He would bring back help. She tried to stand so that she could wave and wish him good speed.

Then the unthinkable happened. Just as Campbell reached the far end of the laboratory building the bike bucked and reared, its front wheel spinning wildly in the air. There was an awful grinding noise and the stench of burning motor. Next she saw something she could not at first grasp, either logically or perceptually. It appeared that Campbell's head in its helmet had come away from his body and flown into the road.

She rubbed her eyes and looked again. The bike lay on its side. The rider, who had fallen sideways with it, still had two arms and two legs. But the head was gone.

A woman was screaming so shrilly Agnes feared her brain would shatter. She saw Kit running, the long red hair streaming like a river of blood behind her. Then she felt all the air squeezed from her lungs as something or someone tackled her from behind and pulled her down and down. Everything turned dim and grainy, then black.

When she came to, she felt both abject and on the edge of shame. She thought at first she had urinated in her sleep. That must be why she had an uncomfortable sensation of warmth between her legs. Oddly, her legs were wide-stretched. She realized she must be lying on her face, which was a way she never slept.

"Agnes?" Whose voice was this? She knew she ought to recognize it, but could not place it. Did it belong to someone in her long-ago past, or might it come from the future?

"Agnes?"

"Pinto." As she spoke his name, the world around her solidified. She grasped that she was clinging to his huge back; or rather that he had been carrying her, for her arms were flung far forward over his chest. Her head lay in the crook of his neck. She could feel his hair against her cheek, close-cropped but with a nap like velvet, and was disturbed by this intimate proximity.

"Let me go," she told him sharply. He released her and she slid down his back gracelessly because her legs had gone numb. The ground was cold and hard. A slip of moon emerged from a grey tatter of cloud. They were in the forest, she saw. She had a moment of blessed ignorance before the agonizing remembrance returned.

"I had to get you away, Agnes."

She was frozen in shock, not even half-hearing him. One picture alone filled her brain, from which she winced away. Campbell had been decapitated. She could not understand why her fingers hurt so much; then she looked down and saw it was because she was clawing at the earth into which the frost had already begun its work.

"I had to get you away," he repeated. "If we got caught, we would lose our scholarships. We're not like the others, Agnes. We can't afford to take that risk . . . "

"Stop it!" she screamed. She tried to stand but her legs were still beset by pins and needles. So instead she knelt and clutched at his leg.

"Tell me. Is it true? Did it really happen? Is Campbell . . . ?"

He bent down and sat awkwardly on his haunches. He tried to cup her face with his hands. She shook him off.

"Tell me."

"Yes," he said. "It did happen. He must have run into a wire stretched across the road. God, Agnes. Don't think about it now. It's too horrible to think of now. We have to get you back safely. Don't you see?"

"No. No. No." She was rocking back and forth on the ground, and biting on her own hand. Pinto took the hand from her mouth and held it between his.

"Hush, Agnes. Hush. There is nothing we can do for him now. Nothing."

"It's my fault," she whispered hoarsely. "Because when I first saw him I thought of the satyr mourning the dead nymph. I saw his face in a painting about death. And now he's dead."

She was aware how unlike herself she sounded; her voice was shriller and tinny, like a piece of clockwork that has been too tightly wound.

"I showed him the picture once."

"Stop now, Agnes, You have to pull yourself together."

She shook her head. How heavy it felt. His head lay beside the road in its helmet. Was it still there?

"He told me," she began to laugh, but the sound was cracked and forced. "He told me he thought he looked more like the dog. 'What's the dog's name?' he asked.

"Laelaps, I told him. He thought that was funny. He kept saying the name over and over. And then . . . " She broke off. "I love him. I loved him."

"I know," Pinto replied. "I know that, Agnes."

She could bear it no longer. The sound that came out of her mouth was curdled; a noise neither human nor animal. All too soon it became a howl she could not control.

TWELVE

The Wire

BACK AT THE ARK, SHE sat shaking at the kitchen table. Her throat was raw from sobbing.

"I need a drink," she told Pinto. "I mean spirits, whisky or gin." She had in fact tasted whisky only once and gin never. But wasn't whisky what characters in novels and films downed in copious quantities to dull their pain; to get "plastered"? That was exactly what she wanted, to plaster the picture over thickly so that she did not see the decapitation happening again and again.

"Why?" she kept asking. "Why him? He was so beautiful. You must have some alcohol in the house, Pinto. Don't you? Oh, please."

"Alcohol won't help, Agnes. Believe me. You don't want to go there."

He looked so sorrowful. His eyes welled up as he hovered over her. She realized then how selfish she was being: that Pinto too had lost a beloved friend. And then there was Kit. Agnes flashed back to Kit running, her mouth stuck open in a blare like a siren's, her hair streaming like his blood in the night. A picture came, fading even as she shrank from it, of Kit reaching the bike and then flinging herself on the earth beside Campbell's head.

No, she thought. I did not see that. I did not see her kiss his lips and cradle his severed head in her arms. I am making this up. This is too ghoulish. I am going mad. How can I bear the loss of him? It should have been me. Her mind slips sideways then. She sees freshly guillotined heads tumbling one after another into waiting baskets. Each head is perfect, noble, the hair delicately perfumed. Each one leaves behind a body with a bright necklace of blood. And above that necklace, there is nothing. Absolutely nothing.

She felt sick. She had no ballast because her heart and substance had been scooped out. What was the point of anything? If life was this meaningless and random, what was the point of going on at all?

"Why, Pinto?" She was crying again, helpless to stop. "Why should we even bother to make an effort?"

His large head swayed like a tolling bell. "Do you mean the Ark's work?"

"Everything." It was difficult for her to speak, the tears were coming so thickly.

"Oh, Agnes." He sighed and sat in the creaking wooden chair beside her. Tentatively, he patted her balled hand with its clutched wad of tissue. "It was a ghastly thing to happen." He stopped a moment and frowned. "It's fate," he continued. "It's rotten what life throws at some of us. But it's inscrutable."

She sees Fate then crouching in the shadowy slot between the wall and the stove. At first it is about the size of a toad, a slimy black blotch. But even as she looks, it elongates, and rears up cobra-like. She yelps, puts up her hand to fend it off.

"Agnes, dear, what is it?" He put his arms about her shoulders, just barely touching her. His solicitous tone helped banish the frightful vision.

"I thought I saw . . . I'm sorry." She did not deserve his patient kindness. Was it just her own self-absorption she saw squatting there, ugly and voracious?

"What about the others?" she asked in a surge of panic. "What do you think happened to Zebra and Minnie, and Perdita and Pablo?"

"I'm sure they're all right, Agnes. Someone would have called the police. We'll all need to support each other through this. And that means being strong. We both need to sleep, Agnes. We need to be calm and resolute and clear-minded to get through this. And sleep's the foundation for all that. I'm not trying to be patronizing," he added.

She nodded. Yes. How concerned and yet rational he was. Like a good parent.

He insisted she sleep in his bed, assuring her he would be fine on the floor wrapped in his duvet. She was grateful. She did not think she could bear to go into the little guest bedroom where Campbell had first made love to her. Pinto brought her a herbal tranquillizer and a glass of water. She swallowed the little brown tablet dutifully, lay down without undressing and pulled up the covers. It was only then she became aware of the various parts of her body that hurt. In her shoulder and her right hip, where the stun gun had hit her, there was a stinging sensation as if her skin had been scored with nettles. The bruising around her ribcage made a dullish band of pain whenever she took a breath. Not that it mattered, of course. She would willingly hurt a thousand times more if only it would bring him back to life.

Pinto breathed deeply and deliberately, cocooned in his duvet. He was so close to the bed she could reach out and clutch his hand for comfort if she wished. By the rhythm, she guessed he was meditating, using some long-practised discipline to subdue the pain. She tried to make her breathing consonant with his.

As the little pill began to work its natural soporific in her bloodstream, the rhythmic sound of his breath transformed into something innocent and sustaining, like a rocking cradle guided by a loving hand. Despite all that had happened, she slept free of soiled and clotted dreams.

The instant she woke, she remembered. The pain was at first a dagger point in her brain; then a terrible numbness came. She pinched the flesh on the back of her left hand hard and registered little or no sensation. Nothing made any sense. It was an accident. Pinto said. It was fate. She didn't care about that. All that mattered was that Campbell was dead. And that shouldn't be, and it hurt and it hurt.

She tried to sit up but dizziness and nausea pulled her back down. She tried again, more slowly this time, and managed to sit more or less erect with her back against the wall. From this perspective, she could see that Pinto had gone, his duvet folded neatly in four on the room's only chair. As she manoeuvered her legs over the edge of the bed and put her feet as solidly on the floor as she could, her eye was caught by the framed photograph on Pinto's bedside table. A lovely red dog smiled at the camera. This visible animal joy helped to steady her.

In the bathroom she splashed water on her face, avoiding her reflection in the mirror, principally because she did not want to see how her head sat seamlessly atop her neck. Campbell's two severed parts were likely laid out now in a morgue. Surely they would have kept him together and not stored his head somewhere apart from his body? This ghoulish notion made her sway violently and she had to clutch the sides of the sink.

She had to grip hard too on the worn banister as she made her way gingerly downstairs. It occurred to her she had eaten nothing for twenty-four hours, which might explain some of her vertigo and weakness. But the idea of food was abominable, and besides, she did not want to impose any longer on Pinto, who had been so tolerant of her self-indulgent show of grief. She must pull herself together and get back to the dorm. There she could shut the door of her room and cry as freely as she needed to.

Afterwards, she would find out how the others were. Had everyone got home all right? She was terrified they might have ended up in jail. And what if they saw her and Pinto as cowardly defectors?

She heard a murmur of voices from the living room and approached quietly. How hushed the house was, as though it had turned into a funeral parlour while they slept. Her steps were so slow; she felt weighed down and yet truncated somehow, as if she were missing some vital body part.

What she saw when she reached the living room door overturned her resolution to leave immediately. Seated on the couch, his knees drawn up to his chin, was a man she knew rationally must be Zebra. But this person looked about thirty years older, his face livid and drawn, almost haggard. Swathes of bandage wound around the top of his skull were coming loose and lengths of white gauze spilled down his neck and over his collarbone. His striped shirt gaped open, exposing a pale thin chest, where each rib pressed a bluish stain upon the skin.

She was reminded of the paintings she had seen of Christ raising Lazarus from the dead, his funeral cerements still clinging to his face and body. She'd always suspected Lazarus would have preferred to remain dead and have the miracle undone. Would he not always have carried a taint of the grave and an indelible memory of the encroaching worms?

She thought then of Campbell's perfect body as it would be worked upon, once laid deep in dank earth, and she shuddered, then reprimanded herself. She must absolutely never think of his physical decay, only concentrate on his enduring flawless spirit.

She willed herself to enter the living room. As she came closer, she saw Zebra's lips were moving. He was speaking so quietly that Pinto, who occupied the armchair next to him, was bent almost double straining to hear.

"Agnes," Pinto said softly. Was there a hint of relief in his voice?

Zebra shifted abruptly, flinging out his arms and legs; then he fell back helplessly against the cushions.

"Sorry," he said to her. "Haven't slept." He rubbed at his eyelids with his index fingers, making them look redder and sorer.

Poor Zebra. She was reluctant to press him about his night's trials; whether he was beaten by the guards while she and Pinto were stumbling through the woods; or had been jailed.

"Are you badly hurt?" she asked, touching her own head at the spot where his was bandaged.

Zebra looked at her blankly. "Me? No. I got some stitches. At the hospital . . . " He trailed off and looked away again.

"Come and sit down, Agnes," Pinto urged her. He patted the arm of the loveseat with its shrieking orange and yellow sunbursts.

She hesitated. On one hand, she simply wanted to flee. On the other, she intuited there was some peculiar geometry of grief to be satisfied here, as if they must all three at this particular time be together in the same room, yet keep a prescribed distance from each other. She grasped that although they were all staggering under a common loss, they each inhabited a distinct grief. Zebra, it struck her, had known Campbell many years longer than either she or Pinto.

"I had to call Leonore, his mother," Zebra told them. "I couldn't let her hear it from the police."

He lapsed into a silence, which boomed throughout the room.

Agnes was shaken as she pictured this unknown woman who had given birth to Campbell. To lose such a son: what could it be but unendurable? She would feel driven to rend her own flesh, to rip herself open where she had carried him. Why does she have such thoughts?

"She didn't say a word," Zebra said, staring straight ahead. "I could hear her breath on the phone getting shorter and raw somehow. She must have put the phone down because in a moment I heard her screaming and screaming in the background. Her husband picked up the phone. He yelled at me. Leonore was still screaming in the background. I told him everything I hadn't told her. I only told her he'd been killed on his bike. He wants to keep this out of the papers. He's coming. Did I say that? Campbell's step-father, Clement Semple, is coming to claim the body. He said he'll look after everything." Zebra made a mirthless little sound Agnes wished she had not heard. "But he can't, can he?" he said. "He can't fix anything, can he? Can he? Can he?"

She was disconcerted when Zebra began to pummel at his upper thighs, as if experimenting with how much he could hurt himself.

"Stop it, Zebra!" She reached out to restrain him.

Pinto made a sign to deter her.

"Zeke," Pinto said. "Take it easy on yourself. That won't help."

"Fuck off, Pinto. At least I'm feeling it. I haven't removed myself to some higher fucking plane."

Her breath was a hot, gritty substance in her throat as she strained for words to neutralize the malign atmosphere that now tainted the room. Then something so inconceivable happened, she was left incapable of speech or clear thought. Pinto drew himself up erect, his face rigid and almost hideous, stripped as it was of his normally benign expression. He glared at Zeke, raised his right hand, turned it so that his palm faced the wall, then brought it down axe-hard on the particleboard table in front of his chair.

Under the force of the blow, the table top snapped in half. Pinto kicked the two pieces against the wall as he got up, his massive chest heaving. He stared down at Zeke, who regarded him open-mouthed.

"Is that what you think, Zeke? You really believe I don't feel it?"

Agnes felt sick again. Was this enraged person really Pinto? Her hands were shaking. She had no idea what to say to either man. Pinto pushed past her, almost knocking her over. She felt weak, and thoroughly disoriented, as if the known world were cracking open everywhere, spilling out horrors. She looked at Zebra, who was shaking his head so slowly back and forth it verged on a pantomime gesture: "I never saw him like that before. Never. I think it's all too much to take in, you know? I'm going to go and lie down. You don't mind, do you, Agnes?"

He did not wait for her answer but stumbled from the room, swaying from side to side like a drunk. She listened as he made his way laboriously up the stairs in case he fell. It was a meagre but welcome relief when she heard him open his bedroom door, go in and shut it behind him.

She sat calming herself enough for the walk back to the dorm. She would do this purely mechanically, one step and then another and another. She would try not to think or to remember anything too vividly. That would be dangerous. She could do these things once she too had closed herself in, just as Pinto and Zebra had done.

She was about to leave, but instead took the stairs at a determined lope to find Pinto. She stood, cowed again, in silence outside his door.

Just as she raised her hand to knock, she heard the sound she imagined a wounded, ravenous animal might make in a desperate search for food, half-snuffling, half-sobbing. She had never heard anything like it before. She went back downstairs and left the house as quietly as she could, and all the way back to the dorm it was the strange noise coming from Pinto's room that filled her head. By some perverse magic, this inarticulate voicing of his pain became the lifeline to which she held fast as she made her way through the horrific, shard-like glare, as sun speared snow on this unreal morning. She clutched at that remembered ragged rope of sound, and it kept her mechanical steps steady so that her cutting thoughts did not bring her to her knees in the public street.

Poor Pinto, poor Pinto. She pictured him crawling on the floor, pressing his broad face into the wood, making those awful noises. She too would have to embrace the pain soon enough once she was alone and private. She knew its demands would be wolfish and implacable.

Although many on campus knew about the strung wire and how Campbell had died, the details never reached the press. The local paper devoted barely a square centimetre to what it described as a fatal motorcycle accident involving a university student. There was no mention of the wire, the protest or the animal laboratory, and certainly not of the decapitation.

Agnes had assumed there would be an inquest. Wasn't someone going to find out who strung the wire there? Where were the police in all this? No officer had approached her. She had envisioned an incident room, and the police reconstructing the scene. She had thought that everyone who'd been at the demonstration would be interviewed, at least once. Had the police interrogated the security guards about the wire? What about the pharmaceutical company that ran the laboratory? Had the police contacted them? Didn't Campbell's death warrant some kind of answer? Give me someone to hate, she thought, and then Pinto will teach me how to purge myself of that hatred. Only tell me. Who is to be held to account?

It was Zebra who set her straight: "It's Mr. Semple's doing. Campbell's step-father is very good at making unpleasant things disappear. He's a born fixer, as well as very, very rich. He's got clout, political connections and what's that word . . . ? Nux? No, nous, I guess I mean."

They were standing outside the library. Zebra gestured that they should move away from the stream of students going in and out of the building. He led her to a bench tented by the branches of a huge blue spruce. Even given this cloistered spot, Zebra kept glancing nervously about.

"Clement and Campbell never really got on," he told her, his tone low and confiding.

Clement Semple. The name conjured up a ruggedly handsome face, a mouth with strong white teeth and the cold blue supercilious gaze of a man accustomed to deference.

"They argued a lot. Campbell thought Clement was basically a capitalist. His own father — Dr. Korsakov — was an eye surgeon, so I think Campbell always saw his real father's profession as more altruistic. That's why he kept his father's surname after his mother remarried. And he made that decision really young. Dr. Korsakov died of a heart attack when Camel and I were still in grade school. It marked Camel out, you know, because none of the rest of us had actually lost a parent at that age. Lost one to death, I mean. But then, Camel always stood out. Even as a little kid, he was special. He really did want to make things better." Zebra stared ahead unseeing and plucked repeatedly at the tufts of his spiky hair. He shivered, then huddled inside his woolen bomber jacket. "God, I miss him."

"Me too."

He gave no indication he had heard her; once again she wondered if he knew she and Campbell had been lovers. Not that it mattered, whether he did or didn't. This was her knowledge, the holy irradiating secret she would hold forever tight.

Zebra shook himself. "Anyway, back to Clement . . . he's very . . . what's the word when a man is really in love with his wife?"

"Uxurious?"

"That's it. Clement is very uxurious. So he'll do anything he needs to, absolutely anything, to make sure Leonore gets what she wants. And if she wants the violent macabre aspects of Campbell's death magicked away, that's what Clement will make sure happens."

"But what about the security guards," she said. "What about the violence they did to you, to all of us?"

Zebra swung around to face her with a look of alarm. The red welt on his brow had a hatching of white stitches. He had taken off the striped peak cap he'd started wearing to cover the wound. "Agnes! We can't any of us talk about that. Don't you understand who we are dealing with? Listen to me, Agnes. It's Big Pharma money behind that lab. If they needed to, they'd manufacture the evidence to make it look like it was all our doing. We all have to keep quiet about what happened, don't you see? For Leonore's sake so that she can bury her son with dignity, and for all our sakes, so that we stay out of jail."

She felt both chastened and foolish. Yes, she reminded herself, it was a nightmare accident she must put away.

Bury it, so that he could be whole again in her mind. Gloriously whole, as he deserved to be.

"You do understand, don't you, Agnes? I mean, Clement made it so clear for me. This really is the best course of action for everybody. I have to leave tomorrow," Zebra said. "I don't own a suit so I have to buy one and the funeral's Saturday morning. Clement has asked me to be a pall bearer."

It was two more days before she saw Pinto, at their first Animal Ethics lecture since Campbell's death. Agnes wondered if Fergus Jonquil might feel in any way complicit. It was Fergus, after all, who had told Campbell about the new laboratory and exactly when the animals were to be delivered.

Impulsively, she wrote the question in her the notebook and passed it to Pinto: "Do you think Fergus feels any responsibility?"

Pinto scored out her question roughly with his pen. Then he put his finger to his lip. That made twice now she had been cautioned by a male member of the Ark to keep silent. Under her defaced question, Pinto wrote in a neat round script: "We made the decision." The double under-score impressed on her their culpability far more cogently than anything Zebra had said.

Her thoughts slid to the vertiginous proposition that she was therefore also complicit in Campbell's death. *We made the decision*. A grotesque picture assaulted her: she was sitting here in the lecture hall with his bleeding head in her lap. *Stop it, Agnes. Stop!*

A solidly built middle-aged woman walked stiffly on to the stage. She wore an unflattering boxy suit of purplish tweed that made her look upholstered. Her hair, which was thin and scraped back from brow and temples, had a glaring burgundy tint.

She faced her audience squarely for several seconds without a word; then boomed: "Good morning, ladies and gentlemen. I am Dr. Clarissa Montridge, and I will be taking over Dr. Jonquil's lectures until at least the end of term."

"What's wrong with Fergus?" someone called out.

Dr. Montridge frowned to indicate she found the manner of the question impertinent. They were made to pay for this discourtesy with another silence lasting some seconds.

"My understanding," she said, "is that he has taken a leave of absence. For further details I would suggest you address yourself to the administration office or to the head of the department."

A buzz of disaffection spread through the hall. Dr. Montridge meanwhile busily arranged her papers at the lectern and took some time positioning her reading glasses on her nose.

"You will doubtless find my approach very different from Dr. Jonquil's," she began, "at least based on my admittedly cursory perusal of his themes and recommended readings. What I intend to present to you, ladies and gentlemen, is a less biased, or shall we say, one-sided approach." To the word "one-sided" she gave a particular emphasis before stopping to stare out at the hall with a look both challenging and smug.

Pinto wrote a single word in his notepad, which he then passed to Agnes: "Ouch!"

As the lecture progressed, Agnes grew increasingly irritated by the professor's sneering tone whenever she referred to the philosophers Fergus favoured, like Sprigge, Sheldrake and Singer. She was also beginning to feel queasy as Dr. Montridge persisted in extolling the biological and cultural benefits of meat eating. They heard a great deal about Vitamin B12 and Jehovah's rejection of Abel's vegetable sacrifice. This ancient story, according to the professor, demonstrated the unassailable truth that the human species requires meat for its physical, mental and emotional well-being.

"Without meat, ladies and gentlemen, we would have no human civilizations."

At least she had said "civilizations" plural. Nonetheless, what a total nightmare this woman's lecture was. Agnes looked at Pinto, who rolled his eyes.

Dr. Montridge then segued into the various ritual proscriptions surrounding the preparation and consumption of various meats observed by religions around the world. What about Buddhists? Agnes wanted to cry out. Why did they have to sit passively and politely listening to this stuff? It was like being verbally whipped for their beliefs. It was like living with her parents again.

The professor had moved on to Indigenous people's traditions of respect and gratitude toward the animals they killed and ate. The ludicrous picture sprang to Agnes's mind of urban meat eaters paying monthly visits to their local abattoir to thank the cows and pigs whose pristinely wrapped remains they would later purchase in the supermarket. Why couldn't this foolish woman see that vegetarianism was an ethical imperative toward which all peoples must evolve?

At last, the lecture was over, which Clarissa Montridge signalled by taking off her glasses and blowing her nose. She then announced that for next week's class, they were to write a 1,000-word essay presenting a balanced appraisal of Temple Grandin's contribution to the more humane handling of stockyard animals on their way to abattoirs. Agnes bristled at the word "humane" in this context.

"That was ghastly," she said to Pinto, while glancing up to make sure Clarissa Montridge was well out of earshot. The sorry fact was she could not afford to alienate this stolid, bigoted woman with her objectionable theories. She had to get an A in the course if she was to keep her scholarship.

Pinto rolled his eyes again. "We'll have to endure, I suppose, and hope like hell Fergus isn't away for very long."

"Do you think he's off because . . . ?"

He stopped her with the same gesture as before, finger to lip. She chastised herself. When would she learn to be more circumspect?

"Can you imagine," she said once they were safely outside, "how Campbell would have reacted to that silly woman's meat-eating propaganda?"

Pinto grinned. "He would probably have leapt up, told her she was talking nonsense and stormed out in protest."

"I wish . . . " she began.

"Campbell could *afford* to do that if he'd wanted, Agnes. He wasn't on a scholarship. If he dropped out of a course or failed one, it would have made no difference. His mother paid his fees."

Campbell the rich kid: the characterization seemed to her to verge on betrayal.

Pinto said: "I hope Zeke gets through the funeral tomorrow all right, and Campbell's mother and Kit."

"Yes." Again, she had to fend off thoughts of his lithe lovely body sealed in a wooden box, the worm-riddled earth pressing against its sides. She strove instead to conjure up a lovely vision of him bounding suddenly into view, the light at play on his black hair, making a natural aureole around his head, the whole world shining on and adoring him.

That night she dreamt he was in her bed, making love to her so lavishly she could feel the warm tracery of his caresses on her skin when she woke. She began to nurture the willfully ecstatic notion that her body retained precise memories of Campbell's touch; a force field of recollection that would stay with her onto death; and perhaps beyond.

And why not, especially since Campbell's love making was one of the most exalted experiences she had ever had? For hours after she had been with him, she lived inside a warm erotic glow that was as actual as any geographic place. Why should her body's memory of all that wondrous sensation dwindle away to nothing?

Even though it was late November, the morning of the funeral dawned fine and clear. She hoped the weather was the same in Boston. It would surely be easier for his mother and Kit and Zebra and all the other mourners if rain was not pelting down on the coffin and into the grave.

When Zebra returned, he insisted she see a photo he'd snapped with his miniature camera. It showed the coffin suspended on its guy ropes, ready for lowering. "I think Pinto feels it was wrong of me to take it," he admitted, opening his laptop. "But it seemed like that final moment, you know, when he was still among us and you could say goodbye."

She was not altogether convinced by this rationale, although she did not doubt his good intentions. Rather than look at the coffin hung upon the air, she focused on the little clutch of people who stared out of white faces.

"That's Campbell's mother," Zeke said, pointing to a slender woman in a black dress with stand-up collar and a little hat with a half-veil. Agnes could make out only that she had a heart-shaped face and her hands near her mouth. To stop herself screaming, she thought, I can understand that. Her eye then picked out a woman with radically razored hair, standing beside Campbell's mother. The near-naked skull reminded her of photos in history books of women who had their heads shaved as punishment for consorting with the enemy.

"Who is that?"

Zebra swallowed audibly, "It's Kit."

Agnes looked at him unbelieving.

"She cut off all her hair," Zebra said. "She's not eating. She's been in hospital. She's in a very, very bad way, Agnes."

"I'm so sorry." And truly, she was.

"Horace is with her," Zeke added. "He is absolutely loyal to her. Like a dog that loves its mistress above everything. I know he can be a pain but he'll see her through this, if anyone can."

Agnes fixed on the photo again. She spied, beside and just a little behind the haunted figure she now knew to be Kit, a familiar small, wiry figure. It was the first time she had ever seen Horace without his hood up. Had Kit's situation prompted some new openness in him?

"Zeke shouldn't have taken it," Pinto declared when Agnes mentioned the photo. "That was a private moment."

He was usually so open and forgiving she was surprised by the vehemence of his disapproval. She sometimes fancied she could see his conscience at work, ejecting rash judgements and preconceptions, making room for empathy wherever it could be brought to bear. So she was certain he would add some remark to soften this dogmatic reaction to Zebra's picture of the graveside group. But nothing came.

Because she saw Pinto's grasp on right action as so far superior to hers, questions begin to tug at her. Was it unseemly to look at a photograph of Campbell's mourners? She consoled herself that she was also one of them, even though she was not physically present for the funeral and interment.

With this rare exception, Pinto continued to be her sterling example as she struggled to accept the fact of Campbell's death. She tried not to lean on him too heavily, and above all, not to babble or to cry in his presence.

"Death sends us to the old labours," he counselled her. Pinto never revealed the source of this gnomic quotation but she took the meaning well enough. Although initially she had to force herself to sit at her desk and get on with it, the habitual compulsions soon reasserted themselves. For twenty-minute spans she could become agreeably lost in a line of thought crowned by an insight and forget that he had gone.

But at day's end, alone in her bed, she would be overwhelmed again by the sudden violence of his going. She had been inducted into the basic lesson of life's fragility and brevity, and she wished with all her heart she might have learned this lesson another way. Not through his death, but another's, even or perhaps most especially, her own. She clung to the certainty her memories of him lived, and of these she had a great store, all of them golden. In this way she learned to placate the demands of her grief, even when it was at its most mordant.

Nonetheless, when the next death came, not one of them — not even Pinto — was prepared. It was the saturnine Clarissa Montridge who was the messenger. When she took her place behind the lectern, it was obvious she was out of breath. Something had happened to dismantle the stolid monumentality she had projected so effortlessly the week previous. While Agnes detested the woman's views, she did not like to see her so distressed.

"I regret to inform you . . . " She stopped and coughed discreetly into a handkerchief. For a deluded instant, Agnes happily assumed Dr. Montridge was about to announce this was her last class before Fergus returned. " . . . that Professor Jonquil has died."

Inside Agnes's brain there was nothing but white noise. Several students in the hall leapt to their feet. Someone's tablet clattered to the floor.

"It can't be," Agnes said three times. She looked around for Pinto but could not see him anywhere in the room.

"Was he ill? What happened to him?" A woman in the front row pressed for the details to which they all felt entitled.

"I'm afraid I'm not at liberty . . . "

"What crap!" someone shouted.

"I will not countenance such vulgar language and discourtesy," said Clarissa Montridge. She then promptly left the stage.

Agnes sat on, benumbed. There was an unpleasant trickle of sweat in her armpits. Some of the others were texting their friends, trying to find out if anyone knew more about Fergus. They all wanted to hear the same thing: a refutation; the confirmation that Clarissa Montridge had it all wrong. The stupid woman had been misled, or she was ill and had fantasized the whole thing. The college would quietly terminate her contract. Dr. Montridge would go away to a rest home where she would recover her health and then go to teach elsewhere.

She decided to go to the Ark, to seek out Pinto or Zebra. *It can't be*, she kept saying to herself, as if this would work some magic charm. *It simply can't be*. But perhaps Fergus had had a heart defect or a brain aneurism. These things happened, even to people as apparently vital and robust as Fergus Jonquil.

If it was true, the fact of his death would surpass the mere uncanny, coming as it did so soon after Campbell's. Either the fates were creating a diabolical garment, stitching one death to the other, or something truly sinister was afoot.

"Agnes . . . you've heard about Fergus, then?" Pinto came to the door looking as if he had not slept. He preceded her into the kitchen, moving very slowly, like a man recovering from a major operation.

"Minnie's here," he told her. "She's on the phone upstairs, talking to a friend of hers who's a policewoman."

"Police? Was it a car accident?"

"They think he was murdered, Agnes. Minnie's friend told her Fergus was garrotted, strangled with a piece of wire."

"My God!" She shook her head stupidly back and forth, a child's gesture that sought to undo what she had just heard.

"It gets worse," Pinto said.

She looked at him in apprehension. Her hands were very cold. "What?"

"He was tortured, Agnes. Burned around his chin and throat. His beard was singed off. And on his chest. And down below as well. His pubic hair. His genitals."

She groaned and slumped in her chair. The terrible idea came to her that Fergus's passion had turned on him; that the roaring intensity of his belief had consumed him. She considered, her mind churning, the awful symbolism of where he was burned: the throat that formed the words of his sermonizing and his diatribes; the chin that moved to utter them; the chest where the deep source of his affections lay; and of course, his sex.

She had always recognized that sexual magnetism underlay his charisma and was instrumental in his power to make them listen to his every word and watch his every physical move. She had never liked to dwell on this particular aspect of his performance, sensing it was too slippery, androgynous and dangerous. It was simplest just to yield to the spell of Fergus leaping about the stage, urging them to join the good fight on animals' behalf, messianic and incomparable in the depth of his passion.

She wondered if he'd thought of animals' torture when he was being tortured himself. If he had seen himself, in the crucible of his agony, as a sacrifice offered up to them.

This speculation was just too horrible to hold long in her mind.

"Who would do such a thing? And why? What about the torture? Who would do that to him, Pinto?" More childlike questions, but she could not stop herself.

Pinto just looked at her blankly, then swung his head back and forth so slowly she wondered if time was indeed visibly running down. There was a new curse on the firmament, so that the space-time net juddered.

Open on the table was a bottle of cheap brandy, which Agnes assumed was for general consumption. She poured some into a mug and drank it down quickly. This time Pinto did not try to stop her, not even when she reached almost immediately for the bottle again.

THIRTEEN

The Rack

"ITHER YOU LOVE ME, OR you do not." So Savonarola daily proclaimed from his pulpit in the Duomo. He was evermore the relentless warrior for Christ, despite being near starved from the severe rigours of his fasting. His sparse flesh was rubbed raw by the hair-shirt girdle and punctured around his midriff by his belt of metal spikes. It was said the Prior's apocalyptic visions gave him strength to endure these mortifications. The divine messages were meat and drink to him. In his sermons he relayed with relish the calamities to come: the punitive famines, plagues and wars God told him He would inflict upon the people of Florence if they persisted in their worldly indulgences and evil ways. He urged his followers to imitate his example and meditate ceaselessly on the oozing wounds of Christ; keep ever in mind the countless ways the Saviour's body had been beaten, broken and pierced through to the bone until there was no part unracked by pain.

This intense probing into the excruciating suffering of Christ the Lord revealed itself in the Prior's eyes, so huge, black and liquid that a wicked man caught in his gaze might fear being sucked into their depths, as a live sheep into a whirlpool. The fearsome orbs under beetling brows were thus one of Savonarola's prime weapons in winning new warriors for the Lord. But his chief instrument in that battle remained his voice, which over the years became even more resonant, compelling and thunderous. It was the clangor of the *Dies Irae* encased in silk and velvet.

"Either you love me, or you do not."

Piero di Cosimo did not. After his first exposure to Savonarola's sermons, and the sublime instrument of that voice with its seductive hint of corvine music, Piero had taken the most assiduous care to insulate himself from the Prior's influence. As he had grasped on his sole exposure, Savonarola's oratory had the power to unmake his artist-self and turn him into a shadow-man shuffling through the streets in penitential mood. He would then become one of those who spied corruption everywhere: even in the clear regard of a new-born child, or in the guiltless creatures of the woods and skies and waters.

Over the four years of Savonarola's ascendancy, Piero had seen the vibrant, boisterous Florence turn grim and grey; even the air was grainier, as if men's obsession with sin-riddled mortality had stirred up a thick dust that coated every surface. There were no more bawdy songs heard on the streets; no more music of flute or lute spilling from an upper casement. The people's garb was practical and drab; Piero found his eyes aching for the sensuous textures of yesteryear, the lucent threads of gold and silver woven through a rippling brocade, the glow of garnets and agates that made the light play lovingly at ear lobes, fingers and wrists, cloth dyed in Lydian purple and in cochineal.

Savonarola abhorred all such decadent, meretricious display. His followers accordingly went about, shrinking inside coarse cloaks, their minds fixed on their grievous faults and the looming Day of Judgement. What Savonarola had created was a city locked in a mood that too much resembled Piero's own worst fits of melancholy, where to die would be deliverance.

Those Florentine nobles who could not stomach the Prior's dire visions and moral strictures had fled the city to live in exile. Piero too sought refuge through his regular rambles in the *contado*. The Prior's gloom could not contaminate the animals and birds he saw there. He wondered sometimes if the company of a loyal and loving dog might cure Savonarola of his hatred of life. But to give voice to such a thought would be dangerous, and might even be deemed treasonous. The ever-swelling bands of Savonarola's vigilant young Piagnoni would soon hear of it. They would batter down the door of his workshop, seize him by the hair and drag him out to the street. There they would cut off his nose, or worse, his fingers.

And so Piero kept close guard on his tongue and diligently carried out the commissions that come his way, which these days were almost always religious works. His patrons asked him for altarpieces which they wished to donate to their family's church, or for circular tondi to grace their homes and inspire their daily personal devotions. Unlike Sandro Botticelli, who was among the Prior's most zealous followers, Piero did not paint the crucified Saviour, either hung upon or newly taken down from the cross. His patrons come to him for Madonnas of gentle regard, with rounded, rosy cheeks as innocent as a country girl's. On their laps, his Madonnas held a chubby, merry Christ child whose pearly flesh showed not the least shadow of the suffering to come.

Savonarola ranted from the pulpit against the shamefulness of artists who depicted the Mother of God as if she were a whore, in immodest dress and with too much redness in her lips and cheeks. Piero was thus ever vigilant to keep the Virgin's robes even more modest than before, and the pigments for her complexion subdued.

The Prior had also now forbidden the painting of mythological and pagan subjects that had been so popular with the Medici and other noble families. Such pieces were an abomination, the Prior said, sprung from the devil and his minions. Piero thought it a great blessing that Savonarola, for all his vaunted gifts of prophecy, could not see men's private thoughts. For inside the sealed sphere of his brain, they frolicked still: the riotous company of goat-legged men who kept drunken attendance on Bacchus and Ariadne; the sprightly satyrs who were so wild and free it was a delight to see them bound into his fantasies; the tritons and the nereids with their naked chests and breasts and glorious curving fish tails who sported and slithered against one another in ways that would outrage the Prior.

To proscribe such artworks was not enough. Savonarola was driven to root out and destroy all worldly things he abhorred. Thus he speedily championed the Piagnoni's plan for a massive bonfire to consume all lewd and frivolous objects that the people of Florence might still have hidden about their homes and persons. This towering blaze, the largest ever seen in the city, was to be called The Bonfire of the Vanities.

It was held at Carnival time. In former years, Florentines had donned astounding masks for Carnival, bejewelled and bedecked with long waving plumes and crowns of stiff lace. They had danced and sung in the streets in a joyous release from the strictures of Lent, and flung themselves at wanton pleasures. Now they yielded up their magnificent masks and gowns and wigs and cosmetics to be put upon the mammoth pyre. Into the fire as well went mirrors, which fed vanity, tapestries of pagan gods that inflamed lechery, and the musical instruments that encouraged idleness and folly. Indeed, any object made purely for beauty's sake must go into the flames, to twist and melt and seethe.

Piero, who knew the drain on artists' health and strength the making of such objects entailed, was saddened almost to despair by this waste and desecration. Savonarola's Bonfire struck him as unholy, for surely it was a sin to repudiate and destroy the fruits of talents bestowed by God? He was shocked when he heard that Sandro Botticelli would willingly consign to the bonfire one of his own paintings he now considered unseemly. It was terrible to think of Sandro standing by, watching with composure, as all his dear labour was rendered ash which the wind then twitched away.

Piero prayed his patron, for whom he'd painted the tender-hearted satyr and noble hound mourning the dead nymph, would hide it well. Were they ever to spy it out, the young Piagnoni would revile this painting on account of the young nymph's naked breasts, the satyr's human face and chest above his furry legs and sharp hooves. It pained him sorely to think these gentle creatures might be seized and put to the torch. She will sleep a while yet, he reflected, this nymph whom he saw, more clearly now than ever, was the human soul drained of her sweet vitality in the dark time of Savonarola.

On the day of the great bonfire, Piero left the city, striking out as far as he could go beyond its walls before nightfall. Surely the reek of the burnt cloth, canvas and wrought bronze would not reach him in the heart of the woods. It was a relief that Savonarola had not issued an edict making attendance at the Bonfire mandatory for every Florentine. Had he been forced to watch the great pyre of destruction, heaped so high no man could constrain its antic, unpredictable raging, it might well drive him mad. His flesh shrank in remembrance of the writhing ox-in-flames he had seen as a boy, when the lightning struck its spine and the beast stumbled blindly, bellowing in its agony, the strings of its charred flesh hanging in obscene tassels. Its boiling blood bubbled through the scorched hide.

When they burned, he fancied, all those artifacts born of artisans' shaping hands and spirits would moan as piteously as did the flaming ox. Piero was perplexed as to why Savonarola perceived the devil's hand in the ever-questing, urgent work of the artist. Was this daily struggle not also a moral one: the perilous and unflagging quest to catch and give shape to fleeting forms: the manifold beauty of the world and its creatures and the wondrous life that thrived in human fantasy?

Saper vedere. His master Cosimo Rosselli was the first to teach him this maxim. *Train the eye. Know how to see.* Despite the Prior's intense black gaze, Piero doubted that Savonarola really saw the resplendent diverse works of vast Creation. With his constant dwelling on corruption and sin, the Prior had blighted his vision. What other reason could there be that Savonarola beheld only foulness and imperfection wherever he looked?

Piero pitied him. How dead the world must appear to Savonarola, for he had deliberately rolled a massive crude wheel of stone over its sublime, intricate beauty, flattening it and draining it of colour.

Come with me, he wished he could tell the Prior. *Let us walk quietly together in the woods. Let your molten voice, with its power to bend the minds of men to your will, be silent a while so that we may sit and wait for the hart and the doe to appear. Let us observe closely how delicately they move toward the emerald moss to graze; how they bow their heads toward the earth and thus become a perfect arc of grace, quivering with a life-force so unsullied that only to observe them might redeem the most sin-encrusted of men.*

Saper vedere. Train the eye. For every wild creature, including the birds of the air, creates by its movement and being this most solemn and potent tracery which holds in place the soul of the world.

Should he make such remarks in reality, rather than within the secure confines of his brain, Savonarola would set the Piagnoni upon him. They would cut off his digits with a sharp blade one at a time, and then pluck out his eyes.

He nonetheless strove to keep in mind the benefits Savonarola had brought to the city during the years of his sway. The poor of Florence no longer went hungry as they had under the reign of the Medici. Under the Prior's counsel, the city government had reduced the heartless burden of tax which the Medici had imposed on peoples of every class, except their closest cronies. And he had used his influence to bring in a fairer, more representative system of government for Florence, similar to the Great Council of Venice and administered by men of upstanding character.

Piero also admired, if he thought reckless, Savonarola's sermons inveighing against the profligacy, bribery and self-indulgence rife at the papal court. Now, with Rodrigo Borgia on the papal throne, a libertine who flaunted his mistresses and fawned upon his numerous children, the tyranny, extravagance and hypocrisy of the Pope were more flagrant than ever before. In his public condemnation of Pope Alexander, the Prior insisted his words came direct from God.

Nevertheless, any good the Prior wrought in the lives of Florentines, he simultaneously cruelly undercut by instilling in the people a hatred of earthly life so intense they were filled with self-loathing and yearned for death. They whipped themselves raw and spied upon their neighbours for evidence of sinfulness or secreted luxuries. Savonarola's militia of young, able-bodied Piagnoni made daily forays through the streets, seeking out sinners. The violence of their punishments grew apace with their vigilance.

How long, Piero wondered, can people live in such a climate of fear before a questing spirit leaps up within them and cries "no more"; before they have the urge to sing again a joyful song with one voice?

It was not a spontaneous outburst of song, but the machinations of the Prior's fiercest enemies that began to loosen his grip on Florence. In May of 1497 Pope Alexander

VI, Rodrigo Borgia, excommunicated Savonarola, who had railed once too often against "the prostitute church . . . the monster of abomination." Savonarola was unfazed. Why should he heed the sentence of Rodrigo Borgia, who was no true pope but a man so steeped in sin he did not hesitate to appoint his own sixteen-year-old son the archbishop of a very lucrative diocese?

Behind the scenes, the Arrabbiatti — the "rabid dogs" that supported the Medici — joined in the plot to bring about Savonarola's downfall. Pope Alexander then commanded Savonarola to cease preaching, even inside his own convent. This command too Savonarola defied, by celebrating Christmas mass in the church of San Marco. He continued to declare that his every word came direct from God.

And so the morning came when the city's government turned against him and sent officers to San Marco with orders for his arrest. The charges were heresy, sedition and uttering false prophecies.

There was always a clutch of enthusiasts to be found outside the tower of the Palazzo della Signoria in whose tiny top cell, the wryly named Alberghettino or "little hotel," Savonarola was held prisoner. These people came, not to pray for his release or comfort, but to listen to his screams while he was being tortured. Savonarola's guards were only too ready to describe to those waiting below the gruesome punishments inflicted each day on the gaunt body of the deposed Prior. The people laughed and thumped their fists in triumph in their opposite hand when they learned the prisoner had been hoisted on a pulley and live coals applied to the soles of his feet. They nodded at each other in glee when told that Savonarola had been stretched repeatedly on the rack, only his right arm left unbroken so that he would be able to sign his confession.

On the day that the screams coming from the "little hotel" were particularly protracted and curdled, jubilant cries rose up from the crowd gathered below. The news soon spread that within an eight-hour span Savonarola had been put upon the rack fourteen separate times.

When he heard of these terrible things, Piero lay on his bed for two solid days, his face turned to the wall and his knees drawn up to his belly. In his blood some peculiar alembic frothed, a mixture of pity and disgust that conspired to thicken his despondency. In those instants when he was able to think clearly, he recognized his pity was purely for the fallen Prior. His disgust was directed at his fellow citizens who clustered beneath the prison tower and smacked their lips when they heard Savonarola's screams. Such feelings of repugnance for his own kind always turned into a vile self-loathing. If this was the depravity to which humans so readily sank, how then was he any different? Was he not by fact of species complicit in their degenerate behaviour?

If only Savonarola had sometimes used the magnificent instrument of his voice to praise, as well as to censure. If only he had allowed himself on occasion to be nourished by the transformative splendours of the world, and not just take horror as his meat. I might have shown him, thought Piero, that passage in Cennino Cennini's *Libro dell'arte* where he spoke of the artist's constant quest "to discover things not seen, hiding themselves under the shadow of natural objects, so that what does not yet exist may come into being."

Was this not the true nature of things, he would have liked to ask the Prior, that they are forever transforming, shifting, coming into being? Leonardo taught us how to paint this coming-into-being, the subtle shift and shading of one thing into another, by the technique he called *sfumato*. And by such technique, we painters are able to show the glow that surrounds all objects and all living creatures.

There came a day at last when Savonarola could bear the torture no longer. He signed with his right hand, which his captors had left unbroken. They then did him the courtesy of executing him by hanging. Then his dead body was set swinging above a live pyre on the same spot in the Piazza della Signoria from where he had overseen his two great Bonfires of the Vanities. His enemies would have had it otherwise. They wanted him to experience the utmost pain, to be stuck like a live pig upon a stake and roasted before the feasters' eyes.

Piero, on the other hand, thanked God that the Pope had seen fit to allow Savonarola this final clemency. Months later, he saw in the workshop of a colleague a painting of Savonarola's end commissioned by one of the Arrabbiatti. It showed a panorama of the piazza with little groups of Florentine nobles in red or cream-coloured cloaks standing in stately disquisition. Two youths hurried across the piazza on the diagonal, bent almost double under bundles of faggots and fresh straw. They were headed toward the pyre whose orange flames were just about to reach the naked feet of the three monks strung together at the top of a wooden cross.

How very small the artist had made the three doomed Dominicans, Piero noted, smaller even than the bundles of wood the two hastening youth were bringing to feed the fire. So diminished were the hanging figures, it was as if Savonarola and his two most loyal monks were already negligible and written out of the city's history.

Had he been given the commission, Piero knew he would have been compelled to make the dangling figures much larger, to show the flickering between agony and prayer on the faces of the two living monks, and the shadow of death on Savonarola's. He would have endeavoured, by some contortion or deliberate disproportion of the Prior's hanging corpse, to convey how many of the man's bones his torturers had snapped upon the rack. Piero would have dared, if his patron was at all amenable, to dramatize the uncanny event many spectators swore they saw that day. The dead Prior's right arm, already engulfed in flame, shot up out of the fire in a rigid salute. Did the dead man intend this harrowing as curse or blessing?

For many weeks to come Piero was haunted night and day by this image of the Prior's rigid raised right arm emerging from his flames. He was dogged as well by the presentiment the mighty shaping power of Savonarola's voice had not been extinguished, but had only gone underground where it smouldered still, a fire in the roots of the earth that could spread insidiously and unseen. Until at last one day it would explode forth and that great puissance would be heard again, the voice with the inexorable power to bend men's minds to its will and compel them to act in accordance with a system of beliefs so extreme they were denatured. So that they would spit out their souls on the pavement and became mere toys of their master's mind.

With the smothering weight of Savonarola's dictates lifted from the city, song returned, and dance and love-making, within and outside the bounds of marriage. Provided he was circumspect, a man could once again adore and lie with another man, without fear of being maimed or executed. The books of ancient learning, of Hesiod, Plato, Aristotle, Ovid, Plotinus, Hermes Trismegistus, again took pride of place on scholars' desks. The luxurious brocades and silks in rich hues, for which Florence was renowned, once again graced the elegant forms of noble men and women. Even those who were poor put on their brightest cloaks and stockings so that they might walk and work with a lighter heart.

All artists were at perfect liberty once more to paint the subjects banned under Savonarola's reign. Some weeks after the Prior's execution, Piero received a commission for a panel for a nuptial chamber. It was to show a naked Venus reclining in a meadow with her lover Mars. He immediately began to sketch the scene in red chalk. He would present the two gods mere minutes after they have been joined in fleshly love together, flushed and sated. Mars, a beautiful young man with rosy cheeks and long auburn hair, was already asleep, his head upon a red velvet bolster, decorated with gold leaf. His sole garment was a woven drapery of delicate wine-coloured stripes covering his sex. In the background, winged putti played with the various pieces of the armour he had flung off in his haste.

A diaphanous silvery band wove around the naked thighs of Venus, beneath her breasts and then, like a christening garment, over the head of the baby Cupid, whom she held close by her side. Piero's chalk lingered lovingly over the details of the magnificent rabbit which also nuzzled against her naked thigh. The rabbit would be a pure snowy white, and his wonderful ears tipped in black. Piero had a fine model in mind and looked forward to welcoming him into his studio.

FOURTEEN

The Christmas Break

THE MORNING AFTER SHE DRANK all the cheap brandy at the Ark, Agnes woke feeling very ill. The light seared her eyes. Her skin felt tight and sore. When she peered with trepidation into the mirror, she felt worse. Her face looked pinched and white, and nasty somehow, as if the heavy drinking had uncovered a foul trait of character of which she'd been unaware. She told herself she would never overindulge in this way again. Drunkenness was degrading and it made her look ugly.

Nor did the hangover help her perspective. Her headache and self-disgust sharpened the still-mordant grief for Campbell and her repugnance at the horrendous ways Fergus had been made to suffer. She was consumed again by the belief she did not deserve to live, when these two, and particularly Campbell, were dead. While she grasped how irrational this conviction was, it continued to plague her. She wondered if any of the others felt this way. But then, apart from Kit, perhaps no one else in the Ark had loved Campbell as fiercely as she did.

And Kit, well . . . the evidence of her love was in that harrowing graveside photo in which she appeared gaunt, shorn and virtually unrecognizable. She looked so fragile and stunned, as if she would have put up no resistance had someone tried to push her into the grave on top of Campbell's coffin. She would have welcomed the heavy earth raining down on her, extinguishing consciousness and breath.

Agnes winced. She should not be thinking these things. It was crudely intrusive to try to imagine what Kit was feeling. It occurred to her that it would do Kit no good at all to hear about Fergus. Surely Horace would be able to insulate her from all the gruesome details, at least until she was stronger again?

Agnes was still very much afraid that Fergus's murder was linked to his activism. She had been surprised, but at the same time relieved, at how few details about the crime appeared in the local news, barely more than Fergus's age and profession and the fact he appeared to have been strangled.

"Appeared!" barked Minnie at a hastily summoned Ark meeting that soon turned into a maudlin wake for both Fergus and Campbell. "He was garrotted, for God's sake! Where's the 'appeared' in that?" Minnie maintained that the college board of governors had pressed the police for a news blackout on the sensational aspects of the murder.

"I mean, who wants to pay thousands of dollars a year to send your kid to a college where professors get strangled and their private parts set on fire?"

"Minnie, please!" Perdita urged. "I don't want to think about it."

"Tough," Minnie said. "It happened. You can't mentally white it out because that kind of sick violence offends your sensibility or religious principles or whatever.

It happened. Fergus suffered hellishly. At least what happened to Campbell was quick."

Perdita got up and left the room. Pablo, Pinto and Agnes all shifted in their seats as if this physical movement would dislodge the image of the vital man they had known turned into meat, sliced and branded. This evening, they had gathered to remember Fergus. They had to forget, for the moment, the grotesque manner of his death. Of course they wanted Fergus's killer brought to justice. With the exception of Minnie, who announced she would gladly "see the bastard fry," they all wrestled to exterminate any instinctive urge for vengeance. When Pablo wondered aloud about a possible link between the two deaths, Pinto shook his head: "There's no point travelling down that road," he said firmly. They then touched briefly, and with a deliberate constraint, on the shocking things done to Fergus. Soon enough, they arrived at what they thought a just conclusion: that the perpetrator was likely clinically insane and therefore deserving of mercy and pity. If this attitude toward Fergus's killer demanded a wrenching effort, they knew nonetheless it was the right one.

But perhaps a murderer would never be found. According to Minnie's friend on the force, whoever killed Fergus had been organized and cunning enough to wipe the place clean of prints. "Absolutely pristine," Minnie's friend said. Nor was there any sign of forced entry into Fergus's home. Because he had lived some miles out of town in an isolated winterized cottage, there were no neighbours to interview, no one who would have heard his screams.

"An absolute dead end so far," said Minnie as she lit a slim joint and inhaled deeply.

Agnes, who considered this rather a poor choice of phrase, sipped more of the peat-flavoured single malt Zebra had contributed to the gathering. As she brought the glass to her lips, she caught Pinto looking at her with concern and smiled at him in rueful remembrance. It was kindly Pinto who had helped her get back to the dorm, without making an unseemly display, after her overindulgence in brandy on that dreadful morning they got the news about Fergus. "Walk tall, and try not to breathe on anyone," were his final instructions as they approached the front steps of her dormitory, where once Campbell had sat waiting for her with his Vulcan parked across the road. It seemed so very long ago now, although it was mere months. How beautiful he had looked that day.

She took a good swallow of the dark amber whisky, relishing its complex earthy taste on her tongue and liquid fire in her throat. What a wonderful drink. It seemed almost immediately to clarify her thoughts and purge the dross of pointless regret. She felt re-energized and hopeful. They would make his memory live, forever and forever. Campbell would be their guiding saint. A very sexy saint, she thought, raising the glass to her lips again.

She glanced up and saw Pinto frowning at her. That silent admonition made her realize she had emptied her glass without being aware of doing so. A flash of rage exploded in her head. If Pinto were not such a genuinely well-intentioned man, she would have strongly resented this unsubtle surveillance. Did he really think she was an alcoholic-in-the-making because she'd drunk too much brandy on one very exceptional occasion?

· She looked across the room at him, put on a counterfeit composed smile, and set the empty glass down on the coffee table in front of her. It was the same one Pinto had broken in half the morning after Campbell was killed. She saw that it had been painstakingly mended, the two halves so carefully glued together that the seam marking the join was barely visible. She pictured Pinto labouring with extraordinary patience to bring the two halves together so precisely. Her eye kept returning to the seam down the centre of the table, where it exactly intersected the base of her empty glass.

She could not deny that the Single Malt, within easy reach on top of a brick-and-board bookcase, exerted a strong pull, as if the lovely dark amber fluid were actually tugging at her will. She wanted very much to pour another inch into her glass, to taste the mysterious earthy components and experience again the golden glow of hope and bliss the sweet fire in her throat had delivered earlier. At the same time, she was uncomfortable with the nagging near-ferocity of her desire to drink more. And so she told herself that the barely visible line down the centre of the table symbolized Pinto's sober moral rectitude, which she must strive to emulate. (She noted that tonight he drank only water.) She must stick with this resolve, for this stage of her life at least, when the wounds of bereavement were still so raw.

In the following weeks she threw herself at her course work, setting her alarm for five and staying at her desk until well after midnight. She had deadline after deadline to meet for end-of-term essays, and the Christmas break was looming. She dreaded the idea of the holidays and her parents' expectation she would return "home" to them and Phoebe. This was her home now: the college and the

Ark. She knew who she was here and she liked herself. She did not trust her parents and Phoebe to recognize how much she had changed.

To her surprise, the essay assignment that most riveted her was the one she had been slowest to tackle, out of concern she could bring nothing new to the subject. The topic was very specific: Explore, through one seminal work, "the yellow high note" on which Van Gogh focused in his paintings in Provence. Of course, she was familiar with *The Sunflowers* and other pieces from his fifteen months in southern France and it was exactly that familiarity that troubled her. She had seen these "iconic" works reproduced so often, on coffee cups, T-shirts, silk scarves and prints in doctors' and dentists' offices, she feared that, for her, they had long been drained of their once urgent vitality.

Then, too, there was the popular image of the man himself, still arguably the most famous modern painter on earth. Everyone, even people who cared little about art, knew about the ear-cutting episode. What Agnes hated most was the way Van Gogh's madness had become a public commodity, and the elements of his sad story so often contorted to belittle his achievement. She found him cruelly caricatured in books and films which showed him raging, inebriated, lurching from failed love affair to love affair, now frenetically ebullient, now desperately despondent. At best, the popular accounts made him a holy fool or idiot savant. They implied it was his insanity that produced the art works which burst full-fledged from his brain despite himself, an uncouth and barbarous man who probably smelled.

As a corrective to this hackneyed caricature, she turned to his letters to his brother Theo. What she found there was a profoundly cultivated and literate man, fluent in three languages. He wrote feelingly of the sufferings of the working poor, whom he tried to help, first as a teacher in London and then as a missionary in the mining district of Belgium. There he subjected himself to such extreme self-mortification, giving away all his possessions, eating only enough to stay alive, living in a squalid hut, that he imperilled both his mental and physical health.

As she read, Agnes saw how he hurled himself into the thick of every consuming passion, including his relentless pursuit of the women with whom he became besotted. When they rejected him, he plunged into the hell-pit of despair. He often referred to episodes of heavy drinking. When he described the overhead lamps in his *Night Café* as "delirium tremens in full swing," she wondered if the metaphor was grounded in direct experience. In fact, she was struck by just how frankly self-aware he was. He knew all too well he was a social misfit, who had "no talent for relations with people."

This passage chimed with her own inveterate social awkwardness, and with Piero di Cosimo's hermetic withdrawal from his neighbours. She still believed that Piero, like Van Gogh, was also plagued by black depressive moods that induced a killing stupor, when the hand could not move to grasp a brush, nor the mind see any point in doing so.

And if she was right and it was wonder at the infinite beauty of the animal kingdom that liberated Piero from despair, then of course it was Van Gogh's enthrallment with colour that liberated *him*. She learned with pleasure how he kept various coloured balls of wool in a special box so that he could try out strikingly unusual combinations, swathe by swathe. What he wanted, in these strange junctures of green-blue, yellow-gold, lilac, cobalt, pink-gold, bronze and copper, was to conjure up in paint the rapturous natural palette of Provence and its effects on a man's soul.

In the landscapes he painted in Arles, the sunlit, flowing fields, the vineyards, the starry skies, the cypresses like green flames, what she saw running beneath the turbulent, swirling brush strokes laden with pulsing colour was the living soul of nature itself — the Anima Mundi she perceived in Piero's best works. Agnes had no doubt this extraordinary ability to reveal the tremulous current moving through Creation came at enormous cost.

For her essay, she chose the painting Van Gogh did of his bedroom in the Yellow House he rented in Arles, just before Paul Gaugin came to stay with him. The gentle warping of the angles of the walls and the outlines of the furniture made the whole scene yielding and welcoming, drawing the viewer into its embrace. Vincent described for Theo the wood rush-seat chair and the solid frame of the soft bed with its scarlet cover as being the "yellow of fresh butter." Here his "yellow high note" signalled his soaring hope for a perfect amity in his relationship with his fellow artist. Everything, including his outlook, was sunny and ordered, from the pale violet walls to the three painter's smocks and the straw hat hanging on the wooden rail.

For many years, Van Gogh had yearned for a community of painters who would inspire each other and provide a sustaining fellowship. Gauguin's coming to

Arles was thus the fulfillment of a long-nurtured dream. It came to Agnes in a flash that that this sensuous depiction of his bedroom was in fact a nuptial painting, much like the canvases commissioned from Renaissance artists to grace the marriage chamber and symbolize a blessed and fruitful union. Vincent desperately wanted a happy marriage of mind and spirit with a colleague whose work he passionately admired, an unalloyed friendship that would extend to the farthest reaches of his observing mind and soul.

Inside of two months, this dream of founding a perfect amity and fruitful partnership in the Yellow House turned rancid and violent. Whatever the root cause of the animosity — heavy drinking, an inescapable raw competitiveness, or the two men's naturally tempestuous natures — it erupted, with ultimately fatal consequences when Van Gogh attacked Gaugin with a razor. Gaugin departed, never to return to Arles, and Vincent, in the legendary fit of despair and self-hatred, cut off part of his left ear. He then wrapped this dismembered piece of flesh and cartilage in a handkerchief and presented it to a local prostitute.

As she pictured this grotesque bloody offering, Agnes was reminded of bullfighters awarded the animal's ear after the kill. In Van Gogh's painting of the bullfighting coliseum in Arles, it was the spectators on whom he focused, and particularly the women with their elaborately piled ebony hair, sparkling white bodices and red parasols. The bullring itself was the merest sketch in the upper right corner; the bullfighter and the bull the barest ideograms of pale indigo. Did he shrink from the gory spectacle itself, just as she would? Perhaps the ear cutting had been an unconscious penance for having partaken, even to this detached degree, in a diabolical "sport."

When he returned to the Yellow House after two weeks in hospital, where they tended his maimed ear, Van Gogh was made to feel the full weight of his neighbours' disapproval. They delivered a petition to the mayor demanding that he no longer be allowed to live there.

It was shortly after this very public judgement on his character and behaviour that Vincent had himself committed to the asylum of Saint-Paul outside Arles. While in the asylum, he painted his bedroom in the Yellow House again. But in this scene, done from memory, the joyous "yellow high note" has all but fled. The wood of the chairs and the bed-frame are chestnut-brown and every object in the room is heavily outlined in black. Agnes much preferred the buoyant, all-embracing spirit of the first bedroom scene. How delightful it would be to snuggle down between the pale lemon sheets and pull the scarlet coverlet up to her chin. The casement window was open at just the right angle to let in the sweet night air of Provence. How happy he must have been when he first painted his room lifted aloft on its triumphant high note.

She wondered if the Yellow House was still there; if the bedroom still perhaps existed exactly as it was. How marvellous it would be to see it and conjure up, in some small way, what Vincent's happiness tasted like at that time, that fresh, buttery anticipatory joy at his friend's imminent arrival. She became so lost in the spell of this image that time contracted. The past undid itself.

Campbell and I could go together, she thought, in all innocence. She was already fantasizing about their rented motorcycle sailing past fields of lavender when the bitter truth returned. A little cry escaped her as she bent over double at her desk, clutching her midriff. Would it ever stop: the loss of him striking her like a physical pain? She took a deep breath, rubbed her eyes and put her fingers back on the keyboard.

The old labours. This essay and then another and another. Then it would be Christmas break. Her unease about being with her parents and Phoebe again was fast becoming a dread, which she knew to be foolish. But as the days passed, the idea of spending the holidays "at home" became no more palatable. The e-mails and texts kept coming, gushy, formulaic, about how much they were looking forward to seeing her. And what day exactly could they expect her? She put off committing herself as long as she could; even toyed with the idea of not going back at all.

On December 22, Agnes sat on a packed Greyhound, cramped and anxious. She had managed to get a window seat but the glass kept smearing with the fug of sixty passengers' moist breath and the steaming damp rising from winter coats. They had all had to line up in wet snow while the various pieces of luggage were shoved into the undercarriage. Agnes pinched her nostrils, trying to shut out for even a few seconds the offensive reek of a wet fur coat somewhere behind her. This smell was rank and sad, not at all as the fur of a live animal would smell under the touch of snow.

Her own coat was one of her more recent charity shop finds: three-quarter-length, made in Nepal of thick ivory-coloured cotton with a sensuous nub, like linen. Stitched into the neckline was a very long double scarf of the same fabric, which was so wide it could be pulled up at the back and worn as a hood. What she loved best about the coat was its bold, black stencilled designs that stood out so clean and clear against the ivory background. There were joyful trumpeting elephants, their bodies painted in ceremonial stripes; stylized rosettes that resembled coronets; and a man-in-the-moon with what looked like a bold capital "W" on his forehead. On both the right and left shoulders of the coat, a pair of elongated eyes stared out at the world from under arching brows. There was a circle with a dot where the forehead would be if these eyes were contained within the confines of a face. But they were not. Instead, they floated in space, as did the sinuous vertical stroke beneath them which might, or might not, denote a nose of some sort.

She had no idea what the floating eyes signified, whether their prototype was on a temple wall somewhere, or if they were a purely fanciful glyph. And this too was part of the coat's charm for her: that the meaning behind its many stenciled symbols was a mystery to her, one she was content to keep company with because the overall effect was so aesthetically pleasing and exuberant. Whenever she wore the coat, on campus or in town, there were always people who looked at it and then smiled widely at her. It was that kind of garment. It made people happy just to look at it. Once, in a line-up at the cash in a drugstore, a little boy kept reaching out to touch the elephants while his mother apologized. His eyes were round with wonder.

This was not at all the case with the angular, frizzy-haired woman who had taken the seat beside Agnes on the bus. She stared frowning at the coat, which Agnes had draped over her knees. Then she focused fixedly on

Agnes's face, her eyes narrowed almost to slits and lips tightly pursed. Three times the woman made her crude appraisal, her neck swiveling as she scrutinized the coat and then Agnes's face in a protracted pantomime of affronted disbelief.

Trying hard to temper her annoyance, Agnes turned to confront the woman eye-to-eye. "Is something the matter?" She strove to keep her voice low and her tone even. She was many months out of practice for coping with this kind of raw appraisal of her appearance. Foolishly, she had let herself be lulled into complacency because she was able to go about unremarked in a benignly civilized college town. Now she was back in the "real world" with its very limited tolerance for peculiar little faces such as hers.

The woman jerked away when Agnes spoke, to signal her offended surprise. Then she drew herself up very erect and said in a voice at once too steely and too loud, "If you don't mind me asking, do you belong to some kind of cult?"

"What . . . ?"

"The weird symbols on your coat," the woman said, jabbing a forefinger at the floating eyes and then the moon face. "And your book . . . that pagan thing."

Agnes was stupefied. Surely this person wasn't serious? The book in question was Edgar Wind's *Pagan Mysteries of the Renaissance*. "It's a book about how ancient Greek myths influenced Renaissance art," she tried to explain, with all politeness she could muster. "And the coat is from Nepal. It's nothing to do with a cult."

"Whatever!" the woman snapped. "It's weird. Spooky. I don't want those creepy eyes staring at me for the next seven hours. What if I fall asleep? People have been decapitated on buses while they slept, you know."

Agnes started at the unfortunate participle. Was the woman insane? She began to wonder if she was the one who should be afraid.

"Look, I'll turn the coat over. Will that suit you?" Agnes held the jacket briefly in front of her, then rapidly reversed it so that only the plain buff lining lay across her knees.

"If you don't mind me saying," said the woman in a stage whisper, "someone who looks like you shouldn't be wearing a coat that makes you stick out even more."

Agnes heard several passengers in the immediate vicinity snigger. Someone guffawed. She felt her stomach swoop in the old conditioned response to derision and worked very hard to hold back an equally rude retort.

"Yes, I do mind you saying," she said between clenched teeth. "Now can we please just ignore each other for the rest of the trip?"

"Well!" With this histrionic exclamation, the woman laid claim to being the offended party. Then she riffled busily in her carry-on bag and pulled out a magazine which she held very close to her face, as if to shield herself from possible defilement.

Agnes inserted her earplugs. On her iPod she had several compilations of Renaissance music, Gabrielli, Monteverdi and Palestrina. The music's meditative rise and fall, full of a dignified yearning, transcended everything commonplace and soiled. Like this wretched bus. She was gripped by a sudden childlike wish to undergo one of those breathtaking Ovidian transformations and soar through the metal ceiling, like a lark or a pure jet of water. Wasn't that the imagination's function? She could go at will into Ovid's and Piero's worlds where the radiant potencies of myth *were* Truth. A truth that had nothing at all to do with the tawdry "reality" that surrounded her now: an overheated, smelly bus hurtling down the highway toward the Canada-U.S. border, sharing a seat with a person who thought she might be a blood-thirsty fanatic because her book had the word "pagan" in the title.

She glanced at the woman who was already asleep, with her mouth hanging open. Agnes could not help but notice the extremely poor condition of her teeth. Several were badly discoloured, both black and yellow, and worn quite thin, like little pegs protruding from the gums. Perhaps she was in discomfort; obviously she could not afford decent dental care. Thinking of the woman with sympathy rather than persisting in anger owed something to Pinto's influence, she realized. She now often found herself trying to emulate his example: the oceanic empathy, the refusal to be snide, patronizing or vengeful.

As she pictured his broad, beatific face with pleasure, it came to her with a start that Pinto was her first real friend. She did not consider this fact pathetic, given that she was now nearly twenty years old. She was simply grateful. She sensed that the unconditional trust Pinto offered her was rare, even among people who were naturally kind and gregarious. I have found a home, she repeated to herself, and in her mind's eye saw Zebra, Minnie, Perdita and Pablo standing on the porch of the Ark. Above them, and the charming sign with its boatload of animals, Campbell's spirit floated, generative and pure.

Agnes mounted the three steps to her parents' front door, dragging her bag behind her. But once she stood on the stoop, opposite the white door with its small inset oval of scarlet and chartreuse stained glass, she could get no farther. She had the key gripped in her palm. Why, then, would her fingers not follow the motion through and insert it cleanly in the lock, and then let herself in?

Was it just weariness kept her standing there? Her shoulders ached, as did the small of her back and her buttocks. But this was more than fatigue from spending the past twenty hours on various buses. It was the peculiar embodied tension where her nerves thrummed taut as overhead wires in the frozen air. The confrontation with the foolish woman on the bus had propelled her back to a besieged vulnerability; the perpetual edgy expectation of odd looks, hissed insults and crude comments about monkey-girls, freaks and paper bags. In truth, the remainder of her journey had not been too bad. Of course, certain people stared at her. But that would always be the case, until perhaps she got too old for anyone to notice her at all.

She felt very cold. Nevertheless, she did not want to go inside, in part because there was so much she must keep secret from her parents. Some days after Campbell's death, she had made the mistake of telling her mother in an email that a friend of hers had been killed in a motorcycle accident. The response she got was trite and unfeeling: "Honey, so sorry to hear about your friend. It must be terrible for his parents. Motorcycles are such dangerous things." The message swung immediately to the latest news of Phoebe and how well she was doing in her drama classes.

Agnes had clenched her fists; then closed her laptop quickly, so violent was her urge to smash the screen.

The door opened suddenly. "I'm sorry. We don't . . . " She recognized her mother's standard lines for politely dispatching door-to-door solicitors.

"Mum. It's me."

"Agnes! My goodness, honey, you look so different. Your hair . . . and what happened to your nice grey wool coat? You didn't lose it, did you, hon? Come in, come in. Your dad's dying to see you too, and Phoebe."

Her mother looked even more fragile, her skin startlingly translucent wherever it was stretched over bone. She seemed smaller too. Or was it that Agnes had grown taller? They were now eye to eye.

Agnes held fast to this new equivalence. She would not let them undermine her, or deflect her from her purpose. Nor would she inadvertently reveal anything that was sacrosanct to the Ark.

"Agnes! You're a sight for sore eyes." Her father's hug was so warmly enveloping, she almost gave way. Was it possible they really did care?

"You've lost weight, haven't you, sweetie? Doesn't she look thinner to you, Meg?"

Her mother nodded. "Are you eating all right, Agnes? And you're very pale too. You know what they say about vegetarians and a lack of Vitamin B12."

"I'm tired. That's all. I've been travelling since noon yesterday." This came out sharply plaintive, a tone she had not intended.

Both her parents looked hurt. "Agnes, we're sorry it was so difficult for you, but neither Daddy nor I had the free time to drive down to get you. If you'd chosen Brock or Queens or even York, the travel would be a lot easier for you. And we'd love having you closer. In fact, your father . . . "

"Meg! Perhaps now is not the best time. Let Agnes drink her tea and have a nap before we . . . "

"Before we what, Dad? Is something wrong? Are you ill?" Her mind emptied of everything but panic on her parents' account. All the time she'd been away, she had never once given a thought to their well-being. She'd just assumed they would continue as they always had, enjoying the rewards of their remarkable good health and looks, charm, intellect and energy.

"Tell me!" she insisted. She banged her cup on the table, harder than she had intended.

"I'm sorry, Agnes. We've handled this badly," her father began. "Let's make it clear. Your mother and I are fine. Phoebe's fine. It's your welfare we're concerned about."

"What!" She was immediately apprehensive. What did they know? Could they have found out about the attack by the security guards at the laboratory? She had never even mentioned anything about the Ark in her e-mails to them.

"We have real fears Bremrose is not a safe place for you to be, Agnes. I know it's quaint old New England, but it's still America. It's simply a more violent culture south of the border."

"Bremrose is just as safe a place as here," she protested. "I live in a dorm with a surveillance camera on every floor and electronic locks. The building is sealed tight by eleven."

"Agnes dear, we're skirting the issue here. We have heard about the philosophy professor at your college who was murdered."

She nodded, staring down at her whitened knuckles. She had not expected this; had not in any way prepared herself for sitting in her parents' kitchen, their eyes fastened on her, trying to probe inside her head. And what would they see if they could? Her imagined Grand Guignol of the naked Fergus, face bulging and distorted as he fought for air with the wire tightening around his neck? Or those unendurable scenes where a fiend charred Fergus's freckled flesh with what — a blowtorch, a hot poker constantly renewed in the woodstove? Or just wooden matches, struck one at a time, for the most lingering effect? Her thoughts too often ran on then to the idea of Fergus as martyr, a characterization that was perhaps slipshod, and of which she must be wary.

Wariness was most definitely called for in her current situation, which was beginning to look like an interrogation. She wished she were not so exhausted; that she did not feel so emotionally raw. What if she blurted something out that made the others in the Ark vulnerable? Why did she feel so diminished in her parents' presence, as though they were systematically draining her of her defining light and all she had gained?

She was aware she was clenching her teeth.

"Yes, of course. It was horrible the way he died. Fergus . . . I mean Professor Jonquil . . . was a crusader. A firebrand." She bit her lip at this last description. What a stupid thing to say.

"Fergus!" Her mother pounced on the familiarity. "So you did know him?"

"I was in his Animal Ethics course."

Her father groaned softly.

"What?" Agnes was nearing total exasperation.

"Agnes, from what I've been told by a colleague who met Professor Jonquil, this man is . . . was . . . dangerous. 'Rabid' is the word Bill Whiterose used and Bill is not the kind of person to make such a judgement lightly. He is a scrupulously fair individual. Did you know this Jonquil was dismissed from one college for inciting his students to get involved in a questionable and highly volatile demonstration? Did you know that one of those students — a young woman — is in a wheelchair today because at Jonquil's urging she joined in a protest outside an abattoir that turned very ugly indeed?"

"Yes," she said. "I heard that story."

"It's not a story, Agnes." Her father's face was stern.

"I'm too tired for this," she told them. "What is it you want? Do you want me to give up my scholarship and crawl back here because some insane person tortured poor Fergus and choked him to death with a wire?"

"Tortured!" Her mother's eyes were wide.

Her father grimaced. "I tried to spare your mother the unsavory elements of the crime, Agnes."

"Then why bring it up at all?" Agnes snapped. "Do you know what I think? I don't think you're concerned about my safety at all. I think you want to pull me out of Bremrose because having a daughter at a college with a potential scandal brewing might pose problems for your career. You're afraid you'll be contaminated by implication."

"That's ridiculous, Agnes. That's wild, hurtful talk."

"Hurtful." Jagged fragments of white light splintered her vision. She knew she should desist. She should just excuse herself, tell them firmly how badly she needed to put her head down and sleep. Then she could get up and have a bath to wash away the stink of the bus and the sourness of this inquisition. But she could not leave it. She could not let them demean and sully Fergus's memory in that way.

"I'll tell you what's hurtful. It's sitting here listening to you tell me that a man for whom I had the greatest respect, and for whom I'm still grieving, was rabid and irresponsibly callous, a virtual psychopath. Neither of you have any idea about his kind of integrity. He lived his beliefs. And I mean literally lived them. He was electrifying. He cared about animals' suffering with an intensity you can't begin to imagine. Being at his lectures was like listening to an archangel."

"Archangel! Do we have one coming tomorrow for the party?"

It was Phoebe, who had obviously just washed her hair, which streamed about her shoulders and almost to her hips. She was towelling it as she came into the kitchen and for a moment, as she bent her small head forward, her pale gold hair completely obscured her face. Then her lovely laughing features emerged again, a naiad from behind a waterfall.

Agnes registered the familiar, yet no less despicable, stab of envy at her younger sister's beauty. Once again, she must confront the terrible unfairness of their contrasting genetic lots. Why, at the very least, could Agnes not also have inherited her mother's small straight finely modelled nose, with its discreet little nostrils?

At the same time, she could never deny the warm tide of affection that drew her to her feet to embrace the guileless, sweet-natured sister who had never consciously done her any harm. The wrenching paradox got no easier to bear. In Phoebe's actual presence, Agnes must continuously struggle to subdue a venomous jealousy that just would not die. She detested this malignant trait in her character, and now more than ever when she believed herself so much transformed.

"Oh, Agnes! I love your hair. It really suits you longer."

"Thanks, Phoebe. I hear you're the star of your drama class."

"Have Mum and Dad told you, then?" She skipped forward and laid her small hand, with its pearly perfect nails, on her mother's shoulder.

"What, Phoebe?"

"I got the part of Cordelia in *King Lear*. The Little Theatre is putting it on in February. Can you believe it, Agnes? There were sixteen of us who tried out for it and some of them even had professional theatre experience. I still can't quite believe it. I feel so lucky."

Phoebe beamed. Her parents beamed back.

"That's terrific, Phoebe. Congratulations! I'm really sorry I won't be able to get back for your performance."

"Oh, Daddy says he'll video it. We'll send it to you."

"Great. I'll look forward to it. You'll make a wonderful Cordelia."

"I hope so, Agnes. But it's funny . . . you know the part I'm really scared about is the death scene. What if I can't keep still? What if I get a fit of the giggles?"

She looked at them all expectantly.

Agnes, seeing Campbell's headless corpse on the road, said nothing.

"You'll be fine, sweetheart," their father said soothingly. "There won't be a dry eye in the house. We're so proud of you."

A jolt of resentment shook her. She couldn't remember her parents saying anything like that to her when she won her scholarship. She had been so happy and astounded at her good fortune, she hadn't noticed at the time. Never once had they said, "We're really proud of you, Agnes."

How she wished she had not come back at all.

"If you'll excuse me," she said, "I really would like to get a bit of sleep."

"Oh, gosh. Wait, Agnes. I haven't even told you about my boyfriend. His name is Georges and he's a French exchange student. He's from Montpellier and you'll meet him at the party tomorrow. I think you'll really like him."

Agnes manufactured a smile that made the skin of her face feel tight and hot. "That's wonderful, Phoebe. What time is the party?" She was hoping there was a way she could justifiably absent herself for most of it. But it would be Christmas Eve, with not even the public library open. And she had no friends here, absolutely no one, about whom she could invent the pretense of a get-together. Perhaps she could plead the need to do some late-night Christmas shopping, although in fact she had already purchased her gifts.

Georges from Montpellier. She grimaced as she went up to her room, picturing him as one of those impossibly handsome models who advertises costly colognes and designer jeans in the front pages of *Vanity Fair*. A chiselled indentation in the upper lip; a pouting sensual bottom one. A spray of fine mist to make the naked chest and prominent cheekbones gleam. People would look at him and Phoebe and immediately think what beautiful children they would produce. No one ever seemed to consider the random factors in genetic inheritance when they saw a flawless couple; that two perfect specimens might have a child with a cauliflower ear or a hare-lip. Or a child who looked like Agnes. Was it frazzling exhaustion making her run herself down so? Or the fact she still felt vulnerable from the inquisition about Fergus and her parents' pressure that she leave Bremrose. Well, she wouldn't! She would not let them chip away at the proud edifice of self she had created. She would protect her hard-won awareness and keep her vows. If that meant having to repudiate her family altogether, she would do so. Not necessarily without a qualm, but calmly and cleanly, because she had another family now who shared her cherished beliefs.

She flung open her bedroom door with a sigh, as if she were about to rush into the arms of a trusted friend. This had been her secure redoubt for so many years, the refuge where the "monkey-girl with the hairy blue ass who liked it from behind" could drop her impassive daytime face and cry until her eyelids turned red-raw. It was her one place of safety where she could dream as indulgently as she wished about a future life purged of pain and aglow with purpose.

Dear room. She greeted it softly, as it deserved. But even as she set her bag on the floor, she saw everywhere the signs of infiltration. Her mother had obviously been busy. The grey-blue walls were now off-white with a faint pink blush. In place of her old quilt of hand-knitted squares, her mother had put on the bed a frilly comforter splashed with rather vulgar red roses. She looked in disbelief at these flamboyant blooms. She could not lie down peacefully on these blood-red flowers. She stripped the offending comforter off only to be assaulted by more pink in the underlying blanket, sheets and pillow case. Her mother knew she detested pink's cloying pretty-girl associations. Or did she know? Was she over-reacting? Yet why did it seem that everything in the room declared: Agnes, be gone!

She pictured her mother humming happily as she did her "clean sweep," pulling pictures off the walls and pitching the newsletters from PETA, the WSPA and the Jane Goodall Institute into the recycling box. It hit her hard that her portrait of Noona was one of the pictures her mother had banished. The morning she'd made her fateful decision to refuse the cosmetic surgery, she had carefully cut out and framed the cover portrait of Noona. She had hung it above her desk so that she would see those empathetic, yearning eyes whenever she looked up. She began wildly pulling open her desk drawers, heaving out books, bundles of essays, and almost-spent ballpoints in fasci-like bundles. She was getting frantic, when at last she opened the long middle drawer where, of course, she ought to have started, had she been thinking at all clearly. There she found the picture of Noona, still in its cheap plastic frame, turned upside down. Even when it was hidden away in a drawer, her mother had had to turn the picture over.

She was hurt and furious, her head full of words like Plunder, Despoliation and Disrespect. She struggled to do the Pinto-like thing and wrench her perspective around.

She might well be misreading her mother's intent. Perhaps she had simply wanted to "brighten the place up," as she liked to say. But why did she have to take away the quilt, which her grandmother had made out of multi-coloured hand-knitted squares? She could remember her mother expressing misgivings that the cover was unsanitary, given that it was "thick with cat dander." Agnes, on the other hand, cherished the idea that placid, dainty Cecilia had likely lain purring on the quilt while it was being put together.

When menstrual cramps had ground in her midriff like broken glass, the handmade quilt tented over her knees had emanated a radiant cure. The agility and tenderness of her grandmother's hands, even the majestic, mysterious life-force of the cat, were knitted into those simple ribbed squares in primary colours. And now her mother had exorcized its spell, as she had exorcized everything in the room that spoke of Agnes and the things she loved.

She lay on the bed under the ugly comforter with its blowzy roses that resembled the greedy, open mouths of human carnivores and was reminded of the smell of meat on her mother and father's breath, so much more evident to her now than when she had lived with them. Even Phoebe smelled of it. Why couldn't they see how harmful and wicked their eating habits were?

She wondered if Pinto's mother was a vegetarian. She hoped so for his sake; hoped too, that his Christmas in the familial home would not be as gruelling as hers looked likely to be. Thinking of Pinto, of his huge, kind hands and embracing smile, helped soothe her frayed spirit. She would be herself again, once she was away from this place that was home no longer. She would go back to Bremrose and be absorbed once more into the sacred body of the Ark.

Pinto's mother did not own a computer nor did she write letters. Communication between them during the school year had been therefore limited to the calls Pinto dutifully made once every two weeks from the landline in the Ark. It had been in early November that he first heard about his mother's new boyfriend, Mick. He could tell she was smitten. She'd spoken rapidly, with an uncharacteristic breathy trill, and managed, in the space of their four-minute conversation, to say Mick's name ten times or more.

For as long as he could remember his mother had maintained a certain distance with the men in her life. "I've been a fool too often, Peter," she would say. He regarded the make-up she wore for her work at the casino — the bold red lipstick, blue eye shadow and false eyelashes — as elemental to her tough, worldly wise persona. It disconcerted him when on the phone she'd sounded more like a gushing girl than the mother he knew. She has put down her guard, he thought. She has made herself utterly naked for this man, and I am afraid for her.

Mick was living with his mother. Pinto had considered breaking with their longstanding habit of spending Christmas together — a tradition grounded far more in convention than any ardent wish to spend time in each other's company — and staying in the Ark, reading, meditating, taking long walks in the snow imagining he was with Agnes; then coming back to listen to Arvo Pärt and to pray for the untrammelled passage of Campbell's soul, and for poor Fergus.

"I've told Mick how smart you are, Peter, and what a fine man you are. He's looking forward to meeting you."

His scruples had prevented him from asking if she had told Mick that her son had an unusual skin pigmentation. It was the humiliating "rituals" of his childhood that prevented candour. His mother still laboured under a burden of regret for all the times she had asked him to hide when she had friends visiting. He had kept his part of the bargain, staying "quieter than a mouse," never coming out to use the toilet no matter how great his need, making do with the plastic bucket she provided. He had complied with all her wishes and been a good son. But that enforced exile within his own home had struck at his heart and fed the self-loathing he so much wanted to surmount. He'd tried often to extend her an unqualified forgiveness, but a residue of resentment made this impossible.

"If you and Mick would like Christmas alone together . . . "

"Oh no, Peter!" She'd sounded genuinely affronted. It was her guilt talking, he thought. They were both still too tangled in its coils. "When you are coming?"

Any cautious optimism foundered the instant he saw Mick. Everything about the man was repellently flashy, from his razored white-blonde hair to the exaggerated pointed toes of his sleek boots. He had what appeared to be a rhinestone embedded in one of his eye teeth. When he parted his lips, its dazzle made his mouth look cruel, if not inhuman. He was wiry and muscular, although a good foot shorter than Pinto. He wore his narrow jeans so tight it was difficult not to stare at the prominent bulge at his crotch. Pinto blinked. He did not like to think of his mother being touched by this person, let alone having sex with him. This thought exacerbated the queasiness brought on by the smell of Mick's aftershave, and the tanned-hide reek of the obviously new leather jacket he had draped over his right shoulder. But the thing about his mother's lover that most shocked Pinto was his youth. He guessed Mick was barely thirty.

"Aren't you going to say hello to Peter, babe?" His mother sidled up to Mick, who stood staring hard at Pinto.

He found it hard to watch as his mother's arm snaked around Mick's waist.

Mick pushed her away. "Nadine, a word." He jutted his jaw toward the kitchen door. "Now, Nadine!"

Nadine was his mother's "casino name." It went with the azure eye shadow and kewpie doll eyelashes; with the stiletto heels and the tight black skirt with the provocative side-slit. But it was Colleen who sent him a look of sorrowful shame as she followed Mick out of the kitchen and closed the door behind them.

Pinto sat down at the table and pressed his knuckles against his eyelids. Why had he come? Why hadn't he obeyed his instincts and stayed away, for this Christmas at least? He knew that for his own sake, and his mother's, he must try not to overhear what Mick said. He was so weary of people like this and fed up with contorting himself to excuse their willful prejudice. But he could not help the fact the walls of his mother's house were thin and he too slow at stopping up his ears.

"You should have warned me, Nadine," he heard Mick hiss. "Did you really think I could sit opposite that and eat my dinner?"

Pinto balled his fists. Was he a disaster-made-flesh from which decent people must shield themselves? He studied his fists. He wanted to smash something, anything. It was a despicable urge.

"I'll be back by six, Nadine. And he better be gone by then. Or I'm out of here for good. Understand?"

The front door slammed. He knew he must attempt to inhabit his mother's distress if he was to salvage his affection for her. Her silence in the face of Mick's remarks told him how deeply she was in his thrall. At the same time, he knew she would be suffering acutely on his behalf, and perhaps be disgusted at her own pusillanimity.

He stretched his fingers out into the empty space beneath the table where Yangtze used to lie while he did his homework. Her presence would have comforted him in this perplexing dilemma and gifted him a quietude in which he could puzzle through how best to speak to his mother so that she was not laden with even more guilt on his account.

He was afraid for her, and of the ultimate consequences of this new love affair. There seemed to be precious little love in it, at least from Mick's vantage point. He supposed their relationship was grounded in sexual need and this worried him because of what he perceived as Mick's innate cruelty. Or was he being unfair? Wouldn't it be possible for Mick to be redeemed, with the right teacher and exposure to salutary, enlightened ideals? If nothing else, surely he could be taught a modicum of civility? His character was so undeveloped, more boy than man; he seemed a self-obsessed and heartless child.

The understanding jolted him when it finally came. Mick was the kind of son his mother wished she'd had.

Not saintly, studious, shy Pinto, but a good-looking, narcissistic, wild boy who often got into trouble but was instantly forgiven because he was so endearing. A son on whom she could dote, foolishly and forever. He had never before considered that he had let her down in this way as well; that she would have preferred him rude and rough-and-tumble, rather than considerate, well-mannered and contemplative. He yearned at that instant, in the kitchen of his childhood with the memory of Yangtze so near, to confess all his sins to his mother; to show her the naked violence of his heart.

She came back into the room with wet eyes and an imploring look.

"I'm so sorry, Peter." She extended her arms toward him, her hands clasped as if she were a disciple asking his blessing.

His mother wanted his absolution. What choice did he have but to give it?

"It's all right, Mom. I shouldn't have come. We didn't think it through."

We. Yes, he will include himself in the culpability. He put his arms around her. He was so large, he engulfed her. He had the momentary illusion she was a tiny child in his keeping. If she were a child, he could forcibly hold her back from the degradation and pain he knew Mick would cause her. Mick would one day depart, with many ugly words and seek out someone younger and more nubile. His mother would then sit many hours at the pitted metal-topped table and smoke until her chest ached.

Yet he could not interfere. He had seen how she looked at Mick; the light of passion in her eyes was undeniable.

"I don't want to lose him, Peter." She wrung her hands, even while he held her. He felt them twisting against his belly. Were he a different kind of man, he could gleefully pummel Mick's face until the flesh hung in strings from his bones. But he is not that man. He is the virtuous and understanding son who says: "It's all right. Really. I have friends in Bremrose who invited me for Christmas Day. I can be back there in time easily."

This too was a lie. It would take him ten hours by train and then bus to get back to the Ark. Where, at least, he would be at peace.

He wished he could say to her: "How can you love this stupid boy? Can you not see that he has traduced me; that his behaviour is beneath contempt?"

Instead, he stood holding her, against the pain to come.

"If I can ever make it up to you, Peter, you know I will."

These were her last words to him as he went out the door, where barely a half-hour previously he had come in. The sharp-pointed snow stung his face. He put on his wrap-around sunglasses, raised the hood of his duffle coat and launched himself headlong into the wind. He longed to see Agnes, to be in the force field of her innocent, questing nature; to gaze on her dear face; to be cleansed and renewed by her quick presence. He would suggest she walk behind him so that, with the great bulk of his body, he could protect her from the wind's teeth and the snow's minuscule daggers.

Most of the young people at the soirée, as Phoebe persisted in calling it, were from her acting class, or so Agnes surmised, based on their remarkable self-possession. As she observed them, she understood this gilded presentation was to some degree cultivated. Here and there she saw evidence of long-studied gestures, perfected with much mirror practice. Some of their affections verged on the comical: the chin lifted just a fraction too high to better show off an elegant little nose; the aristocratic sweep of the head to bestow a winning smile on everyone and no one in particular.

She wondered if any of them appreciated how lucky they were and frowned at their blithe ignorance. Then she smoothed out the loose pleats of her red velvet skirt, which she wore with a black leotard top and dangly jet earrings, all charity shop purchases. In any case, hardly anyone was looking at her and she was content enough to fade into the background. She had resolved beforehand simply to look on quietly and be happy for Phoebe. She would work at subduing the childish envy that inevitably peaked whenever Phoebe was being feted or justifiably adored.

There was one irksome element at the party undermining her resolve to behave as the gracious older sister, and that was Georges. He was not the sensuous brooder of the *Vanity Fair* ad she had imagined but quick and fine-boned, with a pointed chin that put her in mind of a Siamese cat. He had olive skin and thick black hair, sleeked back from a high brow. Even his eyebrows were gossamer-fine and so labile he could transform his face from clown to ardent young scholar in an eye-blink. What most unsettled her when they were first introduced were his eyes. They were so like Campbell's, the same startling almost unreal dark blue. Looking into them, she felt the agony of loss reopen in her, as wide and raw as ever. She pulled her hand away from Georges' firm dry clasp as soon as she decently could.

Was that why he now persisted in staring at her, winking and grinning? She was not at all in a mood to be teased, even if it was meant to be purely playful. Around the room, the pretty children twirled and paraded and tried out silly voices and foreign accents. All the parents present smiled indulgently. She tried to do the same. But how hard it was to tolerate their foolish displays, particularly when she saw these young paragons popping little gobbets of spiced lamb — one of her mother's specialties — into their mouths. She could not, for the sake of the occasion, forget the act of slaughter; the flaying, the hanging, the cold hell of the abattoir.

Georges stepped across the room to her at that instant, holding Phoebe by the hand. She wore a dress of cream-coloured wool, with a close-fitting bodice and a skirt cut on the bias so that it flowed about her like sea foam as she moved.

Georges swung his head back and forth, looking now at Phoebe and now at Agnes, in a faultless pantomime of astonishment.

"Mais, je suis étonné," he said. "That you two are sisters of the blood . . . it is amazing. Is this the right word? A-maz-ing? I am thunderbolted."

Agnes thought how much she would like to send a thunderbolt through his skull. And she found Phoebe's silence incomprehensible. Surely she would say something to moderate her arrogant boyfriend's insensitivity? But she went on smiling at Agnes and Georges as if nothing untoward had happened.

"I'm feeling rather dizzy," Agnes managed. She had to get out. An overly ripe scene of vengeance had possessed her: an imagined scenario so exactingly vivid, she would for years afterwards wake in the middle of the night, put her hand to her pounding heart and ask in a panic if she had indeed done these atrocious things.

It begins with a simple twist of the narrow stem of her wineglass so that she holds a ready-made jagged weapon. Without a qualm, she digs the sliver of serrated glass into the smooth cheek of the peerless, mocking boy. Who is peerless no longer. Who stares back at her aghast, staggers and grabs a napkin to sop up the blood seeping from the long gash that reveals the whiteness of the fine bone beneath. It is the kind of deeply inflicted wound that will always leave a scar, even after the most costly laser treatment. She has utterly ruined his beauty, and this fact fills her with a childish glee.

She moves then with such stealth, she is almost invisible. Her bloodlust — not to kill, but to desecrate loveliness — invests her with a malign magic. She strikes at will with her fang of glass until the faces of every one of the pretty young people in the room are scored and bloody. They all cry out of their little round mouths, like babies torn from their cribs and nakedly exposed to the stinging hail of a hateful world.

How could you, Agnes? How could you? Even as she fled upstairs, the question tormented her; although she knew, in full waking clarity, that she had not really done these vengeful, unconscionable things. She had to face it. This latent desire to strike out, particularly at the self-adoring Georges, was the rank evidence of her resentment and terrible unhappiness. She did not want to be in this house. It was not only a cold and foreign place for her, but perilously undermining.

I want Campbell, she thought recklessly. I want to be in his arms. I want to be myself again.

She recognized she had only the one option for reclaiming who she was, and that was to get out right away. She sat at her old desk for what she knew would be the last time and hastily wrote a little note of apology to her parents and Phoebe: "I am sorry to leave without saying good-bye, but I am still very upset by my friend's death. Good luck to Phoebe."

She left this minimal missive on her bed, together with three wrapped Christmas gifts. Now all she had to do was pack her bag quickly and get out of the house without anyone spotting her. Luck was on her side. When she crept downstairs, there was no one in the hallway and the living room door of hammered glass was shut. She waited until she was on the front step to put on her boots, coat, hat and gloves, shivering all the while.

She found a room for the night at the Y and an Indian restaurant where she ordered a blissfully spicy chick pea curry. It pleased her to think that the dramatic heat of the tumeric and charred red chilies was scouring away her vile and brooding thoughts, along with the bitterness she had fortunately left unspoken.

She was very glad in retrospect there had been no hard liquor at Phoebe's soirée. In that case, she might have overindulged and said or done something irreparably damaging. As it was, she believed she had made a lucky escape. Tomorrow morning, she would be on her way back to Bremrose. The dorm would be open to her, even if there were few other students around. The coming solitude was like a balm. Why did her parents insist on diminishing her, and try to strip away the gains she had made? As for Georges, he was so noxiously self-centred and immature she hoped Phoebe would soon drop him.

She was at the bus station by seven the next morning, anxious to depart. She thought it was unlikely her parents would come searching for her. They would be annoyed; perplexed at best, and ultimately relieved she had gone, if only because her presence at the Christmas feast evoked the unwanted spectre. Her slices of tofu turkey were somehow accusatory, despite her efforts to join in the traditional meal with as much nonjudgemental grace as she could muster. She sat tense as a captive throughout this meal, unable to forget the bird's suffering, as much in its cruelly confined life as in its murder.

The gap between her and her family was just too wide now. Her communion with the other members of the Ark, and the dazzling clear sense of purpose they shared, had transformed that gap into a gulf that was unbridgeable. Unless her parents and Phoebe saw the light at last.

No, they would not come looking for her. And yes, she was elated that her facile, counterfeit bond with them had been healthfully severed. This definitive break gave her courage. She marvelled again at all that happened in the past three months: events both tragic and sublime that had reshaped her as completely as the transformed protagonists in Ovid's *Metamorphoses*. If she had been a tree before, her roots trapped in the familial soil, she was now most certainly a river.

Agnes smiled to herself at this strange thought and found an elderly lady with a tiny face under a Prussian blue knitted tam smiling and nodding back at her from across the aisle. Of everyone in the waiting room, this old lady seemed most alert and alive. Agnes wondered if she was also a traveller or if she was waiting for a son or a daughter or a grandchild coming to spend the holiday with her. It struck her then that there was someone in the family who would be pleased to see her. She had not visited her grandmother for over a year, when their father had driven her and Phoebe down to Gloucester. Nana was in a residential home now, but it was an airy and pleasant place with friendly staff and a huge perennial garden that encircled the building.

Eleven hours later, after several bus rides and a lucky train connection from Boston, Agnes sat in her grandmother's cozy room in the very same rocker in which she had been privileged to hold Cecilia on her lap. She had gotten over her initial shock at how much more fragile and achingly thin-skinned her grandmother was, compared with fourteen months ago. Her eyes, however, were even more questing and percipient.

"Dear child," she exclaimed. "What a delightful surprise. And Agnes, you are prettier than ever." The wonder was that her grandmother genuinely meant this.

As a holiday treat for the residents, volunteers had brought in some kittens to visit the cat-lovers in the home. Agnes and her grandmother got to spend a half-hour with a very active, two-month-old Siamese seal point. The little cat's black diamond face and fine litheness lit up and enlarged the room. Eventually, he decided to climb the curtains and then perched, peering down at them from the top of the pelmet.

Afterwards her grandmother asked: "Do you remember Cecilia?"

"Oh, yes. So very well."

On the evening of Christmas Day, it was therefore a silver grey female tabby, empathetic and sweet-faced, who filled both women's thoughts. She had been a bright lodestar, an unstinting giver of comfort and grace. They sat on a while together quietly, keeping her memory strong and green and giving thanks for her life among them.

Agnes did not check her email until she was back in her room in the dorm. She was reluctant to view any message from her parents, or from Phoebe. She did not want to read that she had been rude or immature; or that she had spoiled their Christmas by her abrupt departure.

Her mother's message was in fact less accusatory than she had anticipated. *It was a shock to find your note, honey. Daddy and I are very sorry we didn't realize how hard the death of your friend hit you. It's so difficult when a young person dies. It seems so unfair. But time heals. The old cliché really does hold true. On the issue of your professor, Daddy and I are just concerned for your safety. Take good care of yourself, honey. And PLEASE keep in touch. We love you.*

Her mother's circumlocution was infuriating. She could not even write the word "murder," but in typical fashion, reduced the killing of a living being and all his attendant suffering to an "issue." She was always doing this. My mother is always shrinking away from human-kind's dark core, Agnes thought. She simply won't look and her denial is all of a piece with her caustic reaction to Piero di Cosimo, and her infatuation with Botticelli's bland perfect goddesses. My mother is a naïve and self-protecting girl who wants everything in her immediate world tamed and prettified. And that's probably the real reason they offered me the cosmetic surgery. It was for her sake, not mine.

How she hated her mother's hypocrisy and willful blindness.

Phoebe's email made Agnes question whether duplicity was endemic in her family.

Oh Agnes, I was so worried you left because you misinterpreted what Georges was saying. He kept telling me how sexy he thinks you are. Allurante. Magnétique. I can't remember all the words he used. He goes much too fast for me sometimes. I felt quite jealous really. I mean about the way he went on about you.

I hope you're okay, Agnes. I'm sorry about your friend. I'm sorry we didn't talk about him. I'll look forward to seeing you in the spring. I'm really sorry you can't see the play and I do hope you believe me about Georges.

The clumsiness of her sister's fabrication both moved and enraged her. Sexy. Did Phoebe really think she was gullible enough to swallow that?

She meant well. Phoebe always meant well. But what she wrote was a lie nonetheless, a naked abuse of language just as unscrupulous as her mother's. It was horrible how people contorted and perverted words to make them cover up a host of hurts and sins and evils. Like "renditions" and "friendly fire" and "ethnic cleansing." Like "humane slaughter" and "experiments for the common good." She wondered how many human and animal lives had been extinguished because of twisted and clotted language.

From a very early age, Agnes had bridled at the precept that humans' ability to speak made them superior to animals. She sensed something badly awry with this self-serving proposition. And what a grim irony if this astounding facility became so corrupted that words were bled dry of their meaning, or became purely a medium for one human being to control another, or a host of others.

Words in the mouths of dictators and demagogues, priests and popes, and misguided, mesmerizing cultists, became lethal, shaping instruments. An entire people could be swayed, by words alone, to regard another as subhuman and therefore ripe for extermination. Under the grip of a spellbinding orator, they would gladly go out and burn their enemies alive in their homes, or tear them apart limb by limb.

Savonarola, whom they'd studied in her Renaissance history class, was reputed to have been one of these compelling, grandiloquent orators. His battering sermons transformed Florence from a highly cultured, questing and exuberant city into a place grim, fearful and sin-obsessed. Agnes was certain Piero di Cosimo had withstood Savonarola's propaganda. He was far too idiosyncratic and self-contained to let another being control his thoughts. Unlike Botticelli, Piero would never willingly have thrown one of his paintings into Savonarola's raging Bonfire of the Vanities.

Nevertheless, living under that repressive regime must have taken its toll, not just on his freedom of expression, but on his mind and body. Savonarola's spies were everywhere. Piero, like every other Florentine, must surely have lived in a constant state of tension, anxious lest his peculiar sins or indulgences be discovered. What dedication and courage it must take to keep one's thoughts one's own; to keep the dance of one's soul alive, in the presence of that all-pervasive power whose very words dealt death.

Once again, Agnes was seized by the conviction this was the real secret behind Piero's magnificent *Forest Fire*. The ludicrously long, vaguely obscene tongues of flame that protruded from the densely green and lacy bush at the near-centre of the painting had an odd rigidity that drew the eye. She saw this as a deliberate ploy on the artist's part, so that we look again and see in these flames the tongues of despots and consummately manipulative men. From this bush at the painting's heart, Piero depicted the tongue of Savonarola at its inflammatory work; and because he was prescient, here also were the tongues of the dictators of the future: Robespierre, Hitler, Mussolini, Stalin, Milosevich. How long was the list? Agnes would personally add the magnates of the meat industry and of pharmaceutical companies whose cunning lies perpetuated the agonies of animals worldwide.

She was more and more certain that Piero meant this bush to be understood as the source of the forest blaze; it was these very tongues that have generated the devastation visible to the farthest horizon where herds of tiny deer flee to the east and to the west.

In the painting's foreground, the remarkable miscellany of animals the painter had assembled — the male and female lions, the mother bear and her three cubs, the boar with the human face, the deer with the human profile, the ox, the heron — all seemed to speak, not just of terror and wrenching confusion, but also of a bond of trust broken. Agnes accepted their judgement with the gravity it warranted. *We spurred you on to speech*, the animals told her. It was our infinite variety, our sleek lustre, our iridescence, our speed, our agility and our beauty that made you cry out in wonder. Human speech began when you looked at us. But what was pure in origin you have made foul.

Agnes wished, perhaps more than anything else on earth, that she might one day do the impossible and converse with Piero di Cosimo. Is this the secret? she would ask. And he would answer yes or no. Or keep silent, only pointing to the one clearly delineated human figure on the canvas: the ploughman who bore on his shoulder the heavy yoke he had removed from the two oxen, so that they could run free and save themselves.

FIFTEEN

The Foreigner

T HE FIRST TIME HE SAW the young woman, she was looking at the caged lions in the Piazza della Signoria. Two things about her immediately arrested his attention. The first was her exotic garb: a tapered tunic and belled leg coverings gathered in at the ankle. They were of a fabric whose whirling arabesques almost dizzied him, a filigree mesh of silver and black. He supposed she must be a foreign servant acquired by one of the noble houses — a Tartar perhaps, or out of Egypt. She wore over her hair a gauzy black scarf, tied at the nape.

Her features had a most peculiar *leggiadria* — a charm due in no small part to the strangeness of their proportions. This was most marked in the distance between her nose and upper lip and slight forward thrust of her lower jaw. It was a face that suggested above all a wide and tender sympathy.

The second thing about her that compelled his gaze was her expression, so jolting in its familiarity. For what he saw upon her features, the shading of grief on the cheek and brow, the lips tightened in bitter indignation, was the very cast of his own countenance whenever he beheld the caged lions. Never before had he seen another being react just as he did to their naked misery and debilitation. The raw blend of compassion and fury on her face was also his, and he felt his blood rush faster to witness her fellow feeling.

She perceived, as did he, how the confining cage crushed the lions' strength and even their will to live. Most days they slept as if drugged and, when they woke, barely roused themselves, only laid their great heads leadenly upon their paws and sighed. It pained him that their eyes were so dull. Worse still was when a fit of restlessness drove them to pace back and forth in a frenzied fashion, a pitiable ritual that made evident how cruelly limited was the compass of their motion upon the earth.

In his view, this violation of the lions' freedom to roam ranked among the most heinous of all his city's sins. It was an affront to their very essence.

He wondered if the young foreigner grasped why the lions' cage sat where it did, outside the city's seat of government; if she knew of the callous tradition that the health of these creatures augured the city's fortunes. So if the female lion whelped, there was great rejoicing. And if the lions appeared feeble and their appetites failed, people became fearful of what disaster might befall them: whether plague, or famine, or the arrival of invading armies who pillaged and raped and left the streets slick with blood.

Conjuror's toys, he reflected bitterly. Such crude usage of the lions' natural majesty enraged him and he often nursed doomed notions of freeing them. But the bars of the cage were as thick as his wrist and he lacked the strength to break them, even with an axe. As to the keys for the padlock, the lions' keeper had them always on his person. This keeper was a man of probity, proud of his office. He clutched the keys as fast to himself as he did his young wife. He would not be parted from them except by violence, and for that option Piero had no stomach.

And so he gave the lions back their liberty the only way he knew how — by sketching them in the wild where they belonged, descending a mountain path to keep company with Saint Jerome in his cave; or in the forest outside the city walls where the male stretched languorously to show off his mane and sinuous waist and the female stalked with teeth bared so that all might be aware of her dauntless heart.

The young women's frown darkened. She clenched her fists; she swayed a little where she stood as if the ignominy of their incarceration dragged upon her spirit. He had an uncharacteristic urge to go and speak with her, even if they must converse in dumb-show. He had just started toward her when someone in the crowd jostled his elbow. He wheeled sharply around, clutching his cloak to himself, for he had ten florins in his purse for the purchase of cinnabar and ultramarine, and the Piazza was a ripe ground for thieves.

Reassured he still had his purse, he turned around again, determined to approach her. But that spot where she had stood was empty and he could not spy her anywhere in the throng. Vanished. But how so quickly? He was impelled to go and stand where she had stood and fancied he felt there a particular softness in the air as if it had absorbed the compassionate heat of her observant spirit.

In the weeks that followed, he began to wonder whether the young woman might have been an apparition, some new species of his fantasia. Had he imagined her because he yearned, despite his reclusive inclinations, to commune with another who perceived these truths to which the mass of men were blind?

Once, he saw her in his back garden where she stood quietly smiling at the riot of tangled vines and profusion of wild mint. But of course that was impossible. No one could scale his high stone wall. Nevertheless, his heart leapt in his chest to see her there.

"Here I am!" he nearly cried out to her — he who would flee around a corner rather than have to speak to his own brother if he encountered him by chance in the street.

He addressed her silently and with a laboured courtesy: "Would you come in and meet this handsome rabbit whose portrait I am painting? Come and admire the incomparable silkiness of his fur, the ebony tips on his ears of purest white." He picked up the rabbit, cradling him in his arms and stroking him all the while to soothe him and calm his quivering as he went into the garden. But by the time they stood amidst the twined emerald cordage of his grapevines, she had gone. He remained there for some minutes, in that cool, green, familiar place which gloried in its own unrestraint. He could perceive a faint glow upon the air where she had been, a sort of living *sfumato* of her form. He went to stand in that place and felt all about him the warmth of her absent self, as if she still watched, in respectful wonder, all this rampant, untamed verdancy that others mocked.

"If she returns, we will be quicker to welcome her in," he told the rabbit. "Whether she be made of flesh-and-blood or spirit, we will greet her as an ally."

He had a most irrational desire to taste the air she had so lately inhabited. By its density on his tongue, he gathers she has not come by her wisdom easily. Her way has been toilsome, beleaguered, and sorely pricked by a Fate pitiless and capricious.

SIXTEEN

May Day

A T THEIR MID-APRIL MEETING, THE Ark members settle on the first of May for their brainstorming session as to what and where their major demonstration will be. They are all to come armed with ideas.

"May first. Cool! We'll be drawing on the most sacred roots of activist history," Zebra said, waxing oddly poetic. "Solidarity. The international workers' movement. The many joining as one to overthrow the system."

He looked so boyish and excited, Agnes felt her spontaneous skepticism to be disloyal. But she could not stop her thoughts turning automatically to the thousands of sweatshops around the world where men, women and children were as good as enslaved, their blood leeched by fatigue, unconscionably long workdays, industrial-strength chemicals and fetid air. Where was their workers' revolution? When would it come?

She liked and admired Zebra immensely, but he did tend to get carried away with lofty abstractions. Or was it naivety? If Horace were here, he would already have injected several snide, leavening remarks. And it did seem to her that Zebra was enthusing about an ultimately empty vision. Hadn't the international workers' movement shown itself to be tragically doomed? All those radiant young faces she had seen in archival film footage, marching shoulder to shoulder, singing the "Internationale". Of course, she wanted to believe. Of course, she found their conviction moving, as she did the bold symbols and slogans on their bright, waving banners. But when one looked at the facts of history — the gulags, engineered famines, censorship, paranoia, the omnipresence of brutalized secret police — hadn't those beaming optimistic youths simply exchanged one form of tyranny for another?

She did not want any such associations polluting their plans for the demonstration dedicated to Campbell's memory. Everything about this exercise must be pure and true and good. It must be nothing at all like the debacle outside the animal laboratory that had culminated in Campbell's pointless death and then the gag of silence Clement Semple had imposed on them. She still found something distinctly dirty about that demand. Weren't they all colluding in a cover-up that would obscure forever what actually happened that night? She could not banish altogether the suspicion that someone had betrayed them. Why else had there been so many security guards, armed and ready for a confrontation?

She wondered if these questions continued to throb in the others' brains as they did in hers. Or were they able to explain it all away as simply appallingly bad luck? What she did know was that nothing like this must ever happen again for the Ark. No blood spilled, either animal or human. Not the least bruise on flesh. There must be a way to make their demonstration a holy act; a ritual untainted by the botched, the tawdry and the impure.

Recently, in her reading about the Ancient Greek mystery religions, she had come upon a phrase that continued to spill its peculiar revelatory light. *To rage correctly.* She saw in these three words an imperative for the Ark's work ahead. Every member of the group, except Horace, shared this rage. When they discussed the barbarities done to animals worldwide and then sat in silence imagining, and shrinking from imagining, the actuality of that suffering, the rage she felt inside her was like a live ticking bomb. Her breath got shorter and faster under its pressure. She often felt physically ill. She clawed unconsciously at the worn fabric of the armchair, or at the cloth of her skirt. She was alert now to the particular signs of this rage in the others: the blanched discs that suddenly appeared on Perdita's cheeks; Pablo's clenched fists; Pinto's barely audible moans; Zebra's pummeling at his thighs; and Minnie's sitting hunched on the floor, drawing her knees ever closer to her chest, then rocking a little to soothe herself. Campbell used to pluck distractedly at his own hair, tugging on the long tendrils at his temples in a way she imagined caused him real pain.

Agnes had not had enough opportunity to observe how Kit's rage manifested itself. Besides, only two primal images of Kit remained to her now: the distraught maenad running, her hair a blood-red veil streaming, her mouth wide open, blaring its single, shrill, unbearable note; and the shorn, gaunt, hollow-eyed Kit, who leaned upon Horace at Campbell's graveside, her beauty seemingly destroyed by an evil spell.

Kit was recuperating at some sort of "rest home." She was still very fragile, Zebra told them. He had spoken with her mother in one of her own more lucid moments.

There were plans to send her to stay with family friends who had a villa in Tuscany. Zebra received a single text from her: *Please tell everyone I will be with them in spirit at the demo.* He relayed this message with a formality verging on reverence, sitting particularly erect, his bony face beaming his delight.

Her message through Zebra is like a shower of gold, Agnes thought. It was amazing how she still managed to wield her goddess powers, despite her illness and debility. But it was Campbell's, and not Kit's spirit, that Agnes yearned to have with them, helping them give their rage the correct form. What they needed was the inspiriting energy of a terrible anger, but not its violence. They had to purge themselves of the crude urge to seek vengeance for all the suffering innocents. Their goal was rather to save — animals from suffering and people from the loss of their souls. The Ark had to find a way to open people's eyes at last. To a peerless clarity.

Nevertheless, in the weeks leading up to the May Day meeting, Agnes found it far easier to think of all the kinds of demonstrations she did not want than to come up with practical suggestions. She sometimes worried that the others might opt for a protest somewhere abroad. Her limited funds simply would not stretch to plane fare to Europe or Africa, let alone money for accommodation and food once she got there.

Then everything changed — for the worse and for the better. In the third week of April she received an official-looking communication from a legal firm in Gloucester. The smooth linen grain of the long envelope, its substantial weight in her hand, the firm's name and address set in a fluid embossed italic, all bespoke a gravity of purpose.

She assumed the letter contained the document her grandmother had alluded to, with a quick, almost surgical precision, when she'd visited her on Christmas Day. Should she have a debilitating stroke, or accident, she did not want to linger in a vegetative state, so would Agnes promise to intercede on her behalf so she could be spared the indignity of a living death? "I cannot trust your father to do this for me, Agnes. He has never really listened to my wishes. Will you do this for me? It is only a matter of signing a power of attorney. Then you can tell them exactly what I want."

Agnes had swiftly agreed. She'd seen her grandmother swept away from her by an inexorable wind while she was then transplanted, like Orpheus in the underground, to a narrow, black passage, its walls compacted by dense love, fear and proleptic grief. All this in an instant. The little Siamese cat clung to the curtain, the potently dark triangular face turned toward her beseechingly. She had held him gently with one hand while extracting his nails from the fabric. He had allowed her to take him on her knee and stroke his fine fur, and this little ritual bonded her again to the earth, and to hope.

When she opened the lawyer's letter, she was sped back to Orpheus's cold tunnel, except this time death was wholly present. She read the words over and over, seeing and not seeing them, because what they told her was impossible. Nana was dead. The lawyer's communication assumed she was already apprised of this cold, incontrovertible fact. He was writing to tell her that her grandmother had willed her a substantial amount of money. Agnes sat, her head swimming, and bit her knuckles. Not Nana. No. She had looked fragile, but well. How could it have happened? Had there been a funeral? Why hadn't her parents got in touch?

She was momentarily furious with them for this callous omission until she remembered that she had been blocking all emails from her mother and Phoebe since Christmas. Now she hastened to her Delete box where she found several unopened messages from her mother. She opened the one with the subject line "Granny" and learned that her grandmother had died peacefully in her sleep (how Agnes hoped the adverb was true and not a lying euphemism) on February 18. *Daddy is going to the service,* her mother wrote. *I can't because of work and Phoebe is busy learning her part for her new play. She's Nora in* The Doll's House. *I know how much you loved Nana and that this will be a hard loss for you, Agnes. But just remember that she had a long and fulfilling life. Get in touch soon, honey. These long silences can fester.*

Agnes shook her head all through this vapid missive. She decided to reply, albeit two months late. She wrote simply: *I visited Nana on Christmas Day. Am extra glad now I did.* She then deleted all the other emails from her mother without reading them. She had been tempted to add a line thanking her parents for being so callous and judgemental on her visit home. If their attitude hadn't forced her out, she wouldn't have visited Nana and had those precious hours with her. Her parents were of no consequence. Nana had mattered. Nana cared.

The first thing she asked the lawyer was about the two cats whom Nana had left with a friend when she moved to the residence. He assured her they were in a good home and that Nana had left them well provided for. "As she did you," he said, "$500,000." This was an amount so huge she found it difficult to take in. He explained the majority of the money would be held for her in a trust fund until she was twenty-one. But she could have up to $25,000 now, should she wish. It was a windfall with which she felt both uncomfortable and altogether undeserving. But she was grateful of course, not least because there was now absolutely no obstacle to her participation in the demonstration. Wherever the Ark decided to carry it out, she could go. To the ends of the earth, if need be.

At the May Day meeting, all the Ark members were present, with the exception of Kit and Harriet and Lupo, who pled ill health and conveyed their "best wishes to their brave brothers and sisters."

"Lilly-livered old farts," said Horace, after Pinto read their message aloud.

"That's uncalled for, Horace," Zebra said, a clipped censure with which they all concurred. No one had expected Horace, who had come at Kit's behest to announce that Kit was contributing several thousand dollars to help defray members' expenses if they decided to go on a demonstration abroad.

"That is very generous," Pinto said.

He looked relieved, Agnes thought.

For the next hour, they vented their moral outrage about the squalid conditions of unregulated petting zoos; captive zoo animals of all kinds; the degrading use of animals in television and other advertising; the deliberate murder of South African baboons that were invading human communities built on their traditional territory; the deliberate extermination of kangaroos in Australia for similar reasons; organized cock fights and dog fights; bear baiting in Pakistan; wolf poisonings and, of course, the tortures endured by millions of laboratory animals worldwide every minute of every day.

This hideous litany of crimes overwhelmed Agnes and made her a little frantic. The atmosphere in the room was highly charged, but it was the wrong charge, dispersed like scattershot. They weren't "raging correctly."

Perdita held up a picture of a baby orangutan whose left hand had been slashed off by palm oil plantation workers wielding machetes. "A baby in his forest home who happened to be in the way of progress," Perdita said, obviously trying hard not to cry.

"The difficulty is the rampant choice," Pinto interjected sagely.

The brainstorming session had already gone on for hours. They all agreed this was sickeningly the case, given the countless situations where the treatment of animals was unconscionable and their lives hellish.

Agnes poured herself another drink from the bottle of Bowmore she had brought to the gathering. She relished the steely confidence the taste of the whisky left on her tongue, and then spread so rapidly and mysteriously throughout her body and brain.

"We're losing our way here," she said, far more assertively than she would have done without the single malt priming her. "It's like we're going farther and farther into an awful carnage, wading through blood, through just heaps and heaps of dead creatures. We have to focus on how we protect their lives; how we make the conscious and unconscious abusers see their wrongs and totally transform their attitudes."

They all looked at her in surprise.

"Agnes is right," Zebra said. "We have to focus, guys. What would Campbell want?"

"Do we know who inspired Campbell?" Minnie asked. "I mean, was there someone in particular whose activism fired him up?"

"Hah!" Zebra struck his forehead with the flat of his hand. "Of course!"

They all wait expectantly.

"Brigitte Bardot," Zebra says, his mouth momentarily mimicking the actress's famous pout.

"Brigitte Bardot!" Horace let loose one of his mirthless laughs. "That's priceless. That's . . . what's the word? That's gerontophilia. Even when he was a kid, she would have been old enough to be his grandmother. In fact, it's darned close to necrophilia."

Zebra leapt to his feet, with his fists bunched. "That's totally offensive, Horace. She's an icon in the movement and she's still beautiful." He advanced on the little man, who continued to sit cross-legged on the floor, smirking, looking as if he could happily be nursing a nest of vipers beneath his shirt.

Zebra seized Horace by the shoulders, pulled him to his feet and begun to shake him.

"Calm down, Zeke," Pinto said. "Ignore him. Rise above it."

Zebra let Horace go and took several histrionic breaths. "Why does he always have to be so damned disrespectful?"

Horace slid back into his habitual cross-legged position, apparently unperturbed.

"Let's all take a breather," Pinto suggested. "Stretch. Go out on the porch and take in the air. Look at the stars."

Zebra resumed his seat in the old armchair, his bony knees drawn up to his chest. "No," he said. "Let's push on. We've got our lead now. Let's look at her site. Campbell would go for this, I'm sure. Let's see what's highlighted on Fondation Brigitte Bardot."

Agnes looked on as Zebra, Perdita and Minnie all get out their smart phones and rapidly accessed the site.

"Hippophagy," Zebra read out. "God! The ritual murder of horses in France. The seal hunt in Newfoundland and Labrador. Dancing bears in Bulgaria. Christ! These pictures make you sick. And bullfights. In France, for crying out loud, as if Spain wasn't bad enough."

"That's right," Perdita chimed in. "Not many people know about the French bullfights. When I was a teenager, my parents took me on a holiday to Provence. We went to a bullfight in Arles, in an old Roman coliseum. When the matador stabbed the bull, I threw up all over my shoes. I hate thinking about it." She was trembling. Pablo put his arm around her.

"I think this is it," Zebra cried, holding aloft his phone so that they could all see the graphic images of the bleeding bull fallen to its knees. "Let's vote!" He was exultant.

Agnes, who could not help thinking of the chance to see Vincent's Yellow House and the fields of sunflowers, voted yes, as did everyone but Horace.

Zebra's face was bright with purpose. "I can rappel from the top tier of the coliseum down into the ring."

"You're absolutely nuts, fetish boy!" Horace barked. "What's to stop you getting gored?"

"Light-weight body armour," Zebra said confidently. "And as I rappel down, up go the banners in different parts of the stadium. Pinto and Agnes hold one up. Pablo and Perdita have another. Ewan and Gerhard have one. And Minnie, well, Minnie can manage one on her own."

Agnes could see it all unfolding resplendent in her mind's eye: Zebra's dramatic flight down into the bullring to end the slaughter, the bright banners rising. This bracing, genuinely evangelical image would go around the world instantly. Their protest will go viral. How many millions of people would see and perceive in a flash what must be done? She had goose bumps at the idea.

"How about August?" suggested Zebra. "That should give us all time to book flights and find places to stay. But we'll have to go separately — except Pablo and Perdita, of course. And leave the same way. We want to get in and out without anyone connecting us through our flight bookings. We want it quick and bold and complete and we don't want anyone hurt."

They all sat amazed. It was done then. They had a plan. But the last word was Horace's. "You're all absolutely nuts. Do you know how many holes your cockeyed scheme has in it? You'll end up in a French prison for years. Or dead. May Day sure enough," he added in a surly tone. "Didn't any of you think of the undertones? Mayday! Mayday!" he cried in mock alarm. "It's the international radio distress signal. Numbskulls." He then left abruptly, screwing his finger into his right temple.

"Good riddance," said Zebra, beginning immediately to search the Web for the perfect body armour, light-weight and impenetrable.

Agnes, rocking securely on her benign sea of whisky fumes, knew that all would be well. They would come through, do all they had to do, and be "safe as houses" as Nana used to say. Horace was bitter and twisted. The Ark had moral right behind them, and Campbell's spirit over them, watching. He will keep us safe as houses, she repeated to herself in a drowsy bliss. She did not consider then all that had gone awry for Van Gogh inside his Yellow House, that domicile of fine fellowship and common endeavour of which he had long dreamed.

SEVENTEEN

The Alyscamps

IN MARSEILLE, AGNES STARED AT the Basilica's bullet-ridden north wall. A lead plaque explained these holes would never be filled in. They are a testament to the World War II battle to liberate this sacred hill on which the cathedral stands. She had never before considered that stone might feel pain. Yet it was obvious these ragged wounds in the dark wall harboured raw memory. This stone was suffering just as palpably as the old men and women, hampered by arthritis and shortness of breath, whom she'd overtaken earlier, one after the other, as they laboured to climb the hundreds of steps up to the Basilica. They were coming to pray. She wondered again if she ought to have offered to help at least one of them, but perhaps their slow, penitent movement was part of their offering to Notre-Dame-de-la-Garde.

Her guidebook told her that this was the most beloved of all Marseille's churches, and that the people called it la Bonne Mère. The Good Mother, in the form of the statue atop the cupola, had watched over the whole city and its port for centuries. Secular tourists like her made the trek up to Marseille's highest point for the sake of the panorama extending far over the tiny roofs to the ships' masts; out to sea the horizon, a wavering, nebulous line, might be the aspirant breath of a sea-god. She fixed on the view below and all around her prompted more by the tourist's duty than by wonder. She took off her sunglasses in an attempt to better study the city's burgundy tiles and stone. A scimitar flash struck her eyes, which she immediately shielded again. The nasty headache returned.

She was badly hungover. She had not meant to drink so many whiskies on the plane, but the alcohol worked so superbly well in allaying her nervousness. She'd been apprehensive, not just about her first transatlantic flight, but also about the protest the Ark would stage in just four days. They had rehearsed the details of their plan so often she thought its components must be written like code in their bones. The schema was simple and flawless, forged as it was by their pure intent; nevertheless, a buzzing anxiety blighted her confidence. What if something went terribly wrong and there was another horrific debacle?

After the second whisky, she'd felt so ludicrously light of head and heart that even had the plane shuddered to a halt in the skies, it would not have fazed her. So potent were the effects of the alcohol in the passenger cabin's rarefied air, the whisky vaporized all her fears.

Now she was paying the price. Her skin prickled. Her body and brain were made of parchment so thin every sensory impression impinged with a merciless intensity. A child's cry drilled into her eardrum. His mother's clinging, hot-pink rayon blouse, patched wet from his tears, was an object at once crass and overwhelmingly intimate, and Agnes turned her face away. Her eyes were still throbbing from their exposure to the Provencal sun. She went into the Basilica seeking a shadowy refuge and stood a moment letting her vision adjust — first to the vaulted gloom of the vast interior, then to the teeming images upon the walls. There were countless little ships, drawn and painted, carved in plaster and in wood: *ex voto* offerings given in thanks by sailors and passengers who had survived shipwrecks and storms at sea.

To the left and right of the main doors, people crowded around portraits of Christ, the Virgin Mary and the saints, each set in its own little alcove. Some worshippers were on their knees. Their lips moved soundlessly as they stared rapt at the framed holy faces above them. She felt both ill at ease in the presence of such fervency, and magnetized by the earnest and unquestioning belief she saw on every face, the frail and the elderly, the vigorous-looking young couples with their babies. She watched a young girl guiding a very old sightless woman toward an image of the Virgin Mary. The old lady's progress across the uneven stone floor was tortoise-slow and tentative. But once she stood before the icon, and the girl helped position her so that she could kiss the ornate frame, the woman drew refreshment there which rendered her visibly stronger.

Blind faith. Agnes was envious. It was just such faith she needed in order to serve the Ark impeccably on this mission, in trusting obedience, without hesitation or fear of failure. She held tight to this idea as she made her way down and around the church's outer aisles.

Once she was outside again, the world impinged a little less harshly. She resolved to drink no alcohol whatsoever that night so that she would be clear-headed and resilient for her train journey to Arles in the morning. If she stayed optimistic and well prepared, all would be well. Zebra's brave leap down into the bullring would constitute an angelic descent. Backed by their raised banners, his controlled plummet to stop the butchery would make ripples around the world. Even if only a thousand people underwent a revolution of conscience as a result of their daring protest, whatever risks the Ark took would be amply repaid.

On her walk back to the hotel, she had to pick her way through the heaps of dog dirt that fouled the cobbled alleyways. The revolting sight and smell infected her mood. Marseille was not at all what she'd expected. The old stone buildings, squares and narrow streets all seemed begrimed, rough-edged and vulgar. She could not stop thinking of the wounds the machine guns had torn open in the Basilica wall. She sensed — through the soles of her feet and the pores of her skin — a hurt in the city that was ancient and obdurate. Was this simply because Marseille had stood so long on Earth, founded long before the birth of Christ? To endure is to gather pain?

But the city's hurt was new as well. She witnessed the evidence of this when she flicked on the television in her hotel room and saw the lean, stoical faces of the Roma people, whom the government was expelling from Marseille. Her French was good enough to grasp that the president regarded the thousands of Roma living in Provence as a "criminal element." The news report showed a Roma man inside a trailer shoving his belongings into a cheap carryall, while a stolid policeman in black observed his every move. The nightstick and a gun at the officer's waist reminded her of the security guards at the animal laboratory. Why did these men always look as if they had been poured into the uniforms; that they were made of molten rubber rather than flesh and blood?

In the newscast's final image, three thickset policemen with closely shaved heads stood with their backs to the camera, watching a bus full of Roma depart. Staring back at them through the bus window was a young Roma boy. His small face had not yet caught up with his adult-sized ears, but his expression was fully a man's: wry and defiant. She guessed he had seen this look on the elders of his extended family countless times and would wear it again in his lifetime countless more.

Whenever she thought of this boy and the three thick-bodied guards surveying his deportation, a shape flitted across her mind. She sensed it might be the classic grim Spectre, brooding and unkillable. Was this the true spirit of History: the oppressive repetition of the same evils, generation after generation? This deliberate expulsion of thousands of people made her feel sick. It was not at all what she had expected of Provence, even if they did still indulge in the barbarity of bullfighting in Arles.

Was she asking too much to expect a little ecstasy on her first trip to Europe, a few moments of surrender to Van Gogh's "yellow high note" or a transporting chambered quiet inside a Gothic cloister? Perhaps tomorrow, on the train to Arles, she would see the fields of jubilant colour that had transformed Van Gogh's palette and helped him channel his manic energy into new forms: the sunflowers, the simple chairs with their seats of woven rushes, the spiralling cypresses that consort with the stars.

Next morning, through the window of the train, Provence yielded up the sublime at last. The sunflowers were a golden sea that flowed to the limits of her vision.

As the train flashed by, she tried to catch their particular character, distinguishing the burnished from the pale, the stout stalks from the slender, the ones that inclined their heavy heads from those that bowed more deeply. As a company, they were prayerful and charged with an energy that quickened her faith. All shall be well. She wondered if this was how Vincent had felt as he made his way toward Arles.

Her pension had the same slatted wooden shutters as Vincent's bedroom in the Yellow House. The walls of her room were not buttery like his, but a pleasing enough blend of terracotta and cream. She was thankful the bedspread was tasteful russet and royal blue stripes, and not one of the garish Provencal prints she had seen everywhere heaped at the street stalls.

Through her exploration of the town, she was already feeling more grounded, in part because many of the scenes were known terrain. She had seen his café, so familiar from the famous painting in which the open terrace is set with table and chairs beneath an indigo sky of parachuting stars. She was not surprised that she preferred the painted version to the reality, with its boisterous crowd of startlingly good-looking young travellers filling every seat. In the brash sunlight, the real café had none of the mysterious intimacy of the one on canvas, where several solitary tables and chairs appear to float invitingly above the indigo-brushed cobbles.

She thought longingly of those magical, empty painted chairs; looked at her tidy, tucked bed and wished Campbell was here. This was a mistake, because the wish brought on an invasive loneliness, that paradoxically grinding hollowness she had known all through her adolescence. She made a fist and pressed it into her belly. She could not afford to be undone by childish vulnerability. She wondered if any of the others had arrived in Arles. And if she should see one of them on the street — Pinto or Perdita or Minnie — could she manage to refrain from speaking to them?

To keep the mission as covert as possible, they had agreed to meet only once before the actual demonstration. Tomorrow at 2:00 PM, they would make their way individually to Sarcophagus Alley in the Alyscamps — the old Roman burial ground which lay beyond the city centre. They had wanted a meeting place not much frequented by tourists, and the Alyscamps, with its broad, treed avenue flanked by empty tombs on either side, satisfied that requirement. They'd be able to review the details of their plan without fear of being overheard or attracting unwanted attention. Until the meeting at the Alyscamp, they were to have absolutely no communication with one another. No emails or texting. Not even a furtive smile should they pass one another by chance. They did not want to leave any incriminating electronic or paper trail. When the demo was done, they were to get out of the coliseum as quickly as possible in case they were arrested for creating a disturbance. Once they were all safely out of France, the Ark would claim responsibility for the protest.

At the tourist office, Agnes learned she could get a bus to St. Remy and the mental asylum where Van Gogh spent just over a year. The hospital was set in the former monastery of Saint-Paul-de-Mausole, a building over a thousand years old.

She arrived at Saint-Paul-de-Mausole just as a red bus was disgorging an organized tour group. The group's guides, a man and woman in their fifties, already appeared harassed. Agnes caught them sending each other looks of mock desperation. There was obvious disaffection in the ranks, most of whom were senior citizens.

"Why couldn't we just stay longer at McDonald's?" someone whined.

Agnes had passed this establishment in her wandering around Arles the day before. The stench of hot animal fat hanging over the outdoor patio had stayed in her nostrils for minutes afterwards.

An elderly woman with thinning, orange hair plucked at the male guide's shirt sleeve. "We'll be safe in there, won't we, Jerry? We won't see any . . . ?" She stopped and frowned.

Agnes wondered what word she had self-censored. Loonies? Crazy people? It had never occurred to her anyone would be nervous about the patients currently at Saint-Paul-de-Mausole, which was still a working mental hospital specializing in art therapy. But there were definite signs of unease among the tour group now clustered about the two guides.

The female guide smiled rigidly: "Those of you who don't want to see Van Gogh's room in the hospital can stay here on the grounds or go back across the road to the Roman ruins."

There was a general hum of approval. Several of them ambled back toward the bus. Agnes decided to wait and let those who had opted to enter the building go in ahead of her. She very much wanted to be alone for this visit, and to give the setting, and particularly his room and its view, all due attention and respect. But she had forgotten how slowly older people sometimes moved, and in her impatience, found herself directly behind this group again in the lobby where they were scrutinizing a stone bust of Van Gogh.

"That's not right," one man loudly declared.

"What's not right, Fred?"

"The ears. The statue has *two* ears." He took a voluminous checked handkerchief from the pocket of his Bermuda shorts and pressed it to the side of his head, groaning.

"You're a card, Fred." His friend clapped him on the shoulder.

The two men laughed, as did the others in the group, although Agnes detected the odd strained tone. She took some comfort in the fact the tour leaders looked chagrined, rather than falsely merry.

Nevertheless, she could not shake off the offence in the contemptible jest, which raised a raw fury in her, and she had to battle to hold her tongue. What could be behind such insensitivity? Perhaps it was simply crude fear. Fred and his cohorts weren't anxious they might be physically harmed. Their unease had its root in an atavistic terror of contagion. She knew how a full-fledged insanity can take a form so alien, yet magnetizing, you are in dread it will take you over. Like demonic possession.

At twelve, she'd seen a man rooted amidst the traffic; he appeared to believe he was a mechanical clock. "Tick tock. Tick tock," he went. He moved his arms in a jerky clockwise fashion imitating the passing minutes. "Time,

time, time," he chanted. "Tick tock. Tick tock." As the traffic flowed around him, car horns blaring, he remained oblivious, his blanched face fiercely intent on his clock-hood, his eyes unfocused.

Agnes had wondered what kind of terrible world he inhabited. She'd felt sorry and mortified for him, that he had so utterly lost his grip on how to behave in a public place. Yet as she'd stood watching, powerless to help, his tick-tock rhythms were so insistent she was afraid she might run into the middle of the road to join him, or start her own relentless time-mime where she stood. When she heard the police siren, she ran away, shaking her arms, trying to rid her body of those compulsive rhythms.

That incident had made very clear to her the insidious, seductive powers of the irrational. How gruelling it must be to have a family member in the grip of such illness — like Kit, who was forced to watch her mother's mind unravel and her behaviour become increasingly bizarre. Did she ever wake up at night in a panic, fearing that next year or the year after, she would not recognize her own face in the mirror; or remember that urinating is something one does on a toilet in private?

Of course, there was no sign that Kit had this cruel disease. According to Zebra, she was recuperating well at her friends' villa in Tuscany. Agnes planned to go to Tuscany after the Ark's protest was finished in Arles. She would take the train to Florence and stand in awe-filled silence before Piero di Cosimo's painting of the sea monster that captured Andromeda. She would look deep into his eye where she was sure she would see evidence of profound love.

To help exorcise the taint of the elderly tourist's crude remarks, she decided to visit the hospital's cloister first. The smooth, cool stone of the ambulatory induced a state of calm as she walked the passageways around the inner garden. The cloister's walls, and the soothing greenery at its heart, would surely absorb a patient's jagged hallucinations and put in their stead an inner well replenished by light and hope.

Was this merely a willful, wishful notion? Hadn't the phantasmagoria that colonized Van Gogh's mind ultimately compelled him to shoot himself, ineptly, in the groin so that even his departure from life was hell-racked? He had four serious manic fits in his fifty-three-week stay at this hospital and, after each one, had to make the arduous climb back to a stability solid enough to allow him to work again. The director of the asylum was unfailingly supportive, giving Vincent a room for a studio and encouraging him to paint outside each day, as long as he was accompanied.

Under his doctor's sensitive care in that tranquil setting, he was able to produce one hundred and fifty paintings. The cool passageways of the cloister gave him easeful shade when he could no longer bear the sun's fire. She had always wanted to see this place that afforded him interludes of peace in a life too often racked by self-loathing and a deranging despair.

She was lucky to stumble on an interlude between tours when she could linger alone in his bedroom, which was preserved largely as it had been in his day. There was the same red tile floor, pale green wallpaper and metal-frame bed. She studied the view from the window he'd so often painted. Where he'd seen a flowing wheat field, there was now a kitchen garden. But the olive trees were there still, and the steadying, jubilant hills whose regnant character he'd celebrated with deepest blue or purple. She was so happy he'd had this respite, with the compassionate treatment of Doctor Peyron, who strove to treat his patient humanely through the healing powers of art.

In the hospital's gift shop, Agnes bought a booklet about Vincent and Saint-Paul-de-Mausole. On the return bus to Arles, she read, wincing, the list of common nineteenth-century therapies for mental illness: opening the patient's jugular vein, applying leeches, pouring boiling water on the nape of the neck, flogging and — somehow the worst of all — ripping out the hair from the patient's temples. All these little barbarities, it was believed, could shake the sufferer out of his or her symptoms. But at Saint-Paul-de-Mausole, they had eschewed such cruelties, and thus Vincent escaped these barbaric assaults on his flesh. Agnes closed the booklet and put her fingertip to the temple of the self-portrait he had painted while at the hospital. The maimed ear was obscured by a blob of white. The eyes were fierce with knowing: both the ecstasy and the abyss.

In Arles, the bus stopped close to the arena. Despite its prominence in the city centre, Agnes had thus far managed to avoid walking right beside its vast perimeter wall. Whenever she'd approached it from one of the radial streets, the massive building, with its two tiers of sixty arches, looked much like pictures she had seen of the Roman Coliseum. Now standing beside one of these huge arches, gazing up at the patchy grey surrounding columns, she felt absurdly small, as if the arena were an omnivorous maw that could swallow her whole. An image overtook her of the towers of bleeding carcasses that had amassed over the centuries inside these walls: the result of murderous spectacles; gladiators against lions, the staged hunts of creatures of all sorts, and now the bullfights. Distaste, and an irrational anxiety about contamination, prompted her to cross to the opposite side of the street. It hit her then how much she dreaded the idea of going inside this building dedicated to ritual killing. The sheer arithmetic of its history sickened her. If the arena could easily hold more than twenty thousand people, how many millions did that make over the years who had paid to see the blood of living creatures soak into the earth?

She stood glaring at the grotesque mammoth structure across the street. Then she recalled the bullet holes in the wall of the Basilica in Marseilles, and the suffering stone. This was no different, she realized. The stone of the arena, on which she had irrationally fixed her distaste, was also suffering on account of the deaths it had been made to witness and contain. It was not the fault of the edifice, but of the men who shaped its purpose.

The Ark would help redeem that blood-soaked history. When Zebra alighted in the ring like a resilient angel to stop the killing, when they all held up their blazoned banners in salute, they would be purifying the past as well as the way ahead. This peerless vision clarified her resolve and she started walking briskly back toward her hotel. She had barely gone a block when she had a seren-dipitous encounter that seemed to validate her renewed purpose. What she saw was a little two-storey stone house with a sign declaring it to be "The Museum of Van Gogh's Room." A reproduction of the famous bedroom in the Yellow House hung in the window. Agnes was perplexed. The house in which the museum was lodged was certainly not yellow. Nevertheless, she decided to visit it, not today, but in the hour just before they were to go into the arena and take their respective positions. She knew she would be very anxious. A good dose of art history — perhaps the museum had the actual bed and the rush-seat chairs? — will help settle her nerves and nullify her tendency to obsess about the risks: the possibility that Zebra might seriously injure himself when he rappelled down from the upper tier, or that they will all be arrested and expelled from college in disgrace in consequence.

Tomorrow morning at ten, the Ark protest participants will meet at Sarcophagus Alley in the Alyscamps. There they will go over the details of their bold undertaking scheduled for two that afternoon. They will inspirit each other. They will speak of Campbell. Agnes was surprised just how keenly she was looking forward to seeing them. *My friends*, she thought. When she was seventeen she had not believed it possible she would ever voice these words with such justification and fervour.

When she arrived at the Alyscamps, she spied Minnie standing beneath one of the huge plane trees lining Sarcophagus Alley. In her scant scarlet T-shirt that showed off the muscularity of her bronzed arms and exposed two inches of solid, toned midriff, Minnie looked indecently out of place amidst the empty stone coffins. She was smoking, staring off into the middle distance.

Agnes hoped Minnie would not unthinkingly use the empty sarcophagi as an ashtray. These vacant eroded stone boxes, stretching in double rows on either side of the alley, made her skin crawl. Their edges were raggedly chipped. They all looked filthy and hulking and sad — like long-abandoned, ill-conceived boats awaiting ghostly rowers. What most disturbed her were the missing coffin lids. Where had these gone? Had the Barbarians smashed them when they plundered whatever grave goods they could find? What had happened then to the bones left naked to the sky in their individual boxes? Did wolves enter the cemetery at night and drag them away? Or had each skeleton simply turned to dust, begriming its coffin's interior?

In picturing the Ark's meeting at the Alyscamps, Agnes had imagined a spacious Elysium where some pulse of the sacred lingered. Once it had been the most famous cemetery in Christendom, a place of pilgrimage where people came to gaze and ponder upon the tiny Biblical figures who acted their stories on the carved faces of majestic funerary monuments. There was even a legend that Christ had visited the Alyscamps and knelt to pray, leaving the imprint of his knee on a stone. The reality before her, however, was broken and desecrated. The gaping sarcophagi were open mouths bemoaning their fate in tones too low for the human ear, but disturbing nonetheless.

"Ag. Hi! Great to see you." Minnie ground her spent cigarette under her heel and wrapped her arms around Agnes.

She felt small and frangible in this embrace. It struck her that the last person to hold her this tightly was Campbell. She sniffed.

Minnie let her go. "Got a cold?"

Agnes shook her head.

"Maybe you're allergic to this mouldy old bone-yard. God, I hate ruins. But I guess Perdita picked it right. The place isn't exactly crawling with tourists, is it? When'd you get here, Agnes?"

"Three days ago."

"Whew! What did you find to do in this town? I'll be so glad to leave. In and out like a surgical strike. Do the deed and depart. That's my plan. I've got a welder refresher course on the fourteenth. Did you know I'm starting up an all-female garage with a couple of friends? There's a lot of women who are sick up to here" — Minnie delivered a symbolic karate chop mid-throat — "with being patronized and cheated by male mechanics. So if you're ever thinking of buying a car, Agnes . . . "

"For sure, Minnie, I'd come to you." She was astounded by Minnie's sang-froid. *In and out like a surgical strike.* Did she have no doubts at all about their protest proceeding flawlessly?

"Hey!" Minnie waved brightly. "It's Pablo and Perdita. Do you ever look at them and think they're just too cute to believe?" she whispered in Agnes's ear. "Sweet though; really good people. How are you guys doing?"

The couple, floating in loose cream cotton shirts and pants, wore identical broad-brimmed straw hats.

After hugs and hand-clasps all around, they all four retreated to the shade of the spreading plane tree and stood watching the entrance to the cemetery. There were still no other visitors in evidence. Agnes hoped it would stay that way, particularly since Minnie's forceful voice carried so far.

Next to arrive were Ewan and Gerhard, ambling with their arms linked and apparently totally at ease. Then Zebra appeared, wearing a black-and-white striped baseball cap, black jeans and a white T-shirt with a silk-screened image of two zebra standing nose to nose. As he came nearer, Agnes felt a stab of alarm. He looked gaunt and the stains under his eyes were the colour of overripe plums.

"Well met, guys." He greeted them all with a grin. "No Pinto yet? I hope the big guy hasn't got stuck in a doorway somewhere. I mean height-wise," he added quickly. "Some of the doors in this town are really low. Anybody else notice that?"

He made no effort to conceal his agitation, shifting his backpack from one shoulder to another; then setting it at his feet; then heaving it up on to his right shoulder again.

"Zeke," Minnie said, "do you want a smoke?"

He looked at her blankly, then shook himself. "No, better not. I didn't sleep well. That's all. But, thanks Minnie. Yeah, thanks . . . "

He dropped his backpack at his feet again and abruptly left them to pace up and down the avenue between the rows of box tombs. Agnes noticed how his shoulder-blades stuck out like rigid little wings under his T-shirt; how he kept having to hitch up his jeans. Or was this gesture a tic? How much weight had Zebra lost? Was the idea of tomorrow's dramatic undertaking, which he had conceived with such upwelling confidence just three months ago, now proving too much for him? "Mayday! Mayday!" She heard again Horace's derisive parting shot, his acerbic tone almost visible, like scissors flashing in the air.

They had staked everything on the purity of their intent, and their unshakeable belief that they were morally in the right. How, then, could anything go wrong? She had unfolded their magisterial schema so often, with such keen appreciation of its component parts and impact. First, the spectators will undergo the emotional and aesthetic shock of witnessing Zebra's acrobatic descent. The angel will suddenly appear and open a tiny aperture in their consciousness into which will flow a wholly nourishing enlightenment. They will see at last, oh glory, and the Ark's banners will rise, reinforcing this adulterated truth: "He Has Rights Too," over the close-up of a bull. "Are We Barbarians?" with the image of a matador holding aloft the severed bleeding ear. And Pinto's choice, "They Are Our Brothers and Sisters" emblazoned over Saint Francis shaking hands with the wolf.

It was all so simple and so perfect. But watching emaciated Zeke pace neurotically like one of his beloved totem creatures held captive in a compound, Agnes was assailed by misgivings. It was too much to ask of him. The banner-holders' part was puny by comparison. Yes, of course, the abseiling into the ring and the body armour had been Zebra's idea in the first place. But when he had ardently embraced this perilous role, he'd been half-blinded by a grief so violent, it battered all reason. He had groped in his churning pain for a ritual gesture large enough to redress the senselessness of Campbell's death. She began to question whether their foray was really about animals' rights at all. What if Zebra's plunge was actually a sacrificial leap into the aching void Campbell left behind? Like inconsolable lovers who threw themselves into the mouths of volcanoes.

This insight, at once trenchant and terrifying, rocked Agnes bodily. She put her hand on the plane tree to steady herself. The touch of the cool, smooth exposed bark calmed her. The unusual mottling of the bark — pale grey and orange and green — was not unlike Pinto's complexion. And he was as steadfast and strong as this tree. Where was he? They were in desperate need of his moral weight and reassurance. Minnie lit another cigarette. Perdita coughed quietly.

"Yeah. Sorry, Perdita." Minnie plucked the cigarette from her mouth and stubbed it out on the lip of the sarcophagus nearest her right hand.

Perdita's lips tightened but she said nothing. She looked away, focusing again, as they all did, on Zebra. The distance he covered in his compulsive pacing was getting shorter all the time, as if his tension was contracting the space in which he could move. In a minute or two, he would be treading a single point on the path, frenetically, like a child possessed.

"Zeke!"

"Zebra!"

Agnes and Minnie both called out to him at once. He had begun to wring his hands.

"We can cancel," Perdita said. "He doesn't have to do the leap. We can still do a protest with the banners outside the arena. We simply can't let him go though with it."

"Get over here, Zeke!" Minnie commanded. "We need to talk."

They all looked at one another, perturbed and pitying, as Zebra approached.

"Maybe it always was a crazy idea," Pablo said. "We got stupidly carried away, wanting something hugely dramatic. Perdita's right. A demo outside will serve our purposes."

"Wimps!" said Zebra. "I've been practising. Lots. From the top of the stands in the gym in my old school. I paid the janitor to let me do it at night. I'm not nervous about the jump. It's just . . . " He stopped. "It's just that I hate waiting. And where the hell is Pinto?"

As if on cue, Pinto's gigantic form appeared between the massive columns of the entrance to the grounds. His dark green shirt hung halfway out of his belt. A barefoot black-haired child wearing a pink tank-top and grubby shorts more holes than cloth clutched the end of Pinto's shirt-tail. A second child — a girl in a mud-spattered yellow dress far too large for her — kept circling him as he walked, badly slowing his progress.

Pinto raised his hand in greeting. "Sorry I'm late."

"Gawd!" exclaimed Minnie. "Please don't tell me he gave them money. Dumb. Dumb. Dumb."

When Pinto joined them under the plane tree, the two children retreated to stand side by side on the path. They seemed particularly wary of Minnie, who glowered, then darted toward them, baring her teeth. "Vamoose, you little shits!"

Pinto stared glumly at the children's backs as they sped out of the grounds.

"They looked so hungry," he said. "I gave them a few Euros. But then they wouldn't leave me alone."

"Pinto, Pinto, Pinto," Minnie sighed. "It's a good thing we all love you."

"Sorry, guys." He was sweating profusely and took off his sunglasses so that he could wipe his face and eyes. The tissues he pulled out of the slot in the blue cellophane package looked ridiculously small against his moon-broad face. Agnes wished she had a proper linen handkerchief to offer him — the kind her grandmother always used to send her father for Christmas and which he would then promptly donate to the local charity shop.

Pinto smiled at her widely, as if he could read her unvoiced wish for a piece of linen worthy of his brow. "Agnes. So good to see you, to see all of you." He took in the whole group with a sweep of his head. "And you . . . come here, Zeke."

They all watched, with a relief verging on joy, as Pinto put his arms around Zebra, engulfing him. He patted Zebra gently on the back and held him a full minute.

Once Zebra emerged from Pinto's embrace, his face was smooth and his eyes clear, his agitation quelled. Pinto had somehow neutralized or absorbed all that chaotic, bristling energy that had made even the muscles around Zeke's eyes twitch.

"He's here with us, Pinto," Zebra declared. "Can you feel Campbell here?"

Pinto's smile was kindly.

"I felt him first yesterday," Zebra continued. He was speaking more slowly and naturally now, Agnes noticed, even given the passionate undercurrent. "I drove out to see some of the troglodyte homes," he enthused. "I mean, how cool is that — to make your home in a cave? And the amazing thing was the colour of the stone on the cliff face where the cave-homes are set high, high up. They must have had to rappel down to get into their front doors, you know? I mean how else could they get into them? But the thing is — the stone is black and white stripes. Beautiful. And I could hear Camel saying: 'Looks like you've found the perfect home, Zeke.' Clear, clear as a bell I heard him. So we've got his blessing for this demonstration. I know we have."

All the time he was speaking, Zebra kept his eyes fixed on Pinto's face.

"That's great, Zeke." Although Pinto's expression was characteristically beatific, Agnes caught the flicker of a shadow on his compressed lips.

"Oh, oh!" Minnie interjected, "happy family at twelve o'clock."

They all turned to see a slender, elegant woman in a navy shift dress enter the cemetery with two immaculately dressed children.

"Do you think that little building down there is open?" Pinto asked. He pointed to the church dedicated to Saint Honorat at the far end of Sarcophagus Alley.

"Let's go and see," Ewan urged them. "We can't afford to be overheard."

They found the church door open. Inside, the air was dank and thickly grey. The floor was littered with cracked and overturned funeral urns and broken memorial tablets.

"Ugh!" Minnie exclaimed. "Can we keep it brief? This place is unhealthy, unwholesome, whatever."

Only Zebra laughed, the sound made even more forced and hollow beneath the vaulted roof. "Okay, Minnie. Here goes. At 1:30 we arrive at the arena, either singly or in groups of two or three. I go in alone. Pablo and Perdita go in together, as do Ewan and Gerhard. Minnie and Agnes and Pinto make up the threesome because they have to hoist the largest banner. You all watch for my descent. I'll be sitting on the very top row, almost directly opposite the main entrance. I'll be wearing a bright red shirt."

"No stripes?" asked Minnie in mock disbelief.

"No. Not this afternoon. The body armour's lightweight but I need a long-sleeved shirt to obscure it and I don't have any . . . never mind. Just remember the blood-red shirt, okay?"

Agnes shivered, but no one else seemed to notice his shift from bright to blood red.

"And when I'm down, the banners go up," Zeke said.

"But how will you get away, Zeke?" It was Gerhard who voiced the concern that sat in their midst like a naked, wailing child.

"Well, there will be mayhem, right? They won't be expecting anything like this to happen. So in the pandemonium, I'll be able to slip away. And if I don't, well, I haven't committed a crime. It's a legitimate protest. It's an uprising urged by the heart. By the heart," he repeated, the glow on his face apparent even in the sepulchral gloom of the defunct church.

"Let's just look at this again, okay, Zeke?" Pinto stepped into the centre of the group, his arms flung wide. He resembled a monumental set of scales, like those held by blindfolded statues of Justice everywhere. He turned his palms upward to signal his transparency; his wide face was open and questing. "There are real risks for you, Zeke — physical and criminal risks. Why don't we just do the banner protest? There are too many unknowns here for you to do the abseiling."

There followed a silence so heavy Agnes felt it pressing on her eardrums.

Zebra took a couple of steps toward Pinto and reached up to place his hands on the large man's shoulders. When he spoke, his mouth was level with Pinto's chest. He had to tilt his chin upwards in order to look Pinto in the eye.

"I have to do this, Pinto. I couldn't live with myself if I didn't do this. End of. Okay? It will be what it will be. But it will be done."

"Leave it, Pinto," Minnie said sharply. "It's Zebra's decision."

Pinto frowned. His arms now hung loose at his sides.

"Is that it?" Minnie demanded. "That just leaves the masks, right? When do we put on the animal masks?"

"Well," Zebra said, "I'm not wearing one because it might move and obscure my vision. But I guess just before you hold up the banners. Okay?"

They all nodded their assent except Pinto.

"Can we put them on now?" Minnie asked, sounding eager as a child at a party.

"I don't know if that's wise, Minnie," Perdita said. "What if someone comes into the church and sees us?"

"I'll keep watch," Zebra assured them.

Agnes heard someone groan. Was it Pinto or perhaps Pablo?

"Come on," Minnie chided them. "I want to go and get some lunch and a beer before I go to the arena. Besides, we have to know who's wearing what mask."

A chimpanzee (Minnie), chow dog (Pinto), gazelle (Perdita), stag (Pablo), polar bear (Ewan), lion (Gerhard) and Siamese cat (Agnes) suddenly manifested themselves amidst the despoiled funerary tablet and jars. The seven masked figures joined hands and raised them in a spontaneous salute.

Zebra laughed as they divested themselves of their disguises, blinking in the dimness.

"That's it!" he exulted. "We're on. We're rolling."

"We should leave here a few at a time," Perdita suggested.

"Me first," said Minnie. "See you guys at 1:30."

Perdita and Pablo left next, then Ewan and Gerhard.

Zebra stood staring wide-eyed at Pinto and Agnes. Twice he started to speak and twice he failed.

"Zeke?" Pinto prompted.

"I have something I have to tell you two," he said.

Agnes's breath was a-flutter in her throat. Was he going to reveal his fear to them and ask for reassurance? Or had the tomb-like surroundings reminded him all too chillingly that his risk could be fatal?

"Okay, here goes. Of everyone that was here today, you two were the closest to Camel. Apart from me, of course."

Agnes started to demur.

"Don't say anything, Agnes. I know about your time with Camel. He told me."

Her hand flew to her mouth.

"He liked you, Agnes. He liked you a lot. Do you know what he said about you?"

She thought she had never wanted to hear anything so badly. Yet she could feel her vanity squirming in apprehension of some clumsy, well-intentioned remark about her appearance.

"He said when he looked in your eyes he could see your soul dancing on the shore beside blue, blue water. Dancing. 'So joyful and clean,' he said."

It was not at all what she'd expected. She immediately hugged these words to herself.

"And Pinto," Zebra continued, "you know how much Campbell looked up to you. 'He's a rock,' he'd say. 'Pinto is probably the most moral man you and I are ever going to meet.'"

Pinto spoke very slowly, as if he had weighed each word on the judiciary scale Agnes had imagined him holding earlier: "Zeke, I really appreciate that, but I want to tell you I don't think you should go through with the jump now. Why don't you just leave it out? Let's do the straightforward placard protest outside the arena as Perdita suggested."

"Yes, I do have to do it, Pinto. I have to do something . . . something irrevocable. I mean an act that makes an absolute mark in our history as a group; something that holds people transfixed, even for a moment. That flight down into the ring is my chance to create a memorial for Camel that he would stand up and cheer about. And that means big and risky and unexpected. It means an act that burns into people's consciousness and makes them really think about the disgusting ways we treat animals. A bold, irrevocable action is my only possible response to his death. So I'm going ahead. And I want you both to stop asking me to reconsider because you're hurting me by doing that."

He stared at them defiantly, his mouth set in a grimace that made him look prematurely old, and even more fragile and spent than before. She turned to Pinto, wanting him to speak the wise words that would pull Zebra back from the brink.

Pinto said resignedly: "If you're absolutely resolved on this, Zeke."

"I am, Pinto. I absolutely am. Like unshakeable. And I can feel Camel with me in this. I really can. There's something else," he said. "Another reason I must do this. It's about the wire that killed Campbell."

"What?" Agnes asked in alarm.

He looked at her with hollowed eyes. "No," he said, "not now. I can't tell you now. Later, though. Yeah, later."

He shook himself as if he must physically throw off this line of thought, then extended his arms. "Give me a hug for luck," he said.

They all three embraced.

"Take care, Zeke," Agnes whispered into his neck.

"You know I will." Then he was gone.

Agnes looked up at Pinto beseechingly. He shook his large head so ponderously he looked like a personification of Melancholy.

"What can we do, Agnes? We can't tie him up or drug him. We can't thwart his will and interfere with what he sees as a moral imperative, tied to his enduring love. I am sorry, Agnes. I am truly sorry, my dear."

She was unclear what exactly he was sorry for or about — the countless lamentable aspects of the lives of humans and of animals? At this moment, these seemed to her so overwhelming she felt a base urge to crawl inside one of the large overturned funeral urns and sleep away all the days ahead. Part of her was desperate for an absolute retreat. She was more and more afraid that Zeke's planned leap was a willed self-sacrifice and that his motives were dangerously muddied. *There's something about the wire that killed Campbell.* And in an hour he would be wearing his own wire, swinging down into a ring of butchery.

But Pinto was right. How could they stop him? She must simply follow through and play her own meagre part in the plan, praying it would all turn out well.

"We should go," she said. "I'll see you at the arena's main gates at 1:30."

"Yes." Pinto squeezed her hand.

[273]

They walked together in silence down Sarcophagus Alley, blinking in the Provencal sunlight that assailed their eyes even through their protective lenses.

Outside the grounds they parted company. Agnes watched Pinto walk away, taking a simple pleasure in observing his long stride and the breadth of his back and shoulders. His sage green shirt was the same colour as the plane trees' foliage. She found this visual rhyme consoling.

At 12:45 she climbed the three steps of the little museum across the street from the arena. Thirty minutes should give her ample time to study whatever relics of Van Gogh's famous room it held. This could not be the original Yellow House, with its yolk-thick paint scraped away. The building was too small and, besides, she had a vague recollection that Vincent's house in Arles stood on a corner, not in a tight row like this slim two-storey edifice.

She was aware how trifling, if not otiose, were these thoughts. Nevertheless, they served her goal of self-distraction. She must keep her disabling anxiety about the looming protest at bay. An unsettling disquiet kept nudging her that their scheme was not only rash, but also arrogantly egotistical. Just as she was opening the museum door with its long vertical insert of plain glass, she suddenly saw the folly behind Zebra's practice descents in the high-school gymnasium. Why hadn't she and Pinto grasped the obvious — that the stands in which Zeke rehearsed were empty?

His faith in his jump was puerile. Because she loved him dearly as a friend, she hated to use this particular word in judgement. Yet it was achingly apt and just as applicable to her and everyone else in the Ark. How could they have been so blind? Across the road in the mammoth arena, the tiers will be teeming with spectators of all ages, turning to talk to a neighbour, gesturing with out-flung arms, standing up suddenly or changing places, shifting a child from one knee to another. No one in the Ark had even considered that there might well be babies and toddlers and elderly people in the crowd: a whole host of the vulnerable and innocent.

"Mademoiselle?"

A woman, whose thick, glossy black hair was swept back from her face and rolled in classic Arlesian style, peered at Agnes from her seat behind a small spare table. There was little else in the room other than a few wrought-iron stands displaying art postcards for sale.

"Billet?" The woman waved a ticket at Agnes, then gestured to the staircase in the room's back right-hand corner.

Agnes stood looking at the custodian, mired in indecision. It was not even 12:50. If she went to the arena now, all she would do is pace and grow more and more anxious waiting for the others to come. She must be supremely calm and reasoned when she attempts to enlist their help in stopping Zeke. "We've set a Juggernaut in motion," she rehearsed mentally, "a blind, insensate machine for destruction. Either Zeke will get hurt or he'll injure someone in the stands. Or both. This isn't the way to get our point across."

She felt better for having composed this little speech. A tour of whatever lay upstairs would help settle her, just as in her original plan. Except that now her goal was to obstruct rather than advance the Ark's agreed-upon scheme.

When she purchased her ticket, the woman had some difficulty counting out the change. Twice she made an error and sighed in frustration. When at last she had it right, she frowned and rubbed the furrow between her brows with her forefinger. Was the custodian perhaps suffering from migraine, or was she beset by some family worry? Agnes stepped quietly and quickly away to the stairs in the corner. When she reached the first landing, she heard voices. She had not realized there were other visitors in the museum and so she carried on up cautiously lest they collide in the perilously compact staircase. It was as well she did, for the room in which she emerged was very small indeed — far too small to accommodate her comfortably, along with the tall man and woman who stood staring at what Agnes could only characterize as a stage set.

She took in the absolute fakery at a glance. It was Van Gogh's room all right, but rendered in painted plywood and Bristol board, right down to the bed covers and rush-seated chairs. Her first reaction was an irritated disappointment. She felt she had been duped and was on the verge of leaving when the percipience and sensuousness of the exhibit began to work on her. She retreated to the landing to give the couple time to finish their viewing without her observing them. It was now 1:00 PM

Some minutes later, the couple started down the stairs. Agnes pressed back against the wall of the tiny landing to give them space. The man glanced at her and shrugged his shoulders and she returned to the exhibit, determined to draw all she could from its clever artifice.

All the elements of the familiar painting were there, including the shuttered window above the bed and the blue door at its foot. Except that neither was real. Like the bed and the little nut-brown table and chairs, they were flimsy, colour-saturated artifacts that drew attention to their own theatricality. Agnes looked long and hard and savoured the point. He was never interested in a simplistic mimesis; what he wanted to get on the canvas was the very instant of collision between the eye and thing seen. Thus lines trembled. Colours throbbed. The light juddered. Not a dead copy, then, but an actual drama-in-the-making where the molecules kept dancing. She thought if she stood here long enough, the stage set would begin to shift and float.

She glanced at her watch and relished her small victory. She had managed to forget about the looming action at the arena for a full seven minutes. Shortly she will leave and take up her stance to watch for the arrival of the first of her cohorts. She will make them see the dangers. Of course she will. It is all so very clear to her now.

She still had enough time to satisfy her curiosity as to what was in the two glassed-in cases on the far wall, a little removed from the main exhibit. In the first she found a much-stained, palm-sized palette, wooden-handled brushes with splayed tips and tubes of paint, contorted from being squeezed dry. The multilingual names on the labels had a pungency that brought him close: Karmin, Blue Cobalt, French Ultramarine. The second case contained remnants of his other obsession — little bottles of vermouth, cognac and absinthe. She remembered the speculative diagnosis in the booklet she'd bought at Saint-Paul-de-Mausole that Van Gogh's heavy alcohol consumption probably exacerbated his manic states and epileptic fits. She hoped he'd never really had to suffer delirium tremens. To shake so uncontrollably that one could not hold a brush — what worse fate could there be for an artist, other than blindness?

And what about the plague of self-disgust that severe hangovers inevitably seemed to spawn, at least in her limited experience? A nasty, doleful, poking creature crouched on her shoulder the morning after her worst indulgences, relentless in its censure. If you drank enough, that kind of daily self-excoriation might well drive you insane.

As if in clinical confirmation, her eye slid involuntarily over the razor which also hung in the display case, along with a pipe and pencil box with a sliding door. It struck her as odd that there was no identifying text with any of these artifacts. She would like to know where they were found. Then it dawned on her that here too she was perhaps being duped. These old tubes of paint and liquor bottles could have been anyone's, plundered from junk shops and refuse sites in Arles or Avignon. The possibility that nothing whatsoever in these cases actually belonged to Van Gogh made her furious. The little display of artists' paraphernalia seemed to her a much more despicable deception than passing off some manufactured, but admittedly witty stage scenery as "Van Gogh's Room."

She wondered how many others had stood here feeling cheated or simply foolish. Not that it mattered now. It was 1:15 and time for her to go.

Downstairs, the woman was no longer at her desk. Agnes assumed she had stepped out a moment for some air.

Then the impossible happened. As she grasped the smooth round door-knob and tried to turn it, she met only resistance. An instinctive panic rose to her throat. She tried again, attempting to turn the knob first clockwise, then counterclockwise. But it remained solidly unyielding. She pressed her full weight against the handle in some magical effort to warm and cajole the unfeeling mechanism. She heard a frantic note when she called out — "Hello! Can you help me, please? I can't open this door."

Her voice rebounded off the high ceiling. She called again, tried the door again. She wondered if the woman was perhaps in the washroom — there must surely be a toilet somewhere in the building — but for some reason could not hear Agnes calling? She searched for another door and discovered one behind the wooden staircase. It too was securely locked. She hammered on it repeatedly. "Is there anyone in there?"

It was now 1:20. She ran upstairs to look for another exit. All she found was the stage set's mocking fake blue door and a skylight through which she could see the very top of one of the arena's grim stone arches. She had the absurd idea that if she could unlatch the skylight and clamber up (but on what?) she could then escape. But the drop down from the roof would be precipitous even if she managed to stagger out there on the slippery tiles. She would fall, break her arms and legs, and conceivably her neck.

She thought again of Zebra swinging down with his wire and harness — a potentially lethal instrument, prone to slippage. She must get out of here. She suppressed, with some difficulty, the childish urge to direct a vicious kick at the bed that was not a bed, but a confection that had seduced her into standing and staring too long, flattering herself she grasped the significance of its blatant fakery. She was trapped here as a result of her own self-indulgence.

She remembered the mistakes the woman had made in trying to calculate her change; how she had obviously been in some mental or physical discomfort. If she had lost count of the Euros that easily, then why not of the number of visitors who were actually in the museum when she left and locked the door? The paramount question was when the woman would return. It occurred to Agnes that she might have missed some clue. Was there a sign on the door with the time the museum would reopen? In fact, there was — a discreet white card suspended from a delicate gilt chain. A little dangling ghost that would announce her fate once she flipped over its blank face. The revealed message was hand-written in a faux antique style with an excess of spidery flourishes: *Ouvert: 14:00.*

She felt sick. By the time the woman returned, Zebra and the others would be in their seats and primed for action. By the time she got inside the arena — assuming she was allowed to enter that late — it was unlikely she would be able to spot Pinto and Minnie easily in the stands. And if she arrived coincident with Zeke's fall, she might witness the catastrophe she wanted more than anything to prevent.

The gory pictures came so thick and fast she had to press her forehead against the cool pane of glass to subdue their hot tumult:

Zeke misjudging his arc and toppling into an elderly couple who fell forward with sharp birdlike cries into the row of spectators below them.

Zeke's abrupt descent triggering a tsunami of panic in the stands.

Zeke impaling himself on the bull's horns.

Zeke falling into the matador and the bull trampling them both.

Pandemonium. Tear gas. Night sticks.

The bull leaping into the stands in its blind terror.

Agnes, in her own unseeing panic, began banging on the door with both fists. But the few people who passed could apparently neither see nor hear her. A man in an indigo shirt with a red tie did glance up at her quizzically; then he smiled bemusedly and moved on.

Perhaps the museum custodian was well known in Arles for her absentmindedness and had locked in visitors before. Agnes clutched at the meagre hope the man in the blue shirt would return shortly with the woman to liberate her.

Time in the little room turned thick as Van Gogh's layered impasto. She paced the bare wooden floor, considering, and then rejecting, the idea of using one of the metal stands, with its overpriced art cards, to smash the glass pane in the door. She soon discovered that these ungainly wrought-iron trees were in any case firmly bolted to the floor.

Several times she nearly yielded to the urge to text Minnie with whom she should now be sitting. At least she could explain her predicament. She did not want her friends to think she had defected out of cowardice. But the agreed-upon ban was absolute: Ark members must not communicate with one another electronically until at least a month after the deed was done, and then only in language suitably oblique or coded.

To calm herself, she tried sitting at the table and took out her notebook and pen. She began to doodle, and found herself writing the name Van Gogh, scoring the paper so violently each pen stroke was like a knife slit. She wondered if this fateful confinement would breed in her an irrational aversion to the painter and his work.

She went again to the door to hammer on the glass, which was so thickly reinforced her fists were soon bruised and sore. She retreated and checked her watch. Unbelievably, it was 2:15. She felt like screaming.

It was then she heard the whoop and wail of a siren, and then another, looping and entangling with the first. Her hands and feet were very cold. All her blood seemed to have rushed to her heart which was lurching in her chest. The Museum was too far down the street for her to see what was happening, but she had no doubt what the sirens signified. Zeke had made his leap. She began to pace, first one diagonal and then another, across the floor. At the diagonals' intersection, she stopped and wrung her hands, imploring whatever kindly powers resided in Arles, *please do not let anyone be badly injured.*

It was in this stance that the museum custodian found her as she unlocked the door. She looked at Agnes in astonishment and began to apologize: "Mademoiselle, je suis desolée . . . "

Agnes fled out and down the steps; then came to a halt, frozen by what she saw. A solid wall of police cars blocked both the street and the sidewalk at the main entrance to the arena. She was at first disoriented by the flashing red lights on the black roofs, like blood splashing on her retina. Then, in the centre of the police bulwark, she was able to make out a solitary white ambulance. She got as close as she could before a policeman waved her back, flourishing his baton. She retreated to stand with a clutch of onlookers who had come out of their homes and shops, pulled by curiosity or concern.

She braced herself against the arena wall and stood on tiptoe straining to see who would emerge from the main gate. Behind gritted teeth she hummed her frenzied little plaint. *Do not let anyone be too badly hurt. Too badly hurt. Too badly. Do not let them take Zeke away. Lock Zeke away. Hurt Zeke. Too badly hurt. Do not let . . .*

She was wringing her hands again. Then came an eerie sound, like a moaning wind caught in a gutter and then freed, and caught again. She rose on her toes as far as she was able and saw two things. Leading the stream of people coming out of the arena was an ambulance attendant in olive green carrying a small figure in his arms. Beside him was a woman whose long black hair was in disarray. Her shockingly pale face looked at first oddly disfigured. It took Agnes a moment to grasp it was the woman's wide-open mouth which created the illusion of a black hole dug into her dreadful pallor. It was she who was the source of the unearthly sound. The people trailing behind her picked up her lowest note; then doubled and trebled it to create a mournful chorus, struck through by darker notes of indignation and rage.

"Mon fils," the woman cried, "mon fils."

We did this, Agnes told herself. We caused this unspeakable pain. And if the child is dead?

She clung to the minute possibility the child's condition had nothing to do with Zebra. Perhaps the little boy tumbled out of his seat and banged his head. Perhaps, like Van Gogh, he was prone to epileptic fits. Or he was suffering anaphylactic shock as a result of a wasp sting.

A multitude of such explanations presented themselves. As much as she wanted to embrace them, she recognized they were each and every one a delusion. Why would all these police cars be here unless there had been some wrong-doing? She shrank from the word "crime."

Then she spied Minnie, still in her chimpanzee mask, her strong, bare arms stiffly resisting the two grim-faced policemen who grasped her elbows on either side, propelling her forward. Perdita and Pablo, in keeping with their Quaker quietude, followed submissively with their police escort. Their eyes were lowered. Their animal masks dangled from their wrists.

"Minnie! Pablo! Perdita!" She dashed toward the phalanx of police cars just as the ambulance siren started up. Once again, the belligerent police officer waved her away, his nightstick mere inches from her face. She waited a moment until he turned to watch the ambulance depart, then tried to get between the two closest cars to reach her friends. This time he made contact, pushing her back hard with his stick against her right shoulder. She fell on the pavement, bumping her head. Someone came to help her up but she was too dazed to tell whether it was a man or woman. She registered only that the hand which grasped hers to pull her up was strong, warm and dry. A large hand. Perhaps a man then?

Perhaps it was the police officer himself. Whoever it was did not tarry, but left her leaning against the wall of the arena, where she waited for her visual field to reassemble itself. Here were the constituent molecules sure enough, but they did not dance nor did they cohere in any familiar shape. A swarm of black specks came at her singly and then in a mass. She had seen pictures of these nasty winged things on Ancient Greek pottery. These were the Furies which pursued Orestes after he murdered his mother, an inescapable curse and proof of guilt. Their ceaseless pricking of the conscience will ultimately drive the sinner mad. The only conceivable relief is through a penitential deed as rigorous as it is perilous.

And what could the Ark possibly do as penance if the child died or remained comatose, forever beyond his mother's reach? She rubbed at her eyes viciously in an aggressive effort to see clearly again. She must try to find Pinto. She must learn where Zebra was and what had happened — and what the police were likely to do with Minnie, Pablo and Perdita. She had not seen either Gerhard or Ewan and hoped they had got away.

When her vision cleared, she saw she was under surveillance. The policeman who had shoved her was watching her closely, together with one of his colleagues. They were frowning at her, with their shoulders thrust forward, as if constraining a violence they would far rather unleash. She thought of the young Roma boy staring out the bus window so defiantly at the two bull-headed officers, and knew that at this instant she could summon no equivalent bravery. She did not want to be hurt. Her body's memory was still too fresh from the scattershot pain inflicted by the security guards' stun gun at the laboratory, and the agonized act of witness that followed so soon after.

She turned away from the officers' contemptuous gaze and started to make her way back around the huge ellipse of the arena where she hoped to catch sight of Pinto or Ewan amidst the emerging crowd. She was surprised at the sponginess of the pavement whenever she set her foot down and at the fact she was listing, even when she stood still. She must have hit her head harder than she'd first thought, although she was fairly certain she had not suffered anything as serious as a concussion.

What if it was only the guilt slowing her, turning her blood sluggish? Why did people used to say "yellow," she wondered, when they taunted others with cowardice? Was that what she was at the core? She rationalized that even if she could find the police station now, she was in no fit state to make a plea on behalf of her friends. People were giving her odd looks and she assumed this was because she was still swaying on her feet. Snatches of their conversation penetrated the fug in her brain. She picked up ugly sounds like "bêtise," "sotisse," "fou," "idiot." The tormenting Furies taking verbal form.

Whether the speakers intended these words for her or whatever had transpired in the arena was irrelevant. It was all one. She was part of the organism that had spawned this abomination.

And if the child died, they would all have blood on their hands. They would be tainted for the rest of their lives. They had utterly botched it. They had not even saved the bull, who doubtless would be trotted out tomorrow for his date with ritual slaughter.

Her head was throbbing. The flickering black specks had returned. The Furies were tenacious. And what of poor Zebra? If she was suffering this sharp-clawed remorse, what was Zeke going through? She had to help him and the others somehow. But first, she had to sleep off the headache and the shakiness. Just a couple of hours prone with her head on a pillow.

Somehow she managed to find the street with her hotel. She curled on the bed in a fetal position and put her hands over her eyes to try to fend off the spectral assault. She was sure the black Furies were capable of creeping under her lids, piercing her retina and from there laying siege to the yielding coils of her brain. She needed a solid rampart, a protective image to gather about her. She tried summoning Campbell, but he came to her headless, his hands scarlet with his own gore. Then she remembered the plane tree under which she and Minnie had stood waiting, still innocent then. It was a canopy, a fastness, a giant distinguished by its subtle multi-coloured bark and its drape of soft greenery, each leaf a little boat to carry her safely over this awful blood-flecked frothing sea that was tilting so dangerously inside her skull. A boat. A little vessel the colour of Pinto's shirt.

When she woke, there was a violet tinge to the light seeping through the slatted shutters. How long had she slept? She was shaken to see that it was shortly after five, which meant she had been unconscious for nearly two and a half hours. Anything could have happened in that time — to the child or to Zeke.

Her head was still sore from her fall, but she was no longer beset by the dizzy confusion. She checked her phone on the unlikely chance someone in the Ark had texted her. There were no new messages. She felt very alone and frightened. She must act and started by changing her T-shirt, which held the acrid stink of her afternoon's anxious fear. Then, on her tourist map of Arles, she located the gendarmerie. The station was southeast of the Place de la République. It would be a long and disquieting walk.

Once she was outside, the pellucid late afternoon light helped her reorder her thoughts. Since she was much closer to the Alyscamps than she was to the police station, shouldn't she try there first? The cemetery was after all their "safe house" in some sense. If anyone of them left at liberty were desperate to connect, wasn't the Alyscamps where they would go?

She arrived at the cemetery half an hour before the gates were due to close. Except for a uniformed guard, who stood smoking a very strong-smelling cigarette, the grounds were empty. In case the guard was watching, she deliberately slowed her pace as she walked down Sarcophagus Alley to the church of Saint-Honorat. If there was no one inside, she would go immediately to the police station.

At first she did not see him, so extreme was the contrast between the clear-edged daylight and the church's crepuscular interior. He appeared to take shape gradually as if emerging from a granular fog. She had some initial doubts that the person standing with his back to her was indeed Pinto. He seemed strangely shrunken.

"Pinto?" Her voice sounded tinny.

He turned slowly, without speaking. His face was so distorted — the mouth agape, the eyes mere slits — that she only just managed to muffle a cry of alarm. His chest was heaving, the noise that came out of his mouth more like an ox's bellow than any human utterance.

She rushed to close the gap between them and seized both his hands.

"Can you tell me what has happened?" These words cost her great effort. She was trying not to scream or to sink at his feet weeping.

He grasped her hands so tightly, she winced. The fact he had hurt her apparently surprised him. He looked deeply distressed and, at the same time, more like himself.

"Sorry, Agnes. Sorry. I've been waiting here for hours. I was beginning to think I would never see you again."

She was perplexed and even more frightened than before. Was he so distraught he had lost track of time? How could he possibly have been waiting for hours?

"I got locked inside the little museum across the street. By the time the woman came back to let me out, the police blockade was up. I saw the boy being carried out and put in the ambulance. And I saw the police with Minnie. How is the boy, Pinto? Do you know? Was anyone else hurt? And where is Zeke?"

He looked down at her vaguely, shaking his head slowly as if he could not understand what she was saying. It occurred to her that he might think she was lying. How unlikely was her story about being locked inside a museum? Did he believe her to be a coward? Was he badly disappointed in her?

"Something terrible has happened, Agnes. Something terrible, my dear."

"Oh, my God! Tell me, Pinto. Tell me, please."

"Not the boy," he said. "Not the child. The boy is all right. Zeke fell into him; knocked the poor little kid over. It was apparently the shock, the fright as much as anything, that made him faint. The boy didn't hit his head. I know this for certain. The concierge at my hotel told me." He nodded glumly. "It's not the boy, Agnes. It's not the boy."

"Thank God. What then?" she asked impatiently. "Have they arrested Zebra?"

He looked at her but did not seem to hear her question.

"Pinto!" She grabbed his wrists to try to bring him back from wherever he had retreated.

"Zeke's dead, Agnes," he told her. "He killed himself."

He lowered himself onto the stone floor, settled his huge frame between a whole urn and a halved one. He brought his knees to his chest and began to make harrowing sounds, the utterance of a wild grief that would never know containment and would forever confound all attempts to move beyond it.

She had heard these inarticulate mouthings once before — when she stood outside his bedroom door the morning after Campbell was killed. Pinto was grunting, snuffling, groaning. His lamentation made the unbelievable true. It could not be. But it was. An onrushing blackness was in her mouth and then her head. She swayed badly on her feet.

Even with his head lowered to his knees, Pinto seemed to sense her imbalance and reached out to steady her. She sat on the floor directly in front of him, trying to banish the hurtling images in her brain. A magpie beat itself to death against a barn door. Naked, emaciated bodies with skull-like heads were shovelled into a shallow trench. She saw Zeke thrown on top of this mass of tangled limbs. She must rescue him.

"How?" she asked. Then: "What d'you mean?"

Pinto wiped his eyes with the back of his hand.

"Zeke panicked. He ran out of the arena as if he was possessed. I think he may have believed he killed the boy. Then he drove to that cliff he told us about. Do you remember? The stone with the black and white stripes where he said he felt so much at home? He jumped off the cliff, Agnes. Zebra jumped down into the chasm."

"Stop," she implored. "Please, stop. This is a nightmare, isn't it? I am going to wake up soon in a sweat and shaking."

"Agnes," he said sternly. "This is a living nightmare. We made it with our arrogance; with our foolish self-delusion that any action we took would be blessed and flow faultlessly from conception to completion. Because we knew we were right, nothing could go wrong. No little barbs or tricks of fate to trip us up. Nothing could impede us. Do you see now how benighted and doomed that notion was? We are no better than zealots. No better than terrorists with bombs strapped to their chests blowing themselves up in a crowded market place. We could easily have killed that child, Agnes. Look at what we've made — a human abattoir. First Campbell, and now Zebra."

"Stop it, Pinto!" She put her fingers in her ears. Why was he being so harsh? She wanted them to cry together, to be gentle with each other in their grief.

"Do you know for sure?" It was a child's voice issued from her throat, small and shrill.

"I had to identify him, Agnes. Pablo and I had to identify him at the morgue. All his bones were broken. He didn't look like Zeke anymore . . . " A shudder passed through his shoulders. He struggled to stand. "I have to get out into the air, Agnes. I have to get out."

It hit her that something was out of joint in what he had told her. How could all this have happened in the space of a few hours? How could Pinto have been to the morgue. Perhaps Zeke miraculously survived. Such things happened.

Pinto was almost at the door when she plucked urgently at his sleeve. "I don't understand," she said. "How can all this have happened in just a few hours?"

He looked at her blankly. "What day do you think this is, Agnes?"

"Wednesday," she answered.

"It's Thursday, Agnes," he told her. "Thursday."

She looked at him aghast. Could she really have slept for twenty-four hours?

She followed him outside where she saw the guard ambling toward them, swinging his key, then making a show of pointing at his watch.

They were silent all the way back down Sarcophagus Alley. It was not until they were outside the gates that Pinto spoke again.

"Did you sleep all that time, Agnes? You weren't drinking?"

"No." She was still stunned. It did not occur to her to be indignant at his question.

"Consider yourself fortunate to have been spared, Agnes. You are lucky not to have been there to witness the debacle, to see the Ark shatter. We are all broken now and we don't even have the pieces of the Ark to cling to. We don't have one another any more. I'm going away, Agnes. I mean I won't be returning to Bremrose. I have to start over. I've so badly lost my way. I have to go somewhere I can purge myself of wrongful pride. I have been thinking all day. I have to beat my ego flat on some metaphorical last; hammer it and hammer it until it is thin and transparent enough for me to bear it. I have to go somewhere huge where I can disappear and then start to see myself clearly: see how tiny and negligible my own life is; and then I must strive to purify that remnant. I know I must sound self-obsessed to you. But how else am I to begin unless I judge myself severely and take my own measure?"

They were standing facing each other now, the day waning. She couldn't stop shivering. How frightened his word "disappear" made her feel.

"I very much want to see you again, Agnes — when and if I can change and find a far better way to help stop animals' suffering. If I send you a message in a year, or however long it takes me to sort myself out, Agnes, I hope you'll respond. That's one of the reasons why I waited for you here today, in the hope you would come; so that I could ask you if you will answer me. I won't be Pinto any longer. Perhaps these names have cursed us as another form of our arrogance. I am Peter now, and it is from Peter that you will hear. Will you answer me then?"

"Yes," she said, "of course." She knew that her affirmation mattered intensely, both to him and to her. Nevertheless, she felt she was speaking into a vacuum; that her words had been rendered insubstantial by a vacancy infinitely beyond the control of mind and eye and tongue.

It is because of this hollowness, she thought, this place where Zeke has been and is no more; a vast, gusty hollowness, painfully and paradoxically full of the dust of the dead, of the debris of their shattered dreams. Zeke is dead and so too, is the Ethical Ark.

"We must each find our own way now, Agnes," Pinto said.

He kissed her on the forehead and she closed her eyes a moment, savouring this human touch in a new time of mourning. When she looked up to ask him where it was he was going, he had disappeared. She could not even catch sight of the green of his shirt, although she stared long and hard down the street.

Eighteen

The Video

S HOT ON SOMEONE'S PHONE-CAMERA, THE video was shown every hour on the French national news program which Agnes watched obsessively in her hotel room. She found it poignant, verging on pitiable, to see Minnie in her chimpanzee mask, and Pinto, whose chow disguise was a smudge of russet, struggling to hold up the banner of Saint Francis. It was simply too large for two. Had Agnes been there, as she ought to have been, she could have helped Minnie hold it steady. She had let them down, and the result was this risible scene, so ripe for mockery, of the North American college kids who could not even manage the simple physical task of displaying their protest sign.

The camera then lurched to focus on Zebra's doomed leap and caught him dangling a moment, his guy wire twisted on some impediment they had not anticipated — a guard rail or perhaps the metal base of the bench. They had been so opaquely arrogant in not studying the details of the amphitheatre's interior beforehand. It was horrible to see Zeke trapped so, vulnerable and humiliated, but, at least at that instant, still alive. He flailed his arms and jerked his upper body, and then he fell, colliding with the seated mother and child. The camera swung to fix on Zeke hastily dropping the harness and racing off the down the steps. But it was the final image, which zeroed in on Zebra's face, lead-white and tight, his mouth and nostrils like holes ripped in a stretched sheet, that made her feel she was impaled on a rusty spike.

She still could not wholly grasp that he was gone. Yet his harrowing expression in this last image told her, as clearly as if he'd spoken, that the Zeke she'd known was already extinct. He could never have recovered his guileless enthusiasm or his unsullied drive for the cause after this ignominious failure, which for all he knew might now encompass a child's severe injury or death.

She could not help but question his craven irresponsibility in fleeing, but sought refuge in the rationalization that his failure had sucked him dry. He'd had no moist vital energy or moral fibre left in him. It was not a man who ran from the arena, but an automaton programmed to carry out its own destruction. Had he already decided on this course when she saw him at the Alyscamps? All that time he was pacing like a frenetic puppet, was he elaborating the contingency plan for his suicide? If he could not make Campbell the perfect ritual offering of a flawless demonstration, then he would give him his own death. Was that his line of thinking? Or could he simply not bear life any longer?

Her hands shook at the invasive image of Zebra poised on the edge of the black and white striped cliff. Did he hesitate at all? Or did the mess they'd made generate a fatal weight that pulled him down? The impact would have broken all his bones. There was a sharp stab behind her eyes as she entered Pinto and Pablo's ordeal of identifying the body. Zebra's lovely angular face would have been demolished, flattened and dehumanized. How she ached for them having to go through that obscene act of witness. No wonder Pinto wanted to go away and try to remake himself on — what did he say? — his metaphorical last? But she could not sustain this idea of beating something flat because it ran too near Zeke's pulverized bones inside a flaccid bag of skin.

She gritted her teeth hard then looked at her watch, amazed to see an hour had passed. And here again, on the news channel she had unwisely left on, Zeke's drained visage loomed. This time she fixed on his eyes. How hollow they looked, as if there was no operative brain behind them, or what brain there was had somehow been corrupted. She flashed back to the conversation at her first Ark meeting about the plaque invading the coils of Kit's grandfather's brain. A thick, toxic paste. She had read a disturbing article some months ago about the brain's potential to turn "toxic" when people witness an event so traumatic they cannot quite take it in.

What if that had happened to Zeke, indeed to all of them, the instant they saw Campbell's head roll away from his body? If that toxicity had eaten into their capacity for reason, just as plaque consumed the brain cells of people suffering from Alzheimer's? Fergus's murder had followed so soon after with the gruesome coincidence of his wire-sliced windpipe. She did not want to think about the torture. Had death been toxic for them and warped their brains in some unalterable way? And the result was the total desecration they'd made of what was supposed to be a salutary and illuminating act: to save the bull and focus the world's attention on cruelty to animals of all kinds.

Instead, they had birthed this reprehensible piece of folly, and shamed Zeke into killing himself.

It was painful nonetheless to see how thoroughly the news channel had recast their protest as pure farce. There was no mention of Zeke's suicide, and only a terse statement that the demonstrators had been released without charge. Gradually, the subtlety of the newscast's propaganda dawned on her: how the police, the city of Arles and indeed the entire nation of France, had been magnanimous and all-forgiving of the youthful, bumbling and misguided activists. The city of Arles, with its ancient tradition of bullfighting and Roman monuments, shone as a paragon of civility and right reason. She found this twisting of the truth unendurable and her heart ached anew for Zeke and for the sunken Ark.

She prayed the video would not spawn itself on other television networks around the world and on the Internet, yet another gobbet feeding people's insatiable Schadenfreude. Global derision: such an end for the Ark struck her as cruel past belief, and at last she turned the television off. She must lie down; her body was so heavy with the weight of unshed tears. When they came, soaking the pillow, coursing and coursing, she remembered King Lear's curse upon his unregenerate daughter that she would one day weep until there were deep runnels in her cheeks. And what would such a deformity matter, Agnes thought, in light of the Ark's accumulated loss? Campbell, and now dear Zeke, who had only ever wanted kindness and respect for his beloved zebras, and every other four-footed, webbed and winged creature.

When she woke at three in the morning, her face was salt-encrusted, rather than scored. She opened the shutters and searched longingly, but could see no stars. Nevertheless, the black night sky demanded an answer of her, as much as would the blinding morning sun. She knew she must leave France. The question was where she would go. She did not feel ready, neither porous nor alert nor innocent enough, to travel on to Florence as she had intended, to seek out and pay homage to Piero's works in galleries and churches.

If there were only a wrinkle of starlight to lighten and hearten her. She wondered under what night sky Pinto was travelling or sleeping. Where on earth could such a man go big enough in which to lose himself? It came to her then where she must go herself — to a city of millions; to the place her mother had gone as a girl and so shamefully passed out in the Met when the docent pointed out to her school group the macabre details of *The Hunt*. In New York City, Agnes could reclaim what her mother had reviled, and look fearlessly on the ripe-red slaughter of beasts, and at the greenish corpse of the hunter, so cunningly foreshortened, with its upturned, rigid toes.

She felt welling in her a desperate need to reclaim her own first principles. That meant, above all, demonstrating how completely she was her mother's opposite. Her insipidly pretty, cosseted mother was a foolish girl; whereas she, Agnes, was a woman who had witnessed terrors and known the kind of shuddering sublime beauty at which her mother would doubtless flinch and then cover her eyes.

How could we bear it, if life were like that? Her mother's obtusely offensive remark when they had looked together at the reproduction of Piero's *The Hunt* had ultimately transformed Agnes's existence and delivered her from her family's grip. She had been hunting in the thickets of Piero's imagery ever since: looking at the mystery of the fleeing animals and the fire, the loyal hound and the slain nymph, and the radiant soul-life so evident in the faces of the gentlest of his hybrid creatures.

What her mother found repellent and bizarre, Agnes embraced. She was by far the stronger, more adventurous and perceptive. She could barely repress a smirk as she pictured what her mother was likely doing at that instant — hemming Phoebe's newest costume or party dress, or seeking out just the right shade of dye for a pair of silk-covered pumps, or tilting her chin upward a fraction so that her little heart-shaped face was displayed to best advantage. How shallow her mother was. It was a great relief to think she would never have to see her parents or Phoebe again. The only home in which she had ever felt truly welcome was the Ark, and it was smashed now, "to smithereens," as Nana used to say.

At present, she could not afford the indulgence of wondering if she might one day find new friends, particularly those who might share her most sacred beliefs. What she must do now was emerge from the wreckage and stand on her own feet.

Who was Agnes? Who was she?

Her mother's opposite. That was the answer that kept bombarding her. And where better to affirm that truth than in front of Piero's canvas in the Metropolitan Gallery that had made her mother blanch?

At Marseille airport she managed to book a seat on a plane leaving for New York City in five hours. The fare was exorbitant and, as she paid with her credit card, she was grateful anew for her grandmother's generous bequest that allowed her to do these things without hardship. She was too agitated to sit and read and so passed the time searching on her new smart phone for a place to stay. By some lucky labyrinthine route, she came upon the website of the Wayfarers and Seekers House, located in Manhattan, a name she associated with safety as much as sophistication. The guesthouse welcomed travellers from all corners of the world, particularly those who had been labouring under trying circumstances and sought "a transformative respite in the heart of New York." It was as if cyberspace had made her a gift of just the kind of warm, responsive accommodation she needed now. The guesthouse was run by Unitarians who obviously had a clear ethical imperative, "called upon to provide travellers in emotional or spiritual crisis with a sure anchorage in the city."

She was amazed to find such language from a hotel in one of the world's most pitiless metropolises. "Called upon" had such a solid, round sound.

She sent an email enquiring about a vacancy. Once again, she was lucky. Yes, they had a single room available. She quickly conjured up these wonderful Unitarians: a man and woman with clear, far-seeing eyes standing with calm, folded hands behind an uncluttered, stripped pine reception desk. They will smile at her as she comes through the door, and understand, without her telling them, all that she has been through. They will show her to her small, clean room where, under their benign influence, she will be healed and find her way, like thousands of sojourners before her.

She twitched as it dawned on her she was picturing her own parents transformed into a fairytale mummy and daddy. It was not just galling but frightening, because this childish fantasy starkly revealed how alone and vulnerable she was, every inch of her bruised, inside and out, by one battering loss after another. Zeke came again, as he kept coming, as a mere a bag of skin full of pulverized bones; and then came the headless Campbell. Gone, and worse than gone, because it was sometimes so hard for her now to remember them whole. It took such an unwavering act of faith, such a transcendental leap, to fetch them back to memory as they had once been. With the wreck of the Ark and its great vaulting vision, she was uncertain she would ever again negotiate such a leap or forge such an act of faith.

What she needed was a stiff drink. "Stiff" was so very apt. Wasn't that exactly what whisky did for her? It stiffened her spine and her resolve; reinvigorated her hope, and took her up, up, up, into a lovely, lofty, glowing empyrean. Sometimes, too, there was a finely erotic undertone, a sensual excitement that played along her nerves and quickened her most secret flesh. And why not? Where else was she to find an erotic charge these days?

In the airport bar she had to settle for Johnny Walker. The French seemed to know very little about good whisky. However, in the duty-free shop she was elated to find a decent selection of Single Malts. She bought a bottle of Laphroaig, whose peat-flavoured elixir she now knew intimately and craved: a roar, rather than Johnny Walker's mundane murmur. She wished she could open the bottle right there, and rehearsed how its sweet burn would feel in her mouth and throat; how, after three or four drinks, she would revel in the sensation of being made new and perfect: like being licked into strength and surety by the warm tongue of a mythical mothering lion. When she reached that blissful inebriated state, not even death had any dominion. I am the resurrection and the life. That was what whisky accomplished in her psyche. It resurrected her and breathed new life in her. Was her pillaging of Christ's declaration sacrilegious? She did not care.

She cared still less once she was many thousands of feet in the air and the plane's cabin pressure performed its perilous alchemy in her blood, doubling the effects of the five whiskies she'd drunk in a row. The nearness of the clouds, at once solid and ethereal, the pure white of freshly laundered, downy bedding, intensified her conviction she had utterly escaped the strictures of earth. Freed from rational bounds, she began to nurture the idea that Campbell, Zeke and Fergus would all come back to life — literally, in the flesh. Why not?

It did not then occur to her that she was sliding into a state wholly self-absorbed and infantile. But eventually she slept, to be jarred awake when the plane landed, and made sharply aware of the thick, sour coating on her tongue, and a headache like an axe blade cleaving her brow. She managed to retrieve her bag from the dizzying carousel and then proceeded through security and customs and immigration in a dogged, mechanistic fashion. She kept telling herself she must be patient in line-ups and answer all questions politely and calmly, no matter how much her head hurt.

Her goad throughout was the vision of the immaculate, Unitarian-blessed room awaiting her, where she would lie down, and drink copious amounts of water. She was badly dehydrated and afflicted by alternating rushes of vertigo and nausea. She had only just manoeuvred through a press of people toward the taxi sign when her phone began to pulse urgently in her hip pocket. There was a little flutter of joy in her chest. Could it be Pinto? She frowned when she saw the message was from Phoebe. She turned off the phone then changed her mind. What if something was really wrong, if one of them was seriously ill?

Indeed, when she opened the message she was confronted by a stark "Urgent!!" in the subject line. The double exclamation mark struck her as accusatory, as did the cryptic text: *Agnes, call home right away!*

It wasn't "home," she reacted petulantly, even as she keyed in the number. Three times she made a mistake because of her trembling hands.

"Phoebe?"

"Agnes! Where are you? Are you in jail?"

"What? What are you talking about, Phoebe?"

"We saw you on TV, holding up the banner at the bullfight in France, where the little boy was hurt. They said the protestors were from Bremrose. You and your friends could have killed somebody, Agnes. How could you get involved in such a stupid dangerous stunt?"

"I wasn't there, Phoebe."

"Don't make things worse by lying, Agnes. We all saw you: Mummy, Daddy and me. It was one of Daddy's colleagues saw it first and told him. 'I think your eldest daughter may be in a bit of trouble.' You can imagine how mortified and worried poor Daddy was."

There was a second's silence. Agnes suspected Phoebe was deliberately staging one of the tricks from her acting class.

"And then . . . he had an accident, Agnes. Because he was upset, he wasn't paying attention . . . "

Agnes's chest was tight. Surely not killed? No, Phoebe would have told her right way.

"He dislocated his shoulder, Agnes. Daddy's in a lot of pain. And it's very hard for both Mummy and Daddy at work. People talk, Agnes."

"People always talk, Phoebe. So what? I'm sorry about Daddy's shoulder, but I've already told you I wasn't there, although it's true my friends were. My friend Minnie was wearing a chimpanzee mask." This was all Agnes could deduce, although it smarted to voice it.

"Agnes! How can you? How can you lie bare-faced like that? We saw you, Agnes."

"It was Minnie, I tell you, in a latex mask."

Phoebe sighed in exasperation. "I'm finished with you, Agnes. I really am. I won't stick up for you any more. It's like Mummy says. You're self-obsessed. You have this stupid, self-pitying idea you look like a monkey. And you don't, Agnes. You don't. It's all in your head. We saw you, Agnes. You. Not someone in a mask . . . So, where are you, Agnes? Where are you?"

Agnes closed the phone, and then looked at it in surprise, thinking how much it resembled a sleek miniature black coffin. A new bout of dizziness besieged her. She had been leaning against a wall while talking to Phoebe. Now she slid down and sat on the floor with her head between her knees.

"Are you all right?" It was man's voice. She tried to raise to raise her head, but it swam so that she saw only his bright blue T-shirt emblazoned with an emerald dragon.

"I'm fine. Thank you. Just a bit dizzy."

"You sure?"

She nodded and caught sight of his running shoes, maroon and white, as he hurried off. It was a human encounter without a face, but nonetheless an unexpected kindness that helped spur her to her feet.

During the taxi drive to the guesthouse, she repeatedly prodded this new wound her family had inflicted on her. She was unsure which aspect of Phoebe's attack rankled the most — that she was a liar, or that her sister really did see her as the "monkey-girl." *She thought I was Minnie in the chimpanzee mask.* The self-image at which she had laboured so hard since leaving St. Catharines and her family was in shreds, just a laughable confection. In truth, she would be the monkey-girl forever. That was really how people saw her. Perhaps even Campbell. Was it pity he had felt for her, then? She needed a drink.

The reception desk at the guesthouse was every bit as pristine as she had envisioned. What was not in evidence was the unconditional welcome.

"We don't allow alcohol here, miss." The receptionist pointed to the transparent bag containing the Laphroaig.

"Pardon?"

"We don't allow alcohol or drugs in our guesthouse. And I believe you've been drinking."

Agnes was seized by two conflicting impulses: one was to stand and weep; the other to pound the desk in a fury. She did neither, opting instead for entreaty.

"You don't understand what I've been through." Even she was disgusted with her tone, querulous and thick with self-pity.

"Everyone who stays with us is shouldering a burden," the woman responded, "or coping with uncertainty. Our goal is to provide an environment with the right supports to help them. And that means no alcohol. The alcohol is undermining your clarity and your strength. Eventually, I hope you will see this. We have programs open . . . "

"Don't patronize me!" What right did this sanctimonious woman have to preach to her? It was not as if she had shown up at their precious hotel drunk, with dried spittle on her chin, her eyes wandering in her head. She was not stinking or inarticulate.

"I must ask you to leave, miss. There are other hotels in the vicinity that will allow you to bring in your bottle."

Agnes bridled at the opprobrium in the phrase, as if "her bottle" were a louche and obviously diseased companion. She bit back the urge to say something cutting, although she had no idea what that might be. Her entire body was swollen with rage, which at any second might burst out in a way she would regret. She grabbed her backpack in one hand, her bottle in the other, and went back to the street where she staggered a moment under the assault of steamy, heavily polluted air. The raw sunlight hurt her eyes. Squatting on the sidewalk, she took several minutes rummaging before she located her sunglasses in her bag. She put them on, took a deep breath, and began to walk, not at all unsteadily. No, not at all.

Half an hour later, she sat on a double bed covered with a lurid gilt-woven spread, in a hotel equipped with its own bar on the ground floor. It was a soulless room, with its laminate surfaces, plasticized curtains and constant rustle of white noise. But she was free to drink, which she did liberally and often, pouring the dark whisky into a glass tumbler "sanitized" for her personal use.

She continued until only a third of the bottle remained. The Edenic lilt of peat and malt had fled many hours ago and she was left with a numbness of body and mind. Her mouth was so slack she drooled, and then used a corner of the bed sheet to mop herself. There was a box of tissues in the room but it was too far away and, besides, her fingers had turned thick and ungainly. Numb, she thought, was a word that sounded like the unfeeling flesh it described. Numb. Benumbed. She tried speaking the words aloud but an unsavoury mix of sweetness and bile spilled from between her lips. Lie still and let the numbness come. If she pricked herself with one of the needles in the package of threads they had left her in the bathroom, she would feel nothing. How did one numb the mind completely so as to obliterate all thought? It was the onrush of "devil" words she wanted most to keep at bay and the bleak, unendurable world they presaged. Depression. Despair. Debility. Depravity.

She must not think at all. But a question worried at the edge of her consciousness, tugging and tugging, as if she had left a thread loose there on which her persistent wakefulness must pull. Until she listened. And so she did.

What if she had hurtled here, to this sterile room, following the same fatal trajectory as Zeke's down the cliff? What if they had both been flung out of the same whirling centre of chaos and this was their fitting damnation? Then she cursed herself because she was alive and he was dead. She tried to sit up but the effort was too much and she fell back onto a pillow that was too yielding and gave off a mocking sigh. She had the remnant of sense, or a grace sent from elsewhere, to turn on her side rather than lie on her back. For she knew if she was sick in the night, she might choke. There was that sliver of rationality left in her.

Then she passed out into a blackness that was total. Even the Underworld would have afforded her more light.

She woke late the next morning to find she had slept in her clothes, which stank of travel and the night's accumulated acrid sweat. There was a taste of stale licorice in her mouth. In the shower, the vertigo was so intense she had to brace herself with two hands planted against the wall as the water thundered down. From room service she ordered tea and dry toast, of which she ate as much as could, only to be violently ill shortly thereafter. She told herself she would be all the better for this involuntary purging. She will stick to her plan and make her pilgrimage to the Met. She will pay her homage to the turbulent power, ethical shriek and superb technical mastery of *The Hunt*. She will look fearlessly and with a schooled appreciation at this painted scene that made her mother quail and faint.

The painting was even smaller than she had imagined, its ornate frame at odds with the roiling carnage it contained. She stood as close as one was allowed, marvelling at the fineness of the execution: the palpable miracle by which oils and tempera applied centuries ago with a brush of squirrel hair could create this heaving, chaotic scene still so densely present; one that gripped her nerves and blood and conscience as much as it did her eyes. They looked so real to her — these brutish hunters with their grotesquely muscular arms and faces hectic with blood-lust. So real that she felt an urge to strike out at them, to stop the slaughter, to save the small grey bear from its inevitable fate, to liberate the strangled horse and give sure refuge to all the animals fleeing to the west, out of the picture's confines. She looked long into the eyes of the solitary monkey high in the blasted tree and saw there what she had never caught in any reproductions of the painting: a despairing quietude, a primordial, abiding knowledge that what was enacted here was both eternal and inevitable.

As long as humans had breath and bodily strength, they would go on murdering animals for their flesh and fur, or for their horns and claws, which they invested with magical potencies. And their tongues, she thinks. Even their tongues. Ox tongues and peacock's tongues, and God only knows what other creatures' tongues.

She became aware that the ominous shadow-work of the painting was steadily seeping out to infect her just as it had her mother years ago. She saw, with a startling clarity, how she had deluded herself as a girl when she first looked at what was happening in the painting. The fact was the animals in flight to the west hadn't a shred of hope. They were all doomed, as doomed as the strangled horse and the massive bear, who lay with its chest ripped open and its heart exposed for whoever wanted to pluck it out.

Even their tongues. Even that. Unbidden, her own tongue and throat begin to shape sounds whose agency she does not recognize. Strange whooping cries loop together mirthless laughter and sobs pulled from deep in the chest. She has a moment's delusional grace when she actually feels sorry for whoever is disturbing the respectful silence of the gallery. Then she knows exactly who it is, and the knowledge is leaden and bitter, but still she cannot stop.

Two security guards seized her by either arm and attempted to lift her from the floor where she knelt and rocked and carried on with her hysterical plaint.

"Calm down, miss, and come with us."

She lashed out at them, catching one of them on his cheek with her nails. Then someone tackled her from behind. She was bundled out feet first, half-carried, half-propelled. She struggled, trying helplessly to kick out at her purveyors, enraged they were treating her like an offensive package that must be disposed of.

"Cooperate, if you don't want us to call the police."

This warning made her quiescent. The police would be bullet-headed and carry nightsticks. She squeezed her eyes tight shut to block out the indignity of what was happening to her. When she opened them, she was sitting on the stone steps outside.

"Go home and sober up." Who was it whispered this in her ear? She'd caught the tone of disgust.

She looked down at her lap and saw she was still clutching her bag. There was money in it. She walked until she found a bar with a sign in the window advertising specialty whiskies. She ordered a Bowmore, for its honeyed, revivifying powers. As the barman poured, she focused on the bottle's label with its familiar picture of Bowmore's iconic white church. It was a round church, built without corners so that there was nowhere the devil could hide. Inside, one was safe, therefore, in a place sacrosanct and pure. All these things she drank down, and the hot disgrace of the recent scene she had made in such a public place, her brush with a precipitous madness, all slid away.

Soon enough she was in that much-desired place where her dear friends rose from the dead; the white horse was freed from the strangler's grip; the hole in the great bear's chest was healed; and the hunters laid down their barbarous clubs for all time. Then the capuchin monkey crept down from the treetop and put out its arms to her to be held. Stay, she whispered, stay.

NINETEEN

A Soured Bacchanal

PIERO RECEIVED A COMMISSION FROM Giovanni Vespucci to illustrate two scenes out of Ovid's Fasti—the first: when Bacchus and his followers discovered honey and its transporting sweetness; and the second: when the eternally drunken Silenus, ancient progenitor of all the satyrs, seized greedily on a hornets' nest instead, causing his fellow revelers great merriment. His instructions were to make both scenes overtly comic and visually arresting, full of vivid and unexpected detail and cunningly hidden allusions to Ovid's text that would afford the family's learned guests fine intellectual sport. Above all, these two spalliera were to serve as windows opening onto a fabled world whose strange inhabitants had such distinctive character, they would charm the viewer into believing they were real.

He seized upon the first scene with a robust delight, on occasion laughing aloud at the odd things that spilled out of his fantasia and onto the tip of his brush. Where had they come from — these fire tongs and common kitchen pots and pans the boisterous company banged upon to rouse the bees from their hive and leave the precious honey unattended? Or the weird codpieces certain of the male satyrs sported: a black feathered concoction that looked like the face of an owl, and a huge scallop shell slung low from a looped waist-cord? What was the origin of their ears, often half the size of the satyrs' faces? — some with the magnificent whorls of rams' horns and others like newly unearthed fungi.

His favourites among the band who circled the tree with its thrumming hive were the contemplative male, who carried a curious baby satyr on his shoulder, and the female satyr who lay on her side in languorous ease in the foreground, giving her infant suck. It surprised him that the god Pan turned out to have the features of a disreputable peddler. Pan sat splay-legged, his outward gaze full of lascivious promise. In his right hand he dangled a bunch of onions. Come, he seemed to cajole the viewer, taste my peerless aphrodisiacs.

The naked Silenus, who entered the throng on his long-suffering jackass, resembled an obscenely overgrown baby. The lardy rolls of his belly drooped over his plump thighs. The excess sagging flesh on his chest created the unseemly illusion of woman's breasts. Yet despite his grotesquerie, the dissolute old god was ebullient and florid-faced. He raised his arm in a general salute, while his followers crowded in close at his donkey's sides to keep him from falling. His expression was doltish, his eyes unfocused.

That he had succeeded so well in depicting this reprobate's stupor gave Piero pause. In reality, he found the spectacle of public drunkenness repugnant. Since the downfall of Savonarola, the streets of Florence were more than ever before coarsened by such dehumanizing displays; it was as if once the Prior's iron grip had dissolved, License must leap from its long confinement with its force redoubled. Piero shrank from the sourly reeking breath of the inebriated, who always had some urgent matter they must impart. But what most appalled him was the vacancy in their eyes. To lose all sure clarity of vision — not to see the dear particulars of nature that could lift a troubled mind, and give evidence of the world's holiness — what worse damnation could there be?

As a young man, he had once foolishly overindulged in an ill-considered attempt to banish a disabling bout of melancholia. He recalled still the horror of his smeared vision, succeeded by an occlusion tantamount to blindness. Perhaps it was his recollection of this shameful incident that infected his fantasia when he began work on the second of the commissioned panels. For here, Silenus, with his bald pate and his paunch, was not one character among many, but the prime focus of the painted narrative. He must show the arch debauchee in three successive plights: falling from his pack-ass when he was repeatedly stung by the hornets he has mistaken for honey bees; being rescued by his attendants who used planks of wood to leverage his great bulk; and finally, having mud applied to his numerous stings while he sat squat and disconsolate. He must also convincingly convey the Bacchic band's reaction to these various difficulties; in every case, an obvious and vulgar enjoyment of the ungainly god's pain.

Piero abhorred men's tendency to delight at another's misfortune. Nevertheless, his discomfiture and frank dislike of the character of Silenus and his unseemly antics inevitably shaped the way he painted the sodden buffoon. The god's flesh was now flaccid as a depleted wineskin; his features drooped to the extent they came near to dissolving. Silenus was sinking into a torpor so extreme he was nothing more than an overinflated fleshy sack.

As Piero pushed himself on to finish the work, he found his will failing. The scene had become despicable to him. He shrank from the task as if he feared the curse of drunkenness he'd depicted would contaminate him. That long-ago morning he'd woken with the sour stench of wine exuding from his every pore, there was a taste of Hell in his mouth. Was this why the satyrs who tried to pry Silenus to his feet looked so like devils, with their pointed ears and cruel lipless mouths?

Vespucci was not altogether pleased with this second *spalliera*, which he considered unfinished, and thus paid substantially less than the price originally agreed upon. Piero accepted this judgement in good grace and felt no need to explain his failure. The second half of the commission had brought him near an abyss he would prefer not to re-encounter. That morning after his self-indulgence, he had come very near self-murder. It was a cautionary lesson that he had wisely heeded since. There were people who should not drink wine at all because it was poisonous to both body and spirit. He had no doubt he was one of these.

And so he clung to his sobriety, with its assurance of clear vision: a clarity of eye and mind that must ultimately steer him through and out of despair. He had no doubt his neighbours regarded his rigid discipline of abstention as merely another of his eccentricities.

The foreign woman, whom he had not seen in the city for some time — now she, he thought, was one who might appreciate his stand and the great maxim: *Cole perspicua*. Study clarity. He hoped she was well and in no way prey to the various abuses inflicted on female servants of noble houses. He found he nurtured a deep care for her, as deep as that compassion she had so manifestly shown for the caged lions.

TWENTY

Laelaps

AGNES WOKE MID-MORNING, STILL IN her clothes from the day before. This time she also had neglected to take off her shoes. She groaned. Coming to consciousness was like struggling to emerge from the mouth of a shark. Her body was needling her, shark's teeth in her temples, her belly, the backs of her knees. *Sécheresse.* She clutched at the elegant French word for a grain of comfort, a poeticizing of her hangover's coarse physical symptoms: the parched throat, gluey eye and cracked lips, a brain in thundering revolt against the dehydration she has inflicted on its gasping cells.

Water will help. In the bathroom, she quickly drank two tumblers, while grabbing the edge of the vanity with one hand to counter the dizziness and stay erect. Her thirst was apparently unquenchable. She avoided the mirror lest what she see drive her back to bed.

After her shower and morning dose of Aspirin, she began the ritual of searching her purse and pockets for credit card receipts. These would reveal the names of the bars she had been at the night before, meagre gleanings from a recent past of which she had little recollection. She had stopped carrying much cash, other than for the taxi back to her hotel. She still wore the money belt she had bought for the trip to Arles, and many times over the course of an evening would check covertly that she still had the passport which was increasingly her sole link to who she was. New York had enabled her to succeed almost too well at becoming faceless. In the bars to which she gravitated — tiny, subfusc places she might consider intimate if she had a companion — no one approached her.

She was grateful to be left alone; to be, in some very needful sense, invisible. Since the incident at the Met, she had begun to dress more conservatively. A plain cerise top with an A-line jean skirt. A black sleeveless shift. She did want to disappear, much as something small and wet and wounded would crawl into a cave to save itself and be healed. Her prime medicament was whisky. It still struck her as miraculous: the swiftness with which the amber-coloured fluid lifted her so high she was made almost unbearably happy; her future was so dazzlingly bright with possibility and the promise of untold wonders, she had an urge to shade her eyes.

After four or five shots, her mind readily overthrew logic and trumped death. Spelled into being by the magical fumes of the whisky, Campbell and Zebra were resurrected intact and glowing with health. She sat in her crepuscular bar nook, always with her back to the wall, sketching their lovely faces just as they came to her mind's eye, quick and so radiant with conviction, the eyes she darkened with her pencil tip had the look of live embers.

When there was the least indication she was beginning to see double or her fingers trembled even slightly as she moved the pencil, she settled her bill and called a cab.

She wanted no repetition of the degrading incident at the Met. She was proud of the fact she had her drinking under control. She would never again appear inebriated in public. When she entered the hotel lobby after her evenings out, she monitored her every move scrupulously. The line she walked across the marble floor to the bank of elevators was die-straight. Not even a policeman would have found fault with her performance.

In her room, she extracted the current bottle of Single Malt from the wardrobe. Her habitually careless decanting of the whisky had left a little pool on the cupboard floor, and this spillage had attracted a stream of ants from deep within the crevices of the building. To the tiny scurrying black bodies in the wardrobe Agnes was mostly oblivious, just as she was oblivious to the breast-high smear of green relish on her T-shirt from the vegetarian burger she had ordered at the last bar. She knew it was important that she eat. Apart from dry toast in the morning, she was managing about one meal a day. Her clothes were beginning to look rather loose on her frame. This fact, too, barely registered.

When she went on Saturday to settle her bill for the week, the receptionist in the immaculate navy jacket informed her that the room would no longer be available after Sunday. He had the air of a judge pronouncing sentence. She smarted under the supercilious chill of his gaze.

"Why?" She heard her own voice with dismay, a child's cry, petulant with an undercurrent of alarm.

He explained very slowly, as if she were indeed a child, that they had a convention coming in, which had booked multiple rooms months ago. As he spoke, he drew heavy score marks on a hotel notepad, then crossed them diagonally, just as heavily. The female receptionist — the hotel seems always to have a man and women in tandem behind the desk — meanwhile directed a tight-lipped smile at Agnes.

"But surely there is another room somewhere in the hotel?"

"I'm sorry, miss. We're absolutely booked up. But there are plenty of other hotels in New York." She could not tell if he intended this remark to be snide. Only when she was back in her room did it occur to her that neither of them had apologized or offered to make enquiries with another establishment. She assumed this perfunctory treatment was the norm for callous New York. She was soon to be disabused of this idea by the chambermaid, Ines, whose insistent knocking and shrill cry of "housekeeping" had often roused her from a late-morning stupor. Agnes's dishevelled and confused state on these occasions had propelled them into a kind of makeshift intimacy. "Bad head this morning, miss? Sit down. Sit down. I will get done fast." For these small courtesies, Agnes was immensely grateful.

On the Monday she was due to check out she stuffed her clothes into her suitcase with a careless haste, having overslept. Ines appeared earlier than usual, closed the door quietly behind her and surveyed Agnes's chaotic packing with obvious distress.

"Oh, miss. I came to say sorry. Sorry I had to tell them about the ants."

"What?" Was this a joke at her expense? Her stomach slid sideways. Her palms started sweating.

"The ants in the cupboard where you hide your bottle, miss. If I don't tell them, I lose my job. Not just the ants, Miss." Here Ines briefly touched Agnes's hand. "They don't like the heavy drinking in the room. For a man, not so bad. But women drunks, they don't like to see that. Bad for business. Other guests complain." She put on a mock grimace and pinched her nose.

Agnes rocked on her feet. *What?* She stared at Ines in defiance.

"I am not a drunk," Agnes declared, even as her stomach slithered and the inside of her head clanged in a clamorous self-rebuke. "I am not a drunk," she repeated. This time she stamped her foot. How hollow her protest sounded. Worse, she perceived a heavy pity in the chambermaid's eyes which simultaneously enraged her and made her want to curl up on the bed and sob.

"Take care, miss."

Agnes glared at Ines. She had intended to leave fifty dollars in the tip envelope for housekeeping. Instead, she inserted a miserly twenty.

Trundling her wheeled suitcase behind her through the lobby, she strove to undo a percolating rage at the management. How the spurned infant in her would love to make a scene and berate the smug desk attendants loudly. But she had made her vow about unseemly public displays and so wisely kept moving. What she needed was a place with far fewer strictures; somewhere anti-estab-lishment and free-thinking. The Chelsea Hotel struck her as a perfect solution. Didn't it welcome junkies and hard-drinking rock stars of both sexes? Didn't it in fact celebrate excess?

She found a quiet coffee bar and settled into a back corner with a double espresso which her stomach soon told her was the wrong choice. She switched to a pot of peppermint tea, Granny's traditional cure-all for anxiety, nausea and cramps. With the help of her smart phone, she discovered that the Chelsea Hotel no longer existed as such. Like so many "heritage places" of character, it was being transformed into luxury apartments. How sad, she thought. But in a city this huge, there must be hotels similar to what the Chelsea once was, the kind of place her parents would shun.

She found a cash point and withdrew two hundred dollars. After several frustrating attempts, she succeeded in hailing a cab. The driver was obese, his bulk exceeding the confines of his seat. When he turned to ask her where she was going, three horizontal rolls of flesh on the back of his neck contracted wormlike. His bald head was covered with purplish spider veins. These things, combined with the cab's reek of pine-scented deodorizer, made her feel queasy and dangerously vulnerable.

"Can you take me to a cheap hotel . . . I mean, low-budget? Something like the Chelsea Hotel maybe."

He grunted. She was perplexed as to what this noise signified. The cab took off and her mood lightened briefly as the rush of air through the open window touched her face. He drove for what seemed a long time but when she checked her watch, she saw that she had been in the cab only fifteen minutes. As so often with her hangovers, time elongated. The entire journey became a protracted agony as she struggled against a rising nausea and anxiety as to where he was taking her.

At last he stopped in front of a decaying brownstone. A stuttering pink neon sign in the ground-floor window told her this was the A-1 Guesthouse. She had not expected anything quite so unprepossessing. Without doubt it was an establishment her parents would spurn. There was a mound of fresh dog dirt on the sidewalk in front of the hotel's pocked stone steps. The orange paint on the door had been deeply scored — perhaps by a knife, or a large dog's claws.

"This is it?" she asked.

"You wanted cheap, right?" His tone was truculent. She did not have the stamina to argue. Besides, she very much needed to lie down. Surely for one night it would do?

"Ninety dollars."

"What?" She assumed he meant the price of the rooms. He could not possibly mean his fare.

"You owe me ninety dollars."

She started to tell him this was outrageous; then desisted. She was just too weak and was feeling increasingly unwell. He pocketed the hundred dollars she handed him without acknowledgement. She sat pointedly waiting for him to retrieve her suitcase from the trunk.

"My suitcase," she prompted.

He sighed. His sodden shirt stuck to the plastic of his seat as he levered himself out of the cab. He deposited her case on the sidewalk beside the dog dirt. Was this deliberate? As he sped away, she tried, Pinto-like, to imagine his life, the sweltering confinement in his unhealthy body and the fume-filled car, hour after tedious hour. Weren't his irascibility and the demand for one hundred dollars understandable?

She averted her eyes from a planter of long-expired geraniums filled to the brim with cigarette butts and pushed open the door, half-hoping there would be no room available. The hallway was long, narrow and dimly lit. There was a faint odour of sewage. What was she doing in this awful place? Why did she ever come to this huge, heartless city? Nothing was working out as she had intended. She had to pull herself together, decide about Bremrose. Should she go back in September? Could she bear it?

A rope-thin old man emerged from a doorway at the end of the corridor. As he came nearer, she could see his grubby string vest, and the bluish exposed flesh which sagged in little runnels, despite his skeletal aspect. He began to cough, so harshly his entire body shuddered, and he did not cover his mouth. Automatically, she put her hand over her face. Was she exposing herself to tuberculosis by being in this dreadful place? Did the taxi driver bring her here out of deliberate malice? But surely that was a foolish, paranoid thought? It was hard to think clearly when she felt so unwell.

"Are you looking for a room?" It was a woman's voice. Although nasal, it had none of the cab driver's abrasiveness. She turned to her left and saw a face framed by a wicket cut in the wall. How could she have failed to notice this aperture, with its rudimentary counter and push-bell?

The woman's hair was the colour of dull brass, densely teased into a rounded pyramid. This rather astonished look was intensified by the severe arcs of her pencilled eyebrows. Her foundation had an orange cast under the flickering ceiling light, and the makeup had already developed tiny fissures, like the craquelure of an old oil painting.

"Do you have a room with a private bathroom?" Then she added rapidly: "This isn't just a hotel for men, is it?" Before she could stop herself, she gestured toward the door behind which the man in the undershirt was performing his cacaphonous ablutions, gargling and coughing by turns.

The woman laughed. "We welcome all genders here, miss, including the in-betweens. I can give you a room with its own toilet and shower. Our policy is that you pay for a minimum of two nights in advance."

Studying the tacked-up laminated card with the various room rates, Agnes quickly calculated that three nights here would cost less than one in her previous hotel. She paid with her credit card and received the toothed metal key to room 11.

"Up the stairs and on your left," the woman told her. "Is this your first time in New York, honey?"

"Yes."

"You'll be safe here. Just make sure you keep your door locked and your eyes on your purse."

Agnes absorbed the perils implicit in this warning as the norm in any big city. She was surprised how pleased she was that the woman called her "honey." Was she that desperate for crumbs of kindness?

She bumped her suitcase up the tight staircase, grateful to meet no men, either young or elderly, coming down. Number 11 smelled of stale cigarettes and was a quarter of the size of the room in Manhattan. Its dominant feature was the double bed with a tangerine chenille spread that had several noticeable bald spots amongst its tufted pile.

She wondered if these were the result of erosion, from the weight of all the bodies lying down and rising over the years. Or had various successive guests plucked out the little tufts, either intentionally or in fits of abstracted despair?

She parked her suitcase against the wall and put the key on the dresser with its haphazard lattice of overlapping water stains. It was only when she had her head on the pillow that she recalled the desk clerk's warning about locking the door. There was a sliding bolt lock, as well as a chain and both of these she dutifully fastened. She even drew back the calico curtains on the window and was reassured to see its inset vertical iron bars. Glancing into the cupboard-sized bathroom, she noted that the small window set near the ceiling was similarly fortified.

She congratulated herself on her move. She was probably safer here than in the bourgeois hotel in Manhattan. Besides, this place had far more character and the woman called her honey. She hugged the word to herself, and pictured Nanny's blanket of hand-knitted squares.

When she woke, it was with a start. Where was she? It took her a moment to recall the morning's gruelling cab drive and her arrival at this less than salubrious guest-house. She was surprised to find that she had slept nearly six hours and that it was now early evening. As she swung her legs over the edge of the bed, she went suddenly light-headed. Her hands were trembling. She felt the closeness of the room pressing, like a hot and thirsting mouth, at her temples and wrists. She needed fresh air. She needed to eat.

She washed her face and tidied herself as best she could in the sepulchral light of the bathroom. The mirror over the sink was small and so high set she had to stand on tiptoe in order to see her whole face. She looked sallow and unwell. Food would help.

At the desk she was pleased to see the same woman with whom she'd spoken in the morning. The reception staff at the other hotel was always changing.

"I know this will sound strange," Agnes began, "but I don't know what part of New York this is."

The woman looked at her and blinked. "You're in the Bronx, honey. This is South Bronx."

Agnes put on as sage a face as she could. She had no idea whatsoever as to where the Bronx was in relation to Manhattan or SoHo or any of the other boroughs. "Thank you. And can you please tell me if there is a restaurant with a vegetarian menu nearby, or maybe a bar with snacks?"

"Snacks," the woman repeated, as if the word were new to her. "Well, you could try the Aardvark. If you turn right when you go out, you'll find it about two blocks down. It has a lime green sign."

It was lucky there was somewhere suitable so close by. She would be able to get back to the guesthouse well before dark. The street was both busier and quieter than she expected. The traffic, although constant, did not halt and snag as it did in Manhattan; nor was there the relentless din of blaring horns. She passed plenty of people on the sidewalk, many of them young couples, but she felt far less hurried and buffeted about in this part of the city. Perhaps the A-1 Guesthouse and South Bronx were godsends after all.

In contrast to its external lime green sign, the Aardvark was predominantly red inside. The walls were cochineal. The hammered tin ceiling had crimson mouldings and the table tops were a shade she could only describe as "ketchup." Because the place was small, Agnes found this mono-scheme overpowering. She decided to sit at the bar so that the vast tract of red was behind her. The bartender was a young man with closely clipped silver-blue hair and a matching earring. Among the bottles on display behind him were two Islay whiskies. She ordered a double shot of Laphroaig, and baba ganoush, the only vegetarian option on the menu. Of this she managed to eat very little; the simple business of chewing and swallowing fatigued her. The whisky, on the other hand, slipped down her throat with its habitual silky burn and sweet promise of trans-figuring joy. Soon her tension dissolved. She was caught up in the play of light upon the shining amber stuff in her glass, but her mind's eye was on the departed and, most especially, on Campbell. Inside her head, he leapt to life again, straddling the Vulcan on the wonderful morning he turned up to take her on the ride to the sea. She rode behind him again in the sun, and inhabited those ecstatic moments as tendrils of his hair escaped his helmet and blew against her lips.

Then suddenly he was there, pushing open the door of the bar. He stood still a moment while she drank his image in. She thought perhaps her heart had stopped and started again. She had to set her glass down because her hands were shaking so. He was wearing a white T-shirt and his face and bare arms were more tanned than she remem-bered. His lovely black hair was longer too, cascading thickly, almost to his shoulders.

He came in and sat at the opposite end of the bar. It was then she saw that of course it was not Campbell. This man was older, perhaps thirty. He had a hawkish profile. The long nose and high cheekbones were both bolder and sharper than Campbell's. But if she focused only on his hair and the proud way he carried himself, the likeness was astonishing — so much so that she had to retreat. She ordered another double and moved to the table in the back right corner. There were still very few customers: only the man and an older couple with two large shopping bags at the table near the juke box. She wondered if the machine still functioned or was only a prop. In fact, there was music coming from the corner speaker above her head, saxophone riffs intertwined with a smoky-voiced tenor half-singing and half-talking the lyrics. "Deep sea," she heard. "Deepest love." She was with Campbell again on the bike, en route to their cave, the whisky strongly powering the vision.

"I didn't drive you away, did I?" It was the man with the hair like Campbell's standing by her table, smiling down at her. His teeth looked very strong and white. She was briefly dazzled, then immediately on edge. Was he making fun of her? Was he some kind of con artist?

"I just wanted to move to a table," she told him coldly.

"Can I join you?" His smile was beginning to work on her. It was so broad and clean. She perceived no duplicity in his face, which was very lean and striking. His dark olive complexion made him look exotic. Could he be Eastern European? She did not like to ask. On instinct she decided she would like to have his company. It seemed like weeks since she had had a normal conversation with anyone. Her last real exchange was with Pinto at the

Alyscamps, and that had been more a dual lamentation than anything else.

His name was Juan. Or was it Guam? Or even Gone? Each time she tried to repeat it after him he laughed so that she knew she had it wrong. He told her he was an artist. When she asked what kind, he would not say. "Maybe later," he teased her. She was already inebriated enough to feel honoured he might yet make her this confidence.

He was sipping his beer slowly. She was drinking her whisky fast. She did not notice this disparity until it was far too late. A wonderful haze formed around his head as if he were holy. She wondered at this; then she decided she was most fortunate that someone so exceptional had chosen to be with her. The more she drank, the more the hard lineaments of his face softened. His brown eyes became larger and more lucent. She imagined she saw in them an extraordinary compassion. She started to tell him about Campbell's death and Zeke's suicide. She persisted in the illusion he was listening patiently, and ventured to describe for him the rawness of her pain.

"Stupid!" His fist hit the table hard enough that the bartender shot him a warning glance.

Agnes smarted under what she assumed was a reproof for her self-indulgence. She got ready to go, vacillating as to whether or not she should apologize for imposing upon him. As she stood up, he put his hand over hers. It was a large, strong, warm hand. She could not help but think immediately of Campbell's touch; of how his bodily heat and strength enveloped and excited her. This man, whose name she could neither capture nor speak, had a touch that aroused rather than comforted her. There was a swirl of something winged and wild in her belly and a fierce heat that spread dangerously downward to her thighs. *Take care.* The tiny inner voice was shrill and insistent. *You are out of your depth.*

"Stay," he said, and the look in his eyes, which glowed with some inscrutable compound of vulnerability and danger, held her fast. She wavered a split-second; the internal admonition was clamorous now. She silenced it as irrevocably as if she had clapped her hand over the mouth of a wailing child. Once the nagging voice was stilled, her mind was blissfully, drunkenly free to imagine in sumptuous detail the sensuous patterns this artistic man would draw upon her skin. Not of course like Campbell. No one would ever make her feel like Campbell had. But she might come near ecstasy again nonetheless.

She sat gazing at the fine sharp contours of this man's face, and when she could bear it, into his eyes. Her body hummed with desire. As if he caught this vibration, he suddenly gripped her bare calf between his legs. This swift, surreptitious claim astonished her. Her legs parted. This opening too he seemed to sense by means of a sexual radar with which she has had little experience. Under the table, he began to make teasing, feathery strokes on her inner thigh. A rush of delight and fear ran through her. The tormenting idea assaulted her that this same amalgam of contradictory emotion might have seized Zeke as he'd stood swaying at the cliff's edge.

"Don't, Zeke." She entered the picture as she so often did these days, to grasp him around the waist and pull him back. This imagined scene, with all its pathetic revisionism, almost made her pull back herself. She did not know this man with whom she was about to plunge into a darkness aglitter with danger. She very nearly retreated, but the enticements — most particularly of the protective circle of his strong arms and the perfect oblivion she would find there — were too much for her.

Suddenly they were outside her room in the A-1 Guesthouse. She had no recollection of how they'd got there. She managed, after much fumbling during which he swore under his breath, to unlock the door. Despite her befuddlement, she remembered to slide the bolt and put the chain on the door once they were safely inside. She turned to face him then, expectant, her arms loose at her sides, as if she were making a gift of herself.

He seized her roughly around the waist and threw her on to the bed. She lay looking up at him, her legs and her lips parted. He sat on the side of the bed and yanked up her T-shirt. He looked angry when he saw her bra. She sat up to unhook it and tossed it on the floor. With her breasts exposed, she greedily expected that his mouth would soon fasten on one nipple, while his fingers caress the other. It was what Campbell had done to her. Already she shuddered as the blood-red cord pulled taut inside her. She closed her eyes to ready herself for the surfeit of pleasure that was about to come, but the world lurched sickeningly as soon as she lowered her lids and she was forced to open them again. His face was very close to hers. His expression had nothing at all to do with desire. His features were contorted either by hatred or disgust.

She sat bolt upright and pulled her T-shirt down to cover herself. He seized her hair and pushed her head back onto the pillow. He put his mouth next to her ear and whispered: "I feel really sorry for you because you are stupid like an animal."

She was stunned, humiliated and enraged. But, as yet, she was not terrified. Then she heard a flicking sound that turned her stomach. He was pressing the tip of a very cold, sharp blade into the base of her throat. She tried to cry out but the pressure he was exerting impeded her speech. She gasped and, as he dug the point deeper, she felt her skin yield and the seep of warm blood begin to trickle around her neck.

"I feel really sorry for you," he repeated, this time between gritted teeth, "because you are stupid like an animal."

She lay rigid, certain that if she moved even slightly, he would plunge the knife in with all his might. If only she could lunge at him or grab something heavy to hit him. She did not want to die in this squalid hotel room. She was tortured too by the idea that the last words she would ever hear from another human being were a calumny. What could be more evil than the assumption that animals were stupid?

Abruptly he removed the knife. She was just summoning her breath to scream when he clapped his hand over her mouth and then straddled her, pinning her arms down with his knees. He made a slashing motion in the air and she understood he was miming the cut he was about to make in earnest across her windpipe.

She pictured Pinto's face and thought how sorry he would be if ever he learned of her death. It was at this instant that the man froze. A look of alarm shadowed his face.

"What the fuck?"

She heard it too then: the low rumbling growl of a dog that was about to strike. Stunned, and disbelieving, she still had sufficient presence of mind to get off the bed and grab the bedside lamp, the nearest object to hand.

The man yelped as the dog, a huge chestnut-brown hound, clamped its jaws into his knife hand. "Get off, you damned bastard."

The hound loosened its hold and took up a position between Agnes and her attacker. Its teeth were bared. Its entire body was tensed in readiness to leap at his throat.

Agnes watched with a kind of crazed joy as the man staggered to the door and undid both locks. She felt faint and had to right her balance by putting her hand on the dog's back. The animal seemed to sense her legs were shaking and kept close as she made her way to the door to refasten the bolt and the chain. Then she slid to the floor and sat with her back against the door. She put her finger to the wound in her throat. It came away red and sticky, but by blind touch alone the hole did not seem large.

The dog sat opposite, watching her sorrowfully.

"Laelaps?" she asked in wonder. "Is that who you are?"

The hound bent his head so that his nose brushed her knee. She stroked his head, worshipfully, and rightly so. Then she struggled to her feet and went to wash out the wound before collapsing on the bed. The dog sat on the floor beside her. His presence steadied her. When she began to shake or feared she would succumb to the hysteria coiled in her chest, she reached out to run her fingers along his silky back.

In the morning there was not the least sign a dog was ever in the room. She scrutinized the bedside mat and the bed cover and found not a single hair. I did not imagine it, she told herself over and over. The wound at the base of her throat was real enough, as was the taint of self-disgust.

She stared unflinchingly into the mirror over the stained and pitted sink and admitted the fullness of her folly. She was indeed a drunk, just as Ines had said as casually as if it were a given. She was grateful to be still alive; to be made to see through her squalid brush with death how her heedless drinking had degraded and demeaned her, and imperilled her intelligence.

No one will ever believe her if she tries to tell them how she was saved. A brown hound named Laelaps, who exists solely in two dimensions in a painting on wood in London's National Gallery, leapt to life and drove a murderer from her bed. What happened defies and vaults over reason. It is both mystery and wonder and she is reconciled to leaving it there. She has never before received such a gift. She has grave doubts she is worthy.

An hour later, she stood at the reception desk at the Wayfarers' Hotel, asking about a program to help her overcome her addiction.

"What is your presenting problem?" It was the same woman with iron-grey curls who had last time barred her entry.

"Alcohol," she said. "Whisky."

This time they took her in.

TWENTY-ONE

On the Fatehpur Sikri Road

WHEN HE CUPPED HIS HAND over the dog's head, Pinto smiled in amazement at how perfectly it fit the cradle of his palm. His was a very large hand, but then this was a very large dog — a Labrador, the colour of well-aged ivory. For each of the three nights Pinto had eaten in this simple restaurant in Pokhara-Lakeside, the dog had come to his side when he was nearing the end of his meal. Not to beg, as other dogs might, but to sit silent and composed, letting Pinto stroke him. Now and then, the dog looked up at him and held his gaze. The lustrous brown eyes conveyed an unmistakable benevolence. He was struck, most happily, by the idea the dog had an ancient soul, continually refined by the holy, rarefied air of Nepal.

All three evenings he had felt a great contentment in the dog's vastly companionable presence. Although it was he who was stroking the dog, he felt it was the dog touching him, and somehow speaking to him, in a language either just above or below the range of human hearing.

"Be well," the dog seemed to say. "You have come through. Now continue on."

"His name is John," the restaurant owner told him as he settled his bill. "He likes tourists."

Pinto thought John a wonderful name for a dog: unexpected, yet strong, straightforward and noble. He was grateful to have it, to hold in remembrance because he knew he was unlikely ever to see the dog again. By noon tomorrow he would be crunched into the too-small seat of the two-prop plane taking him back to Kathmandu. From there he would fly to Delhi where his immersion in something huge, which he had described so fumblingly for Agnes, would begin in earnest. He had wanted to begin his journey with the calmer, emptier space of Nepal; to have the clear-limned might of the mountains clarify his mind for what was to come. For how could India be anything but overwhelming?

Perhaps the dog sensed his anxiety and by his proximity sought to reassure him. In that case, how superbly well John had communicated his good wishes. As Pinto left the restaurant, he looked back to where John still sat by the empty chair. His eyes, fixed on Pinto's face, were benign rather than sorrowful. "Goodbye." He resisted the urge to rush back and throw his arms about John's neck, and bury his face in the thick fur as he used to do with Yangtze. It would not be seemly.

"Goodbye," he said again, only silently this time. He turned quickly away and began walking back to his hotel with its rooftop view of the Annapurnas. They were invisible now, swallowed by the humid black night. At 4:00 AM a taxi would come to drive him up the perilous, rutted roads to Sarangkot so that he could have an ideal view of the sunrise over the mountains.

When he woke to the din of the mechanical alarm clock he had used since he was a boy, Pinto found Pokhara afflicted by one of its regular power cuts. He groped about and managed to find and light the candle the hotel management provided for these situations and dressed as quickly as he could in the murk. Then he carried the candle to the bathroom where he applied a liberal pasting of sun block. He did not want to risk a severe burn once the sun was up. It had not occurred to him when he booked his flight in such haste that he was coming to the subcontinent at the worst possible time for his sensitive flesh. Now he would be stuck with fierce heat and monsoons, particularly when he entered India. But it had to be now. He was compelled, as if by the chart of a ritual dance laid out at his feet, to follow this journey through step-by-step. Or be damned.

His driver was waiting with a flashlight outside. Pinto followed, letting the little pool of light guide his feet on the path to the parking lot. When he got into the car, he was enveloped by the scent of burning incense. He told the driver how good the jasmine smelled. "Every morning I am burning incense and praying to my god," the man replied. Pinto detected not the least hint of self-regard or soured duty in this statement. He had to soothe away an unworthy prickle of envy.

Once out of the city, the car began to climb the switchback mountain road, sometimes veering sharply right or left to avoid foundering in potholes at least a foot deep, and several wide. The driver negotiated all these literal pitfalls with calm expertise. When they reached Sarangkot, the driver parked the car under a canvas canopy and then led Pinto several hundred feet along the village road with its tiny, open-front shops and two-storey houses of pale unadorned stone. He stopped at the base of some steps leading up to a rooftop terrace. "You can watch the sunrise from up there," he said. When he reached the roof, Pinto saw a dozen other watchers, all apparently tourists like him. Several of them were smoking, which seemed to him disrespectful and sullying of the occasion. He sat, toward the back of the group, in one of the moulded plastic chairs set in rows facing the still-invisible mountains. Was he expected to pay his host? Or was this vantage point for the sunrise included in the fee he had already paid his driver? A beautiful, wiry Nepalese woman of about Agnes's height brought him a cup of tea and offered him a woolen wrap of sea green and blue to put around his shoulders. "It is cold in the mountains in the morning," she said.

He saw the lineaments of the mountains repeated in the strong bones of her face and in her lithe movement. He wished his body were that spare. If he were leaner and far harder of muscle, wouldn't he better absorb the natural glory of the world, and the monumental stillness of Nepal's god-bearing mountains? He chided himself. He was doing it again, letting egotistic obsession corrupt the moment and undermine his attention. He must not miss the instant when the mountains first took shape out of the clear dawn air.

He gripped the arms of his plastic chair as the roosters began to crow. It would be soon then. Even with his sunglasses on, he could not bear to look for long at the gigantic fiery ball riding its sea of gold-pink. He was not happy with "gold-pink." Agnes would probably have a precise word for this magnificent drenching colour. Like heaped rose petals threaded with golden stamens, he wanted to tell her.

Then they were coming. The Annapurnas were emerging, the sight catching him somewhere between humility and wonder, shaken to the marrow that he should be privy to such a sight. When at last they were fully there — these dazzling, inscrutable kings and queens at the top of the world — he understood how the world must have looked on the first day of creation.

This is the first day, he thought, and the Annapurnas re-enact it with every sunrise. His eye was drawn, as always, to the extraordinary fishtail peak, which seemed simultaneously to shimmer and to leap into the air. He interpreted this imagined movement as the yearning the mountain instilled in him — to be good and to find God. At that instant the fishtail mountain smote him with a bolt of light that emptied him of all craving.

He blinked and realized he had been absent some time. He was the only watcher left on the rooftop. He got up quickly and folded the shawl in four on the back of his chair as the other tourists had done.

As he was about to descend the steps to the street, he hesitated, uncertain whether he should offer to pay for his tea, or if this would offend his hostess. The woman beckoned to him with her small, strong, brown hand. She showed him the tall, wide wooden loom where a solidly reassuring pattern was emerging from the single, tensile strands enclosing emptiness. This was another kind of marvel, and he stood nodding, hoping this gesture conveyed his appreciation for her skill. The woman tugged a folded wrap from one of the towers of colour against the wall; a burgundy and green version of the one she had lent him earlier. Her slender finger drew his attention to the repeated motif of solid little houses in simple shapes a child might draw. Each pair of homes was connected by an undulating bridge and framed by palm trees. The shawl's deep border was woven in tiny diamonds, as minuscule as fish scales. The cloth was burgundy with gold outline on one side, and green and gold on the reverse.

"It takes mountain women three weeks to make this," she told him. She gestured to herself and to her co-worker at the second loom, her shuttle skimming back and forth through taut strands. She put the shawl into his hands so that he could admire its warmth and weight, and the charm of its design. He appreciated all these things, but was struck most particularly by her sure pride in her work and in the way she spoke the words "mountain women." She was so certain and rooted in her being. He imagined the shawl must have something of her power, and the power of this place, woven into it. He thought it would make a fine gift for Agnes or for his mother.

Just after he had paid the weaver, she brushed the centre of his palm lightly with her forefinger. "Morning is a lucky time," she said. Even if she said this to everyone, he did not doubt her sincerity.

He knew he was lucky — lucky to be here, lucky to be alive. Lucky to see the sun rise over the Annapurnas, and to ponder the possibility he had been visited, while he gazed upon the fishtail peak, by the spirits of the mountains the people call the Dakinis, "the sailors of emptiness."

Two days later, lying sleepless in a damp, truncated cot in a Delhi youth hostel, he began to wonder if his luck had soured. He had been wakened by an unsettling, persistent scratching in the wall behind his head. While he lay rigid, hoping the rats would not succeed in chewing through the plaster, he was suddenly aware of a child-sized hand hovering above his midriff and his money belt. He slapped the hand away before the thief could snip the elastic and abscond with his wallet and passport. The child's shadow slipped from the room before Pinto even had time to prop himself up on his elbows. He was thankful now for the noisy creature clawing inside the walls. It would have been an administrative nightmare to obtain the money and ID to get home again.

He slept until near dawn, with his socks and his running shoes on, his passport inside one shoe and his travellers' cheques in the other. What woke him this time was a noise from within rather than without, a dire rumbling in his belly and a sequence of jabbing cramps that sent him speeding to the toilet. He had tried to be so careful about what he ate, but obviously the foreign bacteria had outwitted him. In the two days that followed, as he repeatedly emptied his bowels into a receptacle whose plumbing was at best desultory, he was sometimes sorry for himself. But he was sorrier still for the men who shared the common lavatory and were subjected to his noisy evacuations and stench. No one in his room seemed to speak English, and for the most part they ignored him, the exception being a handsome, fair-haired man with a Danish flag on his backpack.

"Bad gut?" he inquired sympathetically.

Pinto nodded and tried not to look too stricken. The young man held his right forefinger aloft in a gesture Pinto was at a loss to interpret, and then he left. Half an hour later he was back with two large bottles of soda water and a package of plain biscuits.

"Hydrate. Important," he said, handing the bottles and biscuits to Pinto.

"Thank you so much. Is this enough?" Pinto pulled a rumpled hundred rupee note from his pocket.

"Too much," the young man protested; but he eventually took the money at Pinto's insistence. "Take care," he said as he hoisted the bulky pack on to his back and raised his hand in farewell.

Over the next sixteen hours, the bacteria managed to seed what Pinto could only describe as a pestilence of the spirit. He felt so weak and despairingly lonely he was often on the verge of tears. What on earth had possessed him to travel so far from home, without preparing himself either mentally or physically? He could easily die here in a bare-bones youth hostel in Old Delhi where the rats scrabbled between the walls and he could not even decently flush away the poisons his body kept voiding. In his struggle to surmount this emotional malaise, he revisited the Danish man's simple act of kindness, savouring the simple words "take care" as though they were a healing draught. He had always found it invigorating to be in the presence of goodness.

He held close as well to the mountain woman's shawl, bundling it against his belly or sometimes near his face where he could see the little houses and imagine himself safe inside one of them.

Two days later he was walking, albeit still wobbly, three times around the black marble monument that marked the site at the Rajghat where Mahatma Gandhi was cremated. He willingly went barefoot, as ritual prescribed. The grass was thickly wet and a cramp in his foot soon rose to his right calf. Instinctively he clutched his midriff where he was still so tense and tender. How undignified and self-absorbed such a gesture was, when he had so longed for this chance to demonstrate his respect for his spiritual hero in a small but flawless way.

Within an instant, his circumambulation was made perilous by a deluge unlike any rain he had ever encountered. He found it hard to stay erect in the hot, pounding vertical sea that soon drenched his cotton shirt and jeans and all the flesh beneath. He was almost blinded by the downpour and, despite all his efforts to retain some decorum, he was flailing foolishly against the heavy skeins of water. This was supposed to be his third time around. All the gravitas with which he had hoped to invest his ritual had been stripped away from him. The skies of India had spoken. Yet he was at a loss as to what they were saying. Was he judged unworthy? Did this ancient land recognize his complicity in his friends' deaths; see their very blood soaked into his pores? Or was the relentless, steaming rain washing him clean?

He was doing it again, he thought, yielding to the disgusting prompts of self. It was a monsoon and he was caught in it, like millions of other people all over India. It was a meteorological phenomenon and that was all.

He stumbled on until he was a decent enough distance away from the marble monument before attempting to extricate himself from the sodden straps of his backpack. Even though his preparations for the trip were hectic and ill-considered, he had had the presence of mind to bring several large plastic garbage bags. Holding one aloft as a makeshift canopy, he launched himself through the hurtling rain toward the bench under which he had deposited his socks and shoes. He stuffed these inside his shirt and began to walk to the Gandhi Museum near the entrance to the Rajghat. He very much wanted to look at the Mahatma's books and personal belongings. And now he was impeded, not just by the monsoon, but by a redoubled cramp in his gut. Surely there would be a toilet in the museum? His need was verging on desperate.

The washroom was the most luxurious he had seen since Delhi airport. In a pristine cubicle, he stripped off his sodden clothes. The toilet's scathing artificial light revealed a body already strange to him. He had lost so much weight his belly was concave for the first time he could remember.

It was a relief to be dry again and have some respite from the grinding cramps. However, he was still so light-headed that the floor rebounded with an unsettling sponginess as he walked through the various galleries. He stopped and stared, in as fine a contemplation as he could muster, at the artifacts he most strongly associated with Gandhi's lived ideals: the walking stick that helped support his bird-like body through the punishing miles of the protest marches; the spinning wheels that spurred the people's reclamation of ancient traditions and self-reliance and the throwing off of British rule. A pair of fragile wire-rimmed spectacles — the ones he wore always perched on the end of his nose — briefly conjured up a flickering presence with a beatific smile who mouthed the encouraging words: *Walk on.*

There were some objects on display in the glass cases that Pinto found perturbing. He turned quickly away from several diseased teeth extracted from Gandhi's mouth and saved, he could only assume, by devoted followers. Far worse was the blood-stained dhoti, the garment Gandhi was wearing when his assassin struck. Pinto, who wanted only to be reverent, felt his gorge rise at the sight of this soiled object. Its display struck him as indecorous, if not sensationalistic. But this was not his culture and surely he was wrong to respond with such a judgement?

Was this not one of the reasons he came to India, to be constantly confounded because he was at last in a civilization so vast and so ancient, he must inevitably fail in comprehending even a minuscule part of it? He saw now that his groping words to Agnes about wanting to be lost in something huge were facile and even duplicitous. Was he trying to deceive her or himself? For the truth was he wanted to be extinguished. He wanted the foolish boy who followed his friends blindly into their naïve, ill-thought-out protests to be utterly destroyed. If he had behaved like a man and used his powers of reason far more persuasively, he might have stopped them hurtling pell-mell into the disasters at the animal laboratory, and in Arles. Campbell and Zeke might still be alive. Yet he was so desperate for their friendship and approval he had compromised his principles: never to act on the grounds of heedless passion, but always in the light of moral reason. The boy-man he was had committed utter folly and deserved to die.

If he was to immolate his old self, and be somehow reborn, it could only be here. He knew his chances were meagre and he had limited time. He could not afford to wander the subcontinent for six months or a year, visiting every major holy site. So he had plotted his pilgrimage based on the three places that summoned him most strongly. The first of these was the Rajghat. His next stop would be Pushkar with its holy lake and temple to

Brahma. His third would be the temple of the Jains at Rankapur, with its countless marble columns. Since he'd first read about the Jains as a boy, he had been drawn to this religion which seeks to harm no life form whatsoever, not the least gnat or invisible insect in the air or underfoot. He regarded the Jains as very pure, with their masks of gauze to prevent them from inadvertently swallowing any tiny winged creature.

At the bus station, while washing his hands during one of his visits to the toilet, he met a gaunt young man from Toronto named Eli, who sprouted the longest and most densely matted dreadlocks he had ever seen. And the dirtiest, he speculated, given the frequency with which Eli clawed at his scalp. He had been travelling around India for eight months, he told Pinto, and was on his way south to Kerala to spend the winter.

"Delhi belly?" he asked when Pinto suddenly bent double and had to retreat to the cubicle yet again.

"Meet you outside," Eli called to him through the door. "Got something to fix you right up."

"Fix up" sounded suspiciously like drugs, Pinto thought, as he sat solidly on the toilet, his elbows propped on his knees and his hands clamped to either side of his head. He did not want to be involved in anything of that sort in India, or perhaps anywhere ever again. Smoking pot was a pastime he'd fallen into in order to enter and share the day-to-day reality of his friends. Both Zeke and Campbell had smoked from morning onward. When he had occasionally tried a solitary joint from the household stash, he found it did little for him, other than make him somnolent or disgustingly ravenous.

When he joined Eli in the waiting room, he was surprised to be presented, not with an illicit substance wrapped in tinfoil, but several ripe bananas.

"Bananas, man," Eli urged him. "Boiled rice. Porridge. No milk products, although yogurt's okay. No meat. Nothing fried or spicy. Stick to bananas. Don't eat any other fruit. And no tomatoes or eggs or pasta. Okay? Want me to write it down?"

"I can do it," Pinto said, taking out his notebook and duly listing all the proscribed and endorsed foods.

"I got this list from a doctor in Jaipur early on. Stick to it and you'll be fine. Have a couple of bananas on the bus. Fix you up right away."

"Thanks." Pinto was already unpeeling one of the bananas.

"No problem. Boosts my karma, right? Say hello to TO if you get back before me. Hey, that's my bus just rolled in. Take care, man. Where you headed, by the way?"

"Pushkar."

Eli raised his eyebrows.

"To see the holy lake that Brahma created," Pinto clarified. He was aware of Pushkar's reputation among young travellers as a place to score quality ganja. "The Hindus believe it's as old as creation."

"Right," said Eli. "And the temple with the old, dark-faced god looks like a root dug out of the earth. Yeah, I remember Pushkar. I'm hoping to see the fire ritual in Kerala. Ever heard of that? The words the priest speaks in the ritual are so ancient they predate every human language. So nobody has any idea what the words mean. But just get this. You know what patterns the sounds are closest to? Birdsong! How amazing is that! A human language based on birdsong."

Eli's eyes were wide. He slapped his scrawny thigh in emphasis. "Birdsong," he repeated, shaking his head in a slow wonderment. Then he gave Pinto a high-five sign and sprinted off.

Later, on the air-conditioned bus complete with a clean, well-functioning toilet, Pinto nodded in and out of a dozy haze. Whenever he woke he recalled Eli's enraptured look when he'd described the ritual language based on the music of birds. Pinto automatically pondered the ethical implications. Wouldn't human thoughts, and consequently actions, be purer and less tainted by self-obsession if they were framed by a language directly sourced in nature? Wouldn't such people, at the very least, be free from guile?

The bus abruptly braked. Pinto, who was sitting in the front seat across from the driver, watched three lean brown cows amble across the road. All traffic halted for them and then sped forward again — motorcycles and bubble cars; small buses so densely packed with passengers that heads and shoulders, arms and even feet protruded through open windows; vans with four and five people seated on the lowered tailgates, all of them relaxed and exquisitely poised, holding on to nothing. Pinto looked on amazed as his bus passed a massive transport truck with five young men balanced on the casing over the front left wheel. They were all smiling and at ease, apparently unperturbed by the risk they ran of sliding off and beneath the tire's crushing weight.

The vibrant cartoon colours of the smaller trucks and buses that overtook and passed them made him exuberantly happy. They were painted in swathes of orange and crimson, sky blue and sunburst yellow. And always — in foot-high bold yellow letters on the backs — was the urgent message "Horn Please!" or "Blow Horn!"

The Angel Gabriel would fit right in here, he thought, along with all the thousands of other gods. Blow Horn! He wanted to clap his hands in delight at this brilliant, astonishing flood of life to which he found himself witness. And again the horns honked in a strident discord and everything stopped, in a half-breath, as a black water buffalo loped across the highway. Then everything flowed onward again. Pinto inhaled deeply, a little dizzied by this tumultuous river of vulnerable flesh and hurtling metal. How could he possibly describe this scene if he were asked to do so? All the words that automatically came to mind: teeming, chaotic, heaving, irrepressible, fell far short of what he saw and stirred his mind and body in equal measures of fear and wonder.

The Gabriel horns blew and the pink and orange vans zoomed in and out of focus and young couples balanced sidesaddle on the back carriers of scooters, beautiful as amorous gods carved on temple walls, and the cows and the water buffalo wandered where they pleased, and the homeless dogs lay so perilously close to the roadside, it was a marvel they were unscathed. What a chaotic, miraculous flood of life, always just skirting destruction.

Why were there no accidents, or at least none of which he was aware? The answer was a sudden amber glow inside his skull. It is because the whole precarious mechanism is holy, the whirling spindle of the cosmos recreating itself volcanically each instant. Was what kept it cohesive the radiant threads of spirit he sensed everywhere here, spun out of thousands of years of the people's ritual practice and self-abnegation and their devotion to the countless avatars of Brahman, the ever-fluid, transformative faces of God? He saw two of these faces now, pasted to the dashboard near the bus driver's right hand: Ganesha with his massive grey elephant's head and benign smile beneath his dangling trunk, and Hanuman, the warrior monkey god who flaunted his superhero physique shamelessly. They were both insuperable and potent purveyors of good fortune, portrayed in the primary colours he associated with carnivals. He recognized they were not symbols, but powerful beings whose gaze he could not hold for long, even in their two-dimensional decal form. They affirmed what he had already sensed: that what redeemed India's extraordinary welter of beauty from its peoples' unbearable suffering, instant by instant, was the omnipresence of the animals.

He had a vision of returning to North America; the streets of Toronto look naked and wrong to him, and he aches to register again that pulse of exuberantly sacred life where he has only to glance up to see them: the innocent four-footed, including the cattle and the camels, the delicate drifts of goats and the families of monkeys, holding one another tightly, keeping their own secret counsel, even within the heart of the cities.

Once his bus was past Agra, the traffic thinned, although the honking, kaleidoscopic "Blow Horn!" vans still zipped regularly back and forth across his line of vision. On the Fatehpur Sikri Road, his eye was caught by a woman in an orange sari banded in royal blue. She was talking on a cell phone she held in one hand, while in the other she clutched the lead of a black water buffalo that followed behind.

All his life to come he will be grateful to this woman who has chosen to wear this particularly arresting colour, and to be walking just where she is, as his bus passes. Otherwise he might never have noticed, just after he lost sight of her, the nondescript building set back from the road. It was a stripped-down, functional assemblage of squared blocks that appeared to be made of concrete. The sole concession to design was these blocks' alternating shades of buff and rust. He regretted this charmlessness because the building's name, which he jotted down immediately in his notebook, reverberated in him with a thundering, yet ultimately felicitous shock. He had no doubt he was the recipient of one of those rare gifts chance sometimes offers the unlucky. Had he turned his head, or blinked, he might have missed it. Now he had safely captured this serendipity in his book, whose black covers he clutched tightly between his palms. Writing down these four words had made him as joyful as he had been for some time. He sat straighter and felt his will as one with the speeding bus headed toward holy Pushkar. For the first time in many days, he could conceive of a future life illumined by purpose where he might redeem his woeful part in his friends' deaths.

As the bus approached the desert of Thar, on whose edge Pushkar clung, Pinto saw more and more camels. Some were solitary. Some followed behind handsome men with jewel-coloured turbans and extravagant moustaches. Up close, he saw the camels' teeth were fearsome, which gave their huge, lugubrious faces a sinister aspect. Only now did he fully grasp the ripe irony of Campbell's nickname. He revisited his shame that he had so often envied his friend's flawless good looks, a jealousy so sour he was sure he must have stunk of it. His gorge rose as he saw again that delicate head, still encased in its helmet, sliced from the slim body that shuddered upon the fallen bike, as if in disbelieving grief at this most unnatural severing.

By the time his bus pulled into Pushkar, sweat streamed from Pinto's brow. He kept wiping his eyes, trying to dispel the neurotic notion that the moist clinging air had nothing to do with monsoon season, but was rather the touch of his dead friends' clamouring ghosts.

The white walls of his room in the simple guesthouse offered some solacing calm, as did the blue-green Indian cotton bedspread with its floating, feathery print. The print reminded him of a pretty tunic that Agnes once wore. He remembered how delicate and exotic she had looked in it, and wished she were here with him; that they could pour cooling water over each other's hands in the terra-cotta basin the landlord had replenished mere moments ago. He imagined her lying down beside him on the blue-green spread, and how they would keep quiet company together.

When he woke several hours later he saw that there was still enough daylight left for him to visit the temple. He did not want to go at night, lest he miss anything. His landlord, a lean, striking man with thickly waving silver hair, was visibly pleased when Pinto asked for directions to the Temple of Lord Brahma.

"So good, so good. A young man from America" — Pinto did not bother to correct him — "who wants to go first to the temple. Who does not want drugs. So many." He

shook his head. "In the cafés just for them, in the streets."
The man mimed the smoking of a joint, pursing his
lips, then expelling all the air from his lungs. "Some are
lost," he continued, "cracked, they smoke so much." He
raised his index finger to his forehead and made a vicious
screwing motion. "Cracked."

Pinto shivered, his mind sliding helplessly to Zeke
upon the slab in the Arles morgue, not a bone left unshat-
tered. Cracked through and through.

"It is good you wish the temple," his landlord said.
"I will take you myself. I will show you the Temple of
Lord Brahma — the only temple to this god in India. His
image in the temple is very old." He paused, studied his
fingers as if for numerical confirmation. "Two thousand.
No, more. Two thousand and five hundred years.

"Come, let me take you. It will be an honour. My
name is Mr. Mohindra. And you, is it Peter? Shall we go
together to the temple?"

Pinto nodded appreciatively. He felt light-headed.
Twenty-five hundred years was a dizzying extent of time to
contemplate. As he followed his host through the pungent
streets, with their pyramids of spices, lavish flower
garlands, and everywhere the smell of fried pastries and
ripening fruit, it occurred to him how little sustenance
he has had over the past few days, only bananas, biscuits
and soda water. At that moment, the sun hit him so hard,
he staggered. He reached out blindly, and braced himself
against the sleek flank of a passing cow. He was steadied
as well by its gaze, as the great head swung around to take
in who he was. He was not so sun-struck as to imagine the
animal looked at him any way but blankly. It was enough
that the cow's regard was guileless and creaturely.

The face of the god, on the other hand, simultaneously awed and chilled him. In fact, the Lord Brahma had four faces, staring out in each of the cardinal directions. But it was the foremost face that rooted Pinto to the spot, even amidst the press of worshippers around him, who left flowers, spoke prayers, chanted and swayed, and rung repeatedly the heavy silver bell that hung in the inner sanctum. A filigreed silver casement framed the god in his raised alcove, and his tiered crown was also made of beaten silver. His eyes were a startling white, like little eggs inset in his walnut-brown face. The starkness of the white suggested a wide surprise, like a cartoon character's astonishment. Yet how else would the Lord Brahma look but astonished, as he beheld, wide-eyed, the world he had just created?

"Marble," he heard an English woman's voice behind him. "The idol's made of marble."

This bleak observation left Pinto irritated and perplexed. Marble was white — like the outer temple structure itself, or perhaps honey-coloured or pink. Wasn't it? Could marble really be this dense brown hue verging on black, like an absorbent seed or root hidden long underground, just as Eli had said, gathering and concentrating telluric energies until its power was fearsome and incommensurable? And how on earth, he wondered, could anyone look at the god's face and call it an idol, as if it were a mere doll or an empty husk? His feet were very cold on the black-and-white temple floor. He chafed his hands. He wished he had bought one of the opulent garlands to leave as an offering. There were luscious blossoms looped around the god's neck, vivid reds and oranges that made Brahma's face even more darkly inscrutable. The silver bell rang again. He felt Mr. Mohindra's hand at his elbow and understood it was time they moved on. How long has he stood here?

He followed Mr. Mohindra down the steps and then clockwise around the base of the inner temple. This was part of the ritual all visiting pilgrims performed, Mr. Mohindra explained. He pointed out, as they passed by, the shadowy opening in the outer temple wall that held the image of Shiva, the destroyer. Of course, Pinto thought, destruction must always be just that close. He flinched from the invasive idea that Shiva's fiery feet were as much capable of annihilating belief as everything material. In a bare instant, his apprehension of the carved god's head as a thing of immense, ineffable power might degenerate into rancid doubt. What if the pragmatic Englishwoman was right and it was only an idol made of stone? But even to entertain such a question hit him straight away as barbarous. The intensity of the faith of the people who continued to flow into the temple was palpable. There was no place for doubt here.

As he and his guide came full circle to the base of the steps leading up to Lord Brahma in his filigreed casement, Pinto saw above and through the mass of murmuring, chanting worshippers, the towering pinnacle of the inner temple roof and its thick, round supporting columns. The roof was bright orange and the columns the aqua of certain cloudless summer skies. He was reminded of the bold palette of the trucks and vans' "Blow Horn" signs. If he had a trumpet and could play it, he would go and do so now. Somewhere respectfully removed from the temple he would raise it to his lips and send out a mighty blast of joy. A tremendous Gabriel-like testament to what he felt surging inside him: the certainty that the entire cosmic mechanism was sacred. Not just the earth and waters and all creatures furred, feathered, finned and scaled, but humankind as well, as evidenced by the face of the god. At that instant a bright gleam penetrated the cave of gloom he had inhabited for weeks, if not months. Or was it years?

It struck him that for far too long he had been labouring under the cruel delusion he was cursed because of his disfigurement. How long has he believed this? He saw, as if rudely shaken from a self-induced torpor, how much of his life force he had dissipated in branding himself a man "of evil luck." In a person of Gandhi's stature, the epithet had a noble fittingness, a moral legitimacy. From his young manhood onward, the Mahatma had pitched himself into an epic battle against racism, colonialism, violence of all kinds and the searing injustice of the lot of the untouchables. Gandhi had been relentless, had used himself up, body, blood and bone in the struggle, while far lesser men sneered at him, as some did still, calling him a fake and a fool.

As for himself, what had he ever done except play at being good and gentle and kind, practising his beatific smile in front of mirrors real and imagined? While inwardly he had raged no less. Had he ever forgiven anyone for what he perceived as his curse? Certainly not his mother, nor any of his schoolmates who shunned and mocked him, nor Campbell for his boundless good fortune and for seducing Agnes.

I have been despicable, Pinto thought, as he and Mr. Mohindra retrieved their shoes from the shop near the temple. "One hundred rupees," the shopkeeper said, as

Pinto picked up his running shoes. He dug out the bill willingly, and was suddenly aware of a trio of middle-aged German women who sat perched on little stools, laughing at one another's attempts to outline their eyes with kohl. They paid him no attention, other than a swift glance that took in his height.

On the way back to the hotel, Pinto was assailed by memories of Old Delhi he would shrink from if he could: like the street beggars with bowls balanced on the stumps where once their hands had been. What right had he to think himself cursed? He had all his limbs, his good health and strength. He was a cosseted North American, and rich compared to the families he had seen in India, their homes a stretch of pavement, their roofs a mere lip of tarpaulin held aloft by sticks. No door and no privacy of any kind. You could see their pots and their cooking implements strung on a frayed rope above their heads, and all their haphazard bedding that looked like a jumble of rags. Yet they seemed to bear their wretched circumstances with a consummate dignity. They did not put on a lying face as he did, painting the falsely benevolent smile over a self-pity rankling as a boil. His fakery had undermined his assertiveness and his judgement. He had allowed himself to be enticed by abstractions; to believe that by the study of ethics he would become virtuous; that by being part of a harum-scarum protest group, he would save the lives of animals.

Only now, with those four words he had copied into his notebook on Fatehpur Sikri Road, did he see clearly what he must do. And he must start by leaving behind the curse of his self-absorption, his adolescent obsession with what was, after all, only skin-deep.

At the hotel he gratefully consumed the bowl of dhal Mr. Mohindra produced, together with two airy roti. The charge was far less than the 100 rupees he'd paid the shopkeeper to guard his shoes. The hot food made him feel more solid. The spongy sensation in his legs and arms seemed finally to have gone. He considered taking a stroll through the streets of the town or perhaps venturing to the tent-studded desert on the outskirts. But the instinct was strong to retreat to the simple white room with the sea-green bed cover, to be alone and create a hallowed inner space for the day's images: the face of the ancient god with the astounded eyes; the ceaseless flow of pilgrims giving thanks for the world's creation; the silver bell repeatedly resounding.

Tomorrow, he resolved. Tomorrow he would walk through the town and look at the lake and then get on the bus to Ranakpur.

"Tomorrow," Mr. Mohindra apparently plucked the word direct from his thoughts. "Tomorrow, if you wish, I can arrange for you to receive a blessing by the holy lake. I know a priest who can do this, and who will not cheat you."

Pinto found this unexpected offer unsettling. He did not want to appear ungrateful, but the idea of a blessing agitated him. He groped for the cause of his anxiety. Did he suspect the blessing might be a charade for susceptible tourists? But he could not believe that Mr. Mohindra, who had been so helpful and generous with his time, would be party to a deceit. What then . . . ? Was it rather that he felt undeserving of a blessing, whatever its form might be? I am far too corrupt. These were the words on the tip of his tongue, which he recognized right away as unseemly arrogance, another variation on the self-generated curse he had sworn to shed.

What he did say, and he could not help himself, was that he was "undeserving." A confused dismay curdled Mr. Mohindra's brow. Pinto observed in his host's face ample proof of his own rudeness.

"It is not a thing to be deserved," Mr. Mohindra said with deliberate patience. "It is a blessing not only for you, for your good karma, but for all of your family; for your friends also and all those you love."

For all those you love. That settled it, then. Why might this blessing not be as much for the dead, as for the living?

"Thank you. I am sorry I hesitated. I . . . "

Mr. Mohindra's long fingers performed a fluid combing gesture in the air.

"We shall go early," he told Pinto, "before eight o'clock, before the ghats become crowded."

He left the dining alcove before Pinto had time able to respond. He wondered about the word "ghat" which he associated with ritual cremations. When he consulted his guidebook, he discovered that it simply meant a flight of steps leading down to a river. He lay down and stared a long time at the whitewashed ceiling, half-hoping to see some comforting figure appear, an all-forgiving mother to assure him he has not been flagrantly discourteous, that he has not failed himself badly, once again.

In the morning it was not Mr. Mohindra, but his teenage son Pradeep, who came to the breakfast nook to escort him to the lake. Pradeep, wearing the white shirt and tie of his school uniform, was a shorter, plumper version of his father. His self-introduction, "My father sends his apologies," smacked of an ironic mockery. He was very young, perhaps fourteen at most.

Pradeep walked quickly and Pinto occasionally lost sight of him behind an obtruding chai stand or a meandering water buffalo. It was so early that many of the shops were still shuttered. Pradeep took an abrupt left turn into what at first looked like merely a side street. Then, just a few steps farther on, Pinto found himself standing at the top of a flight of steps. Directly ahead of him was the lake, overhung with a pearly mist. It was as if a casement had swung open on another world where the insubstantial was made substance, but rarefied, having never been polluted by sin or shame. Everything he beheld was compounded of mist and white light. He knew this to be an illusion, just as he knew that the graceful edifices of white marble surrounding the lake were solidly three-dimensional. But he let himself be transported by their present ethereal aspect, and by the silver and blue-streaked mountains in the far distance, whose lineaments seemed to float above the lake.

What came then, on their own light feet, were the words of one of the few poems he had ever willingly taken to heart. A set piece on a prerequisite English survey course, it had been the clear and quiet pool amidst the twisted thickets of the "Metaphysicals." He had been irked by the other poets of this school, who struck him as showy, with their overwrought similes and self-advertising cleverness. Henry Vaughan's work, on the other hand, was both lucid and unquestionably sincere:

They are all gone into the world of light!
And I alone sit lingering here;
Their very memory is fair and bright,

And my sad thoughts doth clear.

Here is that world of light, he thought, this place which he can readily believe took form when a lotus petal dropped from the hand of a god. Could one call this a sublime happenstance, then? Since Campbell's accident and the imbroglio at Arles he has flinched at the idea of contingency. But of course it can go both ways: a petal loosed from a lotus becoming a beautiful lake is as much an accident as a head sliced from a body resulting in a corpse.

How he wished he could banish such thoughts, which were interfering with his absorption of the scene — the sheer web of light and mist; the trio of Indian women in saris of maroon and gold and emerald who walked down the steps of the ghat to his right, and slid silently and fully dressed into the water; the row of young Hindu priests to his left, stripped to the waist, who bowed their shaved heads and moved their lips in prayerful unison. He wished only that he might partake of their guiltlessness for a moment.

Then Pradeep appeared on the step below him, with a short, round-faced man dressed in an immaculately pressed, open-neck indigo shirt and white slacks. Pradeep introduced him simply as the holy man who will give Pinto the blessing. This "priest" was so unlike the lean-limbed Sadhu in a loincloth Pinto had been expecting, he was both embarrassed and wary. Was he being made a fool of? Would the two men demand two thousand rupees?

In fact the fee for which the man asked was a nominal two hundred. Pinto relaxed, dipping again into the warm current of Mr. Mohindra's good intent. After he paid, the man asked him to remove his shoes and sit on the step facing the lake. Around Pinto's right wrist he fastened a string, a twist of dull red and beige. Then he gave him a bevelled brass bowl heaped with rose petals to hold in both hands.

Pinto tried not to dwell on the fact the purveyor of his blessing looked so glossily well-fed and had such plump, moist lips. Yet why would he assume only someone gaunt and self-denying could bestow a blessing?

The man explained that he would translate the words as they went along. Pinto must repeat the Hindi words after each phrasing; or rather, duplicate the sounds he heard as best he could. The unknown phonemes washed over him. He registered many long and short "a" sounds and had an overall impression of potent incisiveness. He could picture the warrior Arjuna speaking this language, or even mighty Ganesha. But so intent was he on properly reproducing the tones and inflexion that he missed much of the English equivalent. He caught, and was automatically oppressed by, the frequent references to prosperity, which he would far rather forego given the inevitable moral pitfalls. Besides, he considered it grotesque to ask for such a thing in a country where starving children begged passersby for a pittance.

Good health, he heard. Well, yes, of course. This part of the blessing made sense to him. At least, armed with good health one might do something useful in the world. But it was the "good karma" for friends and family with which his desires and thoughts were most closely aligned and here, above all, he hoped that he was speaking the relevant sounds correctly.

It dawned on him that this was as close as he had come to participating in a formal ritual since the deaths of his friends. He had not attended Campbell's funeral, and by the time Zeke's body was flying home in a casket decently sealed, he was already on his way to India. He certainly was not seeking "closure," a word he detested for its shallow, quasi-magical allure, and essential dishonesty. He was convinced that no pain or trauma worth its instructive weight was ever fully closed. One's agony might abate or be transformed into good works or art, but it could never be eradicated.

"Good karma," he heard again. He saw Campbell and Zeke transfigured in Henry Vaughan's "world of light," where their largely unsullied souls could take new and wonderful shapes. Oh, yes, bless them and dear, lovely Agnes, and his mother, and Pablo and Perdita and frank, fearless Minnie.

He tried and failed, .as he had failed so often, to generate some small fund of benevolent feeling for Fergus. Of course, he was appalled by what had happened to the man and wished, with all his heart, the grisly murder were undone. It was only . . . he tripped in his own thoughts . . . that the rabid seam in Fergus's lectures had always deeply unsettled him, as had something inflexible and nastily autocratic in the professor's manner. What was it in Fergus that made him push worthy precepts to such extremes they became obscene? Why his ludicrous emphasis on the lives of rats and cockroaches? Ultimately, Pinto had begun to find Fergus's sincerity questionable, if not suspect.

Worse, after the disaster at Arles, he had even wondered if Fergus's dogma had in some very real way polluted their plans, or at the very least, muddied their thinking. Or was he shamefully offloading responsibility here?

The fact was the man had been killed in a manner unbearable to contemplate. Why, then, could he not draw him into this circle of souls he wanted blessed? So tangled was he in his self-reproach that it took him some moments to grasp his "holy man" had finished the ceremony. He instructed Pinto to cast the rose petals in the bowl onto the surface of the lake. When he did so, the look of their crimson splashes on the water distressed him, his mind's eye seeing there the burns the torturer had made on Fergus's body. He shook himself, wishing this foul image banished from this holy place. It was then he remembered he had omitted Kit from his imagined circle.

This was neither the time nor the place to confront himself for this lapse. Unsavoury, he thought. He would leave it there for now, with that single word. Later, perhaps on the bus to Ranakpur, or even on the flight home, he would pluck its syllables apart and face up to his feelings about Kit. He turned to thank the man in white pants and young Pradeep but they had already gone. When he bent to retrieve and put on his shoe, his fingers fumbled with the tying of both laces.

He had ample time on the two buses — first to Jodhpur, thence on to Ranakpur — to examine the root of his unease with Kit. He wanted above all to excise any possibility he was doing her a disservice by falling far short in either tolerance or compassion. What if he had misheard her that night she had returned to Campbell's bed after her time away with her ailing mother?

That night his unabated fury at Campbell's callousness kept pricking him awake. At times he seemed to inhabit Agnes's humiliation; the flesh of his face burned hotly with her shame; he twisted on his bed to escape the sensation he was being crushed by something heartless. To undo his swelling indignation, he decided to go out and walk. A determined motion through the night air, and a disciplined yogic breath, might help the anger dissipate.

Given the frequency of his nocturnal rambles, he was well practised at exiting the house soundlessly. He knew every betraying board in the upstairs hallway and upon the wooden stairs. Campbell's room was at the opposite end of the hall from his. He could see as he made his way forward, his toes up-curled in an exaggerated parody of stealth, a light spilling from under Campbell's door. As he reached the top of the stair, he was aware of a kind of breathy hum emanating from the room. Then came a sound like a stifled laugh.

He remembered exactly how he was standing when the assault began — his right hand gripping the top newel post with its extraneous little carved nipple, his left already in the air, and his depth perception exactly attuned to where he would set it on the first of twenty steps downward. He swayed where he stood. So foul were the words Kit was speaking and so detestable their intent, that the little supper he had eaten curdled in his belly. He knew that if he did not immediately sit down, he was in danger of falling headlong. He no longer cared if they heard him. Had he been a different kind of man, he might have barged into their room unthinking and put the flat of his hand over Kit's face to stop her mouth. Every word she spoke was common and ugly, and every one was applied to some intimate part of Agnes's body.

If he was sickened and shocked by what he heard, he was also dangerously enraged. He recalled cautioning himself, somewhat absurdly — "I am not an Old

Testament prophet," and this was enough to keep him sitting where he was. He cradled his head with his hands as if to protect his brain from her contaminating speech. He wanted many impossible things at once: to make her stop, to wash himself clean of the overheard filth, and to protect Agnes. It was all so horrible and deplorable. He simply could not comprehend how one human being could speak of another's body in this disgusting and disrespectful way.

Sexually inexperienced though he was, Pinto grasped readily enough that Kit was plundering Campbell's deflowering of Agnes for prurient detail that would arouse them both. "Little Aggie," Kit called her. The sneering condescension repulsed him all the more and, at that instant, he hated Kit as much as he had hated the boys who crucified Mrs. Eatrides' cat. His sole consolation, if one could call it that, was Campbell's apparent reluctance to play along. "Cut it out, Kit." Still, his tone seemed to Pinto more cajoling than cautionary.

"Come on, Cammy baby. Tell me everything. Make me hot, honey."

Pinto managed to stand, pulling himself up with both hands gripping the stair rail. He made his way down the steps slowly, a man in a daze, feeling that he had himself been deflowered. He ached for Agnes, whom he prayed would never discover the louche uses Kit had made of her seduction.

He had previously seen Kit as a somewhat tragic figure, given her family history and her dutiful care for Horace and her mother. Now he thought her repellent. As he slipped on his shoes and then out the door and into the night, he knew what he wanted most would elude him: to have her vulgar words purged from his memory. He tried playing devil's advocate with himself. Was he perhaps being priggish and puritanical? Hadn't he overheard remarks intended for Campbell's ears alone? What did he, with his basically ascetic life, know about lovers' tricks to stimulate each other? Maybe this kind of dirty talk about people they knew was the norm.

This line of interrogation had yielded him nothing. He had heard Kit befouling the woman he loved and, by extension, the sacred nature of love itself. He would never be able to look at her again without a wary and frank disgust. This he would endeavour to hide for Campbell's sake.

He'd had little opportunity to put this feigned composure to the test. Three weeks later Campbell was dead and Kit had become the gaunt and ghastly creature in Zeke's photograph from the funeral. She looked like an escapee from a nineteenth-century lunatic asylum. That recalled image still moved him to anguish and an uneasy pity for her.

Why uneasy, he asked himself, as his bus rolled on toward the hills where the ancient Jains had raised a temple inspired by a celestial chariot glimpsed in a holy man's dream. The answer was inescapable. He simply could not forget, or forgive, her sordid remarks about Agnes. The only possible excuse would be mental instability. Perhaps when she spoke those words, Kit was already suffering, as her grandfather and her mother before her, a disease that was undermining her judgement and deadening her sensibility. This was as far as he could stumble toward excusing her. He resolved to let his mind touch on her no more, but only wish her well and healed.

He wondered, and not for the first time, if he put far more store on the moral implications of language than did most people. Shouldn't words, and the sentences we made of them, ideally serve enlightenment and compassion? But of course it was so very difficult when even the simplest exchange between two people could be rife with misunderstanding. The English language — in truth, the only one he knew — often struck him as notoriously slippery. Like the word "cleave," which had two exactly opposite meanings; or "misprision" which could convey either "misunderstanding" or "the deliberate concealment of one's knowledge of a crime."

He was jolted by the awareness it was on these two horns of "misprision" that his own conscience was impaled. Had he not totally misapprehended where the rarefied abstraction of animal rights would ultimately take him? Had he not also deliberately concealed his part in the crime that had unfolded in Arles? Did the others all have criminal records now, Minnie and the pacific-natured Pablo and Perdita? — whereas he had escaped, if not unscathed, then at least without the stigma of wrong-doing in the eyes of the law. He could never make amends to the others, not even if he had several lifetimes in which to try. Yet he might, through his burgeoning and daily more cherished plan, find some measure of absolution.

Certainly he found nothing of the kind as he wandered disconsolately among the plethora of marble columns that crowded the interior of the ornate, turreted temple at Ranakpur. Neither his eye nor his spirit responded to the teeming idiosyncratic shapes of the plants and animals and gods carved into the fourteen hundred and more lofty trunks of marble. He acknowledged, but could not absorb, the wonder of it. All these roiling forms, and the way the way the columns clogged the temple's inner space, went athwart his notion of the pure precept at the heart of Jainism: to avoid harming even the least form of life, the microscopic and invisible.

The wearing of any form of leather was forbidden inside the temple. He was pleased there was this injunction to remind tourists of the Jains' most sacred principles. Otherwise the temple and its famous columns might well degenerate into just another "Disneyfied" experience. He was put out nonetheless by the obtrusive whirring and clicking cameras, as foreigners with showily expensive equipment homed in on particular carvings, whether a sinuous snake or a god's torso, or positioned themselves to commandeer a panoramic view of the columnar forest.

He withdrew to the temple's inner perimeter wall where the marble effigies of Jain saints sat within their separate alcoves. He climbed some steps so that he could walk the raised platform over which the saintly figures presided. Almost immediately he was assailed by a bearded priest in a pleated white robe who asked if he would like to purchase a blessing. The priest's manner was blatantly importuning and the look in his eyes so nakedly avid that Pinto winced in embarrassment. Once he'd politely declined, the priest's face hardened. The effect was chilling. Pinto had had enough.

Outside the temple, he retrieved his shoes and gave the young man assigned to guard them twenty rupees. He had some time before catching the bus travelling on to Udaipur, where he'd get a flight back to Delhi and then home. He decided to meander around the pathways of the temple complex. So it was that he saw, as he turned left off the main thoroughfare, a small temple of red-brown marble whose simplicity of form calmed his perturbation. It was perhaps one-fiftieth the size of the sprawling main temple. Its gentle rounds reminded him of a beehive. Everything about this building beckoned him inside, including the jasmine-scented smoke that commingled with the purple shadows beneath the arced entranceway.

Inside, a small, wiry man in olive green greeted him with the pressed palms of the traditional Namaste. The man stood beside a central stone table on which was set the bowl of burning incense and a brass plate containing some rupee notes and few coins. He gestured expansively to the shallow, shadowy space behind him, the perimeter alight with the sheen of the marble deities. Pinto now saw that these gods ringed the temple's entire inner circum-ference. As he moved deeper within, he had the sensation he was being held, cradled even, in the warm cup of an open palm. Up close, he recognized the benevolent visage of the Buddha — not the corpulent grotesque of bad Western lawn art, but a strong young man whose chest gleamed. "Buddha?" he asked the attendant.

"Balek," the man answered or so the name sounded to Pinto's ear. He could not be sure. He assumed this was the name of a Jain saint.

"Buddha." The man pointed to a recessed figure on Pinto's left.

Pinto could see little difference between this statue and any of the others in the room. They all had a kind of soft ivory patina, and seemed to emanate a long-steeped wisdom and humility. Their temple-house, by its very diminutiveness, spoke to him of the power of small, discrete acts of goodness. He touched the notebook in his back pocket, which contained the four words he'd written down on the Fatehpur Sikri Road, words that would lead him to just such a life of small actions that would work to alleviate suffering. Not the banners or the demonstrations with their sprawling hubris. Not the mammoth abstractions about rights and dignity; but simple practical deeds and work.

"Mahatma Gandhi Veterinary College." This was what India had given him: a purposeful way to dedicate his life. As soon as he got home, he'd see what prerequisites he needed to get into a Canadian veterinary school.

"Thank you," he told the attendant, as he put the most generous offering in the bowl he had given to date.

Through the bus window the langur monkeys stared back at him from the edges of the jungle they roamed at will. He marvelled at their long wise faces. He wondered how it might be to touch one, and stroke its fur as one would a domestic cat. He knew too, beyond any doubt, that he would soon enough be nursing his own split flesh, struck through by adamantine claws. It was foolhardy and reprehensible to sentimentalize animals' beauty and essential nature. It was right and fitting to hold them in proper awe and understand that the working of their minds and spirits would be forever unknowable. In this way, he saw, they taught us the fullness of the mystery of God.

In the washroom of Udaipur Airport he came face to face with the second transformation India had worked in him. Under the glare of the industrial-strength lighting, he caught sight in the mirror of a tall, broad-shouldered man. At first he did not recognize himself and for a moment he was afraid. He leant close in to his reflection, touching his forehead, cheeks and chin and confirmed the astounding truth that his abnormal pigmentation had so much ameliorated as to be barely noticeable. He had no idea how this had come about. He wondered if this change was permanent and, more particularly, whether he was deserving. He had no doubt this unexpected transfiguration would gladden his mother's heart. This knowledge helped to quiet his shock and niggling misgivings about a change he had neither sought nor prayed for.

In Delhi airport, he purchased a *New York Times* which happened to feature an article on the parlous state of traffic regulation in India. He read that each year thousands of people die in road accidents, many of them children. In spinning his fantasy about India's spiritual legacy subduing chaos on the roads, he had succumbed to a spell that was also a willful blindness; just as he shrank from thinking about Gandhi's failings, the man's egocentric obsessions, like sleeping with his virgin nieces to test his vow of chastity. Is this what he had learned from his pilgrimage, that there was no civilization or human being that was wholly exemplary? How despairing and simplistic that sounded. He opened his notebook to study again the evidence of the revelation that had been gifted him on the Fatehpur Sikri Road. How was he to explain this, or his new face, except through ideas like mystery or grace?

TWENTY-TWO

A Familiar Face

SOME DAYS AGNES ATTENDED AS many as three different AA meetings, increasingly desperate to find a group in which she could feel at home. She had not been prepared for their bewildering diversity, nor for the consummately polished turns of certain star presenters. Their testimonies were either chummy and confiding, or hortatory and messianic. She found both approaches equally repellent.

Of course she could not slip out of these meetings, no matter how histrionic or self-aggrandizing she thought these stalwart "friends of Bill." She was the aspiring, fragile acolyte. Vigilant attention to the stories of seasoned AA veterans was essential to her induction. And so she listened dutifully, subduing any urge to squirm through squalid details of their respective falls; the scathingly frank accounts of loved ones alienated and solid careers destroyed; and finally, the degrading scenes of rock bottom with its hurtling peripeteia that led them to the clear light of reason and the vow to stay clean. Twenty-two years sober, they will say. Or forty-two. Or sixteen.

She wanted this happy result very badly. She wanted to be clean forever and to work again and walk with a light step primed by hope. It was only that none of the speakers she heard were compatible role models. They were so patently self-assured for one thing, and their long years of sobriety made her own hard-won achievement seem so puny. She had not had a drink for nine days. What troubled her most was the precariousness of her situation. She felt she was walking across a floor made of particularly brittle glass that an unthinking step would send her plunging through. She conceived of this misstep coming, not so much because she physically craved whisky, but because one day she might simply forget the terrible consequences and reach out for a bottle in a daze. Three times now she had awakened in a sour running sweat because she'd dreamt she had imbibed.

If she had absorbed anything from the witnesses at the meetings, it was the folly of believing you could get your drinking under control. She knew this in her bones. If she had one drink, it would all happen again. She would plunge down through the brittle floor, blood-streaked and doomed. Nevertheless, she was afraid her willpower was not up to the lifelong task. What would happen the first time she was sorely humiliated or rebuffed? Would she be able to control the urge to let the whisky obliterate the pain? She saw she was running into the old danger of overwhelming herself, looking too far ahead. The AA mantra of one day at a time was solid as a life buoy and she must hold to it hard. She had only to make it through this day. She could. Of course she could.

If only she could find a meeting where she saw her own vulnerability and self-doubt reflected back at her.

She knew that when at last she had the courage to get up and tell her story (*Hello, my name is Agnes and I am an alcoholic*), her voice would quaver, her hands tremble. Wasn't there someone like that in this massive city — a recovering alcoholic who had preserved a nervous humility no matter how many years' abstinence he or she had managed?

Many of the meetings she attended were held in church basements and she had come to regard these subterranean warrens as AA's netherworld of striving and bruised transformation. The corridors were almost always gloomy, despite efforts to brighten them with posters or felt hangings with the words "love" and "fellowship" in bold serrated caps.

In the basement hallway of one of the older Catholic churches, she had found herself confronted by a garish lithograph of Christ pointing to his exposed, violently red heart. She had automatically touched the recently healed-over hole at the base of her throat, with its little horizontal ridge of scar tissue. Here was proof of her own miraculous deliverance: the actual evidence she had escaped with her life through the intercession of an ultimately unfathomable otherworldly power. She knew she was not deluded in this belief. Her dog had been no alcoholic hallucination. He had appeared to save her and she had witnessed every minute detail of his intercession. She had felt the strength beneath the fur and his steady, consoling presence after her rescue. What she had not done was slip her arm around his chest to find the steady thump of the heart that had exerted itself on her behalf. And if she had done so? Wasn't it likely there would have been nothing, no answering thump of pumping blood, no proof of corporeal life?

She believed still that the dark brown hound was a manifestation of spirit, or of some rootless, benevolent energy. If she lived to be as old as Nana was when she died, she would not be shaken in this conviction. He was there. He had saved her. His being was beyond her understanding, but not beyond her faith.

The mystery of Laelaps's appearance was one reason Agnes did not run aground — as many newcomers did — on the injunction that AA neophytes get "in touch with a higher power." She was glad the phrase was so elastic because she could not have anatomized the radiant ethereal world she believed lay parallel to this marred quotidian one. Spirits moved freely there — animal and human both. She returned again and again to the idea of "ensouling," of a holy place where everything was always on the verge of becoming. Thus she would puzzle it out in her head, and only there.

She went regularly these days to gallery 607 of the Metropolitan Museum to absorb as fully as her new sobriety allowed Piero di Cosimo's startling visual commentary on these truths. She was often lost in the eventful worlds of the two canvases hung side by side — one strident, one pacific — showing the hunters in the thick of the kill, and then their return home. She had a sketchbook with her and a pencil and a stick of red chalk so that her hours in front of the two canvases were readily justified to other gallery-goers and the guards. No one seemed to recognize her from her disgraceful prior episode and she was heartened by this distance from the drunk she had been. It was a question now of sticking to the last, as she must.

It surprised and delighted her how the act of copying, with the porous chalk in particular, helped her to inhabit the abundant sensuous detail so that she was sometimes inside the painting, looking out. She slipped easily inside the androgynous person, with the little wolf mask settled on her shoulders, whom she believed not to be a hunter at all. From the very beginning, she had seen this admittedly ambivalent figure as well-intentioned, gripping the small, sturdy grey bear around the midriff to stop its blind, doomed attack on the lion who had slain the bear's mate. This angel figure on the bloody field was definitely trying to save the bear, not pull it away to murder it. As far as Agnes knew, this was solely her interpretation. She had never found such a view in any book or article by Renaissance art scholars from Panofsky onward.

Piero had positioned the figure to the left of centre. But the firmly planted naked feet were so near the bottom of the panel that, of all the human protagonists in the scene, this was the one closest to us. Agnes read this illusion of proximity as deliberate on Piero's part. He wanted the viewer to study this figure and enter into her exertions, the way her strong thigh and knee flexed as she braced herself against the bear's back, the steady lock of her arm as she tried to tug the creature away from its piteous attack on the deadly lion. She noted how Piero had given the intercessor's face an ivory cast, in contrast to the shadow-striped, sunburned flesh of the hunters. Her brow is furrowed in determination. Her mouth is open as if she is gasping or crying out, for she is herself in a perilous situation as the grey bear turns its head around, so near her own face, to snarl at her and show its fangs and wide red tongue. Her fine profile shows clearly against the bear's dark fur.

One morning, as Agnes sat sketching the straight nose and the whorled ear, it came to her how much the features resembled the philosophical hybrid boar's in *The Forest Fire* — a human face that spoke of stoicism, yearning and hope in the midst of conflagration, the face she had always believed belonged to Piero di Cosimo himself.

He was here then, too, in gallery 607 of the Met.

She was so shaken by this discovery, she gave a little cry. The nearest guard and several visitors stared at her, and she bent down, under the pretense she had dropped her chalk. How she wished she could tell them what she had found; explain to them that it was in this kindly androgynous figure the painter's spirit lived; that this small painting was not a stomach-churning scene of Early Man's savagery, but rather a painting with a moral centre. Its implicit instruction was as urgent and compelling as when he had set his brush to the horizontal panel six hundred years ago.

Stop their suffering!

Can't you see it? she wanted to call out to anyone in the gallery who might listen. Look at the eyes of the little monkey high in the tree in the foreground. Can you see how his head turns to watch his companions and the other animals fleeing the clubs and cudgels, a great train of deer and ox and bears and capuchin monkeys leaping and racing up the hill? His poignant yearning and his hope, his very blessing of his fellow creatures in flight? And this person who grips the grey bear so solidly? That is the painter himself, Piero di Cosimo. He has painted himself trying to rescue the bear from the lion, who at any moment, will leap up and tear out its throat. Can you see this gesture of salvation and self-sacrifice at the painting's heart? Can you?

How she yearned to take some sympathetic-looking person by the hand, the dark-haired woman in the cream and cinnabar patterned silk dress, perhaps, and lead her to the companion painting where the hunters return home. Do you see how sleekly the slain stag lies along the man's naked shoulders, how reverently the hunter carries the dead creature, as if this very bearing is an act of love? And have you noticed the two animal masks fixed to the mast of the hunters' rude boat? Do you not think those masks might be symbols of the people's awe of the animals' numinous power and a sign of their spiritual kinship? Have you heard what the shaman told the anthropologist Rasmussen, that by eating animals he and his people were living on a diet of souls?

Agnes, you're hysterical. It was her father's voice, with that nasty tone he reserved for reproofs of her "wooly thinking" and "gross sentimentalism."

She flinched, out of long-ingrained habit at the caustic strike, even though he was not physically present.

You have to outgrow this foolishness, Agnes, the voice persisted. *Animals don't have consciousness in the sense we understand it. They don't have rights and if you go on fighting for something that doesn't exist, you'll ruin your life. You're impaling yourself on a falsehood, a childish notion that is woefully simple-minded.*

Had he really said "impaled"? Wasn't that a bit too brutal, and likely far too imagistic, for his ingrained pragmatism?

Listen to Daddy, honey. He has your best interests at heart. We both do. Her mother's words came these days in the form of a mechanical chirping, although fortunately they were less and less frequent.

In fact, the power of both parental voices was dwindling day by day. She knew this had much to do with her family's final blatant betrayal: their refusal to believe her when she'd told them she had not been present at the bullring in Arles. That they would not accept her word was the final stab that had at once killed off any remnant affection for them, and freed her forever from their debilitating influence. She had never before understood that being betrayed can sometimes result in a glorious liberation. And that was very much the case here. She certainly did not wish them ill. Nor did she feel guilt at her intense relief she need never see her parents or sister again.

So when it came to the AA step about making amends to the people you have offended or harmed as a result of your drinking, her family simply did not factor into it. As hard as she interrogated herself, she was unable to come up with anyone whom her alcoholism had seriously injured. It did cross her mind that she might owe the hotel management an apology for the ant invasion, and there was no doubt she had been abrasive with Ines, who after all, had only spoken the truth. After close self-examination, she determined that in both these situations, her faults were too minor to warrant any formal amends.

What major harm she had done, she had done to herself. She had as good as plotted her own demise. She would never understand why she in particular had been saved from death, while Campbell and Zeke had not. It was all so bewildering and contingent. Why hadn't the strung wire snapped or the bike stalled just before the fatal impact? Or in Zeke's case, why hadn't some primal prompt convinced him to stay in this world: a sunburst of primrose at his feet, for example, or the exalted cry of a bird ascending the blue sky above him?

Her new and widening clarity made her very aware the principal threat to her continuing sobriety was guilt. Its peculiarly destructive character, simultaneously corrosive and leaden, could easily blight her energy and will. If she let guilt eat at her or weigh her down, the urge to drink would spring up as fierce as ever. As she saw it, her guilt was rooted first in the fact she had survived the lamentable wreck of the Ark, while Campbell and Zeke had perished; and second in her failure to make a jot of difference in the lives of animals. How was she to impart the truth to others, persuasively and far afield, in order to keep her vow? Was there a way to make herself into a truth-bearing crusader like Jane Goodall, with her saintly works and serene face?

She grasped right away how foolish such an aspiration was in her case. She had neither the long-refined experience nor the charisma to be a universal-truth-bearer. Nevertheless, she still wanted desperately to do more than simply give money to other people's campaigns on animals' behalf. She wanted to act somehow; to manifestly bear witness for those who could not speak for themselves, except through their eyes and their visible marks of suffering. The demands of the sacred bond were so huge and so pressing, she must answer them in kind. But wasn't that exactly the kind of hubristic attitude that had been the Ark's undoing?

Once again, she had tied herself in knots, both ethical and pragmatic. In any event, she would be useless to any living creature unless she stuck with the paramount business of staying sober. *I am still very vulnerable.* She repeated this so often over the course of a day, the words had become as much a mantra as "One day at a time."

One morning the smart phone revealed a category of meetings that had thus far eluded her. These were the "small and quiet gatherings," many of them apparently also "gay-friendly." She resolved to try one advertised for late that afternoon. It was in a basement meeting room of a Catholic church she could reach in two subway stops.

She had come to assume that all AA groups prided themselves on a culture of asperity, perhaps because they did not want inductees ever to lose sight of the difficulties of staying the course. When she found the signposted door in the basement of St. Anthony's, she was therefore prepared for the usual brash affronts to her senses: the fetor of tarry coffee thickening in a glass pot on a hot plate; bleak, stuttering ceiling strip lighting; the screech of tubular metal chairs dragged over stained and pitted concrete. Once she stepped inside, she assumed she was in the wrong place. Instead of an acrid caffeine stench, there were the diffuse scents of various herbal teas, among which she identified jasmine and peppermint. The lighting was an ambient glow. Wooden chairs, with fan-shaped backs and cushions, were arranged in a circle in the centre of the room. Surely she had stumbled upon some other kind of group, dedicated to local environmental renewal or similar good deed?

"Are you here for the AA meeting?" The question came from a tiny elderly woman with a froth of white hair framing her face. She was seated, very erect, and her pale blue canvas deck shoes barely grazed the floor.

"Yes. Am I in the right place?"

"That's us, dear. Come in and take a seat. My name is Ellie."

"Agnes."

"Lovely," Ellie exclaimed. "One doesn't meet many Agneses these days. It suits you. We're just waiting for a few of the other members to arrive. Do make yourself a cup of tea in the meantime, if you wish. It's a dollar a cup and you put the money in the glass jar."

In the time it took Agnes to make her peppermint tea, several others had joined the circle. There were four more women, all older than Agnes. These included Joan, who had very high cheekbones, and her dark hair pulled back in a flawless bun; Mireille, who wore a heart-shaped locket and a smock of lace-edged pink gingham; Helen, whose deft hand movements, chiming with her speech, made Agnes wonder if she was a classical musician; and Clarisse, who kept winding strands of her long straw-blonde hair around her index finger and peering at it, as if hunting for split ends. When she smiled, Agnes noticed that one of Clarisse's front teeth was missing. Her marked thinness and pallor made the midnight blue flesh beneath her eyes stand out even more tellingly. So caught up was Agnes in sympathetic speculation about the trials Clarisse had undergone that she missed some of the introductions of the men in the group. She did catch "Mark": the name of the handsome black man in his thirties who looked like he could be a stockbroker and was the only person in the group with a briefcase. The man with the neatly razored grey hair and sailcloth shirt in vertical cobalt and cream stripes was Walt. Those whose names she missed included a man with a shaven head that had its own five o'clock shadow, an older gentleman with a massive bronze-tinged beard of corkscrew curls, and another man whose face she could not see because of her angle of vision. Only his narrow, elegant hands and wrists extending from deep cuffs of pale lavender were visible to her.

Agnes's jaw muscles clenched in empathy when Ellie announced Clarisse would be the main speaker. Clarisse, who had stopped her compulsive hair-twisting, now repeatedly smoothed down the close-fitting long sleeves of her sage green top.

Today they were celebrating Clarisse's first full year of sobriety, Ellie added. There were cries of congratulation and brisk applause as Clarisse stared down at her magenta-painted toenails. Then, with an almost mechanical effort, she looked up and smiled close-lipped in the direction of the man wearing the pale lavender shirt.

When Clarisse began to speak, her voice was so curdled and raw, it hurt simply to listen to the sounds, let alone the meaning. Much of Clarisse's story could best be classified as unspeakable, Agnes thought, and she sometimes set her mind deliberately adrift when the horrors enumerated exceeded her ability to take them in. Clarisse rattled off parts of her fraught history as if she too could hardly bear to give voice to the soiled catalogue of misdemeanours and mishaps, most particularly the loss of two children: the first, when she'd miscarried after tackling another woman in a drunken, jealous rage and was flung down a stairwell; and the second, when she'd left her two-year-old daughter unattended for two days while she partied and drank vodka straight from the bottle until she saw double, then did several lines of cocaine in order to "straighten out" so that she could drink some more. She had woken with vomit in her hair and a policeman pounding on the door in the company of a neighbour alarmed by the child's fractured cries.

"They took my daughter into care and I never saw her again. Her name was Vivian."

Agnes gleaned that Clarisse might have got her daughter back had she stayed clean and sober, and proved herself competent to the authorities. This she had utterly failed to do. She had gone on the wagon and fallen off — at increasingly short intervals — five times. Clarisse held up her right hand and studied the five digits with a look of stern disgust. She described appearing at one of the custody proceedings inebriated and dishevelled and full of a self-important fury she could not contain. They had to remove her bodily from the hearing in restraints. Agnes shifted in her seat, reliving her own ejection from the august Metropolitan Museum.

"Blind drunk," Clarisse said. "It took me a long time to see that 'blind' means blind to truth and especially the truth of the despicable person you've turned into."

Yes, Agnes understood that. She recalled the swollen certainty of her drunkenness; the implacable rooting of premises that no one and nothing could shake. "I am not a drunk," she had told Ines, stamping her foot. That person she had been, a ludicrous little gnome-girl, seemed pathetic to her now. "He will make love to me the way Campbell did," she had told herself about Guam, sottishly believing that folly until he slid the cold steel across her windpipe.

"I tried a lot of different groups," Clarisse was saying. "But none of them really took—until I found St. Anthony's. You guys made me feel welcome and you didn't judge me. I've made it a year sober with your help, and especially the support of my sponsor, Paul. I've called him at some pretty strange times of night when I was afraid I couldn't hold out any longer. He was . . . is . . . always there for me. And the most amazing thing is that he showed me it is still possible to care for, and even like, the good parts of myself and to see that I do have strength and value. Early on in our talks together, Paul gave me these lines written in the Middle Ages by a wise nun with a man's name. Julian. I recite them whenever I'm afraid I'm going to have a slip. So I'll close today by reciting them and by saying that even though I am still in a rocky place, I am learning to sit quietly and sift through what's important; to know what to care about, like my self-respect, and health and hope, and how to keep these things safe and clean. Or 'sacred,' as Paul says. Here are the lines, very simple but they work for me: *And all shall be well, all manner of things shall be well. The goodness of God is the highest object of prayer and it reaches down to our lowest need.*

"Thank you," Clarisse concluded with a gasp of relief. "Thank you all. And thank you, Paul."

Agnes applauded so hard, her palms began to sting. Then she stopped abruptly, both hands stilled in the air when she saw the man in the pale lavender shirt, the man named Paul, come forward to hug Clarisse. She knew him, recognized his sharp, almost elfin features, his narrow head and sleek black hair immaculately parted on the left. *You obviously have your subject, Ms. Vane, and your work cut out ahead of you.* He was the singularly elegant

[387]

professor, the one on her scholarship board who had seemed most enthusiastic about her thesis. How strange that she should see him again in this place, where she was now so patently unnerved and unhoused.

Paul let go of Clarisse, and turned resolutely toward her. "Agnes," he said, reaching for her hand so that they stood for a moment, palm to palm. "Do you remember me?"

Although he did not officially become her sponsor, Paul Otterly invited Agnes to meet him several times a week for what he termed "free-flowing chats." These conversations were to take place at La Selva, an Italian café in his neighbourhood. The café was dominated by a monstrous, violently hissing antique espresso machine whose wrought-iron embellishments included tiered spires at all four corners, rosettes tinted icing-sugar pink, and two lounging putti with absurdly round faces and protruding bellies, details that reminded Agnes of the worst excesses of Baroque altar pieces.

For their first meeting, where she found Paul ensconced in a leatherette booth with its own hushed atmosphere, she came conspicuously armed with a spiral-bound notebook. On this, he cast an eye either cold or quizzical; she could not decide which. Despite the spare angularity of his face, and the topaz eyes and peg-like nose that made him resemble a Victorian child's wooden puppet, his expressions were so fluid as to be often unreadable. She soon grasped how jealous a watch he kept on his privacy. She never learned where exactly he lived or whether he currently had a partner or lover.

On the other hand, he was unstintingly generous in laying before her the scathing history of his alcoholism: the bottles of Highland Park and Lagavulin "downed at a single solitary sitting," and when there was nothing else in the house, tumblers of metallic blue mouthwash; and ultimately, the dung-hued liquid shoe polish that was to make the inside of his mouth and his stomach lining bleed. He was hospitalized, and his fledgling position at the university jeopardized.

"So rock bottom for me was contemplating an empty container of shoe varnish," he told her with a tight-lipped grimace. "I made myself scrutinize it when I got out of the hospital and there was the little death's head on the label: that discreet skull and crossbones warning, which is of course a classic *momento mori*. In that cryptic sign, I saw the whole squalid tale of my dipsomania encapsulated. The *momento mori* showed me how recklessly I had been sowing the seeds of my own death. Becoming a sodden alcoholic, with a craving so all-consuming I could no longer perceive my degradation — that was my rather banal route to self-destruction. And why? I can see the question on your face, Agnes. Not a greedily curious question, but a gentle, rueful enquiry. The answer is simple. I was destroying myself by degrees ever more pathological in order to mimic the protracted and agonized death of the person I loved above all else on earth. I had been pursuing this woeful, self-damning course unconsciously, or perhaps half-consciously, to punish myself for surviving.

"He contracted AIDS. It was still a new disease then, barely recognized and named. I still wrestle sometimes at three in the morning with the coils of that mocking irony:

thirty years ago my beloved partner was infected by a virus whose invidious speed drugs could easily halt today — in our society and income bracket, at least. Of course, I am aware of the killing inequities in other countries around the world. The sheer arbitrary nature of the infection, the accidents of fate, the awful toll the contingent takes on humankind — dwelling on these things can still rock such foundations as I have, and weaken my will. So I go to meetings and I strive to help others because these disciplines reinforce my faith."

"In?" The question was out of her mouth before she was aware she would ask it.

"In life," he replied. "Therefore choose life. Is that wise injunction from Deuteronomy? I can never remember. As I see it, for a very substantial proportion of alcoholics, drinking is all about death. For us, there's no exuberant Apollonian joy in imbibing at all. We drink to kill pain, or excise unwanted memories, or subvert facts with a perversely shoddy magical thinking. The hangovers tell us the truth about our drinking: that entombed despair and spiritual aridity one wakes into . . . And that is enough of my story, Agnes. Therefore choose life. Now, tell me that you do, and how it is you've come to be here in New York attending AA meetings. You are a long way from Bremrose."

She frowned, stared into the residue of her espresso. The new school year started in less than two weeks and she was still shirking her decision. Could she find the courage to go back, with Zeke gone now, as well as Campbell? Could she face the other members of the failed Ark, particularly Minnie and Perdita and Pablo? Would they believe her when she told them she had been locked inside a museum in Arles and not freed until after everything had gone awry inside the arena? Pinto had believed her. But Pinto was wholly exceptional.

"Agnes? Have I overwhelmed you with questions? If so, I am sorry."

She plunged her spoon into the base of her cup and stirred the turbid dregs twice concentrically. How could she give a shape to the blood-soaked chaos of the past few months and, more crucially, to her complicity in the things that had gone so badly wrong?

"What you were saying about the toll the contingent takes on us? Happenstance? Fate? How everything is fine one moment and then torn to shreds the next . . . ?"

"Yes?"

"What if you feel that you are somehow implicated in these events; that if you had just done something differently, you might have averted . . . ?"

"Well, I would say those feelings are very natural, Agnes. They stem from a deep-rooted sadness and an atavistic desire to blame someone or something for what is in fact chance and uncontrollable."

"And what if it involves a death?"

"Agnes, please consider telling me what has happened. Start wherever you like, but the beginning is probably best. Take a deep breath, and then tell me, step by step, what has led you to these thoughts. You can trust me, Agnes."

She believed this, not least because he had extended her such frankness. She began — as she must — with Campbell and the wire. As she was speaking, it struck her that she had never before recounted the harrowing scene to anyone aloud. Now, as she tried to shape in words that terrible moment, it was ironically delicacy above all for which she strove. She did not want to sully his memory with words suggestive of either sensationalism or crudity. "The headless trunk upon the bike" — how was she to convey this reality without sounding coarse or as if she were parroting the lines from a crass horror film?

Yet, in the end, this was what she said. Then her hands began to shake. She had to put them to her mouth, pressing her fingers hard against her lips, to stop the inarticulate sounds forcing their way up inside her.

"Agnes, would you like to stop now?"

She shook her head.

"Take a breath, my dear, and take your time. I'll speak for a while, shall I, to give you a moment to recover? Was that when you started drinking heavily, after the traumatic experience of seeing your friend killed in that way?"

"No. I wanted to get blind drunk then. But Pinto stopped me."

"Pinto?"

She began to summon the adjectives that would convey Pinto's extraordinary qualities. Kind, generous-spirited, selfless. These all fell short.

"He sounds like a remarkable young man."

"Yes, he is."

"But it was Campbell you were in love with?"

"Yes."

"Was he your lover?"

"Yes . . . No. He had a girlfriend. I was . . . "

"An interlude?"

"Yes."

"You wanted more?"

"Oh, yes."

He nodded. "I have known my own share of unrequited love, Agnes. It can be a purifying and ennobling experience if we allow it to work in us, in full acceptance and without rancour. Perhaps you think that sounds ludicrously mystical."

She managed a smile.

"Good," he said. "And did they ever find out who was responsible for your friend's death — who it was strung up the wire?"

She looked at him open-mouthed. The alarm on his face told her how white her own must be.

"Agnes?"

She collected herself. "Zeke — Campbell's best friend — told us not to ask any questions. He said that Campbell's stepfather had talked with the police and he wanted the accident kept out of the news for Campbell's mother's sake. Zeke convinced me to keep quiet and to accept that it was just an awful coincidence. The wire must have been left up by workmen tarring the driveway or by surveyors . . . "

She jerked back as a dark thought reared up, one so perturbing she was astounded she could have blotted it out till now. On that terrible night, was that not exactly what she'd first assumed? Someone had set up the wire that severed Campbell's head from his body with precisely that murderous intent. Not an accident at all, but a deliberately planned homicide. Was that really possible? She had taken refuge in the idea of Blind Fate for so long, she had blinded herself as well?

An Arles memory now rose to the surface, painfully intact. Maybe she'd lost it when the policeman shoved her back and she bumped her head, or when Pinto told her about Zeke's suicide. Her mind was rent at that moment in so many pieces. Who knew what had fallen out of it? She can see Zeke amidst the broken urns in the Alyscamps mausoleum, his taut, thin body seeming to vibrate as it strained toward its looming dramatic descent into the arena. There was one hectic, horrid change in her recollection of this scene: the words that came out of Zeke's mouth took the form of little bubbles of blood. *It's about the wire that killed Campbell.* Each word a clot sliding over his lips.

"I've just remembered," she told Paul. "Before the demonstration in Arles, Zeke told me and Pinto he'd discovered something about Campbell and the wire. That was all he said. He told us he would explain after we'd finished what the Ark came to Arles to do."

"And what was it that your group planned to do in Arles?"

Sometimes haltingly, sometimes so rapidly he had to ask her to start again, Agnes set before him the bleak facts of the Ark's failures in Arles and Zeke's suicide.

As she spoke, a shadow settled on his face and then flitted away. On occasion, his eyes narrowed or he shut them and placed his forefingers against his bluish lids with a brief, delicate pressure. But these traces of his reaction to her words, whether sorrow or censure, were too mercurial for her to catch and read with certainty. In delivering her shame-filled account, she perceived more clearly than ever before, the galling absurdity of their plans and their utter lack of foresight. She imagined Paul thinking, as she was, that they had behaved as impulsively as children set loose in a playroom, sure that ever-watchful and indulgent guardians would smooth away all dangers.

"We blundered in, not understanding we were blundering. I see that now," she told him. "We assumed our mad schemes would work perfectly because we had just cause and right on our side. What a price Zeke and Campbell paid for our stupidity. We should have stopped Zeke. We all had our doubts at our meeting in the Alyscamps . . . " She twisted her hands, a gesture she was half-aware mirrored the coils of anguish in her chest.

Paul reached across the table and lay a cool hand over hers, stilling her agitation.

"Is that when you started drinking heavily, Agnes, after Pinto told you Zeke had killed himself?"

"No." She hesitated. "The first time I drank myself into a stupor was after we found out that Fergus Jonquil, our ethics professor, had been murdered."

"Ah, yes, I heard something of that unpleasant business. The college undertook some considerable damage control, I understand. I don't think the case has yet been solved, has it?"

"I don't know. I've been . . . away."

"Of course, forgive me. Were you fond of, or close to Professor Jonquil? His views were a touch extreme, I have been told. Or is that an unfair assessment?"

She sighed; studied her interlaced fingers.

"Extreme, yes, I suppose so. Sometimes I thought he was ragingly pure, like an inspired prophet. And sometimes I wondered . . . "

"If he might be mad?"

"Yes." This admission seemed less a betrayal now than it would have done four months ago. Was that because she had learned, at such expense of grief and guilt, how much more difficult it was to advance the revolution for animal rights than Fergus had implied from his elevated platform? Once again, the disquieting notion visited her that his high-minded exhortations were a form of self-glorification, and the passionate lectures largely a preening display. Her nerves could recall the bodily effects of his mesmeric fire, and that fleeting sensation afterwards of feeling vaguely soiled, as if she had engaged in an unsavoury sexual act.

"Poor Fergus," she began. "I got that drunk because I couldn't stop myself dwelling on his agony before he died. The fact that someone would torture him seemed just so barbaric. And then there was the ghastly . . . I mean Fergus was strangled and his throat cut with a wire. It was Minnie who told us all those details," she added quickly. "I would rather not have known. Minnie has a friend who's a policewoman . . . "

"How soon did this happen after your friend Campbell died?"

"Less than a week and a half."

"And the college offered Professor Jonquil's students no counselling of any kind?"

"No."

"In this they were very remiss," he said, his lips a thin line of censure. "Agnes, has it ever occurred to you that you and your friends were in a state of post-traumatic shock when you came up with the scheme for the protest in Arles. Two of your comrades in arms, to speak metaphorically, were killed in a particularly gruesome fashion within days of each other. One of these deaths, of a person much beloved, you all witnessed. In the second case, you were furnished with sufficient description of the protracted execution — again, I speak metaphorically — to produce the illusion you were witnesses. The effects are no different than for soldiers who see their friends dismembered and destroyed in a horrific way on a battlefield. You and your friends were reeling. Your judgement was impaired by shock and deepest distress. And then too . . . "

"We were . . . are . . . very young."

"Yes. Please do not misunderstand me. I consider your group's cause to be admirable and just. Few human aspirations are more worthy than the desire to alleviate the suffering of living creatures. But the fact is that the extent and scope of suffering on this planet far exceeds our ability to moderate it definitively. We do what we can, by increments, and in accord with accepted moral practice. To dwell exclusively on suffering, whether of animals or humans, is unthinkable, perhaps even for the greatest mystics and saints. For most of us such a fixation would drive us mad. It is a question of self-preservation, Agnes, and not moral cowardice. We do what we can, as I said, to lessen the total burden of suffering in the world. But we cannot eradicate it, just as we cannot fathom why those who are most vulnerable, including beings without language, are suffering now, even as we speak. The reasons why there is so much pervasive suffering are beyond our ken, beyond the reach of mortal understanding. But here is what I do know, and I may sound to you like a fusty schoolmaster: we must nurture our talents and use them to add to the store of good in the world. You have exceptional gifts, Agnes, an extraordinary natural insight into the moving spirit alive in certain works of art. This is no small thing, believe me. I recommended you for the scholarship because your talents are remarkable and because I sense you grasp the salvific powers of art. I hold that these powers benefit not just those who practise and study the arts, but the world at large by adding to the store of good. This is our discipline: those of us who are fortunate enough to have the talents and the inclinations."

He switched so suddenly, she was unprepared for the question: "Are you returning to Bremrose?"

Confusion numbed her tongue. "I can't," she managed. "Not now."

"I think you must, my dear. For your mind's sake and your soul's. Do you think me old-fashioned, Agnes? In this theory-driven, secular age, what professors dare speak of souls? Well, I do and I shall. What do you say? Shall we meet again here on Thursday at two? And in the meantime, will you keep going to the AA meetings?"

She agreed eagerly, thanked him and sat on for some minutes after he left. She marvelled at the good fortune that had delivered her to a listener as sensitive and generous as Paul Otterly. When they next met, he would very likely ask her to recount her lowest point, that knot in every alcoholic's story by which salvation hangs. She must tell him how her rampant vanity and drunken delusions had fed the urges of a killer. Can she also tell Paul about Laelaps? Or would he begin to doubt her sanity? She did not want to lose either his interest, or his faith in her. Would *she* believe such a story? She pondered this question throughout the evening, and all the next day, and decided she would be very dubious indeed.

He surprised her by asking, not about the nadir of her alcoholic history, but why she had chosen to come to New York.

"To lose myself in something huge," she said, wholly aware she was parroting Pinto. Once again she wondered where he might be. Most often, she pictured him surrounded by an immensity of space, sitting cross-legged on a sacred mountain. He was communing quietly with God while a warm rain washed him clean of the taint of despair occasioned by the Ark's failures. Sometimes she saw him removing three blood-encrusted barbs from his chest, and then laying them with immaculate precision on a square of white linen. One for Campbell. One for Zeke. She was uncertain about the third.

"And to see the Piero di Cosimos at the Met," she added, although her tongue tripped over the last word. She was putting off telling Paul about her hysterical outburst in front of the paintings; how she had flailed and cursed as the guards bundled her out. To say it aloud would be like admitting to defecating beside the font in a cathedral. She must, of course, tell him. She could not be worthy of his experience and advice unless she lay the most despicable and shaming of her deeds before him.

She determined not to take the cowardly option. She will not stare into her cup as she speaks, but look at him, bearing fully any disapproval or distaste he manifests. Yet as she recounted her disgraceful behaviour in gallery 607, she observed no change in him. He inhabited the same quietude, and his expression was as impenetrable and smooth as glass. It occurred to her then that his composure must be deliberately cultivated: it was his way of reassuring her, without recourse to words, that he was unshockable. He will have brought this same coolly reflective countenance to his sponsorship of Clarisse and all the others he has helped.

The insight flashed upon her that his untroubled face was a mirror; he was letting her see the structural AA principle at work; that, as alcoholics, they shared the same basic story. The plot of his testimony was also hers and every other alcoholic's ever born. Powerlessness in the grip of the addiction; the plummet to a place so black and thick with self-hatred you must either change or die. And then this juncture at which she was now fortunate to find herself: the chink of light revealed; the possibility of renewal and transformation that she might keep and cultivate, if she held as fast to the disciplines as did the fastidiously elegant scholar sitting opposite. Today Paul Otterly wore a shirt the mauve of the violas Nana had favoured in her garden. His narrow tie was a sleek band of silk, a yellow identical to the viola's centre.

"You will not have been the first," he commented when she described the guards depositing her on the stone steps. "You've been back to the Met since, haven't you?"

She caught, for the first time in any of his questions, an urgent undertone. "Yes, every day since I stopped drinking. I went this morning."

"Do you know why you had the outburst in that particular place, Agnes?"

"My mother . . . " This unpleasant word was out of her mouth before she could retract it. Now it was far too late because her mother had inserted herself into the banquette beside her. Even though this was a mere imagined presence, Agnes felt an immediate blight: she was dispirited, her energy pooling away.

You did what, Agnes? — In a public place, one of the great art galleries of the world, you make a total show of yourself! Daddy will be mortified when he hears this.

What if someone we know saw you? I am appalled that any daughter of mine could indulge in this kind of vulgar, aberrant display. Haven't your antics in France caused us enough harm already? Daddy and I can hardly hold our heads up when we meet the neighbours, and as for our situation at work . . .

To cut off this debilitating train of thought, which all too uncomfortably mimicked her mother's accusatory style, Agnes jerked her elbow sideways. This childlike magical gesture served its purpose. She pictured her mother sliding gracelessly off the banquette and onto the floor, her pink lips parted in a look of surprise.

"My mother told me that when she was shown *The Hunt* on a school trip, it made her feel so queasy she fainted. That's how she sees Piero di Cosimo's works featuring the animals and hybrid creatures. She thinks they are bestial and coarse and brutal, the product of a diseased mind. She loves Botticelli. She has a huge reproduction of *The Primavera* on the wall over her desk. I wanted . . . how can I say this? I wanted to stand in front of that canvas in particular and bear a kind of silent witness to all it conveys to me. I wanted to do the complete opposite of what my mother had done. She saw a painted scene that was vile and grisly and blood-soaked. What I wanted to testify to, simply by standing and looking, was the painter's moral outrage and hope."

"Hope?" Paul looked perplexed.

"Hope. Yes." She described for him the intently determined androgynous rescuer, the animals that race away from the bloodbath toward a place of sheltering safety and how they are watched by the guardian treetop monkey whose round eyes emanate creaturely fellowship and concern.

"Hmmm . . . " Paul fussed with his already flawlessly vertical tie. "The moral outrage I can see, Agnes. As for these signs of hope, are you perhaps not grasping at some rather flimsy straws?"

"No, I don't believe that. The more I look at the painting, the more certain I become."

"I would advise you strongly to stay with the iconography of the forest fire, Agnes. You are still working on that, are you not?"

She nodded, but self-protectively drew back from telling him about the consonance she saw between Piero's painted tongues of flame and human tongues that spoke words devastating, dangerous and vile. This idea mattered to her intensely on both a scholarly and personal level. She must protect it, building the case solidly and painstakingly. She must convey convincingly how Piero used the destructive ravaging fire to symbolize the unconscionable damage humans did in their "evolved" form as the "language animal."

She considered again how Fergus had betrayed his students by inflaming them with ideals so rigid, they were unlivable in practice. She pictured a world overrun by the rats Fergus refused to harm. They swarmed the beds of children, the elderly and infirm. She thought too of how, in Florence, Piero witnessed Savonarola's firebrand eloquence turn the city into a police state. Neighbour spied zealously on neighbour and the Prior's band of armed boys roamed the streets, seeking out miscreants to bloody and maim. She was sure George Eliot was wrong when she depicted Piero di Cosimo in the stands watching the Bonfire of the Vanities with a wryly cynical smile on his lips. Agnes knew he could not have borne the sight, not just because of the wanton conflagration of many lovely things, but because of what was yet to come. He had foreseen the killing fields and the crematoriums. Whether past or future, it was all the work of incendiary tongues.

"Agnes." Paul's tone told her their time was running short. "We have strayed a bit," he said. "Can we go back to the day at the Met? Do you know what triggered the hysteria? Were you thinking of the death of your friend in Arles?"

"Yes, of course Zeke was on my mind. But I think what set off the hysteria was shock. I was looking at the painting of the hunt and I realized all I could see was the horror. I was looking at the scene in just the way my mother had. The treetop monkey wasn't watching benevolently over the escapees. He was up there because he was frantic and terrified. The animals fleeing to the left weren't going to elude the hunters because there were more waiting for them just out of view. I couldn't even see a vestige of Piero's moral outrage; just a doom-filled scene by a cold-hearted technician who showed off his skills by painting a superbly foreshortened human cadaver of ghastly hue."

Paul made a sour face. "Had you been drinking before you went to the gallery, Agnes?"

"No, but I was very hungover, and shaky."

"So you'd drunk heavily the night before, after you got off the plane?"

"Yes." She described the raw interchange with her sister in LaGuardia. How she had stood afterwards clutching the smart phone, the sleek black coffin shape pulsing with yet another message from her sibling, insistent in her righteousness. She had gone on clutching the phone because it was suddenly the only solid thing about her. Muscle, bone and blood had all turned to water. That was why her back slid so readily down the wall where she had stationed herself for the fatal exchange with Phoebe. She was deliquescing. The kind man with an emerald dragon on his T-shirt had asked if she was all right and she had lied; then she'd continued sitting on the floor until she had re-materialized enough to stand up.

"My sister would not believe me," she told Paul. Warily she set her espresso cup in its saucer. She could not trust her hands. "I told her I wasn't at the protest; that the image they saw in the video must have been Minnie in a chimpanzee mask. We were all supposed to wear animal masks, you see, and that was Minnie's. Phoebe called me a liar and said that I was self-obsessed and that I clung to the stupid idea I look like a monkey." There, she had said it. She had exposed her tortured, grotesque teenage self to this meticulously thoughtful man whose respect she craved. She uttered a little sound that compounded disgust and sorrow, overcome by pity and frustration at the child she had been and continued to be. It distressed her that this impulse to self-loathing was still dormant in her, feeding on her vulnerability.

Phoebe saw her as the monkey-girl. That was the core of her sister's betrayal; not her resistance to accepting Agnes's word. She looks at me and sees all the names I was ever called. She sees my nights of hot tears and my isolation. She sees a lonely little freak with a most unfortunate combination of features. Whose fault is this situation? Is it mine?

"Agnes!"

She was confused as to why Paul looked so angry.

"Who first put this foolish idea in your head?"

She shook her head vaguely. "I was called names in school. It just went on and on."

"What did your parents do to help you?"

"They told me to toughen up, put on a brave face. Ultimately, they offered to pay for cosmetic surgery to make me look more normal."

"What!" His characteristic repose was momentarily undone as he plucked at his hair and tie. "Wait a moment . . . was this something you had asked for?"

"No. The idea was theirs. Because I was so unhappy at school, I suppose."

"Agnes, my dear, your parents should have been horsewhipped."

She looked at him wonderstruck. The extreme passion of his astringent judgement on her parents was so unexpected she was at first emptied of thought. This state was swiftly succeeded by the sensation she was being filled with a golden light, poured by a steady hand. She felt absurdly weightless and unencumbered.

"You are probably surprised by my vehemence," Paul said. "Perhaps it is because your story reminds me of my own, except that my parents' planned intervention was pharmaceutical. My 'perversity' was to be corrected with the right combination of drugs. I once overheard my mother use the term 'chemical castration' somewhat wistfully in conversation with my psychiatrist. She was a very stupid woman, I am sorry to say, and incapable of distinguishing homosexuality from pederasty. My father simply announced that he found me repugnant.

Thereafter he refused to sit at the same table or even be in the same room with me."

Agnes was shaken by this chilling account of familial cruelty. She tried, and failed, to enter imaginatively the vast continent of pain through which the adolescent Paul had laboured.

"What saved me was a teacher . . . well, several, but one in particular. She praised my talent. I drew well. I saw things in the reproductions she showed us of great artworks, and particularly Renaissance artworks, that others in the class did not see: those beautiful, humane, glowing faces of Fra Angelico, and Ghirlandaio and Raphael, where the spirit is visible in the flesh. I was caught up in the mysteries and the riddles of their narratives painted on wood and canvas and walls. It did not matter to me if the subject was religious or a secular myth; I saw the same miracle happen every time. A world sprang up before me, vibrant and full of a perfect, tremulous light where my eye was gladdened and my mind free and healed. I was rescued from my parents, from their noxious, maiming household, by artists whose physical bodies had long turned to dust. I was rescued by these painters' rigorous discipline, and by their faith in God and their own talent. Like you, I got a scholarship. I was given the opportunity to escape and I was jubilant at the prospect. I am the prodigal who never returned. There can be no forgiveness for the kind of hateful bigotry in which my parents specialized. I would not sully myself, or risk the self-damage of going near them again. I left them behind, and by that I mean totally. Once away from their miasma, I recreated myself. This was easily done, given that as Renaissance art scholars, we are immersed in stories of transformation all the time. We are fortunate to have such mythic materials at hand to help us become who we are. Of course I would never suggest you break as irrevocably with your parents as I did with mine. But there is no doubt in my mind they did you harm, and that they will continue to try to cut you off, albeit quite unknowingly, from your gifts. You know this intuitively, I am sure. You are well on your way. You have escaped the hunters — and unfortunately our families are often our enemies, intent on hobbling us or worse. You have already entered some other dark corners of human experience, bitter, despairing places that left you vulnerable to the seductions of alcohol. Staying sober is mandatory for you now if you are to survive to use your talents wisely and engage in this work of self-creation. Your concern for animals' welfare can come into this work. You will find a practical, legitimate way if you persevere.

"Here ends the lesson, Agnes. I have run on rather more than I intended, and you have not yet told me the incident that made you realize the alcohol had taken control of your life. It was not the scene in the Met, was it?"

"No."

"Well, we can talk of it next time."

She was relieved to have this respite. She still recoiled from relating even the bare bones of the sordid embroilment with Guam and her near death. As for the dog? If she told him, would Paul assume she was halluci-nating? Would she alienate his trust by such a revelation? Was that the quality he extended to her so generously? Trust, or a galvanizing faith in her abilities? She could not presume that what he offered her was affection, although she very much wished it were.

His brusque touch of her hand on parting seemed proof of the professional distance he preferred to maintain. She was the neophyte and he was far and away her superior, in both scholarship and sobriety.

"I may have some news for you next time, Agnes . . . about Bremrose and how we can justify buying you some time and so save your scholarship. Let's meet here Tuesday at two."

She sat on a while after he had gone, chafing at this final remark. He so obviously wanted her to return, even though the very idea made her ill. What if he was mistaken and Bremrose drove her back to the solace of the bottle, and she plunged deeper, and perhaps fatally this time?

To bolster her courage and convince herself of the soundness of Paul's judgement, she pulled from their earlier conversation the words that had most astonished her. She wanted to savour again his outrage regarding her parents' offer of the surgery.

"They should have been horsewhipped." She relished again the ripe fury on his face as he said this. Then it happened again: a scrupulous decanting of the light that is also truth. She sat amazed, drinking it in.

Why did she feel the need to set the scene for him when it would be an affront to his sensibility, and to hers, to conjure up The Aardvark's jarring interior? As she described the grotesque carmine décor, it dawned on her what she ought to have seen the moment she'd opened the door. This was a haunt for hardened New Yorkers, the locals who could handle or were oblivious to its ugly interior with its deliberately ironic resemblance to a new and gaping wound. She had stumbled in, unsteady, untried and unprotected by irony, wit or experience. She had lacked the requisite cynical carapace. On the contrary, she'd been nakedly, perilously needy. She had parted her legs shamelessly for him as he stroked her under the table, inviting her own wounding.

"He looked like Campbell," she explained, quickly qualifying, "I mean, his hair was so like Campbell's . . . when he first came in, his silhouette in the doorway, backlit."

Paul's eyes were closed, his lips compressed. He nodded. Grimly, she thought. Then his eyes opened and she saw a raw grief misted over.

"It goes on happening, Agnes. You must be prepared. I think of these jolting occurrences as the Dr. Zhivago delusion, which is so poignantly portrayed in the film. Zhivago is sitting on a rumbling trolley and he spies a lovely, blonde-haired woman he is sure is his lost Lara. He gets off in high agitation at the next stop, runs after her — we, the audience, see that it is not in fact Lara — and he collapses, clutching his chest. He has suffered a heart attack and dies, there on the street. This is what transpires every time. We catch a glimpse of a person who resembles, in some slight, even negligible way, the one we have lost. And we are made ecstatic, buoyed by the delusion that he or she is still alive. Their death was simply a bad dream and now we have woken into a heady, glorious deliverance. We want to rush over, throw our arms around this beloved person, so miraculously restored to us. Then, of course, the barren, chill truth makes the heart shrivel and we clutch at our chests like poor Zhivago. The worst perhaps is when we dream of our beloved in the warm fullness of being, and then wake into that devastating absence and relive the first knifing of the pain all over again."

"He cut me."

"What!"

"Guam. The man I met in the awful bar. We went back to my hotel. It was in the East Bronx. I was so drunk and so reckless. I thought he would make love to me the way Campbell had. He told me I was 'stupid like an animal.' Then he tried to cut my throat." She unwound her scarf to show him the livid, disc-shaped scar.

"Agnes, my dear."

"A dog saved me."

"What dog? Do you mean there was a guard dog in the hotel?"

"No. He came out of nowhere." She took great care not to sound defensive. "I locked the door after we went into the room. I slid the bolt." She showed Paul a postcard reproduction of the slain nymph with her satyr and canine mourners, pointed to the dark chestnut hound at her feet. "It was this dog."

"Agnes, I look at this painting every time I am in London. The work was once called *The Death of Procis* and was thought to illustrate the sad tale of mistaken jealousy out of Ovid's *Metamorphoses*. And — "

"Laelaps," she interrupted. "That is the dog who rescued me. Guam had put the point of the knife against my throat and the dog growled and bit him on the leg. And he ran. He undid the lock and the bolt and ran. Laelaps stayed with me and let me lean on him. He was very strong. His fur was like silk."

"Did you call the police, or alert the hotel's night desk about the attack?"

She pictured the hole in the wall that constituted reception and night desk at the A-1 Guest House. Had there been anyone there when she stumbled in with Guam?

"No. I ought to have called the police. I suppose I washed out the wound. I did do that. And the dog stayed with me, you see. He lay down beside the bed."

"The man did not enter you? You did not have sexual intercourse."

"No."

"I have one more rather urgent question to put to you, Agnes, before we talk about the apparition. Can you remember if the knife was clean? My concern is whether it had blood on it already."

HIV. Her stomach lurched. She searched the lurid shards of her memory of the galling, transgressive scene that had erupted on the bed. Her exposed breast. His hissed crude invective. The black hairs on his wrist. His Adam's apple an obscene bulge as he pushed his face near hers in a terrible parody of passion. His features hideously contorted by contempt. The fear clawing in her belly and all over her scalp, then behind her eyes. Blackness. Until the shock of his breath searing her cheek as he bent over her, his knees gripping her hips, and his left hand a heavy vise clamping both her wrists to the wall. In that smothering proximity, his pores exuded the stench of imperfectly digested meat.

She'd had a foretaste of her own death then and understood how he perceived her. She was a lump of matter to which he would apply his blade with judicious, discerning cuts. His words came back to her in a newly lethal guise.

"I am an artist." There would be no frenzy; only a cool exactitude, ear to ear, then throat to navel.

She disinterred a shocking remembrance: the moist-eyed gaze of rapture he lavished on the knife. He had looked with a pride-filled love at its glittering edge and the tip he would shortly dig into the yielding hollow of her neck. Briefly, he had turned the knife in the air, this way and that, so that he might better admire its two reflective surfaces.

And yes, she had seen that both sides of the blade were immaculate. The knife was probably the only unsullied thing in the room. Until the dog came.

"The knife was clean," she told Paul.

"A good idea to get tested in any case," he said.

He remained silent for some moments, all the while keeping his long brown eyes trained on her face. She wrestled with the notion he was employing some intellectual probe devised for ferreting out mendacity in his students. But why would she fabricate such a tale? The worst she could be accused of, surely, was reporting on a phantasmagoria. The wound and its livid remnants were real enough, as was the brush with death.

"You are lucky to be alive," he said finally.

"Yes."

"And perhaps fortunate too, to be delivered such a cogent, pressing lesson early on. You willfully impaired your judgement with alcohol and very nearly paid with your life. You see clearly, and will not forget, the depths of degradation into which alcoholism takes us, and how completely it despoils our integrity and our gifts. And now . . . " He closed his eyes and folded his hands. It was a classic prayerful pose, except for the fact he was not on his knees. When he opened his eyes and looked at her, his pupils appeared huge, gleaming with a disconcerting intensity.

She waited, in an unsettling tension, for what he would say. He looked like a master brooding on a condign punishment for a lapsed follower. Did the Twelve Steps make any reference to fantasists? Will he chastise her for her failure to distinguish fact from the projections of an alcohol-sodden brain?

"Would you pass me your postcard, please, Agnes?"

She hesitated a second before complying, wrestling with the irrational fear he would rip the picture in two.

He pored over the image while she waited, lacing and unlacing her fingers beneath the table.

"Has it occurred to you that the scar at the base of your throat anatomically duplicates the javelin wound suffered by di Cosimo's dead nymph?" He tapped the base of his neck, above a crisp collar of cornflower blue.

A strange, exhilarating fear swept through her. Her wound and the nymph's wound: how indeed could such an uncanny coincidence come about? She dared go no further with this unanswerable question. To dwell on it would be to enter a vast territory, perilously charged. Such delving could also be dangerously solipsistic. She must step back and simply yield, as she had done to a large extent with the apparition of the dog. What had happened was inexplicable. Not a miracle. Certainly not that. She was far too flawed a being to merit miracles. What then?

She looked up at Paul expectantly. His brow was creased. An awful thought blighted her perspective. Surely he did not think she inflected the wound on herself?

[413]

She must, and did, ask him this question.

"My dear young woman, most assuredly not. I know you to be honest, perceptive and intelligent. 'There are more things in heaven and earth, etcetera.' Let me tell you about a veridical vision I once had, at a moment of extremity in my own life. It was not a dog, but an angel I saw. This is an experience I have only ever told to a very few trusted friends, and now I will tell you.

"This happened some weeks after my stay in hospital, being treated for the internal damage caused by drinking the shoe polish. The pain of missing my partner had again plunged me into an abyss of despair. I bought a bottle of Jura, produced on that rugged island populated mainly by seals and red deer. It was the place George Orwell spent his last days. Perhaps that too influenced my choice. I was about to open the bottle before me, at the kitchen table, when I became aware of a presence in the room, rather like the heaviness that presses on one before an electric storm. I looked up from the bottle and saw towering opposite me, in the chair where Richard used to sit, a muscular angel. His face was like Raphael's Saint Michael, a beautiful, although undeniably masculine face with a strong jaw and eyes more supercilious than kind. What struck me most, what made me most afraid, were his wings, which were massive and unfurled. I sensed the lethal power lurking in the dense structure of vanes and barbs underlying those mighty pinions. I thought of Leda, and pitied her. The wings were a peculiarly ugly colour, like dirty bathwater or dog urine on snow. He did not wear the typical Renaissance angel's flowing garments with the characteristic sculptural folds. Rather, he was dressed in the drab olive garb of a doctor in an operating theatre. And thus I have always thought of him as the Angel Doctor. He said only one thing to me in a basso profundo that made the room shake. He said: 'Paul, you do not have to drink.' The sternness of his utterance was like a whip lashed across my face. There was no kindness or gentleness in him, as I said.

"I stood up on trembling legs and poured the whisky down the sink. I ran water to flush away the smell. When I turned around, the chair he had filled with his magnificent presence was empty. That was my veridical vision, Agnes. Like you, I have no doubt that what I saw was 'real' and pre-eminently truthful, most particularly for its ramifications on my life. I was irradiated by the vision. I hesitate to call it mine. The appearance of the towering Angel Doctor literally stilled my hand. Although I have often been tempted, I have not purchased or partaken of alcohol since that day.

"It interests me enormously that our visions have a similar source. They spring from the work of painters to whom we devote a scrupulous and passionate attention. I therefore think you will appreciate, as I do, an insight provided me by one of the few friends to whom I entrusted the details of my experience. He is a polymath, whose many areas of expertise include a wide-ranging knowledge of the world's religions. When I told him about the Angel Doctor's resemblance to Raphael's Saint Michael, he asked me if I had ever encountered the Hindu concept of darshan. I had not and this is how he explained the idea to me. The Hindus believe that the more often they go to the temple to look at images of their gods, the greater is the gods' power and their actual visibility. In other words, by paying worshipful attention, by really looking, we intensify the gods' aura and the eidetic clarity with which they are seen in this world. You see what my friend was getting at, Agnes? By my vigilant and often wholly enthralled study of Raphael, I had, in some sense, brought an aspect of his art to life. I offer the concept to you as an intriguing possibility to ponder with regard to your own experience. What do you think? Or rather, how do you feel?"

"Overwhelmed," she admitted.

She found his suggestion marvellous, yet simultaneously so alarming it threatened to overturn the commonsense world altogether. She deliberately drew back from the fearsome edges of this startling precept, so starkly revealed against the quotidian. She would ponder it later, as Paul counselled.

"At the risk of overwhelming you further, Agnes, I would ask that you take this poem and read it." He handed her a copy of *The New Yorker* folded open at a page of close-set text. It was not a magazine to which Agnes had ever been particularly drawn. But once she glanced at the poem, set in its own box at the bottom of the page, her interest immediately quickened. The title was "A Renaissance Monster."

"The author's name is Hugh Massinger-Pollux," Paul told her. "He is in his early nineties, I understand, and he regards himself as a last living repository of the Modernist tradition — a direct heir of Pound and Eliot and Yeats. I gather that in some academic circles he is derided as a quaint, pontificating egotist. In other critical camps, his work is passionately championed as lucid, steely and musical. He will be of interest to you because he has embarked on a series of poems inspired by the secular paintings of Piero di Cosimo. The one I have given you plays with the conceit that the monster in *Perseus Rescuing Andromeda* is in love with his captive."

"Oh!" Agnes exclaimed. She was uncertain whether to feel triumphant or trumped that a well-known poet had seen exactly what she'd perceived the first time she looked at Piero's suffering sea-beast. "That is just what I have always thought," she told Paul, not caring, for the moment at least, if she sounded jejeune.

"Ah, well then." Paul's smile was mild. "The ducks, as an old professor of mine used to say, are lining up."

She looked at him perplexed.

"I am sorry, Agnes. I did not mean to be deliberately obscure. I was simply reacting to this most happy coincidence of your perception matching so seamlessly with the poet's. So I will cut to the quick of the matter. Some days ago I was given a letter of enquiry that Hugh Massinger-Pollux had sent to our Dean of Arts. Specifically, Mr. Massinger-Pollux is seeking the services of a researcher to assist him in his work on di Cosimo. The job would be short-term, conceivably three or four months. I thought at once of you, Agnes. Such a situation would give you a period of justified leave from Bremrose. I can easily substantiate in a letter to your Dean and the Board of Governors that your work with Mr. Massinger-Pollux is essential to your studies, particularly since he is now living in Tuscany, in a villa near Florence. I am sure you see the advantages. You have not yet been to Florence, I think. Simply to walk about the city's historic core, which is so little changed since di Cosimo's time, will fructify your own line of thought as to the character of the man and his creations. You can see the hills and the remnants of the forests where he doubtless sketched the animals and birds we see in the paintings on which your own research centres. Not to forget the Uffizi, which holds the Perseus and Andromeda. You can look, as closely as the guards will allow, at the grand physiognomy of the monster whom both you and Mr. Massinger-Pollux believe to be smitten. I must warn you that time is tight. Although I have no doubt your qualifications are pre-eminent, there may be others who are interested in applying. I understand Mr. Massinger-Pollux has sent his enquiry to several universities. Can we meet again tomorrow? Give me your answer then, and I will email the venerable poet directly. My recommendation will be glowing, I assure you. What do you think, Agnes? Will you read the poem and give this proposal your consideration?"

Her head was reeling. Oddly, it was the prospect of seeing the actual forests where he'd sketched the animals which pulled at her most powerfully. Of course she had qualms. Was she up to the task? What if the elderly poet was irascible or made sexual advances? — No, she corrected herself. That was a ludicrous notion. He was far too old for such urges.

"Tomorrow, then, Agnes?" Paul was already on his feet, glancing at his watch.

"Yes, thank you."

It was a few moments before she was able to focus clearly on the words of the poem. The idea that she would soon see Tuscan *contados*, Florence and the foaming coral ruff framing the lugubrious features of the sea monster, had set off spangled fireworks in her head. Finally, she read:

And Cosimo Rosselli, his godfather, and the master to
whom he was apprenticed
Took Piero with him to Rome where Rosselli was
summoned by Pope Sixtus IV
To paint certain frescoes in the Sistine Chapel —
A Sermon on the Mount and the Healing of the Leper
(1481).
The young Piero did the landscapes for this fresco.
And see! Above green hills surging strongly as song
The rising sun englobes a small and solitary bush in
olden blaze.

Here, this early, is Piero's signal fire.
His origin, his marker and his passion.
The flamey fingers point forward to his masterworks
Where fire behaves in accordance with its most secret
nature
Inhabiting even the eye of the monster Perseus slays
Mistaking its love for vilest cruelty.
That gaze the beast turns on the captive Andromeda
Is tender, truthful — mild.
Love is the flame in the monster's eye.

It was the last phrase clinched it. How perfect was this
synchronicity, so much so as to seem unreal.

By eight o'clock that evening, she had the poem to
heart. How amazing this opportunity should present
itself, almost like a divine dispensation. She would have
the time she needed to heal, in a place of safety and intellectual exchange, and to ready herself for the return to
Bremrose in January. *The ducks are lining up.* She turned
over in her mind this quaint expression of Paul's, picturing

not real birds, but their wooden effigies, like the ones in old films featuring scenes at country fairs. Fair-goers tossed a ball at the row of little wooden ducks set above a trough filled with water, in the hope of submerging them all. Not birds lined up for an actual hunt, then; no bullet penetrating feathers and flesh. No spilled blood; only an innocent game played at an old-time fair.

"Yes," she told Paul immediately at their meeting the next day. "Thank you. It would be a wonderful opportunity. I deeply appreciate . . . "

He waved his hand airily. She was reminded of Prospero. "I am most pleased at your decision, Agnes, and happy to assist you. I do not want to see you forfeit your scholarship. I have an email ready in my drafts to send to Mr. Massinger-Pollux. Why not send it now? It's about four in the afternoon in Italy. *Et voila.*

"I want to touch briefly on the risks involved in this undertaking . . . please do not look so worried. I am referring to the risks posed by alcohol. You will be offered drinks and you must stay resolute in your sobriety. If ever you are perilously tempted, if you feel you are in danger of a slip, call me. Here is my number."

The card he passed with the relevant contact information for Paul Otterly, PhD, Professor Emeritus of Art History, appeared hand-engraved. The font was teal blue on cream.

"Well, Agnes, by tomorrow morning we should have his answer. I forgot to mention that there is a small honorarium goes with the position, plus room and board at the villa. He has a young companion staying with him, I understand the daughter of an old friend."

Agnes was relieved by this news, particularly given her concern about being alone with an elderly poet who might well be cantankerous. She was startled by a looping trill of birdsong emanating from under the table.

"My phone," Paul explained. "The Lark Ascending."

She waited while he checked his messages, thinking how apposite this title was to her present potential good fortune, and all it presaged for the proper completion of what she had come to think of as her "grief work." In Tuscany, with a new slate of duties on which to focus, she could throw herself into the old labours Pinto had advised her were the best response to death. She could renew her vow to live in a way that carried on Campbell and Zeke's ideals.

Paul glanced up from reading his message. "It's from Hugh Massinger-Pollux," he told her. "He is certainly a little prolix. But it's clear he's enthusiastic about your credentials."

At last Paul closed his phone and smiled widely. "You are to go as soon as you ready, Agnes. Mr. Massinger-Pollux says he will have someone meet you at the Florence train station. You have only to call or text his companion to let her know the time of your arrival and she will make the arrangements."

He passed her the page from his notebook on which he had written out these details in a fine script.

A shadow fell across the page as the light in the café was abruptly blotted out, and the whole building shuddered. Agnes looked out the window in alarm, the lurid image of the crumbling Twin Towers and its plunging bodies dominating her mind's eye. What she saw was a huge garbage truck rumbling just outside, its mechanical jaws grinding the refuse tipped into its maw. If this rational explanation calmed her, it nonetheless gave her pause. She realized this was the first time since her arrival in New York that she had paid any mental homage to the people who died in the 9/11 attacks.

She revisited her girlhood's moral outrage at the photographer who had captured the image of those falling bodies, and the world's media that promulgated it. At ten she was old enough to be revolted by the desecration of those last harrowing moments of life, where the only proper response should have been to bow one's head and weep. She believed this still: that the photographer ought to have averted his eyes and left his camera dangling from his wrist. But then, did she not feel the same about most of the images of extreme suffering that were the media's daily fare?

"He shouldn't have taken that photo," Pinto had said of the picture Zeke snapped of Kit standing by Campbell's graveside. At the time, she had thought his judgement a bit harsh. Zeke was always well-meaning, if impulsive. She agreed with Pinto nonetheless. The recollection of Kit as captured on camera, gaunt, haunted and shorn, still evoked the sensation of a hook caught in one's flesh. Kit had looked like a muted cry of hysteria bound in human skin.

As Agnes refocused on Paul's logistic notations for Tuscany, she was startled to see the name Kit McCready beside the cell phone number. For a moment, she allowed herself to doubt what she saw. She closed her eyes, then opened them to see the gorgeous flourishes Paul had added to the capital K and M. Hadn't Zeke told them at the May Day meeting that Kit was staying with friends in Tuscany?

The coincidence was nonetheless so jarring she could feel the milky coffee beginning to curdle in her stomach.

"Kit McCready," she said, surprised that the words tasted bitter to her.

"The young woman, yes?"

"I believe I know her. Is she from Boston, do you know?"

She watched Paul's eyelashes flutter as he scrolled through the text. As she waited, she invented a host of Kit McCreadies, short and plump, blonde and muscular. They came from places like Kalamazoo or Toledo.

"Yes," Paul looked up triumphant. "'My young companion from Boston' is how he describes her. But Agnes! What on earth is wrong? You have gone quite white."

"Kit was at Bremrose. She was Campbell's girlfriend."

"Ah, I see."

She stared fixedly at the backs of her hands, recalling how absurdly lily-like they had looked against the fine dark hair feathering Campbell's chest. Kit does not know, she told herself. Of course, Campbell would not have told her. But what if . . . ? Oh, why must fate stick this barb in its offering?

"Has your risk in going just quadrupled, Agnes? Or is the factor even higher?"

"Higher? — Yes, I think so. But I will go. It is too rare a chance to lose."

Unexpectedly, he laughed. She was uncertain whether it was an entirely happy sound.

"Excellent!" he exclaimed.

She searched his long brown eyes for their habitual reassurance and found instead a coolly clinical regard.

His pupils had contracted. Under the table, she made her hands into fists, in a magical attempt to ward off the sickening notion that she had somehow been "set up."

The ducks are lining up. Had Paul unwittingly given himself away when he dropped that uncharacteristically colloquial phrase into their conversation? Were the ducks perhaps flesh and blood? A mother with her babies ranged behind her, unaware of the invidious presence encroaching silently?

No, she told herself. I am being foolish. She deliberately loosened and flexed her fingers, then carefully folded the paper into quarters, smoothing the creases to a knife edge. Besides, Kit and I are no longer the people we were at Bremrose when Campbell was alive. Grief has battered and scoured and honed us and made us more attentive and responsive to everyone's vulnerabilities.

She gripped this consoling notion hard, and smiled in good faith at her mentor. For the moment, his fine, mobile, child's puppet face showed her nothing but benevolence. Most assuredly, the ducks were wooden, and all manner of things would be well. She pictured how she and Kit would embrace in a spontaneous sisterly fellowship amidst the gentle round Tuscan hills.

TWENTY-THREE

Villa Scimmia

AGNES ARRIVED IN FLORENCE WITH two hours to spare before the car came to take her to Villa Scimmia where her venerable employer waited with his "young companion." It was not much time, but enough to absorb some small aspect of this celebrated city where Piero di Cosimo was born and spent most of his life. She would focus on him, as her lodestar and mainstay, whatever happened in the weeks ahead. For the moment, her apprehension about falling short in the execution of duties for the poet was exceeded only by her anxiety about seeing Kit again.

As the hour of their re-encounter loomed, she saw clearly the empty fantasy behind that imagined consoling, sisterly embrace. She did not really know Kit, other than the obvious facts: the lapidary, almost incredible beauty; the genetic curse of early onset Alzheimer's that had undone her grandfather's competence and was now undermining her mother's; the breakdown after Campbell's death that had sent Kit first to hospital and then here to Tuscany to recuperate.

She sensed how reprehensible it would be to compare her own sense of loss with Kit's. Wasn't it impossible, in any case, to map one person's suffering against another's?

As she exited Florence's dispiritingly functional train station, she was jarred by the thought that Kit might not know about Zeke. Given her fragile state, wouldn't her family have shielded her from all that went wrong in Arles? But the video of Zeke's bungled descent into the bullring had gone viral, as the detestable phrase had it. Surely Kit would be aware of how badly the protest had failed and its fatal consequences?

I ought to have texted her something far more personal, Agnes thought; not just the bald details of when I would arrive, and that I was looking forward to seeing her. I should have said what an amazing and happy coincidence it was to connect with her again. That would have been the "normal," courteous thing to do. Once again, she was forced to confront her appalling lack of social niceties, and the unwitting petty offences to which it gave rise. She had yet to absorb the appropriate cues and responses of human interchange as second nature, as most people did by the time they were in their teens. The repellent armour she fashioned in adolescence had come at a high cost: a self-consciousness so metallically rigid, it exerted its own perverse magnetism. She has too often attracted contempt and opprobrium where she most desired invisibility.

Of course, she was improving. She had changed immeasurably — not least in learning to extricate herself from that pit of inebriated despair she must spend the rest of her life circumventing. One day at a time. She must keep her various pledges to herself and to Paul.

While she was here, she hoped as well to find some way to pay formal homage to Piero di Cosimo as an expression of her gratitude. She was still in the dark as to what shape such a tribute would take. Certainly something far more fitting than the standard trite gesture of a rose laid obliquely on a tomb. Besides, there was no physical tomb. The church where Piero had been buried no longer existed. Perhaps some clearer idea of a suitable offering would emerge from her work with Hugh Massinger-Pollux.

She regretted she had no time today to visit Santa Maria Novella, which was Piero's parish church. Instead, she headed straight for Via della Scala, and started walking down this narrow street, now home to many boutique hotels with glassed-in fronts and marble steps. Although there was no record of exactly where Piero's house once stood, with its legendary vine-clotted garden, she lingered as long as she could. What was she hoping for, other than to murmur some quiet thanks to his prodigious, idiosyncratic spirit, long departed? Nevertheless, against all reason, she stayed alert for any fugitive scent of pigment ground fine in a mortar: madder, cinnabar, malachite, azurite or the rare and costly ultramarine fetched from the Hindu Kush. She stopped and stood stock-still, willing away all extraneous sound, straining to hear the swish of a paint-laden brush on canvas — the brush from whose tip all manner of marvellous beings flowed, including Laelaps, the chestnut-brown hound who was her saviour.

She knew this was not strictly so, and that it was actually the dog's creator to whom she owed her salvation. She has managed to prevail this far because the enigma at the heart of Piero di Cosimo's secular works has lured her on. Without him, she might not be imbued with such a strong life purpose, or indeed have any life at all. Yet now that she was in this treasure-filled city, where he had lived and worked and died, she was newly aware how scant was her knowledge of the man, and of his beliefs. She knew he was a practising Roman Catholic. In his will, he left money for masses to be said for his soul for twenty-three consecutive years following his death. But was he also a fervent animist and someone who really did prefer the company of animals to humans? How can she ever know if her conjecture is correct?

What if the Piero di Cosimo she has come to believe in, intense, mercurial, self-contained, watchful, shamanic, a devoted student of animals' sacred nature, is mere projection? She has always tried in her study of his paintings to use as deft and light a touch as possible; not grappling with an artwork's secrets so much as running metaphorical fingers over a beloved face. When she is lucky enough to have the insights come, they arrive somehow aslant her other thoughts, like spindrift. She feels then neither triumph nor self-regard; just a tremulous thrill of recognition that she is in the presence of a truth-bearing image, with all unbelief banished. At such moments, she seems to see through the eyes of the artist himself; the force and fuse of his creation move in her blood.

She had experienced this thrill when she first saw the love in the sea monster's eye. She'd felt it when she recognized the boar's human face in *The Forest Fire* as Piero's own. It had stirred in her spine when she saw in the elongated tongues of flame, and their destruction of the green woods, a mirror of the devastation wreaked by human words, incendiary or deliberately manipulative.

"Take care not to give your insights about *The Forest Fire* to Massinger-Pollux," Paul had counselled at their last meeting. His admonitory tone so took her aback she did not immediately reply.

"Agnes!"

"Yes. I understand." She was half bemused, half proud that Paul thought she had some glimmering too valuable to divulge before she published it herself.

She had been walking briskly, aware of the minutes speeding by. Checking her watch, she saw she had barely forty minutes left before she must return to the side street near the train station. There a man called Ernesto would be waiting for her in a Land Rover with a Union Jack decal on the bumper.

There was no time even to glimpse the Duomo or the Baptistery, and so she headed directly for the Piazza della Signoria. Here she had vowed to perform a ritual of remembrance.

She spied first the imposing crenellated front of the Palazzo, which was in Piero's time the city's seat of government. Then she stood and stared a moment, taking in the square's ordered architectural elements, and the dramatically positioned statues of gods and ancient heroes. Her eye moved from doomed Laocoön with his sons to the copy of Michelangelo's *David*, where the crowds clustered most thickly. Despite the bright clothes of the swirling tourists and embracing couples posing for photos, she could not abstract the Piazza from its cruel history. A year after Savonarola staged his Bonfire of the Vanities in this square, his body had twisted on a rope above a mammoth pyre. She circled the marble monument that marked the exact place of his execution, his neck already summarily snapped so that he would be spared the agony of death by fire. She tried not to dwell on the two monks condemned with him, to whom the Pope had not extended the same mercy. She hoped they had been very soon rendered insensible by the smoke.

She was certain Piero would not have attended this gruesome public execution, regardless of how much he detested Savonarola's Manichean reign. How could his inventive, anarchic spirit have endured those years of joyless constraint? She pictured him working in secret, producing his chalk drawings of pagan gods and mythic creatures whose images Savonarola forbade. Piero would perhaps have hidden these forbidden pieces under his bedding, lest they be discovered and his fingers broken or severed by Savonarola's thugs.

She was equally sure he would have shunned the spectacle of the Bonfire of the Vanities: the flaming tiered mountain, heaped first with wigs, mirrors, jewels, silks and carnival masks, and then, on top, the books of classical learning and works of art that Savonarola judged to be transgressive and corrupting to the human spirit.

George Eliot's novel showed Piero amongst the spectators, surveying the ludicrous destruction with a sardonic twist upon his lips. Agnes did not recognize this person; he was not her Piero, not least because he lacked innocence and an overtly questing sense of wonder.

She had barely fifteen minutes left before she was due to meet Ernesto. She walked diagonally across the square, in heavy remembrance of the animals who suffered their death agonies here. It was the Medici who had staged the exotic animal fights, pitting lions against horses, tigers against bears, and panthers against bulls for the people's amusement. How shocked she had been when she first came upon a reference to these abhorrent "entertainments." She simply could not reconcile this barbaric feasting upon pain with the Neoplatonic ideals the Medici princes cultivated in their respective elegant *studiolo*. Was this the first time she'd grasped how extremely thin was any civilization's veneer, even one that had produced some of the most sublime art and architecture in human history? What lurks just beneath the skin? She studied the back of her own hand, recalling how she had fantasized these fingers wielding a piece of jagged glass and slashing all the pretty faces at her sister's party.

She had a last ritual stop to make in the square. In Piero's time, the Signoria had kept a pair of caged lions as living augurs of the health of the Republic. If the lions grew listless or were afflicted with mange, Florence's fortunes would suffer. Agnes was perplexed as to how these animals could ever be truly well. No matter how appetizing their meals or solicitous their care, they were captives in a wickedly small space that must have set a killing cramp on their spirits as much as their bodies. She stared into the void above the cobbles in front of the Palazzo where the cage once stood. Soon enough a numbing chill beset her legs and feet. She was rooted there, some minutes longer than she'd intended, her body locked in its own sympathetic response to the lions' bewildered despair.

Her thoughts turned to all flesh-and-blood creatures condemned to death-in-life behind iron bars and in laboratory cages and factory-farms. If only she could *do* something. Her mind churned with the familiar daily torment of the Ark's calamitous failures: two deaths, immeasurable psychological damage, friendships in ruins and not a single animal saved.

It came to her in that instant that Piero had saved the lions by immortalizing them on canvas. She saw in her mind's eye the lioness who paces in the foreground of *The Forest Fire*, a look of outrage and defiance in her eye. Her consort, with his strong back turned, looks into the heart of the blaze. Why had it never struck her before that these lions were based on sketches he had likely made here in the Piazza? He has kept them achingly alive for five hundred years, just as he has the Medici giraffe, who once walked these streets, a living jewel in the ruling family's parades and pageants.

"I am searching for you." As she addressed these silent words to Piero, she felt someone's breath on her bare shoulder. She turned quickly around, but there was no one near her. Glancing at her watch, she saw that it was now several minutes past four. She was going to be late for Ernesto. It was not an auspicious beginning.

She had never been a runner. But now she half-trotted, half-jogged the route she believed was the shortest back to the train station. She had wanted to be presentable for her arrival at Villa Scimmia. Now haste has made her hair wild. A ragged ellipse of damp was darkening the blue cloth from between her breasts down to her midriff.

When, finally, she reached the parked Land Rover, it was in time to see a large, prominent-veined hand flick a spent cigarette from the window. It joined a little pyramid of smouldering butts that told her she was already much later than she feared.

She called through the open window on the passenger side. "Ernesto? *Mi dispacie. Tarde.*" Or should it be *tardo*?

How graceless her Italian was. He made no response, and seemed deliberately to wait some seconds before turning his head toward her. When at last he did, she had to brace herself against the pitilessness of his assessing glare. His eyes were narrowed in a face whose folds of flesh hung heavily, like the runnels in plush drapery. He was absolutely bald. His huge, solid head, thick neck and massive shoulders reminded her of Mussolini. She grappled with the unsettling paradox that Ernesto's features were simultaneously repugnant and sensual. She did not relish the idea of driving anywhere with this man, but what choice did she have?

"Ernesto?"

"*Si*. Agnuzz Vien?"

She nodded. On his tongue, her name sounded like a character in a farce.

He gestured to her to get in and she clambered up the step and sat with her backpack between her feet. He started the ignition and drove off before she had time to locate and fasten her seatbelt. The stench of the potent tobacco from his clothes and fingers penetrated right to the back of her throat. To distract herself, she concentrated on the elemental green of the stately cypresses bordering the road. From their height, she guessed they had stood for several centuries. Piero might have seen these same trees. It was a comforting thought.

Ernesto remained ensconced in a bulky silence she felt compelled to break open.

"Have you worked for Mr. Massinger-Pollux long?"

She immediately regretted this stilted enquiry in a language he might not understand at all well. He might not even be an employee. Kit's text referred to him only as Ernesto.

In any case, he ignored her.

"Kit," she persisted. "Do you work with Kit?"

The transformation was so extreme as to be almost comic. Ernesto swung his gigantic head around. He was beaming, his eyes alight. His bottom lip was wet.

"Ah, Kit. *Si. Bellissima.*" He then performed the classic gesture, which Agnes had seen only in films, of touching his thumb and first finger to his lips and casting off an invisible kiss.

"Kit," he repeated, as if he could not help himself. Agnes pictured him breathing the name into his pillow. He hummed the first few bars of "Una furtiva lagrima," his great head swaying in time on his enormous neck.

Something despicably primitive scuttled across the floor of Agnes's pelvis. She tried to scotch its progress by forcing herself to visualize this infantile emotion: a blind, lumbering crustacean about to spill its viscid eggs of rage. She detested its boiling malevolence. If only her envy really were an object, like a pincer she could pluck out of her flesh. Why was this happening? She hated the idea that jealousy of lovely women, like Kit and Phoebe, was written into her cells, and only slumbering till it woke.

She thought she had outgrown this childishness; that the rigours of sobriety had somehow chastened her; that she had begun to surmount this disabling bitterness.

She turned her glaring flaw around and around, wanting to seize and obliterate it. What kept interfering was the image of Kit as she had first seen her: that day in Fergus's class, mere moments after Campbell spoke to her, inviting her to the Ark's next meeting. She had absorbed Kit's beauty at that moment like a stab to the heart. Here was a woman who would make Phoebe look ordinary. Even if Kit never did or said a single remarkable thing in her life, she would still be legendary simply by virtue of looking as she did.

Agnes relived the awkwardness that beset her that day as she took in Kit's elegant leotard top and long A-line skirt. To salvage her dignity, she had clutched at Campbell's "cute outfit" remark, repeating it to herself over and over; replaying the exact dazzle of his smile and the sensation of falling upward into those eyes of unearthly dark blue. She had slept in her Punjabi outfit that night because of what he said. Although she never wore either the tunic or the pants in public again, she often pictured herself in their lavishly embroidered paisley. It was as if these clothes had become inextricable from her identity. She wondered if that was because the day she first saw Campbell, and then Kit, would always stand out as fateful. She was certain she had been drastically changed by those encounters. The Agnes who went into that lecture hall was not the Agnes who came out.

In large part, this transformation was due to her initiation into a heedless and exuberant infatuation. She was "in love" and her bones were rendered light as air. If Kit's part in her metamorphosis was far less personal, it was nonetheless implacable. Kit made Agnes confront the truth that resplendent human beauty has an almost terrifying power. To see a face like Kit's was to be set adrift in wonder, not quite believing — or in Agnes's case, wanting to believe — that she was real. Kit was, Agnes thought with gritted teeth, the kind of sublime mortal the old Greek gods would have eagerly besieged in the form of bull or swan or a shower of gold, unable to contain their lust. She sensed that here was a woman for whom a man might commit murder in order to have her by his side.

Quite unknowingly, Kit had injected Agnes with the scathing awareness that on the shifting, often subjective, scale of attractiveness, she would forever be on a bottom rung staring up at those paragons the gods loved best. The odd thing was that Agnes thought she had always known this; it was only that her enforced witness of Kit's perfection and Campbell's adulation stripped away any comforting notions she continued to nourish that a face "full of character" might on occasion trump the spell-binding meld of sensuality and refinement women like Kit had in such abundance.

She had managed nevertheless to regenerate the anodyne self-deceit she required in order to function in the world. Yes, of course she was attractive, albeit in an idiosyncratic, wholly unconventional way. She had needed to believe this particularly after Campbell took her to his bed and then dropped her, without a word, the minute Kit returned from Boston. Alone again in her own narrow cot, she'd wept and writhed, deprived of his lovemaking. She thought of this loss as equivalent to being cast out of heaven. Oddly, this maudlin, aggrandized metaphor helped her bear it. She had tasted of glory and although the source had been withdrawn, she knew herself to be transfigured. She had never stopped loving Campbell. She was able readily to forgive him because he had bestowed on her something she had never expected to receive.

On the other hand, she could not in all truthfulness say she had never hated Kit. She had done so intermittently, with an almost bloodthirsty ferocity. Envy was then a hot splurge in her throat, and all thoughts of Kit were mordant. Agnes dutifully fought these feelings, which she recognized as crude and unspeakable. But she never totally succeeded.

Then Campbell died and everything changed. Kit became the suffering widow, ravaged by grief inside and out. No one could envy the shorn, skeletal figure at Campbell's graveside, Agnes least of all. After Zeke showed them that disturbing photo, she had sworn never to indulge in those vile feelings again. Now here she was, moments away from seeing Kit again, fighting the familiar gnawing sensation in the pit of her stomach. How immature, she upbraided herself. And how dangerous.

"Tread carefully." Paul's last words to her. He had not elaborated. She had assumed he meant she should be very cautious around drink. She wondered now if his admonition alluded to something far more personal, like her proclivity for self-denigration. She must at all costs hold fast to the disciplines. Sobriety. Clear thinking. The yielding of self-doubt to the Higher Power. Was the religious impulse behind art really her Higher Power? Where else did she find solace, and the surety that a life purged of malice was worth the effort, fraught with failure as her attempts might be?

Hold fast. Keep your head up. She was baffled as to why these musty clichés still held such galvanizing power. Perhaps because they evoked Nana who made all such hoary encouragements sound newly minted and wholly sincere. As if in tune with her resolve, the Land Rover was climbing, sometimes steeply, an undulating road to a hilltop house. She ducked her head to peer upward through the windshield; she could just make out its russet tiled roof. On either side of this private road she was watched by sentinel cypresses, immaculately spaced. As the Land Rover ascended, the house gradually revealed itself: three stories of dappled tawny stone flanked by two one-storey extensions, each twice the length of the main house structure.

Agnes was surprised by how massive the villa was, far exceeding the needs of three or four people. Perhaps there was a live-in housekeeper or a whole contingent of houseguests. She had not even considered the possibility of having to deal with other people, apart from Kit and Mr. Massinger-Pollux. She quailed at the idea of a crystal-laden dining table where eight people of varying degrees of international fame traded witticisms and drank Chianti with impunity. Surely she will be able to secrete herself, take refuge in her work and station, like a dowdy governess in a Charlotte Bronte novel? She was still too emotionally raw to be always manufacturing a suitable social face, scant as her skills were in that regard. But if she was raw, what must Kit be?

She saw again, and wished she did not, the woman with the flame-coloured hair struggling toward the headless figure on the motorcycle, while Horace gripped her waist, holding her back. This vision prompted the habitual admonition: she must keep a constant check on her self-centredness.

Ernesto parked the Land Rover in front of a flagstone patio whose four corners were dominated by round-bellied terracotta jars large enough for a child to hide inside. A similar shade of terracotta banded the arced shuttered windows and the doors, of which Agnes counted three:

one — by far the largest — in the main structure and one in each of the flanking wings.

She was disconcerted at how cold her hands and feet felt, even though she stood now directly in the glow of the afternoon sun. To quell her anxiety, she turned fully around to study the view in all directions: first, down into the valley whose lush greens, emerald, olive and sage, soothed her, as did the faultlessly spaced farmhouses, their tiled roofs burnished in the clear light. It was a scene that might have been ordered by an artist's hand. She understood that what she saw was the work of centuries of loving cultivation, of both the soil and of the architecture, whose sturdy grace fit the setting as much as did the birds the air. She turned next to her left and right, and then up; behind the house oak and umbrella pine rose thickly as if both to protect and display the ancient villa in its fastness.

Her mother would love to stay in such a place. She smiled ruefully. This was the least acerbic thought she has had about either of her parents for some time. So it was with an expression caught between bitterness and regret that she turned to see Kit on the patio behind her. The sharp intake of breath felt barbed in her throat. How long had Kit been there, watching as she turned around, and then around again, like a schoolgirl in a game with her eyes scarfed?

Kit seemed to open a cleft in earthly time as she commanded Agnes's gaze. She was erect as a goddess. Her naked shoulders gleamed in a high-necked gown of sea-green gauzy stuff that gave the illusion of worshipping her body. Agnes was sure she heard Ernesto moan. How quickly Kit's hair had grown back, thick and long enough to pile atop her head in a charmingly heaped mass, with tendrils licking at her temples and nape. Around the neck of her dress, Kit had looped beads the colour of blood oranges.

It was Agnes who spoke first, determined to break through the numbing spell Kit's beauty cast. "Kit," she said. Only that, because she was at a loss as to how to allude to the events that had blighted their lives, the Ark's ultimate deadly cargo.

"Oh, Agnes." Kit still had not moved from her invisible pedestal. It was as if she was waiting for ritual offerings fetched at great peril.

Agnes approached, struggling with a self-image that rendered her squat, grubby and uncouth. None of these things are true, she chided herself. Hold fast. Keep your head up.

Kit held out her arms.

For one stunned instant, Agnes expected the mutually consoling embrace she had dared to imagine. Instead, she repressed a whimper of pain as Kit grabbed her upper arms, the long fingers digging into her flesh.

"Were you with him?"

Was there a hiss beneath the words? Agnes tried to break away. A winged panic was loose in her chest, and something worse was at work in her belly, rancid and churning. Surely Kit did not mean Campbell?

"Kit, you're hurting me." She spoke each word deliberately, as one would to a child trapped in a fit of temper. The change was breathtaking. The grim rigidity set upon Kit's features dissolved. The repellent glaze left her eyes. Her arms dropped to her sides, limp against the gauzy fabric.

"Zeke," she said, "poor, dear Zeke. Were you with him when it happened?"

"No. He drove to the cliff by himself. Pinto — I mean, Peter — went to the police station to do the identification." She could not bring herself to say "morgue" or the simple word "body". Nevertheless, she winced inwardly again as she pictured the macabre duty Peter had to perform.

"Pinto is a good man," Kit murmured. "Campbell always said he was the Ark's moral compass." She clutched at Agnes's hand. It was a gesture so completely void of tenderness that Agnes instinctually made a fist inside the vise-like grip. Kit's eyes were unfocused as she asked, "Do you think some people are born with a gene for goodness, and some have one for evil?"

Agnes heard the shrill note of desperation, and could find no words with which to respond. If she found the question naïve, it was also undeniably heartbreaking. In her mind's eye, she saw Peter grimace at the suggestion his virtue was innate. She recalled the swift war of light and shadow she had more than once witnessed on his face as he struggled to hold back vitriol and proffer instead some diplomatic emollient to calm the Ark's often-troubled waters. When, the morning after Campbell's death, he halved the chipboard table with a single blow, it was not so much the act that had shocked her as the dawning awareness this huge, gentle man carried within him such a fund of molten rage.

What could she do thereafter but admire him all the more? She had been made privy to a secret recess of his character that revealed how relentless his daily disciplines of self-mastery must be. And in the Alyscamps, when they lamented together the human wreckage the Ark had left in its wake and their own part in that heedless destruction, he had made clear he was equally capable of a lacerating self-contempt. She hoped, beyond all measure, he had not become irretrievably lost in whatever vastness he was seeking.

None of these things about the "real" Peter Dervaig was she willing to confide to Kit. To do so would feel like a betrayal of his private realm. More pressingly, she sensed Kit's mind was still far too tender to readily absorb facts she might construe as harsh. On instinct, Agnes knew she must leave intact Kit's notion of Peter as unwavering moral compass, particularly since it was an image of Campbell's making.

Kit had at last let go the fierce grip on her hand and was gliding toward Ernesto, who waited beside the Land Rover. "*Grazie*, Ernesto." She spoke the words from a queenly distance. Ernesto's head bobbed, his face aglow with a mix of adulation and lust so raw, Agnes had to turn away. Kit said something else in Italian which she did not understand. In response, the large man executed an ungainly bow. Agnes half-expected him to drop to his knees and lay his head by Kit's naked toes, on delicate display in her silvery openwork sandals. It was only when he set off on foot down the hill that she grasped at last that he was not an employee, but a neighbour whom Kit had pressed into most willing service.

"Thank you, Ernesto," Agnes called out. When he turned around, he looked not at her but at Kit, eager to seize a last opportunity to drink her peerless image down. Kit fluttered her fingers prettily in the air. Unable to pull his eyes away, Ernesto tried to walk backwards and so tangled one foot in another and stumbled.

"What an oaf," Kit said. "But he's a really useful neighbour, a farmer and a handyman. We get fresh eggs and vegetables from him and he's the only person who can fix the ancient plumbing in this place. I asked him to pick you up," she added, "because I got one of my horrible headaches this morning."

"Has the headache gone?"

"What?" Kit looked at her blankly.

"Your headache."

"Oh, yes. It's under control. Now, do come and meet Hugh. Then I'll show you the house or at least as much of it as you'll need."

As they came up to the main door, of solid oak set in its own portico, Agnes exclaimed at the exquisite handle carved in the shape of a monkey's head.

"Oh, didn't you know?" Kit said. "He's there because of the name of the villa. *Scimmia* is Italian for monkey."

They entered a white-washed, high-ceilinged corridor with a taint of mould. "I was so happy, Agnes, when I saw your résumé in with the other candidates Hugh was considering. I said 'Hugh, dear, I know this woman and I'm sure she would be perfect for the job.' I was dreading the idea of sharing the house with a, you know," she confided, "you know, one of those people who insist on displaying their brilliance at every possible instant. The ones who sneer at you if you can't tell a Rembrandt from a Raphael. The ones you want to strangle by noon. So I twisted High's skinny old arm. I mean, most of the other candidates had far better qualifications than you on paper: publications, fellowships and awards, that kind of thing."

What! — *Cole perspicua*. Cultivate clarity. Alberti's pre-eminent dictum for artists came floating out of the Tuscan air and Agnes grabbed it greedily. She must remember that even if Kit had a hand in her getting this position, she was not the sole engineer. Paul's recommendation would have carried considerable weight. And Paul had nothing whatsoever to do with Kit. Or did he?

Agnes saw the whitewashed walls flood toward her, an inundating sea of milk — only sour. She could feel her hard-won self-esteem shrivelling; she pictured Kit liberally salting the remnant tail of a brittle, threadlike worm. Had she been always so tactless? Was this belittling deliberate? The floor turned spongy beneath Agnes's feet. She registered with some alarm that her anxiety was in full spate as they stood just outside the door to the poet's study.

Kit said: "Paul is such a sweet man, isn't he? And don't you adore those lavender shirts?"

The little chink of doubt widened; then it gaped. Agnes searched Kit's face for some clue to her intent, but saw only brown eyes wetly gleaming, and a close-lipped smile that suggested unalloyed sweetness. Was it a game? And if so, to what purpose? There were certainly photos of Paul to be found on the Internet, in all of which he would doubtless be wearing a shirt in his favourite colour. Paul would have told her if he had ever met Kit, wouldn't he? His uncharacteristic colloquialism replayed in her brain. *The ducks are lining up.* Had there been a hint of a malevolent undertone? She knew she could not afford to think so.

She set quickly about dismantling her doubts. Paul was her dear mentor, who had vouchsafed her intimate details of his own degrading obsession with alcohol. He had trusted her enough to tell her of the visit he received from the Angel Doctor. He had gone out of his way to help her keep her scholarship and reputation at Bremrose. These were acts of faith on his part, and on them she must anchor herself. She had to persist, no matter how unnerving she found Kit's machinations. With any luck, this was a mere passing mood; the residue of Kit's morning migraine. Besides, it was not with Kit she had the contract, but Mr. Massinger-Pollux. She had never been so keen to meet him as at this moment. She had a crying need for a clear, unencumbered exchange; the assignment of a well-delineated task where innuendo and casual cruelties had no place.

"Hugh, dear, this is Agnes Vane."

They had entered a long white-washed room, whose vaulted ceiling was ribbed with old timber. Glancing up, she saw that the wood was riddled and cracked. To her right, the wall was furnished floor to ceiling with books, packed tight in shelves varnished with the red-brown stain known as oxblood. Directly ahead, in front of a high window with a pointed arch, was a desk coated in black lacquer and inset with tesserae of rose and ruby-tinted mother of pearl.

It was here the poet sat in a green and gold uphol-stered chair, whose high back completely obscured his figure. Agnes could see only his hands, covered in brown-spotted skin of startling transparency, as they toyed with a heavy-barrelled maroon fountain pen. She waited for him to acknowledge her presence, all the while trying to ignore an astringent odour that made her nostrils prickle. It was vaguely reminiscent of hospital rooms and sterilized instruments. She reminded herself that Mr.

Massinger-Pollux was extremely elderly, well over ninety according to Paul, and therefore vulnerable to infection.

Nevertheless, when he turned his chair around to face her, she was unprepared for what she saw. It was as if she was in a museum staring at a totemic stone head that had been buried centuries underground to weather and seal in its power. The weathering showed in the countless tiny wrinkles that seamed his flesh. The power was manifest in the head's small triangular shape and in the still-glittering eyes, perhaps once a dense emerald, and now a compelling malachite. His thick white hair was brushed back from his high brow and temples to create the illusion of a winged helmet of alabaster. His goatee tapered to a cruelly fine point. It was this feature as much as the eyes that transfixed Agnes as she strove to batter away associations she considered conditioned and banal: Mephistophelian, Satanic.

"I am very pleased to meet you," she said, thinking how much she sounded like a dutiful, well-trained child, mouthing empty syllables. In response, the poet made an odd grunting sound while continuing to scrutinize her face.

She tried to neutralize the irrational unease his stony face seeded in her. Groping for a root cause, she came up against the word "pitiless." He is old, she reasoned, that is why he appears inflexible, and as if incapable of anything but the most scathing instantaneous judgements. Then again, perhaps Hugh Massinger-Pollux's character was exactly what he projected: a severe and malicious minor deity, in whose haughty, grim regard was distilled a lifetime of arrogant dealings.

My brilliance coruscates, this face said. Why do you not shade your eyes?

He leapt suddenly from his chair and extended his hand, which was cool and dry and soon retracted. Although shorter than the regally towering Kit, he was still some inches taller than Agnes. He was therefore looking down at her when he said: "Such a bizarre little phizog you have, Ms. Vane. I can see why you would be so drawn to di Cosimo and his outlandish hybrids."

"Hugh!" In Kit's patently false cry of indignation Agnes detected a muted glee. Schadenfreude. How nasty. She was dismayed at the prospect of spending several weeks in this uncivil company. What has she done by coming here?

In an instinctive reaction to the callous remark, she put on the impassive face she'd first manufactured at school, based on an image she'd found of a Kabuki mask that suited her purposes admirably. Projecting an iron-hardness, the mask was painted a thick chalk white, the mouth frozen in a slight twist of disdain. It was a face impervious to harm and yet capable of uttering curses to dire effect. She had hoped never again to have need of that brittle disguise, yet here she was, face to face with her venerable employer, pitting her iron against his stone.

Iron won. Her unvoiced contempt appeared to move the poet to a quasi-apology. "Excuse me, Ms. Vane. I am sometimes excessively fond of hyperbole and indulging in outlandish statements. This stems from my unwarranted reputation as a 'crank,' foisted upon me by certain individuals uncomfortable with true genius. It amuses me on occasion to play upon this caricature. I ought not to have done so at your expense. "Indeed, you have a most distinctive and charming appearance. And Paul Otterly assures me that I will benefit from your refreshing insights into di Cosimo's secular creations. There, am I forgiven?" He made her a mock bow from his chair.

She could not bring herself to voice the polite lie that would excuse him. Nor was she ready to lay aside her wariness. She saw this caution justified when Kit began playfully to rumple Hugh's hair; then leaned in toward him and whispered in his ear. As she did so, her right breast, covered in the sea-green foamy fabric, brushed his cheek. The two then exchanged a smile so intimate, Agnes averted her eyes. When she looked again, Kit was standing behind Hugh's chair with a proprietary air. Stunned, Agnes scotched an automatic picture of their naked coupling, slack flesh against taut perfection. It was none of her business. Or were they toying with her again?

"So, Ms. Vane, shall we begin at once? I appreciate that you are probably suffering jetlag and in need of a rest. But I will prevail on only a few minutes of your time. I want to introduce you immediately to our *methodology*, if you will. I will require from you no conventional scholarly research; no hunting out of recondite debates on the likely metallurgic composition of the pots and pans in the Bacchus canvas, or the preponderance of meadowsweet in di Cosimo's swathes of wildflowers. What I want is a frank account of your sensibility's first flight when I pose you certain questions about the paintings that spark my interest. If you are as knowledgeable about the secular works as Mr. Otterly tells me, I am confident you will give me what I need. To encapsulate, I seek the mental jolt; the freshness of perception with which your eyes will endow me. Shall we begin?"

She nodded. Hugh then fetched a chair which he drew up to his desk, gesturing her to sit. Kit, to her relief, moved to the tall window where she stood looking out at the haze of green. Any distance was a blessing. Agnes sank down, grateful for the apparent normality these small courtesies evoked. Hugh set off briskly toward the book-lined wall. "I will be back presently with the plate," he told her. She puzzled over his choice of word. Was her head to be served upon one? Oh, poor Campbell. She did not want her thoughts to run to death and decapitation. She was terribly on edge, too weary and stressed to summon cogent remarks on demand. She felt as if she had stumbled far too close upon a thrumming hive; she must tread with the utmost care lest she be stung, not once or twice but countless times, and with a venom for which there was no antidote.

Then Kit disrupted the stillness, pulling the bands from her hair so that it fell around her shoulders like a ripe-red cape. She assumed a histrionic pose, pressing her upper body and face to the window glass, and stretching her arms wide and as high above her head as she could reach. Each of her long nails was clearly visible against the glass. The out-flung arms, long legs and torso created the strange illusion she was the letter Y made flesh. So disquietingly still, Agnes was reminded of a bare-bones drawing of a hanging tree. She put her hand automatically to her throat and touched the ridged remnants of her scar, opening the sensation of hot blood spurting under Guam's knife.

The air in the room started to thrum and press at her temples. She has been thrust inside the lethal hive now, into an atmosphere thickly malevolent. Meanwhile, Kit strained harder against the glass, as if she must break it, bend it, or turn it into some new element conformable to her will. Kit crooked a single finger of her right hand and with the very tip of her tapered nail, she began to tap lightly and repeatedly. Why was Hugh not reacting? Was he part deaf or had he learned to seal out his houseguest's annoying tics?

Then again, might she be the cause of Kit's bizarre behaviour? Did her mere presence trigger memories, unbearably vivid and bloodied, that Kit had worked vigilantly to expunge? Did Kit know she slept with Campbell? Was this her punishment — this disconcerting display of Kit's body straining against an invisible force, her sharpened nail tapping on and on as if to summon a primal power to her service? Or was this merely the prelude to a punishment yet to come?

Kit assaulted the window with her nail-tip at a more rapid beat. If she started to scratch at the glass, like a clawed, caged creature seeking a way out, Agnes would find it hard to hold her tongue. Mercifully, Hugh returned to his desk with an old friend: a copy of the book on di Cosimo Agnes had first seen on her mother's desk. He opened it at a place marked by a tasselled cord. Before her was a picture whose details she knew as intimately as she would the body of a husband. She thought of this painting as "the Ottawa canvas" because it belonged to the National Gallery of Canada. Its actual name was *Vulcan and Aeolus* and was the only masterpiece by Piero to be found in her country of birth.

Every living creature in the painting's pastoral world emanated a gentleness that always made her want to step inside, if only for an hour. As she looked down at the familiar scene laid open on his desk, she was restored to herself. No barbed remark from either Kit or Hugh could touch her. Here was the aged Vulcan she knew so well, his dark hair receding and the flesh of his exposed back no longer firm. But he was strong enough still to wield the hammer and smite the molten metal on his anvil. Opposite him sat grizzled Aeolus, god of the winds, pumping the bellows that kept alive the fire to make the metal labile.

She was pulled, as ever, by the benignly curious look of the long-haired young man on the white horse who leant forward to study this new miracle the gods had brought. He and his horse were so easily companionable as to seem one being. In a feat of painterly counterpoise, Piero showed the horse inclining his head at an angle exactly opposite his rider's. Together they composed a living scale: an untrammelled balance that spoke of the harmony that could exist between species. *It could have been like this.* So Agnes always thought when she studied this sublime pair.

The horse bent his head to smile (she knew no better description of his expression) at the man and woman seated on the grass with their baby. Her eye went next to the young man who slept upon the grass in the centre foreground, looking almost as if he might tumble out of the bottom of the painting. His nakedness was prelapsarian. He had bundled his dark green cloak to make a pillow and slept upon his side like a child, his arms folded over his midriff and his legs drawn up to meet them. His evident trust, that he could sleep upon the ground naked and unharmed, confirmed this was a world innocent of crime, deceit and predation.

How far away this world was from the unpleasant atmosphere of Hugh's villa. She had to remind herself that Piero's imagined pastoral was inspired by the landscape in which this very house sat, and that he had painted it mere miles from here, albeit over five centuries ago. He had brought his full panoply of skill, observation and inspired fancy to its creation, paying particular loving attention to the painting's generative source: the creature with the flowerlike head and astonishing neck that stood so quietly on four slim spotted legs in the upper-right quadrant. There was only one possible model for this exquisite animal — the Medici giraffe, whom Piero would have often seen as it was led through the streets of Florence, a living jewel in the ruling family's pageants.

She knew this extraordinary gift to Lorenzo de Medici from the Sultan of Egypt had met a terrible and senseless end when a servant led him beneath an archway too low to accommodate his height. The giraffe's fatal accident was in 1492. Experts dated *Vulcan and Aeolus* to 1495 at the earliest. Agnes therefore believed the gem-like portrait to be the painter's personal memorial to an animal whose idiosyncratic beauty would have thrilled him and primed his spirit as moral being and maker. Of all the living creatures at peace within the painting's green and golden world, it was the giraffe who most palpably embodied the unifying power of Eros. It was his singular glow that caught up and connected the diversity of creation the picture contained, linking the solitary black cricket on his flat stone to the sleeping youth, the mortals to the immortals, the birds of the air to the dromedary emerging from behind a craggy boulder in the far distance, each life joined to life, with Love as Prime Mover.

So when Hugh jabbed his finger at several of the painting's diverse inhabitants — the youth on the white horse, the old gods busy in the corner with their metal work, the builders in their loincloths raising the second storey of a wood frame for a dwelling, and said: "It ought to be jumble. It shouldn't cohere. But it does. Why?" she was ready. She was surprised, first, by her own eloquence; then by the look of delight that made his eyes as bright as she had imagined they had been in his youth.

"Marvellous," he said as she concluded. "I had not known about the Medici giraffe. Very fine," he nodded at her. "That is a deft and inspired reading of the composition."

Kit heaved a histrionic sigh. The layers of her gauzy skirt whispered, gauze catching on gauze, as she glided from the window to stand once more behind Hugh's chair. She looked down at the book with an expression Agnes interpreted as a sneer. It gave her mouth a most unpleasing shape. For the first time, Agnes saw that Kit had very long eye teeth.

"So, Ms. Vane," Hugh continued, "you have already exceeded my expectations of our intellectual forays together. If we progress thus, all shall be well. You can see now how our methodology will unfold. My concise, brisk question followed by your equally brisk response that draws, above all, on your exceptional instincts. Are we agreed?" Once again, he extended his hand.

This time his clasp felt firm and sincere to her, if such a sentiment can be gleaned from touch. At least now he was civil. Nevertheless, she had no intention of letting down her guard. Something was sorely out of joint in this domestic situation and no amount of praise of her "inspired reading" of Piero's works could justify setting a self-protective wariness aside.

"But I have kept you long enough," Hugh said. "Our most beloved and beauteous Kate will show you your room and the other facilities. Won't you, my dear?"

"Of course, Hugh."

The face Kit presented to Agnes was glacial. She lifted her right hand, cupping it in a beckoning gesture and led the way without a word. Agnes followed, newly aware of her heavy weariness and of an unwanted mental porousness which was a side effect of the jetlag. Sensations crowded in, ripe and overripe: the lure of Kit's fire-bright hair, the sea green of her skirt and the silvery sheen of her sandals. The idea came that she was caught up in the slipstream of a goddess, tall, proud and chillingly indifferent to her fate. Or was Kit indifferent? Her taciturnity, her rapid stride, as if she could not get this duty over fast enough, suggested rather that she held Agnes in contempt. Better contempt than hate, she thought, as Kit braked and swirled around to confront her with a face that brought to mind the phrase "a terrible beauty." In her bleariness, Agnes could not recall either the name of the poet or the poem; only that it was a famous lament about a country riven from within, where the young would soon lie bleeding in one's another's arms because they loved their land too well. Kit was riven from within, Agnes reminded herself. She has been broken. I am not. Compassion is in order. Peter would advise me so.

"This is the kitchen." Kit preceded Agnes into a long room, dominated by a scoured table of oak and a blue and orange painted bowl brimming with grapes. Agnes managed not to manifest her disgust when she realized the shadowy shape hanging from the ceiling was a ham upon a hook.

"Hugh's instructions are that you help yourself to whatever you want. You're still a vegetarian, aren't you?" This seemed more challenge than question.

"Yes."

"Then you definitely won't want to eat with us."

Agnes's mind reeled at the implication. Dismay contended with revulsion and there was a terrible taste in her mouth, as if Kit had forced upon her slivers from the ham upon its hook. Had she always eaten meat? And if so, had Campbell known? The very idea of his lips touching those of a carnivore revolted Agnes. She did not want his memory tainted by such a thought.

"In these cupboards," Kit slammed open their doors in a jarring percussion, "you'll find dried pasta, jars of pesto and antipasto. Fresh eggs, cheese and vegetables in the fridge. And yogurt. Loaves of bread are usually here." She pointed at a wooden box on the seamed counter.

"There's lots of decent Chianti. Take all you want. But you're a whisky drinker, aren't you, Agnes? Hugh's partial to Single Malts, but his personal stock is out of bounds, I'm afraid."

"I don't drink any more, Kit."

"Really?" Kit's feathery, flawless eyebrows were two cartoon-like arcs, signalling disbelief.

"Really," Agnes countered, aware even as she spoke that silence would have been the more mature and prudent response. Already, she had put herself on the defensive and exposed a vulnerability better kept hidden.

"If you say so." Kit's mouth had become an odd excrescence amidst all that crystalline refinement, a piece of dough badly baked and fastened hastily to the bottom half of her face. I know you will fail, this sneering mouth said.

Agnes worked hard at superimposing an image of Paul's kind, elfin face over Kit's.

"I'll show you your room now." The tone verged on brutal.

As Agnes turned to follow Kit out of the kitchen's back door, there was a clatter of metal striking stone. She looked down and saw that the toe of her canvas shoe had collided with a crude, jawed instrument as long as her foot and wide enough to engorge it. She had a vision of what might have been: five bleeding stumps poking through rent canvas.

"Oh," Kit sounded more amused than alarmed. "I ought to have warned you about the rat trap."

"Are there rats?"

"No rats," Kit said.

They entered a stairwell no wider than a coffin. The banister was greasy to the touch. A hollow was worn into the wooden steps from the countless feet that had run up and down over the centuries. It must be the old servants' stairway, Agnes realized. Where else would Kit put her but in the servants' quarters?

"The rat trap," Kit continued as they reached the landing and a whitewashed hallway stark as a convent's, "is one of Hugh's little jokes. He enjoys pointing it out to guests as a corrective to their idealistic notions of everyday life in the Renaissance. He tells them how many plagues swept through Florence between 1450 and 1600. Or is it 1560? I can't remember dates. Of course, people then didn't know rats were the carriers. But they didn't want them in the grain, did they, or biting their babies? Honestly, Agnes, I would tell you if there were rats in the house. And the trap usually sits safely inside the hearth. The cleaning lady must have moved it when she was in and forgotten to put it back."

They were standing now at the open door to Agnes's room, which was as characterless as a nun's cell. There was not even a holy picture over the narrow bed with its nubby, fustian throw. The only other furniture was an unadorned chest of drawers, hand-hewn of butternut, and a bedside table with spidery legs, on which stood a lamp with a tightly pleated ochre shade.

"You'll be private here," Kit said, "and you have your own bathroom just two doors down."

"Thank you." Privacy would more than compensate for the room's utter lack of charm. If she was to be nimble in negotiating Kit's feints and genuine cuts, she would need a rooted sense of separateness to nourish her strength.

"By the way, you're not phobic about rats, are you, Agnes? You're not afraid one will get in under your door, even when you've shut it tight?" Again, the mouth took on a shape at odds with the face's perfection.

"Fergus said we should love rats. Do you remember?" Immediately the words were out of her mouth, she wished she could bite them back. Why had she mentioned Fergus when it was he who had encouraged Campbell to stage the animal laboratory protest in the first place? And then there was the ghastly manner of Fergus's death, inextricable from the mere utterance of his name. But perhaps Kit did not even know about their former professor's gruesome end. She had fled to Boston immediately after Campbell died. Who would be foolhardy enough to tell her about yet another hideous death? She was already walking a razor's edge: shearing off her hair and starving herself.

Something strange was happening to Kit, the flesh tightening visibly on her bones. Her face appeared tiny and almost painfully delineated, an ivory miniature caved by instruments of rapier-quick precision. The eyes were far away. Was it Campbell's severed head she saw, rolling upon the earth? She looked so stricken, her hands twisting in the air at her waist, as if grappling with some invisible antagonist.

"Kit?"

"Fergus was an evil man. You must not think of him. Banish him from your thoughts. Banish him." She repeated this once more verbatim in a curdling voice, more male-sounding than female, and as disembodied as a medium's under the full force of a spirit's possession.

Agnes shivered. The tone was guttural and robotic. The words fell so leadenly, they were almost wrenched from their meaning. It was as if Kit had been forced to learn them by rote, in keeping with a pendulum's beat, on a hard-backed chair in a room with only a single beam of harsh light trained upon her. I must bring her back, Agnes thought. This cannot be one of her games. Kit was truly suffering now.

"Kit! Kit!" She waved her hand in front of the unfocused eyes, a perhaps futile gesture she had seen used in movies. Dare she touch that exquisite face? She opted instead, to lay her forefinger, as gently as she could, on the back of Kit's wrist. Immediately she pulled away. Kit's skin was cold and damp, like a subterranean fungus.

Was she in the grip of a psychotic episode? Was Kit psychotic? Agnes knew nothing of the nature of her family's illness. The dire effects of alcoholism and depression she understood, but not the rending of a psyche so severe that another voice spoke through you. She wrestled with the unnerving sensation that a predatory colonizer had seized hold of the most alluring object in the house. I am being ridiculous, she told herself. This is the twenty-first century and Kit is not possessed. She is ill. She blames Fergus for what happened, but knows this is not so. Therefore she is at war with herself. The emotional and rational parts are in fierce contention. How do I bring her out of it? Should I call Hugh?

It was instinct prompted her to whisper in Kit's ear. Perhaps warm breath would dislodge the interloper. A childish and magical act. She smoothed away a few stray strands of Kit's hair, and put her lips close.

Kit's hand flew up as if to brush away an invasive insect seeking entrance through her eardrum. Agnes sprang back so that she stood some distance away.

Kit said in her normal voice: "There are fresh towels in the bathroom for you and a glass. You can drink the water from the tap. That's it, I think. And call if there's anything you really need. Or leave a note on the kitchen table. It's the way Hugh and I communicate when he is holed up with his muse." She grimaced prettily. "Are you all right, then? Got everything you need?"

She was gone before Agnes had time to speak. The afterimage stayed a moment; the lovely sea-green woman in the doorway, her hand raised in a gesture of dismissal. I am done with you.

And thank God for that, Agnes thought as she shut the door.

The room had a single small rectangular window whose shutters she folded back. The view was of the edge of the wood. She let her eyes rest on the surety of the towering, thriving trees, rooted here since before Piero walked this landscape. She lifted her eyes to where the green tips touched the sky, and was drawn ineluctably to the spires of three cypresses planted closer together than was usual.

Her body cried out for sleep, while her mind agitated for a clarity it could not now provide. She slipped off her shoes and lay down. She lay down on that soothing green bed. The day's accumulated vertigo assailed her. She had swallowed an ocean that slipped now this way, now that. If she tried to stand, she was sure she would fall over. She pictured her grandmother in her "gardening dress," gloves and broad brimmed hat, all fashioned of the same lightweight cotton, standing smiling amidst a patch of peppermint.

The dream that prodded her awake had an obscene quality that left a pall she could not shake. She had an urgent need to wash her hands and face and, as she groped for the bedside light, was visited again by the dream's shocking parody of a portrait of the Holy Family. It turned her stomach. There was Fergus in Joseph's place and Kit in Mary's. But the baby, which Kit held perilously near her breast, was a rat.

In the bathroom, Agnes rinsed her mouth and spat into the sink. She splashed water on her face, but avoided looking in the mirror. Why would her unconscious mind spawn such an awful picture? It was as if Kit was about to give the rat suck.

The towel with which she dried her hands and face was thin and rough. She could easily abrade her skin if she was not careful. Were these crude amenities careless or deliberate on Kit's part? She is unwell, Agnes reminded herself yet again. And besides, I am nothing to her, only a readily forgettable member of the crew of an Ark that sank ignonimously, taking her lover down.

TWENTY-FOUR

The Midnight Visit

AGNES WAS WAKENED BY A shrill inhuman cry. A falcon fixed its glassy eye on the pale disc-shaped scar at the base of her throat, sensing the skin was thinnest there and ideal for piercing. By the time she opened her eyes, it had already carved its image in her brain. She saw the remnants of hasty slaughter, bloodied fur and snapped bone, a beak pecking a pinkish, swollen lump which was once a beating heart.

She sat bolt upright and listened to the silence, wide and welcome, at one with the creamy texture of the walls. In the slatted morning sunlight, the room was no longer the hard white cell of yesterday, but cloudlike and malleable. She could work here and begin to shape the flitting thoughts that had come to her over the past few months touching on Piero's fire and human speech. She must be vigilant in keeping these ideas separate from anything she tells Hugh, exactly as Paul counselled her.

Paul is such a sweet man, isn't he?

Of course, Kit had never met Paul Otterly. She said that for the simple pleasure of raising doubt. Agnes then recalled the substance of last night's dream where Kit appeared, not a woman of flesh, but a robot of bolted metal squares, with protruding rivets at temple and jaw. Only the real woman's exquisite mouth and topaz eyes were unchanged.

She must shake off these dark and baseless thoughts. It is a new day, as Nana would say, always with the utter conviction that made you believe, despite yourself, in infinite possibility and untold blessings. Agnes saw one of her grandmother's small miracles when she threw open the shutters on this new Tuscan world. A snow-white rabbit, with marvellously erect ears, was zigzagging across the greensward toward the wood. He or she might well be a descendant of the one curled up on the naked thigh of Piero's Venus. In that painting, the boyish war-god lover slept with his charming head tipped back, but Venus was awake, still caught up in the rapture of the recent coupling that made her body glow with secret knowledge.

I have glowed and hummed with that secret, Agnes thought, under Campbell's hands and tongue and supple strength. But she could not afford to dwell on such memories. Hot, prodding sexual desire might well undo her, topple her resolve to stay clean and sober. Under Campbell's tongue and hands, under the whisky's breathy fumes, she'd been capable of recklessness, loosed from reason. She was an infant, greedy for pleasure, more and more, higher and higher, to the point of oblivion.

So she will stay clean, forgo lovely, quickening whisky in her life, because the alternative was death, preceded by a degradation that would strip her of all dignity. The encounter with Guam showed her how fast and far she could fall. She sensed there were many perils in the act of sex for her personally, not least her awful thirst for appro-bation. *He took me to bed; therefore I am attractive.* In the furnace of sex, Agnes the Monkey Girl was extinguished. But was she really? Or will Monkey Girl live on, until Agnes's last breath, asking to be killed again and again, but never dying, not really? The doubts would linger: that she was only the physical means for another human being to satisfy a natural hormonal urge. Nothing more. And if she ever considered a sexual relationship again, what would save her from empty and conceivably squalid encounters? The answer was obvious — the sure steerage shared love provides. Might she one day be lucky enough to find that? For now, she could not entertain such dreams.

At Villa Scimmia, she was being tested and must not fail. She must be chaste of thought and firm of purpose, even if her time here proved to be penitential. Sobriety was its own reward, was it not? She pictured Paul, probably asleep at this moment, in freshly laundered pyjamas of mulberry Egyptian cotton.

No, of course Kit did not know him. Her machinations were another bump in the stretch ahead she must negotiate. Stay firm. Cling to the mast no matter what emotional storm Kit fomented. I have made my own little craft now, Agnes told herself, and yes, craft in the sense of cunning too. If Kit, under the contorted stress of her illness — for yes, this must be what it is — tries to undermine or humiliate me, I will not let her bring me down.

The water for her shower was tepid and intermittent. She tried to read nothing into this; to excise the picture of Kit's hand in some shadowy crevice of the house, playing with a stopcock.

She was relieved to find the kitchen brighter and less dank than her initial impression had suggested on Kit's perfunctory tour. The steel jaw rat-trap was safely stowed in the hearth. Where the ham had hung upon its hook was now a blessed void.

The coffee in the large espresso pot on the stove was warm, if not hot, and bold enough to vulcanize her resolve to see the day through with dignity. It was not until her third sip that she spied the note tucked under the china fruit bowl. The calligraphy was idiosyncratic, muddied by a preponderance of dashes, heavily scored. She pictured Hugh slicing at the congealed ham with the same leaden strokes.

Finally, she unravelled: AM sess'n. Any tm. Wlk in.

Nana always said it was proper etiquette to knock, even when one had been granted a symbolic passe-partout. So Agnes was uncomfortable in her flesh, a child assaulting a norm, as she followed Hugh's instructions to the letter. Walk in. Once the study door swung wide enough to reveal the room's interior, what she saw so shocked her she was drained of all clear thought. The half-formed idea came that she had been drained of blood as well; that she was merely a stretched white sheet etched with droplets of acid.

Kit sat in front of the window where yesterday her fingers had drummed their maddening staccato, naked from the waist up. Her breasts were two perfectly moulded ivory globes, with a faint tracery of fine veins as blue as Hugh's ink. Each pink nipple was set in its own golden aureole. Her rich, thick hair was drawn back from her brow and wound into a dazzling confection of looped braids, studded with baubles and interleaved with strands of pearls. A green toy snake was twined with the slim gold circlet she wore at the base of her throat.

[465]

On this theatrical duplication of Piero's portrait of Simonetta Vespucci, Hugh fixed a regard that was by turns coolly appreciative and patently lecherous. Agnes was outraged and disgusted, not least by the mocking appropriation of an image that was chaste and idealized. Piero's Simonetta was an embodiment of exalted Love, whose nature was almost divine. There was nothing at all louche or voraciously sensual about her.

Not like this cheap display that dared to corrupt the sublime. Not at all like this coarse pantomime which reeked of an urgent eroticism to which Agnes felt pulled, despite her resistance. She was afraid of Kit's powers on all levels. This self-admission dizzied her, and then she was angry again.

Kit gazed at her from across the room with a bemused arrogance, as if to say: "If we asked, you would, wouldn't you?"

Hugh meanwhile feasted his eyes on Kit. Beside her flaunted glory, he looked perilously fragile. If Kit snapped her teeth upon the air, his bones would surely snap.

It was at that instant Agnes saw the snake quiver. The thing around Kit's neck was real, and full of venom.

"Kit," she screamed, "for God's sake, it will kill you."

She was halfway across the room, ready to pluck the snake away by its tail when Kit threw back her head and laughed. Then, in a gesture as bizarre as it was contemptuous, she unwound the length of green rubber from around her throat, dangled the tiny head above her parted lips and then bit the toy snake neatly between the eyes.

"Oh, Agnes, if you could see your face. You didn't actually think it was real, did you?"

Her laughter had the shrill grinding aspect with which Monkey Girl was so familiar. Purged of all true mirth or delight. Just a cutting instrument. Agnes wondered if there was a strictly feminine equivalent for puerile. She must keep in mind that Kit was unwell and therefore crude and consummately controlled by turns. *Kit is unwell.* This had already become an ingrained mental chorus, excusing flagrant rudeness. Kit is unwell. Have compassion.

Hugh had not joined in his houseguest's hollow merriment.

"Kate," he said. "Kate, be calm, my dear."

Kit swivelled to face him, the moth-wing eyebrows knotted to suggest an umbrageous mask. With her magnificent breasts still uncovered, and the dead-eyed stare, she was like a ship's figurehead surging over a vast, black sea rife with alien creature life. Then she shrugged and pulled the russet merino shawl about her shoulders and clasped it in front of her chest.

This restoration of simple decency to the room was a relief. If Kit were not ill, Agnes thought, I would never forgive her for this mockery of a portrait full of sacred intent. Or was this judgement priggish? She definitely felt contaminated by what she had just witnessed: an old man's lust fixed on its shameless object. Why did they have to draw her into their tawdry erotic game?

"Our little tableau has rather misfired, I fear." Hugh deliberately weighted each word in a cadence at odds with his usual rapid speech. It was as if he was trying to repress an invasive sigh, or even a sob.

"It was a shock," Agnes said. She resisted any apology.

Kit stood up, a proud beacon at the window, the baubles and fake pearls in the ornate hairdo played upon by the light. The snake dangled from her left hand.

"Oh, Agnes, you are still so gullible. We used to laugh about it. It's sweet really." As she strode glittering and imperious from the room, she paused just long enough to rumple Agnes's hair. "Sweet."

Such condescension packed into a single word and careless parting gesture left Agnes's scalp feeling scalded. Sweet. Sour rather, like the acrid broth boiling in her stomach. But worst was the poison of that pronoun. "We used to laugh." This loaded plural brought Campbell speeding back from the dead to lay his head between Kit's breasts and join in the mockery of silly, pitiable Agnes. How subtle, as well as coarse, Kit's unkindness could be.

Kit is ill. Kit is traumatized. Kit is broken. So went the dutiful little chorus, which now had an appended refrain: I will survive this. I will see it through. Here again came the question that seemed always to be lurking, and which she dared consider only long enough to immediately refute it. Did Paul know he was sending her into an emotional minefield? Of course not. No. How could he?

She sat on the chair she had used the previous day and asked the obvious question: "Is it the Simonetta portrait you want to focus on today?"

Hugh looked at her in a stricken surprise, as if he had forgotten she was in the room, or indeed who she was at all.

"She is the consummate Muse," he said, "but her volatility, I hesitate to say ferocity, can take its toll."

Muse. It simply had not occurred to Agnes that Kit's beauty would serve this function for him. And at what cost? Hugh still looked shrunken and somehow friable, the stone face of yesterday quite demolished.

She tried again: "Do you have a question about the Simonetta portrait?" The book on his desk was open to the profile portrait of the girl-woman with the budding breasts, her gaze serene, despite the live viper twined in her necklace. If her smile was enigmatic, one could see nonetheless that her most secret thoughts were benevolent. It was the turned-up nose, so unexpected and idiosyncratic in the portrait of an iconic beauty, that made Agnes sure of this idealized woman's essential kindness. There was no evidence of cruelty in this face, nor could it ever have been tainted by any malign thought.

"The cloud," Hugh ventured, his voice faint.

"The brooding one directly behind her head?"

"Yes. I see it offsets the flushed alabaster of her complexion. But why just there, massed around her high brow, and then again down to her chin?" She was relieved he sounded stronger now, more like the arrogant man she'd encountered yesterday.

She had hoped not to talk about the strange cloud. She had seen it or one very like it — the day Campbell took her for the ride along the coast on the back of the Vulcan, the day she ceased to be a virgin. Whenever she looked at Piero's portrait of Simonetta, she therefore tried to avoid looking for long at this sky-smirch with its louring threat of bitter wind and hail. It was burgeoning, even before her eyes, with a terrible power. This was the risible superstition which taunted her: that the appearance of the malformed, malign cloud that day foretold Campbell's death, and if only she had been alert to its ominous message, she might have averted the disaster. Ludicrous.

Now she must look again, cleansed of these childish thoughts. She saw that the swollen storm cloud was a contorted mimicry of the woman's profile, bulging behind the markedly high forehead, and again in a bulbous protrusion adjacent to her nose and mouth. Its entire mass was the intense plum of a new-laid bruise. To study it was to see it throbbing; to acknowledge its tangible ache to explode and do its worst.

The sheer contrast between the smooth, cool plane of the woman's brow and the turbulent cloud revealed what she had missed thus far: that it was Simonetta's high-mindedness and her purity of thought and speech that was holding the storm at bay. The evils of the world were seething in that cloud, like Pandora's box flung skyward, and Piero's Simonetta was stilling it by means of her virtue, reflected in every thought and word and deed.

All this she explained to Hugh, who listened while tracing the immaculate lines of the lady's profile with the tip of his bony forefinger.

"Good!" he said. "And the snake. How do you read its symbolism? Not surely as a foreshadowing of Simonetta's death at twenty-three? That would be too tritely transparent for di Cosimo, would it not?"

She tried for a moment to inhabit the painting's dramatic counterpoise: to be the woman wholly calm and clear of gaze, while the snake's scaly gold belly rasps against the thin flesh covering her breastbone. The barest millimetre separated the threadlike darting tongue and the infinitesimally tapering tail. Should the two touch, the resulting charge might well jolt the woman's heart into fatal spasms.

Electric, venomous and with a stealth and quickness surpassing any creature's on earth. Its slightest torque could mean instant death and who knew where a serpent would strike next? This meditation led her to the certainly it was the embodiment of quivering fate that Simonetta wore looped about her neck; the facets of emerald on the rippling body flashed now here, now there. Agnes confronted again, with a sore heart, the slight contingencies on which destiny depended.

If Simonetta had not been born with a genetic predisposition to pulmonary disease.

If the doctors Lorenzo de Medici sent to her bedside had managed to save her.

If the wire had been an inch lower and sliced Campbell's leatherette jacket and not his neck.

If he had zipped the collar up to his chin.

If at the Ark's frenetic May Day meeting, they had not tumbled upon the idea of the bullfight protest.

If Zeke had not been enthralled by Brigitte Bardot and the example of her relentless activism.

If they had heeded Horace's warning. *Mayday! Mayday!*

If she had not gone to the Aardvark Bar. (But then she might never have sought sobriety.)

"Fate," she told Hugh, "the absolute arbitrariness of its twists and turns."

He nodded. There was even a flicker of a smile.

"But for this instant, frozen in time," he said, "her serenity and spotless character stay its tortuousness?"

"Yes."

"Yet we know the actual Simonetta will suffer a strike and be cut down far too young."

"Yes, and thousands will line the streets of Florence to pay her homage as her funeral cortege passes."

"With di Cosimo among them?" Hugh asked.

"He would have been only a child. It is possible he never saw the real Simonetta."

"And did the actual woman look at all like this one, do you think? Hers is a charming face, of course, but hardly the kind of beauty that makes one catch one's breath and gaze in silent awe."

Like Kit's. She could almost hear his unspoken thought.

She told him what no doubt he already knew. "Many scholars believe that Botticelli's Venus on the half-shell and Flora in his *Primavera* are portraits of Simonetta, drawn from life. So, yes, Piero's Simonetta is wholly imagined; she is not meant to resemble the actual woman whom he perhaps never saw. Botticelli, on the other hand, likely saw her often, given his favoured position in the Medici court."

Hugh said, "The first time I saw Kate, her resemblance to Botticelli's sea-born Venus astounded me. I never thought to see that paragon alive and striding into a room whose air I also breathed. Kate's hair is a richer, more arresting red than Sandro's goddess, in keeping with her passionate nature. Exposure to the peaks and valley of her moods can nonetheless be draining. On that note, I must admit to being wearied today, Agnes, and I have a nurse coming shortly to give me one of the injections that, regrettably, I have come to require. So we will close now. Once again, your insights have had a most freshening effect on my perception of the painting and will serve me well, I am sure."

Three things surprised her in these remarks: for the first time, he had addressed her familiarly as Agnes; he had been disarmingly frank about his current fatigue and frailty; and he had implied that the vagaries of Kit's moods might be harmful to his health.

"I regret I am unable to drive you to Florence for the art appreciation I am sure you are eager to undertake. And Kate, I fear, is not likely in any state to take you. But by all means, walk. Explore our lush and classic Tuscan countryside. You will be quite safe, too, if you choose to wander in the woods behind the house. Only keep watch for the vipers, identifiable by their diamond pattern in gold and black."

This warning and formal show of concern were also unexpected. Perversely, she thought she preferred Hugh's rebarbative manner of the previous day, perhaps because she could not help mistrusting kind remarks.

Paul's attitude toward me was not kind, she reflected, but steely and pragmatic. "I abhor waste," he had grimaced at one of their sessions. "It would pain me to see you squander your talents."

Later today, also thanks to Paul and his swift, privileged diplomacy with the Bremrose administration, she would be able to register online for her courses and get the reading lists. When she returned to college she would, with any luck, not be too hopelessly far behind. Apart from her mandatory art history and iconography classes, she needed a language and had decided on Italian, plus Modernism for her literature option. Because Fergus had left his rabid taint on the subject, she was hesitant to take another ethics course. Nevertheless, she felt a strong compulsion to do so.

When she tugged at the obscure roots of this inclination, what she found was a desire to imitate Peter. She wanted genuinely to understand what it meant to be selfless and good and then follow through, even if she repeatedly stumbled on a path of her choosing. Peter was the only person she knew who had made his dedication to this quest explicit. They shared a common guilt for their part in the wrongs perpetrated by the Ark. She wondered if he had succeeded in expiating his, or hammering its corrosive power into a new and productive element of character.

When she pictured Peter, it was now always from the back, as she had last seen him, walking away from her in Arles: a huge man of uncommon strength who contained his own forge, its operation ceaseless, as he smote and refined and perfected, casting off arrogance and self-regard. He made everyone else she knew seem crude and infantile. Yes, even Paul, with his inveterate academic rivalries and dilettantish habits. It seemed a wrenching betrayal to admit this, yet she saw it was so. On the other hand, this made her realize just how rare a person was Peter Dervaig and that she would probably never again meet his like.

It was late afternoon by the time she ventured out for a walk under a tyrannical sun. Its spear-like heat would soon fell her without the broad-brimmed green hat of cloth imbued with its own UV protection. Her drawstring pants were fine-weave azure Indian cotton. Her loose, long-sleeved shirt was a shade of terracotta. Mindful of the vipers, she had put on fawn canvas shoe, rather than sandals. She was halfway down the hill on which Ernesto nearly tumbled before it registered that she was dressed in the constituent colours of this perfect world, so long husbanded and cherished it had become a prototype of Rustic Paradise. She removed her sunglasses the better to take in the sweep of vineyards and amply spaced hilltop farmhouses, all with their attendant rows of sky-skimming cypresses. There was not a single false note for miles — no crass dazzle from a conspicuous electric blue swimming pool cut into the hillside, despoiling the view, nor any of the gaudy orange beach umbrellas, or lemon and purple deck chairs, of which she had seen several examples on the drive with Ernesto. She thought these excrescences terrible, part of the awful move to turn Tuscany into a consumable. Here, thankfully, there was none of that sad spoilage, and the barking dogs, alert to her presence from their hilltop lookouts, told her these were still working farms.

She walked for just under an hour before she decided to return, mindful of the small quantity of water left in her bottle. Turning sharply around, she stirred up the dust of the road with her foot. When it cleared, she noticed a network of fissures, some spidery and some actual cracks, which the sun had opened in the hard-baked ground. The soles of her feet prickled at the idea of all the secret life teeming deep in those crevices: the slithering coils of the vipers' nests and the hosts of beetles relentlessly feeding; perhaps even some centuries-old miasma, the remnant viral matter of the plagues that periodically had stilled Florence's throbbing life, the people either fleeing or bolting themselves in.

Piero had died of plague. He was sixty and therefore likely less than robust. She always resisted picturing him old. The person who came to her imagination was at most middle-aged, consistently quick of movement and thought, sometimes literally awhirl with his brush as he worked to keep pace with the speeding visions before they vanished. On the other hand, he must have been capable of such watchful stillness that his figure could turn spectral, transparent as leaf shadow.

When she entered the woods behind Villa Scimmia, she found her way often blocked by bramble thickets. She had not expected the forest to be so dense and unkempt. Once, she had to get down on her hands and knees to crawl beneath the slant limb of an oak, newly cleaved by a summer storm. She was looking for a path she could follow farther tomorrow, but if one existed it continued to elude her. What she did find unnerved her: a ring of stones with a heap of warm ash at its centre. Had some wayfarer camped here for the night? Or was Villa Scimmia and one or more of its inhabitants being watched? Kit was the most obvious attraction and Ernesto the most likely candidate for voyeur. But surely, even for Ernesto, such surveillance would be excessive?

She decided to let Hugh know what she had discovered. But his study was empty. After a light supper, she wrote him a quick note, which she left on the kitchen table. She then checked that both the back and front doors were securely locked. She pushed away the paranoid idea that the villa was now as unsettled without as within. The campfire was likely made by a wanderer passing through.

Sitting gingerly at her laptop set on her spindly-legged table in her room, she retrieved some of the required texts for her Modernism course. She began, perhaps unwisely, with the first of Ezra Pound's *Pisan Cantos,* written while he was imprisoned by the American military in post-war

Italy, on charges of treason. She recalled Paul telling her that Hugh had deliberately modelled himself on this uncompromising literary maverick, right down to the goatee and the jewel in his earlobe. But surely Hugh's admiration did not extend to any facsimile of Pound's radio broadcasts made throughout the war extolling Mussolini's achievements?

She found the poem almost impenetrably difficult until she decided simply to yield to its grand rush of imagery. The striking juxtapositions brought her a finely tuned sensuous pleasure. Fragments entered her like discrete prayers: the smell of mint under tent flaps in the rain, and the sight of a lizard upholding his spirit. This simple acknowledgement that a wild creature had sustained the elderly man confined in his wire cage moved her and quickened her respect for his ordeal. Then she went back to the poem's opening and discovered, with the help of the editor's annotations, the historic truth behind the ghastly human abattoir depicted in the first few lines. Pound's vituperation centred on the indignities done to the corpses of the executed Mussolini and his mistress Carla Petacci, hung by the heels in a public square in Milan.

She wondered if Hugh ever delved into iniquity in his work. If they looked together at the bloodthirsty protagonists of *The Hunt*, would he see the dark stain of sin on their naked arms and straining backs? Or would he find the hunters' physiques magnificent, just as Mussolini would have done, when he extolled the youthful male body as consummate death machine?

For the rest of the evening she read an essay on Russian Orthodox icons. She spent a long time looking into the eyes of Andrei Rublev's Virgin Mary, which were doleful yet consoling. Mary's head, covered in a hood of indigo and gold, inclined to the right and the tiny Christ Child touched his face to hers. The scene in the bullet-riddled church in Marseille returned to her, with the line-ups of the faithful waiting their turn to kneel and kiss the image of their favoured saint. She had been hungover, she remembered. At least she was no longer doing that daily damage to herself, although she must take nothing for granted. The fact was she still dreamt of whisky, where its peat-scented fumes and promise of bliss were enticing as ever. Such dreams woke her in a panic. It always took some minute before the sick anxiety subsided. No, she had not actually had a drink. She was still sober, thank God.

That night she was cursed with a whisky-dream so realistic she could taste as well as smell the lovely, ultimately ruinous spirits. It was a Skye whisky, the Talisker. How soon she had forgotten its sensuous numbing of the lips. In her haste, she had spilled her drink, as she so often had in life. There were drops on her chin which she wiped away and the front of her nightgown was wet. How could this have happened? She cried out at the gravity of her self-betrayal. Had she raided Hugh's drinks cabinet in her sleep? Who could help her now? She threw out arms in an operatic gesture of despair.

"Ouch!"

The back of her left hand had clipped Kit's cheekbone. Kit was holding a squat, cut-glass tumbler nearly full to the brim to her lips, and was regarding her with her habitual hauteur. She looked magnificent, like an eroti-cized angel, with her hair loose and rippling over the filigree lace straps of a nightgown of cotton so fine it was transparent.

"What are you doing, Kit?" She was trying hard to temper her outrage. This was tantamount to rape. As she struggled to control her trembling hands, interlocked in front of her like a breastplate, she realized she was more than a little afraid. What if Kit overwhelmed her physically and forced her to drink? What if she was already corrupted by those drops spilled on her lips? *I did not swallow it.* She saw herself standing in a court with Paul seated in judgement, his left eyebrow raised. Did that mean he was sceptical? *I didn't, Paul. I didn't.*

"Oh, Agnes, I just wanted to wake you nicely so that we could have a talk. I thought you might be missing your whisky. I remember how much you enjoyed it."

"I don't drink any more, Kit."

"Don't be silly, Agnes. Drink with me. Be sisterly. Come on." She proffered the tumbler again and Agnes only just managed to stop herself knocking it from Kit's hand. As she turned her face away, she saw that Kit had brought Hugh's entire decanter, which stood emanating a lurid glow beneath the bedside lamp. She set about imagining a dead plague rat festering in its depths. *Noli me tangere.* Was this thought sacrilegious? Probably, but at this juncture she would grasp at any fragment that would hold her steady.

"You have to help me." Kit's face was pressed so close Agnes could see the silken layer of moisture on her skin. Her pupils were extremely large, their magnetic pull disorienting. "Help me, Agnes. I can't tell you what I have to unless you drink with me."

"I'm an alcoholic, Kit." There, she had said it.

"What! Don't be silly, Agnes. You're far too young. People our age can't be alcoholics."

"Yes, they can. And I am." The strained cords in her neck and shoulders eased as Kit at last put the glass down.

"Okay, I'll plunge on then. Only hear me through because you won't want to believe what I'm going to tell you. But I swear it's true."

Kit now sat erect in the bedside chair, hands folded neatly in her lap. Agnes pulled the sheet up to her neck in an empty symbolic effort to insulate herself from whatever unpleasantness, manufactured or otherwise, was about to be revealed. She had no doubt it would touch on Hugh.

"That disgusting performance this morning with me half-naked and my hair in those horrible little braids and the junk jewellery and the stupid plastic snake — he made me do that, Agnes. There are lots of other things, debased and degrading things, that he makes me do. Things that make me ill. Like sucking him off. And lying down with him naked while he tries . . . "

Kit stopped and buried her face in her hand.

A self-protective instinct prevented Agnes from reaching out to comfort her. Was she witnessing yet another performance? How on earth could Hugh force her to do these things? In addition to her abrasive emotive power, Kit was by far the physically stronger of the two.

"You've got to believe me, Agnes." Kit had uncovered her face, on which Agnes saw no evidence of tears. "He threatens to tell my father my mental state is deteriorating, that I need to be hospitalized again. Last time they gave me four electro-convulsion treatments. I can't go through that again, Agnes. I'd kill myself rather than go through that again. You feel like your soul is being fried. You can hear it screaming."

She covered her face again. Her shoulders heaved. Agnes watched appalled, picturing Kit strapped to a metal trolley, her beautiful body juddering as a jagged electric current passed repeatedly through her brain. She had supposed such torturous "therapies" had long been banned. Was it possible this was another of Kit's lies? Would it be heartless to doubt her in this case? If her claim was true, it was unconscionable that Kit's parents would subject their daughter to such a barbarous treatment.

"You have to help me, Agnes."

"Tell me how, Kit? What is it you want me to do? Can I help you get away? Can you not simply leave Villa Scimmia?"

Kit regarded Agnes blankly, as if this idea had never occurred to her. After a moment, she said in a leaden tone: "He's hidden my passport. He took it from me the first day I arrived. For safekeeping, he said."

"Well, we'll find it. Or we'll simply ask him for it."

"Ask him for it! Agnes, you are so naïve. Haven't you got it yet that Hugh Massinger-Pollux is an evil man? Can't you feel and smell his wickedness when he comes anywhere near you? Did you know he belongs to a Neo-Fascist group that wants to put an end to democratic systems everywhere and bring in programs of enforced eugenics and extermination of the mentally disabled?" She hissed this damning revelation, her eyes gleaming slits. "Did you know he makes me kiss . . . ?" She stopped, made a show of wiping her mouth with the back of her hand. "There's only one way to deal with him, Agnes, one perfect solution, and that is to kill him. That's what I want you to help me do."

It was as if Agnes had gone snow-blind. Her eyes pained her and she groped, directionless, amidst the white granules that flew thickly about her head. She blinked and saw Kit leaning forward in keen expectation. Her expression was grave, her skin so tautly stretched on the fine bones it looked sore.

Agnes could taste her own alarm. How did one handle someone who ruptured all reason? She would welcome Kit's braying jubilance at this point, the display of demonic glee that she had once again played upon her gullibility. What tended to persuade her of Kit's sincerity now was her sense that everything mild and humane had been drained from the room. She clutched at the fragile proposition that words were not actions, and risked a cautiously phrased reproof.

"Kit, you realize that what you're saying is just talk, don't you? That you could get in very serious trouble if . . . "

Kit's eyes blazed, all molten fury. "God, Agnes, you sound like an old woman. Have you ever considered that it might be unhealthy to spend all your time on a weird painter who died hundreds of years ago?"

There was a condescending contempt in this last remark which Agnes readily deflected. But the mere voicing of the judgement had vitrified Kit's hauteur. The eyes turned glassy, fastened solely on the live quarry of Agnes's face and the tender self lodged within. On this front I am unbreachable, Agnes thought, while registering nonetheless the insistent pulse beneath her throat-scar, her body's now automatic drum of alarm. Was Kit as insane as Guam?

How could she possibly gauge the weight behind Kit's wild words? Even though she was sober and Kit apparently already inebriated, she felt like the one undone and floundering. She recalled the man who believed he was a clock, executing his crazed tick-tock measure in the middle of the road, and how she had fled, fearing contagion. Was that possible here? Did Kit's madness, if it was not feigned, have the power to invade her and make her a collaborator?

Of course not. Ludicrous. I am a depressive, she told herself firmly. At worst, I sink into a bog of despair and inaction. I am infinitely capable of harming myself, but unlikely to injure others willfully.

Nevertheless, under the sheets she wrung her hands. She must throw off this galling disadvantage of lying in bed like a child in the clutches of a malign yet mesmerizing storyteller. But as she started to get up, Kit gripped her shoulder hard.

"Ow!"

Kit retracted immediately, but Agnes's physical relief was undercut by the sight of the woman's mottled cheeks and unfocused eyes.

"Here's what you'll love about it, Agnes, the most wonderful, exhilarating thing that no one can know until they experience it. Can you guess? It's an art form, Agnes. Murder's an art form and you feel godlike, filled with a power you can hardly contain as you make your first cuts and lay the heavy bruises and the bright burns on your victim's skin. Even if you gag them, the sounds they make — the groans and sobs and cries for mercy — they intensify the pleasure and goad you on to hurt them more and in clever new ways. And when you put that final touch that stops their heart altogether, it's such a high, such a high . . . "

"Stop it, Kit!" This must be fantasy; just a sickly chimera her poor brain was spawning. It must be.

"It's a high, Agnes. Don't you understand? The act of murder is better than the very best sex you can imagine."

"You've got to get a grip on yourself, Kit."

"Grip? What are you talking about?" She looked genuinely affronted. Then her expression turned minatory, the upper lip curling back to expose the long eye teeth. "You're a coward, aren't you, Agnes? A boring, conventional little coward. What can we do with you? What, oh what?"

There was no muscle in Agnes's body that was not strung tight as a ligature. What weapons did she have, forged of cool reason and compassion, to combat Kit's aggression and unreason? Only one. It was a risk she must venture.

"What would Campbell think, Kit, if he heard you talking in this way? It would hurt him badly, wouldn't it? He would want you to stop saying these foolish things and go to sleep so that tomorrow you will see everything in a clear light."

"Oh, my beautiful Campbell. Oh. Oh." Kit buried her face in her hands. When she took them away, Agnes witnessed the naked anguish, the black cavern of her mouth stopped up with her fist. "Oh, Agnes, if you knew. If you only knew . . . " Kit began to gnaw at her knuckles. It was like watching a terrible ritual mourning where women tore at their own flesh.

Obedient to impulse, Agnes slipped out from under the covers and sat on the edge of the bed facing Kit. How pitiable the woman looked, her delicacy carved away by raw distress. Her nightdress smelled of sweat and spilled whisky. "Stop it, Kit, please."

Agnes succeeded in gently taking the abraded fist from her mouth. Bravely, she stroked Kit's temples. She had to reach up to do so because of Kit's height, the gesture thus striking an uneasy blend of obeisance and solicitude.

"Try to calm yourself, Kit dear." The "dear," which had been Nana's standard endearment, came to her tongue unbidden.

Kit seized Agnes's wrists in a manacle-tight grip and held them fast in her lap. She leant forward so that her forehead touched Agnes's. Her heavy hair, now in disarray, covered them both. Agnes fought the irrational notion she was smothering and managed to emerge from beneath the shrouding weight. She sat as erect as she could, taking long, deliberate breaths and tugging in gentle resistance to Kit's grip.

In response, Kit tightened her hold. "I left something out, Agnes, and that's the sweetness. It really is true what they say about revenge. Sweet. Sweet." She seemed to lisp the repeated adjective, made harrowing in this context.

"Please stop this, Kit. You're just imagining all these terrible things. Grief does that." How facile she sounded. She was grasping at what? Not straws, but some bare-boned verity on which to haul herself out of the ever-quickening morass.

"You can't tell me anything about grief I don't know, Agnes. The claws at the heart. The black cell where no light comes. The vengeance helps, you see. It eases the pain a little because you've made restitution to the person you lost. You do see, don't you? That was why I had to kill Fergus and I did it lingeringly, the way he liked to make love, if you can call it that. Fergus liked his sex heavily salted, with blood, I mean. So I gave him plenty of salting at the end. I drew the pain out for him as long as I could, as imaginatively as I could. In winter he liked to couple — another of his nasty words — naked, near the woodstove, where the overwhelming heat brought you close to fainting. So once I had him securely bound, I got the fire roaring, even though it was spring, and I heated up the tongs until they glowed. And then . . . "

"Please stop this, Kit. You're . . . "

"Are you going to say raving? Well, I'm not, Agnes. I'm only telling you what I did, and it was glorious. The pièce de resistance — and oh, how he resisted — was the wire I strangled him with and then sliced right through his windpipe. It was from the same spool of wire he used to kill Campbell."

"Kit!" Agnes was inside a thundering void. Her face felt wet, as if with blood spouting from an unspeakable fountain. "It cannot be." She was uncertain whether she had spoken these words or even if she had a tongue to utter them.

"Yes, it can, Agnes." So she had spoken, and with this affirmation, Kit's face came back into focus, pale, intent and exultant. "He told me he wanted me purely for himself; that I had to give up Campbell. I told him I couldn't, I wouldn't ever do that. But I had no idea, Agnes, that Fergus was that crazy. He wouldn't kill an animal, but he had no compunction about murdering Campbell."

"It was an accident, Kit, an awful, inexplicable accident."

"No it wasn't, Agnes." Her nails dug in. "Fergus was gloating afterwards, strutting up and down. You know, the way he did. He set Campbell up first, telling him what night the animals would be delivered to the lab. He tipped off the pharmaceutical company about the demonstration, told them the Ark members would be violent, that they were bringing homemade incendiary devices. That's why there were so many security guards. Fergus strung the wire there . . . He calculated exactly how high it should be and how fast Campbell would be going. He wanted a flawless decapitation. That's what he said, Agnes, a flawless decapitation." Kit shuddered; then jerked back and clawed at the air.

This time Agnes succeeded in pulling away altogether. She was beset by the ghastly image of Kit raking her nails down Fergus's fair, freckled face, about to gouge out his eyes with their tapered points. She was in shock, her hands and feet numb. A lightning bolt had split open the room and in its cruel light she saw her bones beneath the skin. She wondered if this might be a good thing: to leave her human flesh behind because this was where sin resided.

She did not want any of it to be true, but most especially Campbell's murder. The idea that he was plotted against and deliberately executed soiled his memory in a way that made her want to run from the house screaming to the heavens. But not to drink. Never that. Must not. She looked at the decanter of whisky and conjured up again the repulsive, bloated plague rat with the festering purple sores on its flanks.

There was still the very real possibility that all these horrific things Kit had told her were phantasmagoria, chimera generated by trauma or a congenital mental illness. In that case, she would be heartily sorry for this woman's suffering.

"I know you cared about him, Agnes. Campbell told me you slept together. That's why I believe you'll see why I had to do it."

Mere hours ago, having her most intimate, sacred secret exposed so casually would have made every cell in her body ache with loss. Now, in the context of bloodlust, unbridled impulse and a welter of burnt flesh and splintered bone, this divestment seemed a meagre thing.

"You do see, don't you, Agnes? What I did to Fergus was perfect justice. And believe me, Hugh deserves the same. You can help me, Agnes, help me to kill him. There are other wicked and unforgivable things he does, right here in this house, not just to me, but . . . "

"Please, Kit, please. I can't. You know I can't. You're overwrought and not yourself. You must try — "

"You're talking like an old woman again, Agnes." The eye teeth were on full display. "And why do you presume to know what my 'self' is. You haven't a clue about life, have you?" She stopped, seemed to reflect a moment, then smiled slyly. "I know you were a virgin. Campbell told me everything. Absolutely everything, Agnes. I know what you like, how you want your nipples nibbled and his tongue darting in and out of you. You would beg him to 'spread you wide.' So cute."

Was the furnace scalding Agnes's skin mortification or some emotion impossible to name, with a cankerous betrayal as its root? Can the dead betray us? Apparently.

"Go away, Kit."

"I could give you the same pleasure, you know. I am very good, very good in bed."

Agnes did not doubt it. While Kit's unseemly offer appalled her, it stirred a humid, churning desire. She despised herself for this low instinctual craving, born of her cells and nerves. She was so much more than this yearning of the flesh. If that were not so, she would be drunk now, the contents of the decanter demolished, along with her dignity, will power and lucid reason. Her tongue would be lolling in her head and her chin flecked with spittle. She might be ready to follow Kit, God knows where. But not there. Surely never to collusion in a murder.

Even as she erected this mental bulwark, Kit slipped her hand inside her nightgown. Against the firm cupping of Kit's palm, her nipple stiffened. Kit reacted immediately, pulling and pinching so dexterously that Agnes was overwhelmed, her vagina already wet and pulsing.

Quickly. "I can't do this, Kit." She grasped the hand that threatened to undo her and pushed it away.

Kit's fleeting look of surprise was succeeded by an arrogant scrutiny.

"No one resists me for long, little Agnes."

If Kit intended the diminutive to be withering, it left Agnes unscathed. She felt only relief at the restitution of a small island of calm as Kit swept from the room, her hair swinging in a heavy arc, first left, then right, then settling along her spine.

She sat hunched on the edge her bed, listening to the slithering of Kit's bare feet as she ran down the stone steps of the servants' staircase. Once she heard the door to the kitchen open and then shut again, she leapt to her feet, closed her own door and wedged the back of the chair under the doorknob. This was sheer symbolic protection, but for the moment she needed to muster whatever defences she could. Her hands were shaking and there was a muted nervous trill in her throat that threatened to become a full-fledged ululation. Veiled women in faraway lands made such sounds, at times of crisis and of death, an ascending looping whoop that married lamentation and alarm.

She was desperate for some comparable ritual structure to contain the roaring in her head. She wanted banished as well the lingering erotic charge of Kit's counterfeit caress. She felt tainted by that touch, and corrupted, even though she had not succumbed.

Every aspect of Kit's revelations reeked of the irredeemable. The best Agnes could hope for — although damning for Kit — was that this unspeakable tale of murder and revenge was factitious, either hellish delusions arising from a genuine illness or a superbly duplicitous performance. There was no doubting Kit's fervency, but such dramatic intensity might also be cunning practice.

And if madness or mendacity was the best that could be hoped for, then the worst was that it was all true, including Campbell's casual mockery of her sexual inexperience, affection and trust. She did not believe such a Campbell ever existed. Kit had invented him, just as she had invented the Fergus who killed him. Or had she?

Agnes could still call up the physical and emotional unease she had experienced when Fergus was in full messianic flight, urging them to love the lowly worm and despised sewer rat. Those extreme diatribes had suggested a mind off-kilter, if not unsound. Then there was the disturbing lewdness he seemed always to exude, a sexuality so flagrant and pressing you found your eyes drawn repeatedly to the smooth bulge below the plastic belt. She recalled her dream nightmare of Kit suckling a rat. Did it prefigure, and corroborate, the truth of Kit's account?

And what of the plague rat she had pictured decomposing in the whisky? She must get the alcohol out of her room, and remove that tangible threat at least. She slipped a loose shirt on over her nightgown and, after dismantling the chair barricade, picked up the decanter. The cut glass and substantial stopper made it heavier than she had anticipated. Like Kit, she went down the stairs barefoot, but because of the decanter's burdensome, awkward weight, she could not run. The cold stone made her arches curl. To compensate she rose on the balls of her feet and nearly tumbled headlong. She righted herself, gripped the decanter grimly and proceeded slowly down, aware that what she bore was her own fate in a glass casket. Her own lovely, liquid fate where she could find not just solace, but a quick, much-needed shot of unalloyed joy.

She has been without a drink for so long. Over two months. Surely by now she has learned moderation? Hugh will not mind if she has a sip or two. After the night she has been through, who would blame her for indulging in a little whisky?

It was not until she reached the kitchen and set the decanter down that she saw clearly how close she had come to folly. To cast off her hard-won sobriety so carelessly would be tantamount to self-slaughter. What had she been thinking? If she succumbed, she would let down both Paul and the Higher Power from which had emerged

Laelaps, her saviour spirit-dog. She would let down Piero di Cosimo, whose enduring corpus had inspired her to break open the constricting cage of her life.

She picked up the decanter with its forever-tempting Talisker and carried it through the maze of hallways to Hugh's study. She remembered exactly where it had sat on top of his ebony drinks cabinet with its ornate lacquer-work of grapes and drooping fire lilies. Once she had safely deposited it, she glanced around, absorbing the steadying influence of the scholar's room, the desk, the solid tubular pen, the walls of books.

I too am a scholar, she reminded herself. I have a task that is sacrosanct—to me, if no one else. Nevertheless, standing there barefoot, newly braced and chastened, she had to confront the blighting doubts Kit's febrile outpouring had seeded in her. If she could not tell if Kit was lying, how could she be certain that Piero di Cosimo had indeed cared about the lives and well-being of animals? How could she be sure there was an enigma at the heart of *The Forest Fire*, an enigma many-layered and profoundly truth-bearing; how could she know that the painting was not just a spectacular virtuosic display by an artist who had a peculiar talent for depicting animals? Perhaps it was no more than that, and there was no moral or spiritual significance to the animals' poignant expressiveness. Only paint and cunning artistry, an ultimately hollow mimesis.

It was then she heard a car door slam and an engine turn over. She ran out of the study and down the milk-white hall to the front door. She opened it in time to see Kit starting off in the Land Rover, her hair unbound and streaming though the open window. There was someone seated beside her. Agnes feared at first it might be Hugh, trussed and gagged in readiness for execution near some water-filled quarry. Then she saw the passenger was a much slighter person than Hugh. Although the night was warm, he wore the hood of his jacket up.

She knew even before he turned and looked at her, expressionless, whose pale pinched face she would see shadowed by the little hood. Horace Fairhaven.

Mayday! Mayday! Her perplexity thickened.

She watched until the Land Rover's rear lights dipped below the hill. That Kit was gone, at least for now, gave her some respite from curdling anxiety in the face of a manic power whose compulsions defied her understanding.

She re-entered the villa, locked the front door and set the bolt fast. She was relieved to think of Hugh sleeping soundly in his bed, ancient and intact.

Her own room had been transformed, and transformed again; now it was purged of Kit's presence. Before she lay down, in faint hope of sleep, she packed her bag in case there was need for a hasty departure.

TWENTY-FIVE

The Flight

FOLLOWING THE INSTRUCTIONS ON THE note Hugh left for her in the kitchen, Agnes entered his study at precisely ten. Scant sleep and a tinny ringing in her ears made her feel uncommonly brittle. She had to take conscious note of how to set one foot in front of the other. What if it was all true and Hugh was in real danger? And the antithesis? But on examination, she found she could not seriously entertain the idea Hugh was a party to Kit's baroquely unkind jest, if jest it was. He could not be that uncouth or sadistic. Or amoral.

It was on this word Agnes leant more and more to characterize Kit's shocking disclosures and proposals. Whether true or untrue, these ugly outpourings had to be rooted in disease — perhaps full-blown schizophrenia or very early onset dementia, an illness indelibly set in the brain's cells. Not Kit's fault then; only a randomly imposed curse whose cumulative wasting of a life Agnes shrank from imagining.

Hugh was sitting at his desk, his figure completely obscured by the high-backed, upholstered chair. Only his left hand was visible, his thumb clamping down the single sheet of creamy vellum. Agnes waited, in a yearning tension, to see if the spotted hand would move the merest fraction. She was desperate for some simple proof he was not already dead.

He coughed; she let out a long pent-up breath. "You wanted to see me . . . " She hoped he would not remark on the tremour in her voice.

Hugh's chair swivelled around to reveal an unnerving sight. His skin was an opaque grey and he seemed to have lost weigh overnight, all of it from his face. The veins at his temples stood out like icy rivers. He folded his gnarled hands and brought them level with his chest. It was not a gesture she had seen him use before. She had the impression he was shielding his heart from her offensively youthful gaze.

"I fear I must cancel our session today." These few words cost him an obvious physical effort. "The injections sometimes leave me drained for a day or two. And so once again, you are at liberty. You have work of your own to pursue without doubt."

"Thank you."

He did not acknowledge her empty courtesy; only swung his chair back to face the desk. This time, not even his hand was visible to her. She could understand his desire to seal himself away; it humiliated him to expose his frailty, even to her.

Nevertheless, she had no choice but to press him for some clarity now. If she did nothing, he might be murdered, and then she could well go mad. There, she had thought the forbidden, impolitic word, which evoked a Bedlam of fouled sheets, manacles and gibbering mouths pressed to iron bars. In daring to entertain this damning word, she confronted her own fear of contamination. How ductile might her mind be, subjected to the repeated hammering of a formidably persuasive power that could turn black white, and make evil deeds appear to be essential salutary measures?

"Is Kit . . . ?"

He cut her off, swirling back to complete her sentence. "Gone? Yes. To Siena. She has a counsellor there who provides some succour. 'Stabilizes' is darling Kit's word.

"A ghastly thing for her to have witnessed. Were you also there?" He asked this as if the idea had only just occurred to him.

"Yes."

"An unspeakable shock for all of you, no doubt. But then, you did not have Kit's strength of attachment to the young man."

The tiny, loudly protesting figure that sprang up inside Agnes was solider-like in bearing. Thus she discovered that her love for Campbell was undiminished, even if he had betrayed her in heartless pillow-talk with Kit.

"No," she dissembled, in face of the enraged interior solider who sent out clarion blast after blast. "I saw her drive away," she blurted out. "It looked as though there was someone with her. I thought it might be her relative, her . . . " She groped for a term to dignify the soiled origins of the blood connection, the child engendered on a small-boned Irish nurse in a rape committed by an old man with a diseased mind. Was Horace Kit's uncle? He seemed rather to be her gnarled, grimfaced knight at arms, without the physical weaponry. Agnes saw him again on his knees, imploring Kit not to go to the sit-in at the animal laboratory. And later, when the truck disgorged the aggressive security guards in their riot gear and Campbell was trying to make his escape, Horace had physically restrained Kit from getting on the bike. His two companions had looked so like bodyguards he'd contracted for just that purpose. Why? Had Horace known the wire was there, strung so taut it hummed Campbell's death-song? Obviously, he was still obsessed by Kit, as evidenced by his presence here. Had he always wanted her for himself? Was Horace, with his habitual malignant glare, capable of murder? No, surely not. This was far too tangled a thought. Her weariness was casting shadows, shrouding her reason.

"Yes," Hugh said. "An eccentric little man. Always wears a jacket with the pointed hood up, whatever the weather."

"That is her cousin. His name is Horace Fairhaven."

"I did not know of the blood relation," he said gravely. "There is certainly no family resemblance. He could be a creature of the underworld, a haunter of culverts, in comparison with our glorious Kit. How dark and shrunken the house seems without her resplendent presence. I intend no offence," he added.

This uncharacteristic apology confirmed for her how ill he must be. She left him, without another word.

On the way back to her room, she considered the unintended mocking irony of Hugh's phrase "at liberty," given that all her thoughts were dungeons. Perhaps if she walked, made a show of striding off into the sunlight, she could cast them off. She put on her hat and, prompted by an overriding caution, took up her money belt with both wallet and ID. She remembered then that she not asked Hugh about Kit's passport. For now, the idea that he would seize and hide it away struck her as absurd, even obscene, as she mentally posited his sad debility against Kit's rampant vigour.

She closed the front door behind her so forcibly that the monkey-shaped knocker rattled. She studied the tiny, forlorn brass face with its widened eyes that conveyed both anguish and alarm. The fact he wore a chain made her wonder if the monkey might be modelled on an actual macaque, kept long ago at the villa as a plaything or conversation piece. If so, she hoped he was never tormented with sharpened sticks or made to perform antic dances decked out in baby's frills.

She decided to go into the wood and then to the top of the hill the forest flanked. Looking down on the villa might give her some perspective on Kit's perverse confession. It occurred to her again just how easy it would be to run, hand in her notice, call a taxi and go to Florence where she could lavish her attention on Piero's paintings in churches and galleries throughout the city. Why did she persist in staying? The answers that came were the same ones she had thrashed out during the night. She had made a promise to Paul. She must see this penitential course through until her eight-week contract was up. And she must decide what to do with the information she now held. If what Kit had said was the truth, didn't she have a moral obligation to seek medical help or legal counsel on her behalf? If she left now, she would never know, really know, what had transpired. If she stayed, she could perhaps clear away the murk so that she *could* do something — to help, to purify, to bring tortured Kit some ease. She had no idea how. What would Peter do? For reasons she did not fully understand, she had begun to see everything that transpired at Villa Scimmia as an integral part of her personal Twelve Steps. Unless of course, Kit embarked on some misadventure that would make her stay impossible . . . but Kit had gone for counselling and would be better on her return.

Kit will come back, calm, rational and self-contained. She will have forgotten the substance of midnight's delusional ramblings. Agnes realized she was talking to herself in the soothing tone Nana had used when she was a child and forked lightning had turned the world livid and terrifying. All is well, Nana would say, stroking her temples.

As she skirted the left wing of the house, she heard the shrill squeal that had penetrated her dream on the previous night. She stopped and was reprimanded by silence. The piercing sound was only her nerves playing tricks, sorely stretched from lack of sleep and chafing anxiety.

She entered the wood at a point directly below the hill's crest. Here she found a well-trodden path, which looked promising and likely to lead her surely upward. It seemed a fine portent. She could not entirely expunge the fancy that Piero once had walked where she did now, following the same switchbacks, seeing the same laurel, yew, elm and oak. At times the foliage above and around her was so dense she was enveloped by a gloom that sent a chill foreboding through her blood. She recognized it was the atmosphere of Piero's *Hunt* that reigned in these lightless passages. Here the shadows were thick enough to slice with a knife and the trees, stripped of all apparent fluidity and grace, were stolid columns bounding a murderous ground.

In the painting, it was not at all clear that any of the animals would escape alive. Only her girlish, ardent wishing saved them. At the top of the hill to which they fled, there was a naked, brutish hunter waiting, his cudgel hoisted high to smash them as they came. If she could make a single change to Piero's work, it would be to paint over that muscular hunter on the hilltop because he ate shadows and bloody meat and slaughtered hope.

When she reached the top of the hill she found no hunter, but the surprising gift of a small meadow, whose grass was still a rippling green despite the advancing autumn. The remnant wildflowers, cinquefoil, yarrow, saxifrage, had preserved their lively colours and she settled down carefully among them to look down at the red-tiled roof of Villa Scimmia. From this remote, tranquil perspective, she could imagine it was Kit she saw there far below, her hair bright in the sun and her arms flung wide. A newly healed Kit, whirling in delight to be so transformed.

In the afternoon, Agnes turned to the always "tantalizing ambiguities" of *The Forest Fire*. How could one small, jewel-like canvas, with its marvellous predominant menagerie, contain so many teasing enigmas and paradoxes? Why did this sublime pastoral scene on the very edge of extinction, with flames lapping at its periphery and exploding at its core, nevertheless have the power to delight and console? She kept coming back to the notion there was an abiding joy at the painting's heart. She derived such pleasure and renewing wonder from looking at the diverse company of animals assembled in the foreground like a diplomatic contingent, even if some, like the ox and the crane, cried out in alarm, while others, like the deer and man-faced boar, stood silent and serene. Stark against the opalescent green-gold fields, the hares that fled the encroaching conflagration were the merest Zen-like stroke of the brush. Yet Piero had so exactly caught their fluid movement, she heard them rushing by.

In that certain vital flicker his brushstroke captured, she perceived how the joy co-inhered in the terror. So the hasp sprang in her mind at last: the truth the boar's calm regard prompted her to examine was Heraclitean. She had misread the long tongues of flame as purely destructive, like the duplicitous, fear-mongering words of politicians and demagogues. In fact, the flames were mutable. "For he is like a refiner's fire," she remembered Nana warbling, her accompaniment lagging a little behind the sure bass on her recording of *Messiah*.

Fire had the power to purify and refine, as much as it had to raze and destroy. Which aspect of fire will you seize upon: to illuminate or devastate? That was the question the boar with Piero's face asked. How will you use language, your defining human tool? She looked approvingly and with admiration at the ploughman who shouldered the yoke so that the oxen could run free. He knew the answer.

She was quietly exultant and grateful to have stumbled on this new and far more fluid understanding of why the painting had always filled her more with innocent felicity than fear. She celebrated by opening a bottle of San Pellegrino to accompany her dinner of arugula salad and linguini spread with the barest tracery of pesto, greenly potent as spring.

She was jolted awake. Someone was driving an iron spike into her shoulder. She struck out blindly and opened her eyes to find a world awash in blood.

"Agnes." The name hissed in her ear brought her fully to consciousness, the torrent of blood first contracting, then congealing, to become Kit's loosened hair covering them both. The spike, Kit's nails — again.

"You're hurting me, Kit." The gruesome thought came that Fergus had spoken these same words to her on his last night on earth, initially in a drawl, his speech sodden with pleasure; then more and more shrilly, until the terminal screech.

But, of course, that was all nonsense. Kit did not really do it. She was delusional when she said she had murdered Fergus.

"Get up, Agnes. There is something you must see. Get up now."

The merciless fingers digging into her shoulders had the power to bruise, even to the bone. I may bear Kit's imprint forever, she thought. This irrational fear of such contaminations generated a surge of uncommon strength. She was able to push Kit away and leap to her feet.

For an instant, before Kit closed in on her again, Agnes had a clear view of the mottled complexion and, above all, of the wide, eerily unfocused eyes. She had no doubt the inner scene Kit beheld was a protracted torment. If she had indeed been to Siena to see her therapist, then she had obviously found neither lasting comfort nor clarity there.

"Get dressed, Agnes!" The command had the force of a slap, so much so that Agnes instinctively averted her cheek. "Move!" Kit pushed a fist into her sternum.

"Stop it, Kit. What's got into you?" She immediately regretted the foolish idiom. Insanity had got into Kit and there was perhaps no way ever to get it out again. But surely there was hope? If she could stay sober, Kit could be made well. She frowned, aware this was facile, a child's line of thinking. Clumsily, she tried to clasp the hand that had just punched her. "Try to calm down, Kit. We don't have to race out into the night."

Kit glared. "Oh yes we do, Agnes. And we won't be going far. I need you to *see* why you must help me kill him. I want to bring you into the presence of his evil. Unless you witness it, you're never going to believe me."

The oddly Biblical phrase, "the presence of his evil," intensified Agnes's alarm. Unwanted pictures crowded her mind: of Hugh, naked and slug-white, hunched over a computer screen on which were played out deeds so repellent they ought never to have been conceived. Or was it something far worse Kit would show her? Agnes plumbed the scale of human iniquity, hit vivisection, both animal and human, and chose to go no further.

"Hurry!" Kit snapped as Agnes pulled her loose cotton pants hastily over her nightgown, thrust her arms into yesterday's T-shirt. When she fumbled putting on her canvas shoes, Kit prodded her in the shoulder.

Tomorrow, Ages resolved, tomorrow I will give Hugh my notice. I cannot bear this any longer. I do not have the resources to withstand the toxic atmosphere Kit creates. It is too vast and riddled with pockets of hatred and horror. If I were able to help her, I would. But the root and reach of her illness are insuperable. It is like trying to grapple with a hurtling meteor. These inane thoughts came far too late; the spectre of fear was already grotesquely swollen in her chest, corded tight.

"Hurry!" Kit shadowed Agnes so closely down the stairs she could feel feverish breath on her nape. It was to her advantage that she knew the topography of the steps so well, which treads had worn away in a smoothed bevel and which narrowed as the winding stair curved, once, twice, three times. Otherwise, she might have stumbled and fallen with Kit's relentless harrying behind her. The planed wooden handrail was noticeably damp. She did not want to admit this was because her palms were sweating profusely. She could not afford to dwell upon her fear.

Once they passed through the kitchen, Kit took the lead, gesturing Agnes to silence with a finger to her lip, then beckoning her onward toward the front door. This mute instruction brought Agnes untold relief. She had been dreading a forced march up the main staircase to the sacrosanct second floor where she had never yet set foot, where Hugh and Kit slept — separately? But who was to say?

So her spirits rose with an unwarranted lightness, as she and Kit went out into the night. The first thing she saw was the moon, so full and low riding over the hills, it appeared a thing unreal. Its pallid sheen had a greenish tinge, like the febrile complexion of a restless patient too long confined. She grasped at the crude explanation it was the moon making Kit unwell. There must be some truth in the old idea of lunar influence, the planet's gravitational pull working upon the watery vapours of the brain, so that it overheats and madness ensues.

Kit ran ahead to the villa's single-storey left wing with its shuttered windows. There she stopped, demonstrating her agitation by leaping from foot to foot, then scrutinizing the ends of her hair, holding the individual strands close to her eyes as if seeking out some microscopic life form to exterminate.

"Hurry!"

When Agnes caught up, Kit seized her by the shoulders and gave her a shake. "Now, you will see," she said, her hand on the doorknob, which she twisted forcibly counterclockwise. Then she pushed the door open and flicked on the light. Immediately, there was a high-pitched shriek, a rustling sound and the grind of metal.

"Look!"

Kit pushed her into the raw-lit space of the long, low-ceilinged room. At first, Agnes could see nothing. The glare of four bare light bulbs strung from the ceiling momentarily blinded her. But worse, her eyes were streaming in reaction to the potent stench of urine-sodden sawdust, feces and formaldehyde.

When at last she did see clearly, her deepest, craven desire was to flee. Six macaques clung to the crossbars of a cage perhaps six feet by ten, wincing and blinking in the light. As their eyes adjusted, they fixed on her a look that spoke of a desolate sorrow and bafflement. They resembled pathetic little men—an image she at once throttled as denigrating to their essence. Three of them wore gauzy bandages, stained and stiffened with blood and lymph, taped to their groins.

Agnes's nails were embedded in her palms, driven there by a bolt of useless outrage, pity and self-disgust. It was of no consequence that she had not personally kidnapped and imprisoned the macaques then sliced open their scrotums for some vile purpose. By the fact of her humanity, she was complicit. Besides, she had twice heard their screams and done nothing to investigate.

"We have to get them out of here, Kit. Call the authorities. Now." Her fury was infecting her speech, the words slurred as if she were drunk. She repeated: "We have to call the authorities. What's the equivalent of the Humane Society in Italy?"

The monkeys had retreated to the back of the cage in reaction to her strident tone. She was intensifying their distress, which was unforgivable. She must stay calm and think clearly.

Kit rounded on her, eyes narrowed. "I don't know, Agnes. First, you help me. Then we'll deal with the damn monkeys. You wanted proof he's evil. Now you see it. This is the kind of thing you care about, isn't it? You and the idiotic Ark. He's using their hormones to pump up his own failing virility. That's what the technician's visits are for. He deals with the monkeys and gives Hugh the injections. So, just help me kill him. You won't have to do much. Just hold down his skinny old arms."

"Kit, you're unwell. You don't know what you're saying. Our responsibility is to help these . . . "

"Shut up, Agnes!" Kit shoved her outside and shut the door behind them. She strode off, then abruptly stopped and turned to face Agnes, her features stark and blanched in the glaucous moonlight. "One last time, will you help me?"

"No, of course not."

Kit raised her arm as if to strike, then let her words serve that purpose: "You're a pathetic coward, Agnes. One of life's mistakes."

Agnes watched benumbed as Kit re-entered the house. She pictured the fettered brass monkey fixed to the front door and winced at his newly revealed portent. At least the little figure fashioned of metal could not be made to suffer. *This is the kind of thing you care about, isn't it?* That Kit could divorce herself so completely from the macaques' plight appalled her almost as much as did Hugh's callous use of them. She felt increasingly frantic. She must stay rational; go back to her room and find the right number to call.

She entered the house warily, alert for any sounds of disturbance, the creak of the old man's bed or a floorboard as he rose to greet his alluring flesh-and-blood succubus. It occurred to her that Kit had been dressed all in black: matador pants and one of her scoop-neck leotard tops. Her "killing clothes"? *She will not really harm Hugh,* Agnes reasoned. *She would not keep asking me to help her if she felt able to act alone. And of course she may only be raving, or taking a bizarre vengeance on me because of Campbell and my part in the Ark.*

Sitting on the edge of her bed, she was overtaken by a tremor that convulsed her head to toe. She lay down and hugged herself, trying to quell her body's reaction to this fresh horror the inhabitants of Villa Scimmia had spawned. If this were a nightmare . . . but it was not. There were indeed six of them, bleeding and terrified in their cage, while the vainglorious and contemptible old man lay in his bed, indifferent to the pain he caused them. From the welter of thoughts crowding her brain, she plucked out the most self-damning: that she might take pleasure in seeing Kit slice Hugh open. How hot and raw and despicable the atavistic urge for retribution was.

Was this how it was inside Kit's head, all rational constraints eaten away? She must remember that Kit was ill and broken. The tormenting notion returned that she had been an unwitting agency in Kit's regression; that her mere presence had summoned up far too vividly the primal scene of Campbell's death. She ought never to have come to Tuscany. Yet if she had refused the chance, who would there be to act on the macaques' behalf?

Her smart phone soon displayed the phone number and address of the Italian State Animal Rights Office in Florence. The Italian name, Officio Diritti Animali, was reassuring. *Diritti Animali.* Backed by the full force of law. Their officers, with gentle hands inside protective gloves, would liberate the captives and tend their wounds in a healing sanctuary. The office opened at 8:00 AM. She began hunting in her phrase book for words to piece together a semi-articulate and compelling case for the Officio's immediate intervention. *Scimmia. Maltrattato. Imprigionato.*

Around two she succumbed to a sour sleep. As she went under, the successive hypnagogic visions were all mimetically detailed portraits of the macaques, except that their baleful eyes stared out from their groins. This surreal obscenity forced her to wake fully. There was a smell of burning in the air, which she at first assumed was dream-residue; her unconscious had conjured up the stink of Hugh's corruption. But when the odour turned palpable and caught at the back of her throat, she could taste the smoke.

For a split-second, her head emptied, a dead husk on a stalk. There were ice pellets in her blood. Then her skin prickled and instinct drove her on. She stuck her feet into her canvas shoes, grabbed her pants and shirt, her packed bag from under the bed, and her money belt with passport from the nightstand. When she opened the door, she was relieved to see the smoke in the hallway was a thin, swirling grey, not the dense black it would surely be closer to the fire's source. Keeping her head low, she started down the winding stair. She kept crying out to Kit and Hugh, but as she descended the smoke thickened, invading her eyes and lungs. If she continued calling out their names, she might choke to death.

Thirty-five. Thirty-six. She counted each step mentally, nearly doubled over now as she tried to catch the less polluted air near her feet. Forty. This meant she must be standing near the entrance to the kitchen, but all she could see was an opaque grey murk ominously streaked with black. She groped blindly, seeking the rasping texture of the rough-hewn stone wall she could follow with her fingers to the back door and the glorious promise of sweet air beyond. To her far left, where the kitchen opened to the hallway leading to the main quarters, the smoke was an unadulterated black, and just behind it was an unnerving lurid orange-red glow. Were she to turn that way, she had no doubt she would asphyxiate.

Where were Kit and Hugh? She prayed hard they had already escaped. From somewhere in the house there was a crash and then a roaring, as if a vast furnace had leapt into life. She reached out in panic into inchoate nothingness and lurched on her feet. Taking little sideways steps to the right, all the while striving to steady her frantic heart and thoughts, she dislodged with her foot an object that made metal clatter on stone. The cursed rat-trap. She took two baby steps left again, well away from the serrated jaws that could so easily have maimed her. But at least she now knew where exactly in the kitchen she was, with the ancient hearth immediately to her right. She reached up and grasped in triumph the protruding ledge of the mantle. She progressed slowly along its length until it yielded to the stone wall. Every few seconds she had to clamp her hand over her mouth and nose to control the amount of smoke she was taking into her lungs. There was an uncomfortable pressure in her chest. Its very lining hurt. Her brain was befuddled, and for a foolish instant she considered lying down and resting a while.

There was a sudden bang behind her, like a cork drawn from a vast bottle. When she turned her head, she saw a wedge of crimson filling the far door. This solid wedge was soon rent apart to become a mass of darting flames. In the light of their demonic dance, she saw how pitiable her resources of breath and brain were against the fire's power.

Terror pricked her onward and at last her fingers touched the wood grain of the back door that would open onto sweetest air, air that heals the lungs. She will be able to seek out Kit and Hugh and free the macaques. She must do these things. Her fingers scrabbled over the door, seeking the old-fashioned latch. When at last she found it and managed to depress its little tongue, the door would not budge. She felt sick. Could the wood have swollen or become fused to its frame? Then she remembered the high-set bolt. She strained upward on her toes, cursing her temporary blindness, her weakness and the ever-encroaching fire behind her. Its ferocious heat was already scorching the back of her head. She drove the bolt back, out of its housing. Now the tongue on the latch obeyed her touch. The door flew open and she fell on her knees outside in the night air, gulping it down. Then she was up and stumbling toward the trees. Here she dropped her bag. Surely the flames would not reach that far? Besides, help would soon be on its way. Ernesto, in his doting wakefulness, will have spotted the fire and called in an alarm. Or Kit or Hugh will have made the call.

The flames surged from every window of the upper storey. Did they both get out of that inferno in time? Please, oh please. She rushed around to the front of the villa, in time to see the oak door burst open under the incendiary pressure. The fire that roared out appeared first in the shape of a ball, then became a many-tongued hydra. Even at that distance, she felt its terrible heat on her face trying to peel off her skin. She ran toward the left wing but the flames outstripped her, racing along the horizontal wooden ridge of the roof. She could hear the terracotta tiles cracking. She reached the door behind which the macaques shrieked, a cacophony that made her nauseous and deathly cold. Although the actual wood of the door had not yet caught fire, both the lintel and the frame glowed red-hot. The roof directly above them was fully ablaze. She must free them before it collapsed and burned them alive.

In her desperate haste, it did not occur to her that the metal of the door knob would be hot enough to sear off her skin. She yelped and pulled her hand away, only half aware of the disc-shaped blister oozing in the centre of her palm. She bundled her T-shirt around the wounded hand for insulation. With this ungainly fist she succeeded in gripping the handle and turning it strongly clockwise as she had seen Kit do some hours earlier. The pain in her hand was excruciating, but removed from her, a trivial matter that belonged to some time she might never attain. Then she was through the door, the thick smoke invading her eyes and throat. She unthinkingly switched on the light, only to discover that the flaming interior roof beam cast sufficient hellish light upon the captives. Everything seemed to be on the edge of combustion — not least the monkeys, whose shrill screams would surely rupture their brains if she did not free them soon. There was a padlock on the cage door. With her left hand she tugged at it in the faint hope it was unlocked. It did not give. The monkeys wailed and retreated to the back of the cage. She detested herself for making them more afraid. She must find the key. Her eyes swept the walls, which flickered in the reflected light of the burgeoning flames above her head. As one licked low, she was forced to her knees, and so she spied it, tiny as the elusive passe-partout in a fairy tale, hanging from a hook beneath the bench on which the cage was mounted.

Her right hand proved useless for manipulating such a featherweight instrument, and she was not at all adept with her left. Three times she fumbled, while the monkeys fixed on her their huge eyes hollowed by terror. When at last the padlock responded with a melodic click, it was the most wonderful sound she had ever heard. She lifted out the padlock, opened the cage door and positioned herself behind it lest their claws tear at her as they emerged. For a second, they all stared at the open cage door, quivering.

"Go!" she yelled, gesturing to the black night beyond.

They leapt out, two at a time, and there was no hesitation as they fled to a freedom whose pitfalls she could not dwell upon now. She followed after, rushing as they did, toward the protective cover of the forest. She strained to catch a last glimpse of them, hoping the moon would illuminate their progress. But they had disappeared. How would they survive in the Tuscan woods? What instincts would protect them from wild boar, ravaging dogs, the dreaded viper and curious humans without conscience? What choice had she had but to free them?

By way of moonlight and firelight, she was able to find her bag, from which she retrieved a shirt to cover the stained and soot-smeared nightgown. Then she started, as quickly as she was able, down the steep drive that led to the main road. Help would be coming soon and she'd get news of Hugh and Kit. She was halfway down the drive when she fell, clutching the throbbing hand to her chest. Several hundred feet above and behind her on its hilltop, Villa Scimmia groaned as the crumbling charred beams brought down another wall of stone.

"Agnes!"

She was roused from her stupor by a familiar voice, from which she flinched nonetheless. *Mayday.* It was Horace Fairhaven extending his hand to help her rise.

"She told me you had gone to Florence," he murmured. His sigh hinted at a genuine sadness and perplexity. Agnes could not doubt the gravity of his expression, nor his solicitude as he steadied her when she stood up, his hands cupping her shoulders.

"Kit? Hugh?" she pressed.

"I got Hugh out in time," Horace said. "He is in hospital on oxygen, but otherwise unscathed. Kit is sedated in the back of the van." He pointed to the white vehicle parked below, his arm writing a smooth arc upon the air. She understood this gesture signalled his obeisance and complete fealty to the sleeping princess the vehicle contained. "What did you do to your hand, Agnes?"

She tried to show him, but the cloth of her makeshift bandage was stuck to the raw flesh.

"You need to get that treated. I'll take you now. How did it happen?"

When she told him, he looked at her severely, his narrow face etiolated in the moonlight. "Why?" he challenged. "What do you think their chances of survival are in the woods of Tuscany?"

"Wasn't it better than them burning alive?"

He shrugged. Then something like a smile flitted across his face.

She missed her footing getting into the van. Horace steadied her, with a firm grip under her elbow. She was struck by the almost professional assurance his touch conveyed, and understood then how thoroughly practised he was in dealing with frailty. His habitual charge so often faltered and fell.

Once settled in the passenger seat, she turned her head to gaze at the recumbent Kit, who slept curled on her side in the back seat. She noted the gentle rise and fall of her breath. If one did not know, Kit would seem the embodiment of quiet virtue and undefiled mind. When Agnes turned away, she saw that Horace had also been watching Kit's untroubled sleep. The beatific glaze upon his face told of a love that had no need whatsoever to explain itself.

"The fire," Agnes asked as Horace started the van. "Did Kit . . . ?"

His look was austerely assessing. "You have a right to know. But the price of that knowledge must be silence.

Lifelong. You do understand that, don't you, Agnes?" Did his tone carry an underlying threat? Or was this bizarre exchange all founded on pure reason, as his almost clinical calm implied?

"I understand," she said.

"Yes, then. She set it — but to say she did it deliberately begs the question of agency." He contorted his mouth in the sneer that had always accompanied his most caustic critiques of the Ark's airy resolutions and schemes. "Hugh had a brocade canopy over his bed, and she put a candle to it while he slept. Fortunately, I was ready, anticipating a major incident. Her symptoms sometimes peak markedly. It never was Alzheimer's. She has the behavioural variant of fronto-temporal dementia. This past week she had been particularly unstable, as you know. I did not get there quite soon enough to stop her. But the old man is largely unscathed, and perhaps ignorant as to the fire's cause.

"As for the house," he gestured vaguely to the back window, "it was a rats' nest, metaphorically at least. Not at all a good place for her. But her father has no clue what to do with her, none at all. He never did. Electroconvulsive therapy . . . did she tell you? Now how is that going to help her? I would hate him, if I had the energy. He put his wife in an institution . . . "

It was as close as he had come to admitting how onerous his burden was. But she must ask. She had to know. The clawing pain in her hand intensified, the nearer she came to articulating the question.

"She told me she murdered Fergus. Is that true?"

He did not react, even with an audible breath. She scrutinized the prematurely wizened gnome-like profile, which appeared similarly unmoved. She might have made some facile comment on the weather.

"Did she?" This insistence took all her courage.

"Agnes, I will tell you only on the understanding that this exchange constitutes a pact between us. It goes no further. You are an intelligent woman. I do not need to spell out the terms of our agreement, do I?"

There was no mistaking the threat this time. "I understand."

She recognized that in years to come she may find this affirmation burdensome. This was the price of forbidden knowledge. She had asked for the box to be opened and must live with the consequences.

"I am placing my trust in you, Agnes, because you are also an outsider and therefore expert in self-containment. So the answer to your question is, regrettably, yes. She called me after she'd done it. I had never thought she would go so far. I went to Fergus's house and cleaned up, made sure all her fingerprints were obliterated. Not a hair left. Nothing. Complicity is not a moral issue for me, not at least, as far as she is concerned. She was the only member of her family to treat me humanely. They made me eat in the kitchen and when she was a child she took her meals with me. I am devoted to her. I am . . . " He stopped in order to control a quaver in his speech.

"Her courtier?" She clumsily attempted a word that would elevate his servitude.

"No, I am her dog." He made this assertion with a touching pride. "And I am grateful to be so."

I also had a dog, thought Agnes, but he was of another time and made of paint.

Two days later she stood, with her hand professionally salved and bandaged, in front of Piero's sea-monster in the Uffizi. She was amazed by how small he was, set inside a scene of Andromeda's rescue that resembled a jewelled miniature. When he had first arrested her attention so long ago, on a book cover on her mother's desk, it was the magnified detail of his commanding portrait she'd seen: the tusked, grotesque head in whose ugliness she recognized herself. She approached the painting as closely as the guards would allow and saw the confirmation of her original girlhood intuition. It was love gleamed in the monster's eye as he gazed at the captive princess, while the human hero Perseus mounted his back, making ready to stab deep into his heart's blood. The monster's passion for Andromeda was much-abraded and woefully misdirected, but it was love nonetheless. Like Horace's love for Kit, she thought sadly, or the Ark's for all the suffering species it sought to rescue. Even misbegotten passions have value, when the intent is pure.

This too, Piero di Cosimo had taught her. She was newly astounded how far one could travel on the blessed conveyance of an extraordinary artist's work. Her gratitude was without bounds. She had returned, thus far, such stores of it as she could.

TWENTY-SIX

The Painter, April 12, 1522

H

E IS SOMETIMES GRANTED A few moments' release from the clutch of delirium and fever-soaked dreams. It is then he becomes aware of the purple-red inflammation of the buboes in the armpits and groin. Madder. That would be the base pigment to catch the doom-filled hue plague has painted on his body. The swellings are hard and as large as chicken eggs. What they cook inside is an ever more rankling pain.

Death crept nearer and nearer his bed, a skull-face shadowed by a hood, and long fingers of bone beating a soundless tattoo upon the air. This rhythm served to thicken the viscous fog that occluded Piero's outer and inner eye. He feared he would go blind altogether and could conceive of no worse final curse upon an artist's life, even one grown old and afflicted by a palsied hand.

With so little earthly time left to him, his fiercest longing is that his inner eye clear long enough for him to see again the dear companions of his spirit. How often they have freed him from a petrifying despair. Their grace, speed and unparalleled idiosyncratic beauty manifest God's glory more surely than do any human face or form.

He wanted what was perhaps a sacrilege: to blend his spirit with theirs and apprehend the world through their senses and with their wisdom. What he most abhorred was to see them suffer. Thus where he could in his commissions, he set the animals loose, where they might wander at will and, when danger loomed, flee and escape the bloody cudgel, the knife and death by burning.

Now he sees, with a vision so crystalline it verges on mystery, six more who have been liberated and by a hand other than his. Their silvery capes shimmer in the moonlight as they race surely over the hill and into the sheltering canopy. Their excited chatter convey to him a fear-filled joy. What better perspective can there be on God's creation? Teach me, he implored. In his lifetime, he wanted this above all. Teach me. Teach others.

Their flight confirms it has begun at last. He has unknown cohorts dedicated to this peerless truth and quest: that the animals be free and cherished; that our human spirits await their coming, and the redemptive mingling of our souls with theirs.

TWENTY-SEVEN

Three Years Later

T HEY HAD ARRANGED TO MEET in the National Gallery in front of Piero di Cosimo's *Vulcan and Aeolus,* a place that had fast become her favourite haunt since moving to Ottawa to do her master's degree. The gallery guards were used to her now. There were no more perturbed or vaguely minatory looks when she sat, sometimes a full hour, engrossed in this masterwork almost exactly her height that contained some of her dearest friends on earth. She did not regard this assertion as in any way pathetic. She knew Paul would understand. Nothing in her life had sustained her like the figures, animal and human, that made their way from Piero di Cosimo's brain to the brush in his hand and the wafer-thin layers of paint on his canvas.

The canvas in this case had its own idiosyncrasies and these, too, she seized on with the intense pleasure of familiarity and because the endearing quirks brought the artist nearer. First, there was the evident lozenge pattern in the weave still visible beneath the meticulously applied tempera and oils after almost six centuries. Then there was the noticeable seam that ran through the sky just above the giraffe's horns, where the artist had obviously stitched two pieces of cloth together. He had used what was at hand, perhaps a linen tablecloth or even a shroud. She pictured him seated near a window in his studio, the swathe of white fabric enveloping his knees, and his small, quick hands, like swallows in their harmonious busyness, darting in and out of the snowy folds.

It still struck her as miraculous that he had conjured, from materials as inert as cloth, wood and pigment, these beings, who in their ever-present life, appeared to breathe the same gallery air as did she. But the sources of the linen, frame and pigments were also once alive, she realized. In this earthly paradise he had made, where the aged gods laboured in their corner to teach humankind the metal-lurgical arts, and the beautiful youth sat astride the white horse with a light grace that spoke of love bestowed and returned, there was nothing at all forced or artificial.

She saw, always with the same joyous pang, how it might have been — a holy consonance among species that had been the Ethical Ark's dream. It was this vision Piero made manifest, today and forever, and she fed upon its truth with the hushed respect due a mystery whose profundity defied words. She had learned to temper her bewildered disappointment when gallery visitors skirted this lovely, ever-freshening world with scarcely a glance. However, very young children were often drawn by the white and brown horses, the luminous giraffe and the tiny camels in the background and she was grateful for their unsullied wonder.

Today when she passed through the European gallery's steel and glass doors in search of Peter, she was delighted to see a group of Buddhist monks in maroon robes clustered at the base of Piero's paradise. They were in the company of a docent who was just finishing up an account that would no doubt have highlighted the artist's most egregious eccentricities as perpetrated by Vasari: the curmudgeonly reclusiveness, the unvaried repasts of hard-boiled eggs, and the terror of lightning.

Five of the monks were tall, robust young men with immaculate shaven heads. The sixth was an elderly man Agnes assumed was their teacher, who bent down to examine a detail in the painting's bottom right corner. When he turned around to look up at his charges, his face was beaming; then he pointed, drawing their attention to the cricket on its stone. He was still smiling, caught in rapt communion with this tiny, winged fellow-creature, as the group filed out after the beckoning docent.

One man remained behind, staring up at the painting. Although his head was shaven like the others, he did not wear the brightly declarative monk's garment but a long-sleeved shirt and loose-fitting slacks in neutral cotton. He must, she thought, have newly joined the order. Perhaps he had not yet attained the level of discipline that merited a robe.

Then he turned around and she registered, with an anguished surprise, that the man was Peter. She was spun in a momentary confusion as the light in the gallery shuddered and the years since she had last seen him contracted. They were standing, not in the National Gallery of Canada, but outside the forbidding stone wall bounding the Alyscamps. The despair that had tainted that last encounter was with her again. It had exactly the weight of Zeke's corpse multiplied by a guilt of monstrous proportion. She had failed Zeke and the entire Ark by not being present at the protest. And she had failed Peter who had been forced to fulfill, without her support, the grim duty of identifying Zeke's shattered remains in a frigid morgue in a foreign land.

She swayed a little where she sat, on a low bench covered with black, padded leatherette, whose yielding sturdiness was such a familiar aspect of her weekly vigils in this room. She dug her fingers in, seeking anchorage. As the man took a step toward her, she wondered if she was mistaken; if perhaps this was not Peter but someone who resembled him in height and in the breadth of his shoulders and cheekbones. If it was Peter Dervaig, he was changed in some way she could not immediately grasp.

"Agnes." The voice left her in no doubt. She stood to greet him and they clasped hands in a spontaneous move they just as quickly abandoned.

"I thought," she blurted out, "that you were with the monks; I mean, that you were one of them." As soon as she spoke these words, which she had no conscious intention of uttering, their import struck her a heavy blow. Could she have found him only to lose him again for good? She felt unaccountably cold, picturing him sealed away in his crystalline quotidian virtue.

"I might have been," he murmured as they sat side-by-side on the bench. "I considered the monastic life very carefully. But in India, I was shown a sign, and I mean a literal sign that told me the obvious; that I should become a vet. So now I am in my third year at Guelph. I'll do another year specializing in feline and canine neurological disease."

"India," she echoed, in the dazed understanding this was where he had gone after the wreckage in Arles, the "huge place" he'd sought in which to lose himself.

"Yes," he said. "I was doubly blessed there. Unexpectedly blessed." He put his hand to his cheek and she saw then why it was he looked so different. The unusual patches of pigmentation had disappeared and his complexion was now uniformly pale. She wondered what new freedoms this change had brought him and if he was at ease with them all. "My mother thinks it is a miracle," he said, "and perhaps it was, although in that case I do not think I was deserving."

She was about to say something trite yet heartfelt, along the lines that no one could be more so, but stopped herself in time.

"I have also been blessed," she told him. "I have a wonderful mentor who was my guide when I stopped drinking — a professor of art history in New York. He is supporting my application to do a doctorate there under the world's foremost scholar on my painter." She worried that this sounded boastful and fell silent. Then she gestured to the painting on the wall in front of them, forgetting as she did so, that she would expose to him the livid circular white scar that marred her palm.

"What happened to your hand, Agnes?"

She recounted, as concisely as she could, the bitter tale of Kit's immolation of the Villa Scimmia and Horace's rescue of Hugh.

He listened attentively, and in complete silence. Only when she was finished did he say, "That poor troubled woman. But it is Horace who probably has the hardest life of any of us. His love for her is like a devoted parent's for a damaged child incapable of returning affection."

The peculiar emphasis he gave the word "damaged" alerted Agnes that he was aware of the worst of Kit's crimes. "Did you know . . . ?" She turned to him with the naked question in her eyes.

"About what she did to Fergus? Yes. Horace confided in me after the May Day Ark meeting. 'I know you can be trusted, Jolly Green Giant,' he said. I suppose he felt he had to tell someone. He swore me to secrecy. Then about three years ago, I got an email from him that said simply: 'Agnes knows.' That was all. But I think Zeke knew the whole story too, or at least he guessed. Do you remember when we three talked in the crypt in the Alyscamps? You and I were trying to dissuade him from attempting that foolish stunt and he said 'There's something about the wire . . . ' Do you remember that? I think he had found out it was Fergus strung up the wire for Campbell."

"If only we had managed to stop Zeke."

"We blundered badly," he answered. "It was a kind of group megalomania."

"And we will spend the rest of our lives making restitution," she said.

"Yes, but it will become habitual — through small, discrete acts of goodness, day by day."

"I walk dogs for the Humane Society," she told him, "and I have applied to foster cats." Small indeed, she thought, if not pitiably meagre.

"And we will both make monthly donations to PETA and WSPA until we die," he laughed.

"And even afterwards," she added.

He asked: "Did your painter ever have lions in his work?"

"Yes, magnificent, contemplative lions."

"Do you know what Wittgenstein said about lions?"

She shook her head.

"He said that if lions could speak, we wouldn't be able to understand what they were saying. I don't believe that," he declared with a hushed gravity.

"No," she told him, "nor do I."

"Roar," he whispered. "Roar," again.

She laughed, thinking what a marvel these seamless thoughts were, his fitting into hers and hers into his, like the cricket into its stone, and the stone to the cricket.

He had taken her hand and traced with his forefinger the outline of the doorknob burned into her palm.

"You did well," he said.

Agnes bit her lip, just hard enough to stop herself demurring or denying. With his hand still in hers, she looked straight ahead at Piero's pacific, prelapsarian world, forever receding, yet ever present in its blazoned power to keep their striving constant.

Acknowledgements

I am grateful to the poet, Robert Duncan, whose "Pasages 13: The Fire" introduced me to the work of Piero di Cosimo. Duncan's vivid description of the animals in di Cosimo's *A Forest Fire* inhabited my imagination from my first reading of this poem. The vision of the "Angel Doctor" who helps Paul Otterly is based on a story Robert Duncan told me; in his case, the Angel Doctor said: "Robert, you don't have to smoke," and he stopped thereafter.

Three works in particular gave me invaluable material on the painter's life and works: *Piero di Cosimo: Fiction, invention and fantasia* by Sharon Fermor, *Piero di Cosimo* by Dennis Geronimus and David Franklin's chapter, "Piero di Cosimo: A Renaissance Eccentric?" in his *Painting in Renaissance Florence 1500–1550*. I also drew inspiration from *The Forest Fire by Piero di Cosimo* by Catherine Whistler and David Bomford.

I learned about the concept of darshan from Geoff Dyer's *Jeff in Venice, Death in Varanasi*.

Through the process of writing this book, I was helped immeasurably by the interest and encouragement of my family and friends.